THE ESTANCIA

THE ESTANCIA

Martín Cullen

ADELPHI

First published in 2018 by Adelphi Publishers

Text Copyright © Martín Cullen, 2018
This edition © Adelphi Publishers, 2018

The moral right of the author has been asserted.

ISBN 978-1-9995891-0-3

A CIP catalogue reference for this book is available from the British Library

All rights reserved. Published in the United Kingdom by
Adelphi Publishers, 50 Albemarle Street, London W1S 4BD
and distributed by Penguin Random House UK,
20 Vauxhall Bridge Road, London SW1V 2SA

Typography and typesetting by Peter B. Willberg
Typeset in Monotype Walbaum

Printed and bound by CPI, Moravia

For Harriet

Araignée du matin, chagrin

MIRAFLORES

La Paz

mid XVII century

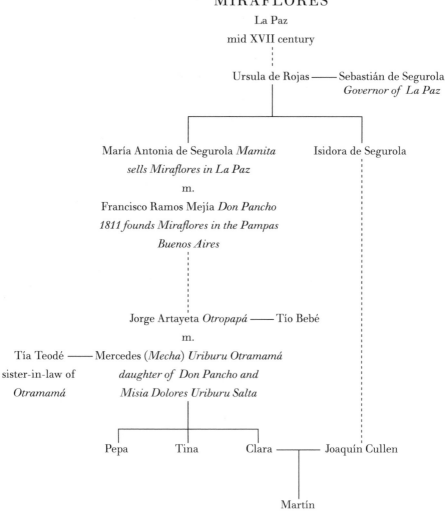

Ursula de Rojas —— Sebastián de Segurola
Governor of La Paz

María Antonia de Segurola *Mamita*
sells Miraflores in La Paz

m.

Francisco Ramos Mejía *Don Pancho*
1811 founds Miraflores in the Pampas
Buenos Aires

Isidora de Segurola

Jorge Artayeta *Otropapá* —— Tío Bebé

m.

Tía Teodé —— Mercedes (*Mecha*) Uriburu *Otramamá*
sister-in-law of   *daughter of Don Pancho and*
Otramamá   *Misia Dolores Uriburu Salta*

Pepa   Tina   Clara ——┬—— Joaquín Cullen

Martín
Narrator

LIST OF CHARACTERS

CULLEN
Martín – narrator
Joaquín – father

ARTAYETA
Jorge – *Otropapá*
Clara – mother of narrator, daughter of Jorge, wife of Joaquín Cullen
Pepa – eldest sister of Clara
Tina – second sister, Godmother of narrator
Tío Bebé – brother of Jorge

URIBURU
Mecha, Mercedes Uriburu de Artayeta – *Otramamá*, wife of Jorge
Tía Teodé, Teodelina Lezica de Uriburu – sister in law of Otramamá

ESTANCIAS

COUNTY OF MAIPÚ

THE ESTANCIA
Francisca Madero Ramos Mejía de Lynch – *Niñita*, founder of the
estancia, aunt & guardian of Otropapá and Tío Bebé
Clara & husband Joaquín
Martín – narrator

MIRAFLORES
Bebette – second cousin of Otropapá
Adela – grand-daughter of Bebette

SAN CARLOS
Tía Justita, Tía Juana, Tía Lula – first cousins of Otropapá

KAKEL
Lola María, the Elía, Madame de Mailly – cousins of Otropapá

SAN FRANCISCO
Tío Sebastián & wife Cuca – first cousins of Otropapá

PART I

THE CITY

1

OTRAMAMÁ didn't take off her rings to put cold cream on her face. She would stick two fingers into the jar, then work the cool, white paste around the corners of her mouth, puffing out each cheek in turn to make them smooth. Then she would oil her forehead and her crows's feet.

My grandmother – I called her Otramamá, my other mother – had the huge earlobes of an old person, and at bedtime she replaced her pearls with two tiny blobs of cream that filled the empty holes. This intrigued me. My mother's ears weren't pierced, and I socially demoted the girls I saw in the park who wore earrings. To have gone through all that pain, I thought to myself, only to be looked down upon. But Otramamá was born in a less complicated age, when distinctions were clearer and the Argentine was divided simply, between rich and poor. Some colonial customs lingered on in the 1950s of my childhood. When Otramamá had a fever, they would call old Benita Flores to sit up with her. Benita was the granddaughter of family slaves, and as long as the fever lasted, she would be there, fixed between the bed and the wall like a dead star.

The scent of the cream, a pink smell that clashed with the great shadows of the room, made me sleepy. But my grandmother was impatient; she was merely following a ritual she had copied from her three daughters that she didn't believe in. Just as she got cream all over her rings – the woman who came in to clean the jewellery had to scrub them later with a tiny brush dipped in soapy water – so she massaged the stuff into her face without any particular care. Then she climbed into bed with me.

Propped up against the scratchy lace pillows, she read to

me from *Les Malheurs de Sophie*, whose striking gouache illustrations showed a series of ever more unbearable disasters befalling Sophie, a poor girl whose only defect was greed. She paid for this sin by losing her name. De Réan, that beautiful, aristocratic surname, was demoted to Fichini, a name that sounded like the haberdasher's around the corner from our house on the Calle Juncal. At least they didn't pierce her ears.

Otramamá would embroider the stories as she read in the soft French she had improved at the Couvent des Oiseaux in Paris, intertwining her own memories with the words on the page.

'One of my school friends was the granddaughter of Madame de Ségur, the author of this book. She was a good girl, just like *Les Petites Filles Modèles* of Fleurville, but I can't remember if she was good and stupid, like Camille, or good and sensible, like Madeleine. Ah, Fleurville! That house was so pretty and simple. It makes me think of a real house, Brunoy, and the warmth of its owner Pepita Balcarce, San Martín's granddaughter. On Sundays she would give us puchero stew for lunch, although she'd never set foot in Buenos Aires.'

'What was Pepita Balcarce like?' I asked.

'What do you want me to say?' Otramamá shrugged. 'An old woman.'

Why was it that the one children's book in my grandmother's room was so nasty? Its blue leather covers, square-ruled in gold tooling, with heavy pages and tissue-paper guards that whispered like bats' wings and protected pictures painted in purple and emerald green and grey, with the occasional turquoise flame, turned the volume into a worthy object, like Otramamá's red velvet dressing-gown and silver bedside lamp. Why then did it make me uneasy?

And yet the tone Otramamá used to describe Pepita Balcarce's smile as she served broth to her guests to help them digest the puchero, was also the one she used to describe Sophie's tears to me as her wax doll melted. She did not seem to notice – or rather, it did not seem to matter to her – that Sophie, whose life had begun so auspiciously in the cheerful air of a French spring morning, would be shattered by that drive in her which made her break whatever she touched, and would end up destroying her mother. Otramamá's voice seemed to imply that at such an hour, there was no difference between pleasure and horror. And although I'd heard there was another of Madame de Ségur's books in which Sophie was freed from her suffering, I dared not ask about it. There was only that one book in Otramamá's rooms, and for me it occupied as inexorable a space as the bed, or my grandmother herself.

From the middle of that vast bed, between sheets so fine they wrinkled like handkerchiefs as I slid into them, feeling to my right the gleam from the bedside lamp passing from Otramamá's spectacles to the perfumed pages under her shiny hands, I perceived still more deeply the presence of the silent room whose walls I could not make out but the size of which, rather than isolating the pool of light with its two heads and book and threatening me, enveloped us like a dark skin, and made me feel as if the house was dropping off to sleep with us.

The last sounds were of Otramamá moving about the bathroom, clinking jars and then pulling the chain, again and again. Five times before bed she sat on the loo, five times it would flush, and five times or more it would be echoed by my grandmother's own plumbing, the effect of the powerful Inca brew she took each evening. Then, silence, save for the tick-tock of the clock out in the hall, and its chime every quarter of an hour.

Now I could go to sleep. Otramamá put the book back on the bedside table and began to turn a rosary very quickly between her fingers, reciting not the mysteries, but short, ejaculatory prayers. 'Jesus, Joseph and Mary, protect me in my last agony. JesusJosephandMaryprotectmeinmylast-agony,' one after the other, always the same, adding millions to the millions she recorded in a little black oilcloth notebook. As she began, I dived down between the sheets, saying goodnight to her body stretched out in the yellowish, aquatic tent which moved with me, and which grew dimmer as I burrowed towards the foot of the bed.

I think it was my grandmother's skin that gave me greatest comfort. It was the skin of a thing, not of a person. Except in her armpits, where two or three long, transparent strands sprouted, she had no offensive hair anywhere. Here and there were a few flat moles that must not be scratched in case they became cancerous, the odd scar from a clumsy injection, and a network of meandering rivers on the neat relief map of her legs, so colourful that they were the best part of my journey. At the end of them, the skin began to change, the rivers, born blue at the thighs, finer and more tortuous and menacing as they descended, stagnating at her heels, where they became purple and yellow. I swam to the bottom of the bed, then turned, kissed each knee and swam back to the surface. Unconcerned at what was growing at her margins, Otramamá was waiting for me with a smile on her face.

Just as the felt of the maid's gloved hand slides over the shiny wood of the dining room table, spreading the wax until the smell of the unguent seeping into the veins of the wood evaporates and sends her into a sleep beyond her tiredness, hearing only the music in her ears as her hand travels around the oval of ebony and imagines she is dancing, so my immersion to reconnoitre my grandmother's body put me to sleep. From that becalmed flesh, ribbons unfurled that brought order to the house, to the servants, to the estancia, to the past. That darkness which embraced me was the same nocturnal space where the watchmen of the great banks could be seen patrolling the corridors, safe-guarding the vault, ensuring its protection since the guardian of the watchmen was the city itself, and the guardian of the city was God.

As my eyes closed, I saw other incarnations of Otramamá, leaning over a balustrade and looking down at me from one of those damp, round heavens that decorate Italian bridal chambers. I saw the Countess de Ségur against a backdrop of clouds, a pious figure surrounded by floating streamers, each baring a dedication to her grandchildren. She was virtuous, garrulous, filial, and she missed Russia, just as my grandmother in her Paris convent had missed Buenos Aires. I saw the Mother of Jesus, lifted on high by angels, but no higher than the others who danced before my eyes, since although she was the Queen of Heaven she had relatives on earth. '*Je vous salue, Marie, ma cousine,*' they prayed to her. And then to match this I saw Otramamá's aunt, Santa Teresa de Jesus, looking straight down at me. And Sophie, whom I included so as to avenge her. And Pepita Balcarce, the exiled purveyor of puchero, whose name was on everyone's lips that year, 1950, the year the government had dedicated to her grandfather, the Liberator. I fell asleep under the beatific smiles of these ladies, whose heavenly eyes bore a single message – Isn't he sweet! – for me alone.

I always dreamt the same scene. It was summer, and I was in our house on the Calle Juncal. All the windows and doors were flung open so as to catch even the tiniest current of air. The only perceptible movement was the breathing of its sleeping household. It was strange to see these living islands stir in their sleep, turning away from the yellow beams of streetlamps that were reflected in the mirrors and polished floors of that hot, dank atmosphere, amidst the furniture stifled in its white summer covers, in rooms stripped of carpets. From time to time the headlights of a car climbed the walls to the ceiling, and this sudden illumination only strengthened the sense of torpor. From out on the street came voices – tired, hard voices that swam in through the open windows, swirled around the rooms, and made the sleepers shudder.

The house was no longer our stronghold. It had been invaded by the city, and the city was hostile. The voices forced their way inside, the watchmen cowered in their sleep. Wrapped in white bandages, the furniture stood quiet and alone on the light-streaked floor, while the obscene voices seeped under the covers like a mob rounding on a condemned man and burst into raucous laughter, echoing the rage of bodies accustomed to living among butchered animals that dripped blood, grease and excrement.

'Come on che, give it to me.'

A woman's laughter welled up, sour, cutting, shrill. I could feel her egging the men on with her plump, manicured fingers.

'Closer, that's it, give me more.'

The cloying voice seized the flesh and tore it, with the sound of rent silk. Beneath her perfumed powder, with its rancid smell, droplets of sweat glistened on her painted face, framed by a wig of platinum curls. Her teeth, tiny and pearly, nestled within fleshy pink gums flecked with black and gold and her blindly painted, stupid, horrible mouth.

'Piss off, you greasy wog. Go fuck your sister.

The man began to beg, but with a cold insistence, as though he might at any moment slit her throat.

'Come on, you whore. Don't play hard to get. You won't regret it. That blonde hair drives me crazy. You look just like Evita.'

'Bastard, don't you dare speak like that of the Señora.'

Her silver spangled dress, her sweaty cleavage and her fat white neck shone in the oily night like a submarine on the attack. The poor are horrible. With the squealing acid of their poverty, and their false, dirty faces filled with fear, they defeat the goodness of those who want to help them; Otramamá even, but not me, never me. I didn't want to know they existed.

Now they were in Otramamá's room and had tied her up like a parcel. I was afraid of their fear. The women sat on the bed, and passed round bottles and jars from the dressing table, dabbing their chapped lips with lipsticks, painting enormous mouths, playing carnival chasing one another with sprays of perfume. The men began to slice up Otramamá as if she were cold meat. Their voices grew louder as if the radio was spitting them out, and we couldn't switch it off, the horrible booming voice of that whore, that Evita, goading the squalid poor, those sons of bitches, by giving them clubs with which to destroy everything and yet leaving them with nothing.

Rigid, I lay beneath the thin scab of the sheet, waiting until they had finished with Otramamá and came to tear it off me.

2

WHEN I look for memories of my father in the house where I was born, I find none. Almost nothing of him remains in the Calle Juncal. His room was my mother's — Señora Clara, or niña Clara, as the servants called her, depending on how long they'd been with us. His bedside table was crammed with things that couldn't have been his, like balls of newspapers used to keep hats in shape. I, who was always looking for people in drawers, hoping to find beneath letters and photographs and cuts of cloth a heart of flesh and precious stones to speak to me, didn't even go near his, which smelled of medicines.

Almost nothing was known about my father. He seemed to have had no parents, and never took me to the places of his childhood. He had one photograph on his bedside table, just a few brown stains on a pale background in a round frame, which pretended to be his mother. To build a face with those blotches was almost impossible. I could tell the big one was a cloche hat, the smaller a gloved fist, in the space between the two, Papá saw his mother's face, but I could never find the features of my grandmother. She was a lady of the 1920s, her eyes hidden beneath the shadow of her hat. It was a sudden image, a snapshot, as of someone caught open-mouthed on the front page of a newspaper. I could not see her, because I was missing all those parts of a life that only memory can understand. There was for me no child's face, no troubled adolescent eyes like those captured in the few pictures of my real grandmother, Otramamá.

'It's the best photo we have,' my father said, when I told him I found it difficult to make her out.

'What was your mother like?'

'Your grandmother, you mean. I don't know, I don't remember.' He seemed a little annoyed, and confused.

'But Papá, you must remember something.'

'I was only twelve when she died. I didn't see much of her, she was always in Buenos Aires with my elder sister, Beba. My mother hated living in the suburb of San Isidro. Anyway, I was never at home.'

'Where were you? Did you visit your friends in the other big quintas?'

'What quintas? I played around in the streets with the greengrocer's boys, or I was fishing in the shallows of the river by the Sarandí. I remember Mamá was pleased when I got good school reports. My brothers were lazy.'

'What else?'

'My grandfather used to say that your grandmother was the most intelligent woman he'd ever known.'

'What else?'

'What else do you want me to tell you?'

'How did she die?'

'She died six months after my father – of flu.'

It was impossible. I had to force every detail out of him. Orphaned and with no immediate family, my father seemed to have been invited into the household at the Calle Juncal, perhaps because he was a distant relation of Mamá's. But he didn't settle. There were those who came every week to eat at Juncal, the table was always laid for certain cousins or anyone my grandfather might bring without warning from the street or the Círculo de Armas. Every Thursday Malena García came to eat her *poule au riz à la crème*, always without sweet corn, which gave her a cold, and to gossip with her sharp tongue and Parisian precision of the comings and goings of our loose society; Tío Pedro, the handsome bastard cousin of my grandfather, who arrived the following day and was allowed to tell one dream during lunch in the unmistakable voice of Mademoiselle Maillard, a voice shared by all the Maipú family who had had her as their governess. These people appeared to me much more permanent than Papá. Though not indispensable, they seemed unmovable. Whilst my father, despite his three children, his wife, and his position as the only young man in the family, came and went, good humoured, animated, kind, but always elusive, like the lover leaving at the end of the night. His dangerous beauty kept him aloof. I thought of him as a puma, sulkily licking itself. He spoke rarely, and when he did, brusquely, with a naïve optimism. His words seemed often to contain a challenge, as though he were throwing down a trump card. Whenever he opened his mouth he frowned.

He was six foot tall, solidly built, and had the luck to have been born with the sombre macho looks fashionable in his day. He had a white smile like Clark Gable or Lady Chatterley's lover, but with eyes that didn't look straight at you. Sometimes they seemed vulnerable, but mostly he would narrow them, concealing all but a bright, hazel glimmer behind half-closed lids, warm but mocking. He was so unpredictable that I was constantly in fear of some rage within him. He would come into my room, throwing open his arms, offering me his big body to embrace, but he remained beyond reach. The orphan, the poor boy, the man who didn't know how to pronounce French, the man whose bad manners I mustn't copy, was the treasure of the house.

I think he had already realised that he was bored by the Calle Juncal. Once he felt secure of the place he had won for himself at the centre of his new family, he lost interest. It was a good place to return to at night, tired after the day's adventures, to Mamá's fresh, welcoming and anxious face, shining like a lamp against the outside darkness. I suppose he vowed to come back every evening to that lamp, with a child's earnestness, by-God-and-the-Holy-Gospels-till-the-day-of-my-death, in memory of those parents who broke their promise by dying. But he expected us to celebrate his return.

He came up to our nursery on the fourth floor every evening. As he opened the lift door he would whistle, a long, low sound, almost absent-minded like a wink that could be mistaken for a tic. And I — and later my brother and sister — had to drop everything and run to him. If we were not there immediately, the sulkiness would descend. 'Papá, Papá!' we would scream as loud as we could, our beaks wide open as if his cheeks, cold from the outdoors, were sweets to be gobbled up. He would catch the one who reached him first, lifting him or her up to his face, while the others made do with his legs. The power with which he manhandled us was a delight. Mamá, ashamed of her own hands, said his were those of a surgeon. I thought them beautiful, skilled, and innocent of the knowing edge that frightened me in his eyes. Broad and never still, they were worked with tendons and veins, his fingers curving backwards at the tips, unexpectedly fine in their strength.

His hands seemed to be a separate, tranquil part of him. I liked to believe they were independent, bringing him home to us at night of their own free will. They were also perhaps the unused hands of an artist.

In the last two generations of his family, an aesthetic side had emerged, surprising in a line of politicians and landowners who had known only how to fight, to seize power for a while, and then lose it to a firing squad or to a knife in the throat — even as late as 1878 a Cullen governor of Santa Fé had his slit by a gaucho. They left behind hastily composed wills, whose sole interest lay in the drama that had forced them to be written. But in 1900 an uncle who had studied sculpture at the Ecôle de Beaux Arts in Paris began to get commissions on his return to Buenos Aires. And then Papá's twelve-year-old brother won a local prize for painting. The uncle became a clubman, though, and my father's brother, who married money, didn't make much of his talent either. Papá was proud of this artistic strain, and when he spoke of his family it was this that he talked about and not, like my mother, of battles or governorships, although bloody misadventures were a recurring theme on both sides of the family.

One day, when we were walking in the park next to the Recoleta, Papá pointed to a statue under one of the ancient rubber trees, saying, 'Uncle Hernán sculpted that.' This sudden mention of someone of his own family whom I didn't know, as my mind was on the ice cream I'd been promised, brought his past back to me abruptly and incomprehensibly, like his mother's snapshot. But also I was hungry for his words, and the way he shrugged them out so lightly made me feel I was being let into a secret.

'My brothers took turns posing for it,' he said. 'Hernán sat them in an armchair and gave them a cigar to hold, but they weren't to smoke it, they had to hold up a hand to the temple, and not puff out their cheeks. He grew tired of them after a while and kicked them out.' It was typical of Papá to give a calm recollection of childhood a violent ending.

To accept another family as one's own can take a lifetime. But with another family's house we can coat in the spittle of our routines until finally it ends up smelling of us. Nevertheless Otramamá never grew to like the family estancia in Maipú, and although the half-century of summers she spent there should have thinned her distaste for that house she ended up inheriting, still it never felt her own. I can see her now, at the end of her life, sitting on the terrace in springtime against a wall of acid green ivy, shivering in spite of the black shawl and tartan rug she was wrapped in, gripping the bamboo arms of her rocking chair as if they were coming to pluck her from the womb, and saying to my grandfather, 'It's looking lovely, Jorge, lovely. But you know me, nothing beats the smell of tarmac.' And in those first years of his marriage, the Calle Juncal must have appeared to my father less of a disappointing prize, more a cave full of hostile animals. That he didn't have his own cave to go back to increased the hostility.

But perhaps without being altogether aware of it, he was attracted to the elegance of the house. When he entered the hall after the closing of the street door, as he smelled the opulent darkness, he gave in to a repeated sense of wellbeing. A vast silence received him, mixing with the tang of wax, leather and wood ash. Glimmers of light from polished oak, bronze, old leather, lacquer and mirrors – the eyes of the house – emerged slowly from the shadows to meet him, he who held in his hand the same key as the owners. Money had built the house, and its submissive eyes reminded my father of the strength that had brought all these elements together, and provided a life sealed off from the chaos of the world behind the street door. The sheer scale of it was its force. Its beauty was not relevant.

Juncal was order imposed on a grand scale. Within, the house wore a public face that kept the heart at bay. My father was excluded somehow from the pride the house demanded. That pride lay in the house itself, in its criollo resonance of European palaces older than its own sixty years. My father was not a man to look deep into himself, and even if he had been he would not have accepted that it was the exclusion rather than its pomp that drew him to the Calle Juncal.

I suppose he loved me like something inside him that was trying to escape, and in his stuttering way he used his charm to keep me where he wanted me. He would scoop me up in his macho grip, and drop me as soon as I wanted to talk, claiming that he didn't know how. It would have been better for a father incapable of answering his eldest son's questions to simply leave him alone.

A distant dreamy light connecting me to him, both intimate and elusive, dims slowly on and off in my memory. The cosy yellow glow of a corner grocer, with the cheap perfume of Le Sancy soap and the rough, grey smell of laundry soap. It is the light that shines as the barrio settles into the night and the small shops brighten, becoming rooms offering themselves like the fruit they still display on the pavements in the lengthening shadows of tree-lined corridors. I associate this light not with Juncal, or its women, but with my father.

I remember, or I think I do, my father taking me with him on his rounds as doctor for the Electricity Board. I like to imagine that I was left on the front seat as he rushed into the depths of a narrow tenement to save a dying patient. My father was shy, but he was always showing off, and when the distraught women of the tenement discovered that a foundling – the child of that Clark Gable in the white coat – was at their door, they ran breathlessly across the courtyard to my small, illuminated bulk. Those breasts, which smelt of cooking, and against which I was crushed, may well be the source of that light, which owes nothing to Juncal.

If this did happen, no evidence of it was to be found in our house. After our escapade my father returned me to those four powerful, bored women who surrounded me with their babble, and whom I obeyed, too confused to keep anything to myself. I swallowed their memories whole, so that when I grew up theirs became mine. Even my memories of Papá seem somehow an echo of their voices. Papá was so poor. What did he have to counterbalance the brilliance of the Calle Juncal and its women? His looks, his smell of medicines, and his silence.

3

OTRAMAMÁ and her three daughters all sat together in Otramamá's white bathroom during the long time that it took her to bathe. They didn't just drop in but treated the room as their own, taking the opportunity to paint, comb, pluck, dab under their arms, and massage their thighs with a rubber roller to combat cellulite. Within those steamy walls they were Moors in a harem, untempted by sweets, protected by a virginal dryness. Never quite naked, they covered themselves with dressing gowns or petticoats. Otramamá bathed in her nightgown while around her the daughters gossiped, marking out their rules of life, precise, inconsequential and cruel. They shared out scissors and combs in a business-like way, without touching each other. If they wanted a back-rub they asked their maids to do it.

'Look at this horror,' said Tina, the second daughter, one morning. She was pinching a fold of skin on her hip with two fingers. 'I'm getting enormous, even though I eat like a bird.'

'You're making yourself ill with your diets,' said Otramamá. 'You've been at death's door four times and you're still obsessed with being fat. You let this little glutton gobble down the ham I buy specially for you, so I'll think you've eaten it.' She indicated at me with a tilt of the chin, giving me a look of complicity that reminded me we'd awoken in the same bed.

That morning something happened that had left me uneasy. Whilst I bit into Otramamá's dry toast without enthusiasm – in this at least I wasn't spoilt, and didn't like that the only prize of having slept in her bed was nothing more than an extra cup on my grandmother's coffee tray

– and as she twiddled the dial on the radio in search of her news programme, I heard amidst the flurry of chopped words, a woman's voice say the word luna. I promised myself I would never forget it, for the rest of my life.

'Since the government banned travel, people are letting themselves go,' said Clara, the youngest. 'If I were you, Tina, I wouldn't worry. One can get away with anything these days. You have no idea the hats people are wearing. Look what happened the other day in the park. The children were in those boaters bought for us in San Sebastián thirty years ago. An elegant woman came up and said they were adorable and that the children looked just like the poor little Tsarevitch.'

'Clara, don't exaggerate,' said Tía Pepa, her voice still hoarse with sleep. She was the eldest.

The women of Juncal followed Parisian fashion with rigid devotion. They liked to look good, but even more, they liked to be correct. Tina was the most fastidious of them all.

A three-panelled full-length mirror showed me I was not as cute as they would have me believe. It revealed something that did not resemble me, something squat, swarthy and sad-eyed, when I expected to see that brilliant plaything of my mothers: an only child, blue and dressed in blond silk. Who was lying then? Not them surely, the fault was mine, the *botarate*, the *meterete*, the *tragadalbas*, the *majadero*, the precocious twit, expressions I half-understood but all pointed to the same fault. They had said it once and it was enough. Why shouldn't I believe them, after all my docility was the price I paid for the enormous love they had for me. By following them blindly in all they did, I would be deserving of their love and their love alone. The point was to be the only one. The two years my brother took to come out was enough time for those Moors and their voraciousness. Yes, there is no doubt they chose me – what else was there – and I brought with me a certain hope. With a single kiss, they had branded me. I belonged to the girls of the Calle Juncal.

There were two types of legs in that bathroom. There were the long ones, which came from my grandfather, slender in the thigh, and round in the knee like the button on a shield, and then the short. Reluctantly lifting her nightgown, Otramamá inspected her short legs in the unforgiving mirror, out of proportion with her long torso, and seeing how her calf bulged out straight from her ankle – those ankles that I found deliciously martyrised by varicose veins – she consoled herself for not having transmitted them to her elder daughters.

'Sometimes our children save us from ourselves,' Otramamá said, but then regretted it as she glimpsed Clara's young legs, which had the same defects as her own.

'The-short-leg'. A term that even now jumps from my mouth when unawares, I see a new body of unremarkable proportions, and mechanically apply the obsessed eye of my mothers. Those are the legs I love and want to forget. They make me feel comfortable and caught. The long ones didn't console me, in that bathroom they were the legs of those who had not had children, and their sterile svelteness seemed to be of an artificial beauty like the shoulder pads fashionable at the time. My mothers took them very seriously, not only their length but their shape.

As a girl my mother had hung herself from trees, trying to lengthen her legs, but unsurprisingly it was her arms that grew. My sister's legs were bandaged to keep them slim from the age of seven. When she couldn't avoid having her picture taken, Otramamá stood on tiptoe, and afterwards tore up the photos. The bleeding vanity of these women, who had already found or even discarded their men, could be better understood if one saw the drawing rooms of Buenos Aires as slaughter houses.

But the importance Otramamá claimed as her own was

not physical. The famous intelligence of the Uriburus, together with their short legs and Indian features, had been handed down to her from both sides, as she was the daughter of first cousins. She brought to Buenos Aires a dowry of colonial cities isolated by miles of desert, a courtyard overlooked by a brow of mountains, fifteen static generations, and a hatred of our port city. That history, common to the rest of Spanish America, did not cut much ice in the white bathroom. She was born in the Calle Corrientes, at a time when her father, who had left their northern province twenty years before, had already amassed his millions. From that courtyard in the province of Salta all he had kept were a few family portraits, School of Cuzco, as stiff as dolls, and a silver maté kettle with feet in the shape of mestizo angels, which he used as a pattern for a tea set he had made in England.

The fixity of life in the hacienda of Salta, where in three hundred years not a roof tile had been changed nor a hectare bought, had turned into a frenzy of acquisition: a villa with a copy of the lantern of the Château de Chambord and of the gardens of the Monte Carlo Casino, a palace under construction in the Calle Lavalle, and a fine mausoleum in the cemetery of the Recoleta. Buenos Aires had become too bountiful to be hated any longer. Otramamá's father would be appointed Chancellor of the Exchequer, an uncle had succeeded to the presidency, and her brothers would take wives from the Casa Rosada.

When Otramamá spoke to me of the past, it was of Paris rather than Salta. Of Salta she knew only the spa at Rosario de la Frontera, which the Salteños couldn't afford and where the guests felt as immune to the Creole ways as they might in Vichy.

Although my grandmother did nothing to hide this family triumph, something finely tuned in her intelligence found the excess not only vulgar but banal. Success tends to be embellished by the optimism of memory, but it left her unmoved, as a girl sated with toys pines for a rag doll. Her indifference to Belle Époque opulence didn't mean that Otramamá was attracted by the simplicity of the thirties, with its revival of viceroyalty-style furniture and white walls. She couldn't tell, or didn't notice, the difference between the fakes and museum pieces she'd inherited from the Calle Lavalle. She wasn't exasperated by the provincial torpor of those colonial days, it just meant nothing to her. It was the same with anything Spanish. 'Why bring the majas back to life? As if were't sick of guitars,' she said disapprovingly when her cousin had her portrait painted by Zuloaga. Her own portrait, hidden in the servants' quarters, was painted in front of the Tuileries and showed her perfectly correct in a Worth gown and Reboux hat.

Still, she always spoke of her Creole forbears with pride. But did so discreetly, and laughed at what she saw as the pretensions of Tía Teodé, her sister-in-law, who described a Mamita who sauntered through the Gallant Indies, and a Papito straight out of Candide. Unlike Teodé, and unlike her cousin Pépé Uriburu, military president during the thirties, Otramamá didn't believe that the blood of the Conquistadors gave our class the right to govern. The people of the Calle Juncal were far too frivolous and Francophile to fall for the fascistic dreams of their relatives.

Otramamá never wavered from these convictions. When she had only a few months to live, and a stroke had reduced her speech to gibberish, she was given a poncho from Salta. 'Sacatuseco, viastuseco, sacatuseco,' she babbled her thanks, fingering the cloth and attempting a friendly grin. Later, alone with me, she pushed the poncho from her lap, muttering with unexpected clarity, 'What rubbish!'

In the white bathroom, I searched the mirror for an image of myself that matched Otramamá's stories, which always insisted on the 'best'. Instead, I found myself, a squat little boy who seemed to have nothing to do with her tales, or with the bleached, elegant bodies of the women surrounding me.

A harsh laugh cut through the steam. 'This boy is becoming rather common,' someone said. That disappointment, which I too felt, could have been voiced by any one of them.

There is one photograph that Otramamá didn't manage to tear up, of a group of dignitaries standing in the window of the Chambord villa. Beneath the window, lost amongst the flowers, is a little Indian in a dustcoat – my grandmother as a child. Those features were my own, the face I struggled to recognise in the bathroom mirror. When I pointed out our resemblance, Otramamá wouldn't acknowledge it, just as she often ignored my remarks on her mother's looks, which she liked to describe in adoring terms. 'But Misia Dolores was ugly and fat,' I said, taking the portrait framed in silver petals from Otramamá's bedside table. 'Here she is, look at her.' Otramamá snatched the oval miniature, covered it with the hand on which she wore her beautiful rings, and said, without looking at me, in a rather defeated voice, 'She was pretty, very pretty. You just don't know how to look.'

My aunts, the two 'girls' who had no children of their own, weighed less heavily on me. Tina, my godmother and my favourite, was tricky and hard to pin down. One day Otramamá heard her humming as she sat at the dressing table.

'Tina Bosch,' she was saying, 'Tina Bosch, Tinaboschtinaboschtinaboschtina. Why don't I call myself Tina Bosch?'

'Why would you want to be called Tina Bosch?' Otramamá asked. 'Why is a fancy Catalan name better than your own? You've always wanted things that don't belong to you.'

'Mamá, you keep getting things wrong. It wasn't me, it was Catita on the radio being her usual mad self.'

Her lie was so preposterous that it left my grandmother in doubt. Had she stopped to think, she might have understood her daughter's increasing detachment from the world around her. Tina was the second girl when they had hoped for a boy. Her face was so like her mother's that Otramamá was reminded of her own imperfections each time she looked at her. Tina contracted tuberculosis soon after becoming engaged to the heir of a tram company, whom she didn't love. She had spent the best part of fourteen years in bed with Pott's disease, enduring a spinal operation involving a transplant from the tibia, a recurrence of the TB, and the removal of a lung. She broke off her engagement after four thousand days, when she sensed that her fiancé was about to give up. Soon after this, streptomycin was discovered, and she began to recover. But her illness had left her isolated, and although she never said so, for she was the most submissive of daughters, she began to look down on the improvident ways of Juncal.

Tina inherited Otramamá's face, but not her chaotic intelligence, her flair, her colourful language. She had a tidy mind, and her humour was constructed from fragments of her mother's, which sounded sharper alongside the rambling wit of Clara and Otramamá.

She was hardly out of her teens when the illness took over. It embalmed her, preserving her immaturity and revealing her weakness for the surface of things, which took the form of collecting expensive editions of French classics. She didn't read them, she just used their bindings to furnish her virginal bedroom. The effect was of a sober luxury, the discretion of an absent minded bibliophile and of a natural and fastidious young woman of fashion, already composing her wardrobe, which culminated in that most admired of uniforms, the New Look tailleur of Christian Dior. She also sent off every year to Smythsons in London for a gold-edged appointment diary. This was a city where no one committed to anything more than two hours beforehand, but she filled it with a Sisyphean doggedness in her ant-like handwriting.

In her dealings with the outside world she was constantly ingratiating, far too polite, or so it seemed to her proud family. They saved face by sneering. 'Tina has become so smarmy,' they would say. But she was the only one who got things done.

She shared with my grandfather a fascination with social life. Otropapá was only alone during the siesta, when he would nap on the chaise-longue in his dressing room, a volume of Saint Simon's memoirs propped on his chest. Tina, when she was well again, took to accompanying him to the diplomatic receptions my grandmother had long since refused to attend. My aunt dressed with the same attention to detail as her father, and the two would leave the house looking like mannequins, a reminder to the outside world of the family's taste.

Even so, her social crawling was an embarrassment. If no one was better than her family, why did Tina worry about being nice to people who were not even blood relations? But she didn't care for money or blood, she cared for position, and was enthralled by nobodies who boasted of yachts and parties in Punta del Este. The worst thing was that when she offered herself to these people, she became like a woman possessed. Her attractive criollo voice, usually so dry, would turn into honeyed tones of banalities and genuflections.

However there was an edge to these social antics. As though she were playing an elaborate private joke, pushing to see how far she could go. How could she expect to be taken seriously when her politeness was so extreme? Sometimes I'd see her put the phone down on the table whilst the recipient of this sweetness would go on talking, as she continued to file her nails, winking at me as if to say, 'If you believe what you're hearing, you're an ass.' That love of the street was the sign of Tina's revolt against the Calle Juncal.

Tía Pepa slept a lot in those days. I used to wake her at noon, from a bed foul with cigarettes and an Indian smell that the Uriburus carried like a recessive gene. She would run long fingernails over the back of my neck, half-awake, a sensation like a bee that made me dizzy, and sing in her sticky voice,

> 'Amor, amor, amor.
> Nació de Dios
> para los dos
> nació del almaaaa...'

Then the two of us would grope our way as if sleepwalking to the bathroom, her eyes heavy like a seal's, and she would begin to brush her teeth. She wore a white dressing gown, which revealed her slim hips and her father's long legs. After a good deal of mouth rinsing, she'd sit in a white armchair, the first cigarette of the day in her mouth, and carefully passing the depilatory wax from the top of her foot to her knee with a languor that heightened the sleepy atmosphere, she wondered aloud to herself what pudding there would be for lunch.

Unlike Tina, Pepa had been married but was separated. 'Separated' was the first word that hurt me. Because I heard it unexpectedly from the very mouths of those half naked heroines in that bathroom who ordained the world. I realized that one of them was branded with a stain, with a wound that went on suppurating even though the blood was staunched with creams, which had been inflicted by a husband. Pepa had married and had been sacrificed. The sacrifice had been made to a monster. 'That Monster Caró.' In the steam of the bathroom That-Monster Caró was enough to silence them. My elder aunt's life had been wrecked before she was thirty and from its debris she had rescued one interest, the pudding of the lunch she had for breakfast. The refined disgust with which That-Monster Caró was uttered by those voices came nowhere near to expressing their feelings.

That-Monster-Caró was the only man who entered the bathroom. And with him the affront that the first-born should have returned to her spinster's bed robbed of the jewels and the furniture of her dowry, 'and even the linen he had carried off, the cad, the sheets which are meant to be the gift of the bridegroom. That he could steal her things one could accept, but to take back the bed-linen he had given to his wife, that is totally unforgivable,' twittered Tina, while Pepa, oblivious, went on rubbing the rubber roller over one thigh and then over the other, without lifting an eye.

There it was, so constant and indelible, the stain within the steam, lingering like something both mundane and awful. It was mentioned as a matter of course, as something that would eventually mend or be forgotten, but it was something I sensed as more dangerous than Tina's eternal illness, because it was the doing of a living monster, rather than God. He was pointed out to me once walking in the Calle Arroyo, dark, well dressed, with big grey eyes, a bit bent by the evilness, I thought, that had left them all vulnerable. That was why the word 'separated' had lodged in my memory as an illness, a shameful, incurable and humiliating infection, which only that hopeless Pepa could have contracted, despite the warnings of all her family, brought on by an inexplicable passion.

The ten years before my birth had gored them. This expression, more of Sancho Panza than his master, was my mother's. The words she'd heard as a child were engraved on her memory. She could barely spell, and probably even less understand what she said, but there the words lay, gold dust for her restless tongue to sift, as though she sought to protect words which would soon disappear. She spoke with a colourfulness that made me proud, even though her old Spanish and Quechua turns of phrase were sometimes cheapened by the rugby jargon of the husband she so admired.

First came the bankruptcy of the Uriburus. As with so many families who inherited but did not control their fortunes, being rich was something they took for granted, like being alive, and never really exploited. They spent the way they ate, without real pleasure. And since Buenos Aires society was made up of a network of cousins, all of them more or less of the same standing – no one else existed – they had no outlet for their vanity. One day, the estancias in the province of Buenos Aires, the vineyards of San Juan, the silver mine of Salta and our city properties would begin to produce as they should, and then the girls of Juncal would be really rich. Instead, one day, seven years after the Wall Street crash, they discovered all at once that they had become poor. Tina pinpointed it to the moment when Otramamá asked Maison Carraux whether she could pay for ballroom gowns in instalments. Otramamá dated it to a few months earlier at the Bristol Hotel in Mar del Plata, when she received a telegram from her husband that read: BROKE STOP CHANGE HOTELS STOP VERY SORRY STOP MUST TIGHTEN OUR BELTS.

They took the crash without much fuss, perhaps even with relief. In the end, it was the change they were longing for. Disaster was something in their bones, even if they had no memory of it. The chaos wrought in the Viceroyalty of the Río de la Plata by independence had robbed them, exiled them and cut their throats, many times over.

Otramamá didn't speak about the crash as easily as about other things, but it fascinated me, and I badgered her to tell me about it.

'Well, my darling, I'll tell you if you'll stop nagging me. After my father died my brother Enrique, who was very clever when it came to other people's business, and was President of the Banco de la Nación, looked after our fortune. Your grandfather went to his office every day, terribly nice but weak as always, and Enrique, who was very bossy and temperamental, wouldn't let him get a word in. Your Tío Pancho, my eldest brother, didn't help matters, he was up to his ears in politics and *La Fronda*, that bottomless pit of a paper of his. And the vineyards failed to produce. One day a friend of your grandfather, Count Marone, who owned Cinzano and was married to the Infanta María Cristina, offered them a partnership; he wanted to use our Caucete wines to make vermouth, but Enrique sent him packing, saying he preferred to be master of his own house. We had two thousand hectares of vines back then. Then came the Thirties. The governor of San Juan was a Radical, so he cut off our credit. Enrique, Don Quixote that he was, didn't think of pulling any strings. Anyway, that's all I know about it.'

I learned later that my grandmother had said to my grandfather, 'I would rather a thousand times over – a thousand times, do you understand – lose everything, than have harsh words with my brother.'

It didn't cost her much, this detachment, for she had been born with not one but a handful of silver spoons in her mouth. Her father, who had a grandson older than she was, bought her emeralds when she was twelve – as he might have done a mistress – and satiated her for the rest of her life. I never met anybody more disinterested than Otramamá, I don't remember hearing her ever really longing for anything. She wanted little things that she could have afforded to buy, despite her impoverishment, but to keep herself eager she did not: a crocodile handbag, a Breton dresser to replace the Art Nouveau one in the estancia dining room. But that was a lie, she spoke her wishes for the sake of speaking, out of courtesy, to resemble the rest.

She liked travelling by tram, and one of her extravagances was to pay twice for a journey. We'd take the tram from our front door, travelling three blocks further to Retiro Railway Station, the last stop. There, at the foot of the slope leading up to the Calle Juncal, we'd wait for as long as fifteen minutes, until the empty tramcar was full again. The Señora wore a hat with little black feathers, an Astrakhan coat, and white kid gloves; I, a grey overcoat and cap. I admired myself in the windows, Otramamá did not, but people getting off the train and on to the tram stared furtively. Otramamá would tell the ticket collector to keep the change.

'Como aves precursoras de primavera,
en Madrid aparecen las violeteras,
que pregonando
parecen golondrinas que van piando,
que van piando...'

she sang in my ear. The tram made her sing. Her nose wasn't the swallow's beak in the song, but a bird of prey, and her eyes — half-closed, surrounded by a thousand wrinkles — were those of an eagle whose hood had just been removed. We were on our way to the cinema in a click-clacking gondola that climbed from the river flats by the English clock tower, up the steep and narrow Calle Tucumán, just the two of us.

We glided along, the other passengers ranged around us like cushions, and the smell of the river mixed with petrol fumes added to the adventure. The tram's bell, the metallic creak of the conductor's ticket machine, and the tiny snip as the ticket was cut, the genteel voices, the coarse ones with their sibilant immigrant accents, saying, 'One ten cents, please,' or 'Three twenties' or 'Just as far as the Obelisk', all combined to serenade us from a separate gondola that I pictured floating a little behind ours, and which embroidered my grandmother's thin, finely-pitched song. It wasn't that we didn't want to acknowledge the others; we didn't see them. Just as the black limousines of those Peronist days blew across the city like a high wind, scattering traffic with motorcycles and blaring horns, so Otramamá and I entered the centre of Buenos Aires with the same impunity, on the ebb and flow of the breeze of the tram we had made our own, singing.

4

LUNCH was at one-thirty. Everyone gathered in a little sitting room a good distance from the dining room where the sole purpose was this – to wait for lunch. Family and guests alike would sink comfortably into armchairs, without much to say to each other.

Otramamá passed the time knitting. She made us children untidy jerseys from the cheapest wool, and I sulked whenever I was forced to try one on. My great-uncle Bebé Artayeta, Otropapá's only brother, who had never married, sat in a hard chair against the wall, coughing up phlegm from time to time. Pepa chain-smoked, sitting straighter than the others and self-absorbed. She stood out from the rest, her fine long legs half-crossed in a ladylike way peculiar to her, as to the flautist of the Ludovisi Throne, and I could feel my eyes drawn to them, to not lose any of their repose or movement, as if something important for me depended on it. Otropapá would enter the room and pour himself a glass of sherry that he hardly touched. My grandfather's elegance was his armour, not because he showed it off but because his height, his mildness and his good looks would have to be ruffled in some way in order to make them bearable. I sensed an edge beneath those perfect manners that I studied carefully, hoping to copy them, as if the cut of his clothes expressed him better than his warm and absent hugs.

I had to be careful about copying my grandfather. Once when I was small I told Tía Teodé that when I grew up I wanted to be a gentleman with a flower in my buttonhole. Everybody laughed – everyone but my mother, who said darkly, 'We'd better watch him, we don't want him turning into a useless dandy like my father or my grandfather Artayeta who couldn't keep a coin in their pockets.'

Otropapá set the tone of the Calle Juncal, which had been built by his grandfather. It was he who gave the house polish. It didn't pretend to compete with the most palatial houses in the city, but it challenged them with its refinement. My grandfather strolled the streets of Buenos Aires in suits the colour of dead leaves, and even those who didn't appreciate his subtlety — something porteños were seldom capable of — said that there was no-one more exquisite, as his coats fell from his narrow shoulders, flaring out like a dress in a Watteau drawing. After much deliberation, he had placed the 'best' of our rather formless art collection in the drawing room, a room so stark it made visitors shiver. Otropapá had a Florentine restraint, the origin of which was a mystery, had been educated by the Jesuits in Buenos Aires, learned French in France, eaten puchero in his childhood and then later French food, had read López's history of the Argentine, Eugène Sue, Balzac and the letters of the Marquise de Sévigné, dressed in clothes made for him in London, and had lived, in short, just like his friends and relations, but still felt deeply that roses should be shorn of their petals, hats of their plumes and mirrors of their sheen.

When he had to deal with the ceremonies of death, he would send back the undertakers' candelabra and orchids, hide the lace fringe of the coffin, leaving the lead inside the mahogany exposed, and allow only a single bunch of violets to be placed in the hands of the corpse, with an everyday rosary. 'There's no need for frills,' he would say, before he started to prune. But he was chaste rather than dry — although this proud word applied to his taste, and not his morals.

Tina would come down to lunch from her sick room. Fine and pale, her aquiline face looked more than ever like Otramamá's. My mother often arrived home at the last moment, coming straight into the dining room. I remember once being so struck by her entry — she walked in still wearing her grey Astrakhan jacket, belted like a trench-coat, fresh from her morning adventures – that as she removed her gloves and apologised to the family, all so bored with each other and the daily ritual of lunch, smiling at me, smiling at them, my fork slipped and my egg squirted, landing on my grandmother's black sleeve.

'Caracho!' cried out Otramamá. 'Casimiro, bring a cloth, please. This child should stay out of the dining room until he's learned how to eat.'

'Mamá I'm sorry, it was my fault,' said my mother, producing her handkerchief in her usual keenness to help. 'I distracted him, blowing kisses. He was looking so sweet. But you'll never guess what La Negra told me just now at the florist's. The government has taken the Pereyras' estancia.'

'I heard the same thing from Matías at the Círculo,' said my grandfather from the head of the table, wiping his mouth with a napkin. The Círculo de Armas was his club, of which he was president.

'And a good thing, too. They were Rosistas, and thieves. They deserve it,' said Tío Bebé in his phlegmy voice. 'They made their fortune paying Rosas peanuts for the confiscated properties of Unitarians who'd fled the country.' Although he was speaking of events that had taken place over a century before, the whites of his bulging blue eyes began to redden.

'Perhaps, but it'll start with the Pereyras and finish with us,' my mother answered. 'Agustincito Elía has heard that Tapiales may be next.'

'First Rosas, then Perón. So what? We'll have it all back again when Perón gets his come-uppance,' cut in my grandfather. His wife's lost fortune seemed to have made him either too generous, or indifferent.

'How?' spluttered Tío Bebé, who owned nothing but his share in our estancia. 'In 1855 they gave us back Maipú less sixteen leagues of land. Do you realise how much that is?

Forty thousand hectares! We were left forty thousand hectares short! And who kept them? Piñeyro and Anchorena, Rosistas just like the Pereyras. It's their turn now, and if they never get their land back, it's only what they deserve.'

Otramamá smiled. Turning to her brother-in-law she laid her ring hand, the hand that winked at me, its green and white eyes exploding with light, on his worn sleeve.

'Bebé, *du calme* – please. Don't go on again about the robbery of Maipú. Just the other day I was at the Rocas' reception, and Angelita said to me – in a perfectly nice way, thank goodness – that whenever she sees you, you carry on about the grounds of San Simón being right in the middle of our land.'

'But it's true my dear, it's the truth,' Tío Bebé answered, gripping the edge of the table with both hands. 'San Simón and El Chajá, too. How could we forget the theft of forty thousand hectares?'

'Forget? Certainly not. But it's slightly complicated by the fact that your uncle married the thief's granddaughter,' said Otramamá, in the special tone she reserved for her in-laws.

'Perhaps Tío Bebé would feel less strongly about all this if he still had his hectares,' said Tina, smearing her egg over the plate to make it look eaten. 'Tina! Don't be cheeky,' Otropapá scolded her.

'I'm so bored with my mornings since the Sociedad de Beneficencia has been taken over. The knitting only helps for a while,' my grandmother said, changing the subject with that knack she had for keeping hold of the thread of what she was feeling.

The dining and drawing rooms were squeezed into two widths of the ten-metre frontage laid down by the city's founder in 1580. The dining room had been inspired by a grander model, and so its furnishings fitted rather tightly. At one end was a muddle of columns, at the other an agglomeration of doors. In a picture between the windows, an English wood was sinking into romantic darkness, and in front of the trees, on a beach hardly enclosed by a sea which disappeared into the frame, two of Jonathan Swift's intelligent horses – one a grey, the other a dark chestnut – twisted their fine heads to speak to each other. On the opposite wall Gulliver joined his hands in supplication, begging asylum of a meek-eyed chestnut, while behind him a boat unfurled its sails. But it was the frames round these over-sized paintings that I really liked. Their faded gold branches and loops were like a battle, like the wind. They whirled around the paintings as though around the eye of a storm. Carved by someone with more passion in his hands than Gilpin, the painter of the pictures, ever had in his head, I believed that without them Gulliver would never have been granted the asylum on which his life depended.

Otramamá focused intermittently on the big horses within their sumptuous mounts: 'I don't want to exaggerate, but they hate us. Those doctors with their Italian surnames and their smart houses in Caballito and their cars, they see us as an obstacle...'

'To what? An obstacle to what?' Pepa interrupted her. She felt sleepy, it was only the first course and too early for worries. At that stage she could only manage some patience for her father, of whom she was the favourite.

'What a bore your sleepiness. You don't get it do you. We're an obstacle to their illusions, to their fantasies of the promised land, where time begins with their arrival. They see us like the *signori* they left behind when they embarked in Genoa. And here we are, we jump up like Jack-in-the-boxes *pour les désabuser*, even if they are perfectly happy with the salaries we paid them. We, owners of the Sociedad de Beneficencia, bossy and ignorant, but worse still, rich. If they only knew that they live so much better in Caballito than my cousins in Salta.'

And she fingered deliberately and absent-mindedly the edge of her plate of the Compagnie des Indes, whose little bumps reminded her of tapioca soup.

'Sometimes I feel as confused as them. Who are we with our four hundred years in America? Mama Casiana Castro, my grandmother, who presented a bouquet of flowers dressed as an angel to Bolívar when he entered as a conqueror in Potosí, the great Liberator, knew it much better than I do with her patio life, simple as the earthly paradise. But when my mother's turn came, she lost her way. Too much money, Villa Elisa, the Calle Lavalle, dinners for thirty with maître d'hotel and a footman behind each chair. It was all too sudden.'

She laughed. 'In the end we're as parvenus as Doctor Culaciatti.'

'But prouder,' said Pepa.

Otropapá raised his eyebrows, bored. Meanwhile Tío Bebé started to choke as he stared at his sister-in-law, irritated and confused as he always felt when faced with her intelligence.

'I'm not sure what you are getting at, Mecha, but I seem to remember that at one point you said they hate us. Well I do feel something like that at the estancia. Not the gauchos, no, they accept us like the bad weather, but the people of Maipú, the immigrants. Those tenants, Italian or Basque, it doesn't matter which, who take advantage of the frozen rents, we'll end up selling them the land because we won't be able to afford the taxes. On top of everything they allow themselves to hate us.' Us, for Tío Bebé, meant the family, and not the class, as it was for Otramamá.

My great-uncle was perfectly aware that his class was limited to two hundred families more or less related to each other, but his narrow mind held only the horizons of Maipú populated by his maternal cousins, and that was enough to fill his world. As for the Artayetas, there were only Otropapá and himself. The frontier neighbours were easily lost beyond the vastness of those sixty square miles. They were few and far between: the Ortiz Basualdo of Las Armas, the Iraola of Labardén, the Peña of Madariaga. The Rosista intruders, Anchorena and Alzaga, who had married into us, were accepted but were frequently reminded of their depredations. The others, those intruders who had bought up our land, were now so close that they had swallowed Yamoidá, El Arazá, Pichimán, and a good part of Miraflores, of which they had even changed the name, were rich but for us they didn't exist. If by chance they came to call they would be received on the terrace, like the tenants.

We were not the only ones. The criollo clans were vast, and like the Scottish they vied with each other jealously. Our only difference was to have been Unitarians, at a time when the other great estancieros had thrown in their lot with Rosas. And so my adorable uncle full of phlegm basked in the glory of being a Unitarian, even more than in the glory and myth of our possession of the land over three centuries rather than one, like the others, the Federals.

Because the mystery of that myth worked on my uncle's mind like the dogma of the Immaculate Conception on the mind of Benita Flores, descendant of slaves, our guardian. For both of them, the Parthenogenetic Virgin and the womb of silver that gave birth to the estancia were the essence that gave them distinction, that helped them to live.

'I don't know why, I don't know why,' Tío Bebé snorted, then he fell silent.

Otramamá smiled: 'Because we blot out their sun. Don't forget that the immigrants come from Spain and Italy, lands of envy.'

'They came to where they were needed,' Pepa insisted. 'It's all very well, but if we hadn't let them in, who would have worked the land? *To govern is to colonise*, etc.'

'In Maipú there's no land worth cultivating, there are

only cows. And horses, of course,' Tío Bebé added more gently.

'They might not like us, but they work harder than our gauchos. If not, why does Samuel Basualdo only employ Basque puesteros?' Pepa once awake had embarked on a subject nobody supposed would interest her.

'Twenty thousand sheep is what Samuel Basualdo has. With that many it's hardly surprising,' concluded Otropapá in that neutral voice so neutral that it always distanced him from me; as if beneath the bonhomie, so much appreciated by Buenos Aires – as Otramamá liked to inform us every now and then in the little tone she used to cut short the vanity of others – there lurked a rejection, or worse, an indifference, more damaging than my father's.

Unlike his older brother – whose society was reduced to the family and evenings at the Jockey Club, rather the Círculo which was Otropapá's domain, surrounded by five friends all as nice and dim as himself -Otropapá lived in the world. And though he carried his share of pride like every child of the Calle Juncal, albeit more discreetly, he was aware of the fortunes of others.

Silence took over the dining room, the air trembled with things unsaid, silver cut against china in a desultory rhythm. There was something heartless in those repetitive clinks, a load that cannot be spoken of and that my family were not aware of. This unvoiced sadness was no more than a vague indigestion for them, the well-known heaviness of midday. And the voices shifted to the horses, to their frames, to the columns, to the shiny laugh of the great silver tureen.

This must be why my voice breaks in public. Because I need to express what they didn't bother to mutter. My tongue was spoiled by those lunches at the house of the Calle Juncal.

'Poor Mamá,' Tina said, relieved that her mother had failed to notice her untouched plate being taken away.

'Do you think you'll be missed at the children's hospital?'

'Who knows, my dear,' Otramamá said. 'I certainly miss it. They said we used to stick our noses into everything, that we stopped work from getting done, that we behaved as though the hospitals were our own homes and the doctors our servants, that we were stingy with the coffee and humiliated the poor with our furs.' My grandmother's sarcastic laugh made her seem a little mad. 'If only you knew about That Woman's behaviour on her trip to Europe. Seven times a day she changed her outfits, the exhibitionist, and on charity visits she'd look down on her hostesses if she found them too simply dressed for her taste. "You're wearing that?" she'd say. "The poor will only respect us if we dress like royalty." Eva actually had the nerve to say this to the Roman princesses whom the Pope had forced into receiving her.'

'What do you expect, when the woman spent her life between two Juníns?' Clara said angrily.

'What are Juníns?' Otramamá asked. 'Or are you attempting a *jeu de mots*?'

'Don't you know that Junín is the street where all the brothels are, and she was born in a slum in the town of Junín?'

'Ché, the only thing I know about brothels is that Maneco Demaría liked to go there to drink maté.'

'*Ces dames s'échauffent,*' cut in my grandfather. 'Enough! Has the government's vulgarity turned all your heads?'

Otramamá stared at him. 'But Jorge, it should amuse you when we talk like this. I know you like talking dirty with Pepita Errázuriz, she told me so. So why not in your own house?'

'Pepita's like a Frenchwoman,' said my grandfather coolly.

'*Alors quoi?*'

'In France, the women speak like men.'

My grandmother's fingers began to drum on the table, like a tap dripping faster and faster, punctuating her words. 'That's because they can talk to men. Ever since the time of Marguerite de Navarre – no, what am I saying, since Christine de Pisan – they've been treated as equals,' she said. 'But men are paying for it here, my dear, they're paying all right. This Evita is the demon your machismo created. The whore you've longed for has arrived to take her revenge. There she is, decked out in Dior, dethroning ministers. You deserve her.' And she started to hum *De triste coeur chanter joyeusement*, adapting with her good ear the tune of Las Violeteras to the poem of the daughter of Pisa. On the whole, Otramamá felt that she had been taught and packaged well enough as a girl to set her up for life, so she surveyed her family table de haut en bas, and never looked again at a book, other than her missal.

My grandfather gasped mockingly and raised his eyebrows, half-surprised, half-amused. 'Quiet, Mecha! Where have you learned all this nonsense?'

Pepa, halfway through the chicken pie, suddenly woke up and joined in. 'Don't worry Papá,' she said, 'They aren't her ideas.' Otramamá's daughters treated her without much respect. 'She got it all from that sissy Englishman Victoria Ocampo brought to La Armonía. He wrote about Berlin in the twenties and he's a friend of the Atuchas. I think his name is Ishterwood, or something like that. I remember him telling us everything Mamá's just said, in that reedy little voice of his. He said we were blind to the importance of Eva Perón, that we're subject to prejudices this country should be free from. That Eva was a phenomenon, a combination of San Gennaro, Pachamama and Greta Garbo, that she fitted the Argentine like a glove, and that Victoria was judging her as if from some airy-fairy salon in Paris.'

My grandfather gave his daughter the grimace of disgust

usually reserved for badly cooked food. 'What on earth are you saying?'

'I'll tell you, word for word, what he said,' Pepa said, biting and sucking her lips.

'You and your elephant memory. What did he mean?' asked her father.

'I'm not sure really. Victoria and he were arguing, Victoria was very flustered. He was as cool as a cucumber, sipping whisky after whisky. He told Fina Unzué that La Armonía was like Newport in the middle of the desert, a mirage, and he was a mirage too, and perhaps all of us were. And then he let out this respectful little laugh. And Fina said to me, "This Englishman might be a darling my dear, but he's got a sting in his tail." He was small, a bit insignificant, with a crew cut. Well bred though, and intelligent, full of kowtows and beg-your-pardons. I didn't like him much.'

'Desert – such *culot*!' Otramamá murmured.

'Shut up, all of you – shut your mouths!' shouted Tío Bebé. 'You're wrong. We're on the edge of an abyss, and none of you can see it. We're surrounded by the mob Sarmiento brought into the country. What does Perón have to do with Rosas? Rosas was one of us, yes he was a criminal, but he was a gentleman. Perón is a thug. This country is now a nation of thugs. And it's going to stay that way. Listen to the people on the streets – they talk like Italians. Perón is Perone.' He spat the words out with contempt. 'It's all the fault of that pedant Sarmiento, that penniless provincial. General Roca was right – he warned us what would happen to our country if it was governed by immigrants.' Tío Bebé's face had turned dark red, his blue eyes even bloodier than before.

Just then one of the dining-room doors opened a crack, and an old woman scuttled in. Dressed in liquorice black, shuffling very quickly in flat shoes, she had on a little hat, stained gloves and carried a large handbag, and pinned to her breast was a brooch of the Argentine flag made from precious stones.

'Hello, Blanca, sit down,' said my grandmother over the noise of scraping chairs, as all the men made to get up. 'Casimiro, a chair for Señora Blanca. Where have you been?'

'Where do you think? At the Mass for Tata Justo. Today is the anniversary of the battle of Pepirí Guazú. I had a Mass celebrated at the cathedral. There's not much point in waiting for the government to remember.'

'Bebé's a bit cross with the Federales today, so perhaps it's better we leave Tata Justo Urquiza out of this ... How did you get here?'

'On foot, my dear, on foot. Not a single tram came by. I walked down Esmeralda, and stopped in at the Santa Unión for one minute to say hello to the Mother Castísimo Esposo. The poor thing is terribly worried. She told me an awful story, although these days what else can we expect?'

Blanca Campos Urquiza de Amadeo Artayeta, as she announced even to her fellow passengers on the tram, was very ugly, and reputed to be malicious and mean. She ignored me, and I hated the sight of her.

'What, my dear? Tell us.'

'They've made it compulsory for the nuns to read La Peróna's book to the school children.' Her voice barked, like the otters of the laguna of the estancia.

On the days when there was no afternoon school, I was allowed to lunch in the dining room, while my brother and sister ate an hour earlier in the nursery. But in the evening I had to go back to eating supper with them off Beatrix Potter plates, sitting down at eight, when lunch had finished only at three. I found this humiliating. I'd tried to teach them to eat a banana with a knife and fork, as Tía Teode had taught me, but they paid no attention. *Martín has become quite pompous since his grand lunches,* said Miss

Judy, the new governess. My role as emissary of the powerful made me unpopular not only in the nursery but in the servant quarters also.

We children seldom ventured to the reception rooms on the first floor. They weren't out of bounds but I never explored them on my own, and if I did, I felt I had to explain what I was doing there. Those darkened rooms, twice the size of the others in the house, filled me with awe. The dining room and small sitting room were the only ones we used, and the recent presence of humans made them more interesting than the embalmed and abandoned atmosphere of the darker drawing rooms, where even the fabrics smelt metallic.

In the dining room the table and chairs seemed arranged in accordance with a canon. Crumbs remained as evidence of the diners, just as the dust of the host survives at the bottom of the chalice, and the room held a degree of the terrible that our overpainted parish church of the Socorro lacked. Once lunch was over, it lay empty, nobody was left. The black table shone like the bottom of a well, on its polished surface the silver dishes glimmered like aquatic flowers, and as the reflections deepened in the still water, their silver bellies trembled. Light filtered through lace blinds as thick as wax and the colour of butter, bringing the grey horse into relief, and sinking the English wood into a black as dense as the table. But the picture frames absorbed the light, their dark gold brightened and became transparent and fluid, softening their power. As the afternoon sun flooded in, the dining room of Juncal swelled like a cathedral filled with light. Only the table kept its cool. The two chairs with arms remained at each end, the rest had gone back against the wall.

5

M Y GREAT aunt Teodé wasn't as affectionate as Otramamá, but she was more consistent. She kept her
promises and finished her stories. Her monologues had a
greater authority than my grandmother's and one day —
after she had suffered the first of the strokes that would
kill her — I realised that I had never learnt how to talk to
her. She's never really been interested in what I had to say,
I thought, as I sat next to that poor, twisted, mouth, that
latched on to the world, implacable, like a cupping glass,
wondering why she didn't get on with it and die. Finally she
did die, at the age of ninety-two, after hanging on for years,
angry and mute. And once she was dead, her voice became
more present, and young and easier.

The four fingers of her right hand bent over at the tips
like the top of a Phrygian cap, ever since the night when as
a girl she had run out into the garden after a bath wearing
only a towel, at the wedding of an aunt. They were the most
special part of her, and their calming rigidity — like the
beak of an eyeless parrot — reminded me of the bodies of
old people which resemble old people's gifts. But Tía Teodé
had a commanding manner, and the voice of a judge which
conferred undue rigour to her intelligence, much given
to gadgets and novelties. Her Pharaonic pride sustained a
rather undistinguished body, unlike Otramamá, who with
her opaque bulk and aquiline features looked like an Inca
ñusta. Ironically, despite her old porteño blood Tía Teodé
could pass for a Spanish immigrant. Her skin was very
white, her face round, her eyes round like two black buttons,
her eyebrows thick, with the frown line so deep it cut into
her short nose like an angry wound. She had shiny white
hair that grew out of her temples like an egg, the measured

gait of a duck, full legs, and an ample bosom, and although she had not much money left, she had pearls. A great many of them, big ones in her ears, coils of them around her neck, and long strands in her cleavage that emerged every now and then down at her navel, from between the buttons of her fur coat.

For a time I loved her more than anyone else. This was during the two months that we spent together in Paris. Tía Teodé had no children of her own, but she was godmother to a number of her nephews and nieces, and took each in turn to Europe for their education. I, the first grandchild of her husband's sister, was the last of the chosen. When we arrived in our rooms in a hotel on the Rue du Faubourg Saint-Honoré, the Señora was over seventy-five and I not yet ten.

'Get dressed. We're going to see Monsieur Gimpel, so you can try on the *pélisse*. And don't rumple me!' said the Señora, batting away my embraces.

The windows opened into the empty, leaden light that signals the imminence of snow and that awakens in people a kind of delicious impunity. Tía Teodé's deformed and efficient fingers spread butter on the light bread. Our rooms were tall and red; her bed had a roof and walls. Suddenly the silence became intense, and it began to snow. I'm in Paris, I thought. How am I ever going to pay for it?

'Totola, I would like us to go to Lourdes before my birthday,' I said. 'Do you think we could? There's so little time left. That's what I want for my birthday – and a rosary, one like yours with silver medallions.'

'There's time, my treasure. But why before your birthday?'

'Because I'm going to be ten.'

'And what will you ask of the Virgin?'

'For her to help me become a saint. Do you think that's too much? She might think I'm a pest who never stops asking for things.'

'Ask her only to make of you what she wants.'

'No, Totola, no, what if she wants to use me as an example of evil, like Judas? What if she tries to put me at the edge of hell, just to see if I can escape? I only want to be a boy saint, like Ceferino Namuncurá or St Louis Gonzaga. And to be free from temptation.'

'Ooh la la, what a clever little so-and-so. How little he asks for, how little he expects.'

'Totola, don't laugh at me. I'm really scared about my birthday. Can we take Communion in the grotto at Lourdes? Will we take Communion together? How will I confess in French? The priest may not speak Spanish.'

'You can just say to him, "*Mon père, je m'accuse de vouloir le ciel dès aujourd'hui.*" He'll give you the full four mysteries as a penance.'

'The more I pray, the more I'll save my soul.'

'And the world? And the flesh? Just wait till they get hold of you. I'd like to see you then.'

'But you won't see anything, you'll be dead.'

'I'll watch you from heaven, poor love, struggling away, and I'll pray for you. Now, put on your beret and let's get going.'

'Totola, I think I should give up the *pélisse*. I have to begin to deny myself things, since I'm going to be ten. You don't mind, do you? It's not that I don't want it – I'm dying to have a fur-lined overcoat just like Otropapá's.'

'Do as you like my dear, I know you didn't like the fur I was going to buy you. "Otropapá's fur is *loutre*," you said, you ungrateful boy, turning your nose up and fingering those furs Monsieur Gimpel showed us. You're a complicated little thing, and you're pretentious with it. But you have charm, and that'll land you straight in hell.'

'Don't confuse me with your intelligence – you take advantage because you're grown up.'

'All right, that's enough. If we're not going to the furrier, we'll go and change my galoshes in the Avenue Victor Hugo.'

'And then can we walk down the Rue de la Pompe?'

'How odd you like it so much, but yes, if you want.'

'It reminds me of Buenos Aires.'

'But it's the least charming street in Paris.'

Tía Teodé laughed at me, but I loved her all the same. My love for her was different, more intimate than my feelings for my parents and real aunts, who were all in Paris with us that winter thanks to a permission to travel issued by the government God knows why. I loved her because she was old, alone, because beneath that pomposity she was soft. It was as if I had as my captive a lioness even older and more glorious than the Argentine Republic – after all, our national anthem had been created for her great-grandmother to sing. I told myself that the poor dear had only me to love, and the thought made me cry. This made me feel so virtuous that I asked for another present.

'This boy is very mixed up,' I heard Pepa say, on the day she and the others set off for Brittany and I chose to remain with the Señora, who was coming down with the flu.

When Teodé was better, she and I strolled in the Bois de Boulogne. There was snow on the ground, and the landscape seemed alien. I didn't recognise these browns that froze into purple, sucking away the sun and leaving only stone-like trees. Tía Teodé wanted to pee, so she opened her umbrella and crouched down behind it in the snow. I was mortified. My great-aunt shouldn't need to do such things. She should read, and stroll through Paris, down the Rue du Faubourg Saint-Honoré, recalling her life. That was what she was meant to do, to remember. It was normal and beautiful that La Señora de Uriburu remembered, and that walking with her in Paris was a way of witnessing her memories. If not, why was I here? How else could I be expected to accept those horrible, purple browns, getting colder and colder, other than by seeing them through her eyes? But here she was, squatting behind her black umbrella on that strange field of snow, my great-aunt peeing like a little girl.

'Keep an eye out, my treasure. Don't worry, I'll be quick. Ooh la la, how cold it is, my bottom's freezing. Don't look – you'll only see an old bottom behind an umbrella. Poor love, I'm embarrassing you so, you think we're like angels and have no human frailty. What a bore that this old woman who takes you to see the Bois can't cope with the call of her bladder. I shall have to pay you for the shame of it. I'm going to take you to tea at the Georges V.'

We stopped at our hotel so Tía Teodé could change her clothes. I had nothing to keep out the cold of that European February. My grey suit had short trousers and so every day I wore a pair of twenties knickerbockers my godfather had given me, and some yellow lace-up boots that were rustic and fully waterproof. I thought them marvellous. Tía Teodé had bought them for me in Aux Trois Quartiers when my brand-new Buenos Aires shoes that had cost a fortune in Harrods got soaked through in the first snow. I also wore a black beret – a Basque beret, which my aunt considered essential to mark me out as a first-class tourist, and made my father laugh – more proof of his ignorance, as far as I was concerned. And I also had a brown overcoat and a bright green tartan scarf. Since the Señora approved, it never occurred to me to consider whether my attire might be less than perfect. She donned her mink coat, pushing out the pearls beneath her buttons, put on a hat trimmed with birds that seemed a bit much even to me, put on her glasses and picked up her umbrella. We strolled across Paris at a leisurely pace, for although the Hôtel Georges V was some distance from the Hôtel Bristol, we went everywhere on foot.

Inside, the light was yellow, as if the sun were shining through alabaster walls. A *maître d'hôtel* of paralysing politeness led us over the thick carpet, between rows of small tables covered in linen, silver, crystal, pastries, lap dogs eating sandwiches, dainty cups and red fingernails. On and on we went, making for the invisible end of the room. I felt as though Tía Teodé and I were getting married and our walk was the procession up the aisle, between rows of guests who eyed us vaguely while continuing to speak to one another in loud voices.

I glanced up at Totola and saw that she was puffed up and serious, her fur coat too pale against the black *tailleurs* of the women at the tables, her bird hat too much, sumptuous but suspect, like a ceremonial toque in a dream. And yet I felt proud. I knew that our arrival at the altar did not depend on me, but somehow an awareness of my ignorance gave me strength. I had never before been taken to tea in such a vast room, I had never been married, but Tía Teodé, who had been through both, seemed to be asking for my help. Beyond the silence which engulfed us a piano was playing 'Smoke Gets in Your Eyes' and the slender, painted ladies, their hats tight-fitting helmets among glossy curls, shifted their dogs about like chips on green baize. At last we reached a table at the back and she sat down, exhausted.

'I've been walking between rows of Parisian women for more than fifty years,' she said, smiling, 'and they still make me feel like rubbish.'

6

Now I am no longer following the granddaughter of the
national anthem as she waddles like a duck through
Paris, but trotting through the barrio of Caballito, in the
wake of a tall woman with the palest eyes in the world.
It was the autumn two years before those scenes in Paris,
and our new governess Miss Judy and I were walking along
pavements scrawled with leaves of the paraíso tree, on our
way to an old people's home run by the Russian Orthodox
Church.

I was borne along on a new wind brought by the European war that was changing the routine of the Calle Juncal.
This wind was incarnate in Miss Judy, who had replaced
grumpy old Miss Amy whom Mamá had sent packing when
her maid Matilde found her tippling Mamá's perfumes. It
appeared that in an unexpected rush of benevolence, the
Virgin had decided that we deserved the gift of a young
guardian.

The Virgin of Perpetual Succour, constantly in my
prayers, whose bejewelled icon stood in our church, would
not have been out of place here. The old Russian Orthodox women, warming themselves in the strong sun of the
porteño autumn, with their frayed furs, their thick noses
and grey eyes, crossed themselves fervently – in reverse –
before icons that were festooned with little candles. But the
home represented too strange and poor a world for me to
like. The women were beautifully polite and melancholy.
Miss Judy told me that they had lost everything because of
the Russian revolution.

The shabbiness of the Orthodox home made me sad,
above all when the ladies took out some yellowing photographs of their old estates and described them to us in

French with r's even hoarser than those of Otropapá, while looking at me out of eyes so lost that I shivered, despite my hat and overcoat. It was as though they were telling me, between sighs, 'Take care, take great care of what you have, for what happened to us can happen to you.'

But the ordeal of these visits was a small price to pay for Miss Judy. Her presence, with the wind that seemed to billow around her, pulling back her blonde hair to reveal an Aryan profile straight from a totalitarian propaganda poster, made the rituals of the Calle Juncal seem old-fashioned. Miss Judy had arrived from heaven, sent by the Virgin of the Socorro, and she would protect us even more than the ten thousand miles that separated us from Communism.

I realised that the English governesses who had come before Miss Judy had paid us scant attention, and we'd had good reason not to like them. Carlos and Mercedes, my brother and sister, more needy than I, attached themselves to the servants. Mercedes chose Gilda, the Irish nanny who had been born in Capilla del Señor and spoke a sort of gaucho English; Carlos, as ever, did not choose but was chosen, by Matilde.

Over the months after her arrival, I learned that Judy Wjugow had been born in Riga, thirty years before the wet morning in 1949 when a French cargo ship brought her and her husband Anatole, son of a White Russian officer, to the port of Buenos Aires. Anatole got a job as a concierge at the Círculo de Armas, thanks to a letter of introduction from a fellow Russian exile. Otropapá, president for a quarter of a century, was now almost honorary proprietor of the club, and so it happened that Miss Judy came to us. Anatole quickly made friends with the manager, the brother of Vicenta, Otramamá's maid. Anatole had a second job, playing the piano in a bar in Calle 25 de Mayo, where he often took Vicenta's brother to get drunk, Russian-style, and to open his heart to him. It was by this roundabout route that we found out what Judy felt about us. Her views came to us through the cruel filter of Vicenta's gallego resentment.

Miss Judy was surprised by the warmth with which the family received her in that house she found large and bleak, devoid of coziness even in the bedrooms; and she soon realised that we responded with curiosity and affection like children, but like children we could quickly withdraw it. She complained to Anatole, saying we all shared these traits of spontaneity and fickleness.

'All they do,' she said, 'is gratify themselves physically, all day long, with their prattling and kisses and sweets.'

'Are they so spoiled?' Anatole asked.

'I don't know if that's the word. They're idle rather than spoilt. Bored, sick of their own flesh, their eyes shiny and sad, like their cows. They haven't yet learned to calm themselves through work.'

Miss Judy spoke English, French, Italian, German, Russian, Polish and of course her native Latvian. We soon became greedy for her talents. Once, my mother asked her to draw up a sort of roll of honour, in which we were to be awarded points for performance in English, French, table manners, gymnastics and bedtime prayers. Each week the family were to scrutinise our progress. On the first Friday, Miss Judy presented a poster that had been decorated with birds and flowers and cut outs in the Baltic tradition. It was received with wonder. But Otramamá never looked at it again. Clara diligently read it each Friday at breakfast, but didn't even bother to scold us if our marks were poor.

Her appearance was noted beyond the walls of Juncal. At a family wedding, one of our poor cousins approached my mother, wearing a fierce smile.

'Clara, where did you find such a treasure? I saw her in church just now with the children, looking like a Russian princess in those funny fox furs and that wide-brimmed hat.'

'Yes, we're delighted with her,' answered Clara. 'She organises theatricals and has the boys do gymnastics. And she adores the country and riding too.'

'That's exactly what you always wanted, my dear. You with your passion for languages and culture. I do envy you.'

Miss Judy and Anatole lived in the attic of the Círculo de Armas, in one of the servant's rooms, which was too large for the thin light that filtered in through its single *oeil-de-boeuf* window. It had only two iron bedsteads and a trunkful of their possessions that now seemed very threadbare amid the solid luxury of Buenos Aires. After years of poverty and migrations, the Wjugows were astounded to find themselves in a city where steaks were given away in beer cellars to make the customers thirsty.

Our family's ignorance didn't bother Miss Judy; it was our frivolity that troubled her. It confused her that we saw culture as snippets of national history that revolved around our estates, or the recital of verses by Verlaine and Gérard de Nerval. And there was our weakness for elegant portraits by Blanche and Boldini. Their *fin-de-siècle* chic made her aware of her straight legs, her Baltic roots, and her suffering during the war. But there was one thing she loved us for – what she saw as our openness.

Once she told Anatole she was afraid we were going to grow tired of her. It wasn't that we weren't fond of her; we children cried when she went home to sleep with Anatole, and my mother paid her the rare compliment of calling her Miss Emily, the name of her own beloved governess. But her even-tempered nature, her sense of justice – she disapproved of the way Otramamá fussed over me – made the family nervous. She was vulnerable and alone, and perhaps she needed us more than she realised.

Miss Judy could choose to stay the night at Juncal when she couldn't face returning to the squalor of the Calle Corrientes. Often if my parents were out she would stay on, reading us one of Grimm's fairy tales in her galloping, Brünnhilde voice before putting us to bed. Then she would go downstairs to the library, place another log on the fire, and sit with a book.

Late on one such night, settled in a large leather arm-chair with her feet propped up on the brass fender, as the brass and leather returned the blue glow of the flames licking silently at the quebracho logs, Miss Judy allowed herself to dream. She had told my mother that she missed the crackle of pine logs; that this tropical wood, consuming itself like the slow fall of sand in an hourglass, the fire mute and half-smothered with a snow of ash, seemed to symbol-ise her new life.

That night, returning early, Clara noticed a light in the library, and heard Miss Judy speaking in an odd, intense way. As she approached the door quietly, Clara realised our governess was talking to herself.

'What am I doing here? What am I trying to teach these children? These people look up to us Europeans, but they seem wiser than we are. If only I could let myself go like them. They feel they must have this grand house, but they neither use nor admire it – they would feel more at ease in their old courtyards. Ah yes, to let oneself go! To sit after lunch in a rocking chair, and to babble on and on, to fall asleep while the flies buzz and the tap drips and the sea of grass stretches out all around and grows solid, blurring into a horizon of mirages. How can I ever learn to let go?'

Clara pressed her ear to the door.

'I was taught to keep busy,' Miss Judy went on. 'To do anything, so long as when evening came I could give a clear account of my day. I wrote letters, embroidered cuffs, fried dumplings, all so that I could lay my hands before me with-out shame, rest my head on them and sleep. Is this what I should teach these children? What for? Why tear them away from their dulce de leche? It would be better if they remained curled up together, easy, warm, naïve. But what about me? If you grow a rose, the neighbour will see it, if you write a letter it is answered. But these people rub up against each other without noticing, without answering. What am I doing here on this pampa? Will I go to seed like the foreign oaks on the estancias?'

'Miss Judy, is everything all right?'

The governess looked up dumbly at my mother. Clara swept into the room and saw the book on Miss Judy's lap.

'That's what I should have been doing tonight, instead of decking myself out and going to a ball where I hardly danced, and spent the evening drifting from room to room so I wouldn't look like a wallflower.'

'But madam, you look so lovely.'

'Yes, my dear, I don't look too bad. Even that sissy José Uriburu told me so, and he never thinks anyone in this city is smart enough. "Very chic, the combination of coral shoes with that grey dress. You look good. You remind me of Chita Castellane at the Escandóns' dance in Biarritz." But real men don't notice the colour of my shoes, only that I'm too serious. They find me a bore. Anyway, I'm not going to change the habits of a lifetime to be successful at a ball. Joaquín had a wonderful time, just like all the men. He danced almost the whole night with that music hall artiste, that mulatto in green sequins who Lalo Palacios dug up from somewhere. I was so fed up I left without telling him. I might not even send the car back. And now I've come to find a book, because I'm not sleepy.'

Miss Judy made to get up.

'No, please don't go. Why don't we have a whisky and talk? If you're not too tired, and I'm not boring you.'

'Madam, how could you think such a thing?'

'Fine, you sit there and I'll get the whiskies. I'm a little tipsy, which makes me grumpy. It's not that I'm jealous of that idiot, but I envy him his freedom. If you could've seen him, flirting in that cocky manner he must use with his patients. Doctors can be more ingratiating than whores. When he asked me, his voice up in the clouds, "Are you enjoying yourself?" I could've throttled him. But poor you, listening to me go on like that at this hour. Tell me about yourself – we've spoken so little. How do you find Buenos Aires?'

'I don't know how to answer that yet, I was thinking about it when you came in.'

'Well, you can rest assured that we're delighted with you, and that we're all very fond of you,' Clara said, rather pointedly.

'Thank you so much. I can't think why, I'm comfortable here, but I'm not sure how long I ought to stay.'

'What a pity, what a loss that will be to us, especially the children. But I suppose a person with your talents needs a more stimulating job. Summer's just around the corner, why don't you come with us to the estancia and then think again in the autumn? You'll love it there. Friends of my fathers, the Gortchakoffs, say that it reminds them of their estates in Russia, which went up in smoke, of course. My father likes to think of Balzac being dazzled by the vast horizons of the Ukraine when he went out into the countryside with Madame Hanska.'

'We were at the estancia at Easter, madam. But I'd rather become better acquainted with the gauchos than find myself among the muzhiks of Yasnaya Polyana.'

'Ah, of course. In any case, the gauchos aren't really like muzhiks. First, there aren't many of them, and second, they're not servile. They refer to the master amongst them-selves as El Hombre. They've never been tied to the land, you see. You know, because you ride so well, they treat you quite differently from poor Mr Overington – the eternal family tutor, whom you must meet. He tries to keep his horse at an English trot, with his bottom going up and down in the saddle. The gauchos call him "The Misti of the merry-go-round," and drive the young bullocks towards him in the corral to see if he'll get knocked off. Don't worry, they'd never do that to you. They'll feel they must protect you, and although they're very shy, they'll offer to tighten your girth for you, or appear out of nowhere to open the gate. They hide, like children. But you ride through that gate, and they'll reappear and close it again. They and we are the only things in this country that remain as it once was.'

Clara leaned against the mantelpiece and looked at Sorolla's portrait of her grandfather, painted after his death. It was as though she'd never seen it before. 'When my mother said that my grandfather had come out a little too thin, the painter, vulgar Spaniard that he was, said, "You want more belly, then you'll get more belly."'

Her eyes on the picture, Clara went on speaking to the governess. 'By now you must have a clear idea about us. I hope it's not the same as that of the horrible Frenchwoman my Mamá forced on me in exchange for my beloved Miss Emily. She was always quoting Diderot at us, "*Vous êtes devenu pourris avant d'être mûrs.*" But you're more subtle than that, and good-natured too. I hope you've found something positive about us.'

'Señora, Señora Clara, I'm so lost and frightened,' Miss Judy said. Clara's amnesiac babble was suddenly too much for her. She covered her eyes with the tips of her fingers, and began to sob.

Clara went to her without hesitation, embracing her and stroking her hair. 'Miss Judy, my poor dear Miss Judy. Don't feel so alone. Of course you'd feel lost, in a strange country, and especially after everything that's happened to you in Europe. It never crossed my mind that you were troubled, you always seem so tall and sure of yourself. I'm so insensitive! But tell me, what is it? Do you miss your home? Or is there some problem with Anatole?'

'No, the worst of it is that there is no reason for me to feel bad. I like it here and I'm fond of the children. Anatole seems happier than me, even if he has troubles at his bar. I don't really miss Europe. I don't know what it is.' Miss Judy took one of Clara's hands, and began to cry even harder. 'Are they coming? Have they found us?' Her pale eyes focused on the door as if she were staring at death.

'Who, my dear, who?'

'*Kommunisti*,' said Miss Judy, a long way off.

Clara didn't know what to do. Had the governess gone mad? She held her closer and tried to get her to move, but Miss Judy was almost six-feet tall and weighed a good eleven stone. Clara was barely five-foot two and kept her weight down below eight. Miss Judy seemed to have gone into shock. She was trembling, her big face had turned livid and blotchy. She moaned in Latvian, and every once in a while her body arched back in a contraction, forcing Clara against the chair.

Clara hung on to her. When she could, she took her head out from Miss Judy's armpit. She slapped her cheeks, saying in a soothing voice, 'Don't talk nonsense. How can you imagine there are Communists here? We're in Buenos Aires.'

Little by little Miss Judy began to recover, the animal moaning slowly became more like a human sob. Her fingers sought out Clara's, who let go of Miss Judy as soon as she could, bringing her a glass of whisky, which she drank with her eyes closed. Clara sat before her in her ball dress, watching that big, hurt body that seemed to have no place anywhere. First she felt shame, then revulsion, then guilt. This woman is like a whale with a tummy ache, she thought to herself.

'Do you feel any better, my dear? Come, let's get you to bed. You mustn't think any more about those bogeymen you left on the other side of the ocean.'

7

CLARA decided to keep her epileptic governess; a diagnosis she arrived at without the need for a doctor. Not just because she couldn't be bothered to find a new one, but now she felt more sympathy for the old one. To have seen her so lost didn't make Clara love her any more, but fear her less. Now, as she watched her devouring the creamed chicken, she encouraged her with a smile.

Eat. Go on eating, my sweet, my blonde whale. Restore yourself, calm yourself, go on growing, and getting uglier, I've lost the fear I had for you, I'd paint your toes if you allowed me, from sheer joy.

'Where are you taking the children this afternoon, Miss Judy?'

'They're going to a party, madam. Had you forgotten?'

'A party, where?'

'At Señora de Castro's.'

'Ah yes, Bebette. It's bound to be quite a party, she gives into Adela's every whim, she's her favourite grand-daughter. Tell Matilde, please, to have Mercedes' frock ready for half-past three. I'll dress her myself.'

Matilde and Gilda appeared, laden with riggings of mountainous white and pink, starchy whites that shone and held the promise of icing sugar; and pinks that gave off a thicker and more placid light. The maids lifted my sister on to a commode, naked on the marble top.

'Mamá, make the boys go away,' said Mercedes. 'They're spying on me.'

'But we want to see her being dressed,' I shouted from behind the door.

'I'm freezing. Can't someone put my socks on?'

'Gilda, put the lacy socks on, please. Matilde, have you threaded the pink ribbon for her knickers?'

Clara inspected the only daughter of the family coolly, without a mother's weakness. She saw an object that was hers, that would be judged soon by her rivals, and that with a bit of work she could improve. The child was plump. At the estancia she was called gordita, little fatty, a compliment that mortified both mother and daughter. But Mercedes was pretty, with big lively eyes, a nose like a sofa button and little pearls for teeth that showed her winning smile, and she had curls. People called her a Shirley Temple – 'a criollo one' my mother would point out.

Having been born last and with the least trouble, Mercedes was treated both by her mother, her grandmother and her aunts without enthusiasm, less like a daughter than a younger sister, and abandoned in the corners to play alone. She emerged on party days when she was required to show off the family's good taste. It was confusing for her to be paid so much attention all of a sudden, and moving to see the docility with which she allowed herself to be transformed into a doll, a patriotic rosette, a Virgen of Lujan. Maybe she hoped that one day she would be transformed into something so precious, they wouldn't be able to stop loving her.

There she stood like a trussed bird on a carving board, the pink light from the lamps touching the curve of her belly and her little bottom, her smile half fearful, half lost, her spongy curls like a halo. The marble slab on which she was displayed had been the tombstone of great-great-grandfather Artayeta. His wife had retrieved it from the Recoleta when the family mausoleum was built, and had used it, face down, as the top of the commode in which she kept her widow's mauve petticoats.

Matilde had the bodice and knickers. 'Come on, lift your leg, niña. Now your little arm, that's right. And the other one. Miss Clara, the niña has put on weight. These knickers are too tight, they fitted perfectly last month.'

'They do fit, Matilde. Pull me tighter.'

'Yes, pull, Matilde, pull. And you, my dear, you mustn't eat so much bread.'

'I never eat bread, Mamá.'

'She doesn't do anything else,' Carlos shouted through the crack in the door. 'The other day I caught her in the pantry, all alone near the fridge, she ran away of course but inside there was a big piece of bread with her teeth marks in it.'

'Lies, Mamá, all lies. Tell him to go away,' said Mercedes bursting into tears, and covering her face with her tiny hands. She sank down, crumpling her puff pastry petticoat. Matilde threw her hands in the air, and Clara began to grow impatient. Not knowing what else to do, Miss Judy rolled up a discarded ribbon.

Still to come was the dress, the topping of the cake, the snap of the poppers and the winking of candles for the sacrificial offering.

'Mamá, let us look at the little darling, I'm begging you. She looks so cute,' I pleaded.

My brother and I appeared from behind the door, dazzling in our white piqué, and knelt at the feet of that weary little cake that was beginning to melt, our hands joined in supplication. Matilde started to sew the pompons on to Mercedes's shoes.

'All right,' said Clara. 'If you promise to be good boys at the party, and not pinch her.'

The niña looked at herself in the mirror, terribly pretty in her broderie and lace and bows and pompoms. But she was afraid Clara would not be satisfied.

'Well, that's about it,' Clara said a bit apprehensively. 'Gilda, let the chauffeur know they're ready now, and put her coat on – carefully.'

The niña was encased in a white, rabbit fur coat. Her face emerged from within, and she gave her mother a wan smile. 'Mamá, do I look pretty?'

'Yes darling, you're all right.' Clara gave her a perfunctory kiss. 'The dress is perfect. Mamá had it brought back for me from Paris.'

Miss Judy sat in the jump seat opposite us. We sat stiffly and as far apart as possible, hands folded, shining cheeks, eyes fixed. My brother and I were dressed in navy-blue coats with velvet collars and between us, the niña, in a ball of white fur. Every now and then I looked at her and felt proud. The three of us felt so smart and so strange that I didn't look at Miss Judy for fear of being found out. But I could feel her looking at us. I wished the car would never reach the Calle Arroyo, that this drowsiness so full of hope might never be broken. I went on feeling so pretty and so good, and Miss Judy never stopped scrutinizing us.

The car pulled up at a portico before a brilliantly lit glass door. I got out without saying a word, and stood by the car awaiting Miss Judy's instructions, barely able to hold the present in my hands because my gloves were too long in the fingers. A footman was opening and closing the glass doors, as the nannies and children bearing presents went up the stairs. I came to all of a sudden and felt terribly tense.

'*Please, Miss Judy, I don't feel well,*' I said in English, taking her hand. '*I want to go home.*'

'*Come on darling, come on poppet. Remember the story of the little prince. You'll be all right.*'

Miss Judy herded us towards the stairs, me in front and the others trailing behind. I thought about the prince, and his friend the groom, and as I climbed I started to feel an excitement stir in me. All great stairs had the same effect, even the one at home, producing in me a feeling of waking up, as if ascending slowly towards something new and vast and clean, and clear like the morning, but more precise than the feeling of awakening, and the expectation was less uncertain, one was going up to lunch or tea, rather than into a new day, and the dark yellow light was soft, and not sharp like the light of the morning.

On the landing, a lady with orange eyes set in deep melancholy sockets was receiving the guests with an absent smile. She was Bebette, one of the owners of Maipú and Otropapá's first love. Her granddaughter Adela stood beside her, dressed for her First Communion.

'The Cullen children. How nice. Come and kiss your cousin,' said Bebette, pushing Adela towards us. 'She's had her First Communion today,' she added, unnecessarily.

Adela came forward, kissed us, took her gift and thanked us. Her deft fingers examined the parcel before she passed it to her nanny without looking at her, like a queen.

'The children of my cousin Clara!' repeated the señora de Castro. 'How delicious, the little girl's dress. Come here my love, let me give you a kiss. Here is Adela,' she insisted. But when she turned to look at them together, she felt the displeasure of recognising that the communion dress of her granddaughter was damp and lank compared with the frothy stiffness of Clara's concoction. Mercedes had never looked more like Shirley Temple, never more appetizing, never more shy and well-intentioned.

The moment we entered the drawing room my nerves lifted, and I felt at home. I recognised the icy tone of the drawing room at Juncal. Like Juncal, the room was designed around two large tapestries. Ours depicted scenes of castle life in the days of Louis XIV and had been part of my grandmother's dowry. We had a game in which she used to take me to visit a little black-and-white dog she called Cucumeco that was woven into the foreground of one of them. For sixty years, paralytic and silent, Cucumeco had waited for her, the only dog she had ever had time for. Otropapá had played down our tapestries and treated them as wallpaper, but Adela's grandmother preferred to show hers off. That spirit of contradiction was absent in her, and she allowed herself to be carried away by the opulence of the Belle Époque. Her French decorator had been encouraged to mimic Versailles, setting hers among an excess of bronze and pink-and-grey marble.

An upturn in the Atlantic's economy had pushed certain unkept Argentines to move along halls of mirrors, and it would be unjust to blame them. Suddenly they felt obliged to inhabit houses whose splendour didn't compensate for their boredom, and when they felt the pinch they sold them at a loss. Adela's party took place towards the end of these endeavours, that had lasted no longer than fifty years, and her grandmother's salon shone with the melancholy halo of a sun setting on a day swallowed too quickly, with much avidity and no merit, whose twilight held the sadness of what is not ready to die.

The room had filled with children and their nannies. The English ones sat stiffly, mournful rocks scattered in a foreign sea. The Germans were fewer, less genteel but more jolly. The two or three French ones held themselves apart, detached from their surroundings, their precise speech and dress gave them a secretarial air. The children came in a range of complexions from Swedish blonde to Sicilian black, and although we were all connected one way or another by blood, we were not melded into a recognisable type.

Before Miss Judy, the Calle Juncal had witnessed a succession of these mournful rocks, the Miss Wilsons and Miss Amys, who, unlike her, had never got close to us. What they had bequeathed us was nursery English. *Nursery English!* That language carried by the rhymes of Mother Goose in spite of those sour mouths – the rhymes more intimate than the Our Father – and more so their illustrations, the other face of *Les Malheurs de Sophie*, illustrations of books whose pages hid castles and woods and beaches and shoes full of children, until opened when they revealed themselves suddenly, truthfully, in flesh and blood, like the walls of our bedroom where Papá had drawn in dotted lines Mary had a Little Lamb with Mercedes' face, and Little Jack Horner with Carlos's blue eyes. That joyous English where pale lupins and pale roses don't melt like Sophie's doll, in that blissful garden of eternal childhood. What a curious contradiction it was that made my adored grandmother speak the language of loss, and our hated English governesses the language of beatitude.

In Buenos Aires nurseries were boats that leaked. For one, parents came in and out, breaking the most careful plans with irresponsible incitements to disobey. But there was another voice, softer and much more insidious, that buzzed incessantly from the back of the house long before the ship woke up, and went on long after the ship had gone to bed, buzzing and humming, from the nursery, or the sewing room, or the laundry room, or the kitchen. You could say it was the voice of America, were it not that it sometimes came from a Spanish or an Italian mouth. It was an unfailing voice, twangy yet stony, that resonated like an undecipherable hieroglyph in the nightmares of Miss Amy or Miss Wilson.

In the Calle Juncal with its zeal for emblems, the voice was without question the voice of America. Benita Flores, twice widowed, who had watched over Otramamá's fevers back at the beginning of time, decided to give up her house in Floresta and come to die among us. She was almost a hundred years old and had a hairy mole beside her nose and the surname of one of the French cooks of the Calle Juncal, Monsieur Robert. Her mother, Mamá Isabel, was the daughter of slaves and the wet nurse of the two first Uriburu cousins who coupled to beget Otramamá. In other words, we belonged to her. And what Benita did, like the other voices in the other houses did, even if they had been born in Logroño or in Basilicata, was to establish an intimacy with the bodies of the children unimaginable to the northern governesses, indeed much to the confusion and embarrassment of Miss Amy and Miss Wilson. Not only did they spend their lives cradling us, touching us, scratching us, and putting cold compresses on our foreheads or hot cloths on our chests and taking thorns out of our feet with pins and squeezing boils, they also put a finger up our bums to loosen our constipation and exercised the elasticity of the foreskin of the penis. We knew that Benita allowed us everything, but we didn't know that this idol who hardly spoke was re-enacting an old American custom, observed by Pizarro's henchmen in the Cajamarca of the last Inca.

Miss Judy struck up conversation with a Frenchwoman who had been a governess in St Petersburg in her youth. Every once in a while, without much rhyme or reason, she exclaimed, '*Ah, les officiers russes!*' in the same tone in which the English nannies might say 'Oh dear.'

'As you know very well, *ma chère*, the Russians are mad, perfectly mad. But what generosity, what panache, such extremes! So very different from here, *hélas*. At least they have a culture. I compare the Argentines to the Macedonians, who borrowed everything from Athens. *Ah, les officiers russes!* I once worked for a countess who presented me to her son's colleagues. She was terribly romantic and so I'd tell her about my conquests. But she wanted me to die of love, and that was too much. What do you make of your little charges, Madame Wjugow? They seem to me a bit like Russian children, they become meaner as they get older, and acquire a ridiculous fear of ridicule.'

'Why do you think that is?'

'Because they're nothing but Spanish peasants, these great gentlemen, these cattle barons.'

'*Mademoiselle Thibaud, de grâce!* Why do you say such hard things?'

'Because I'm sick to death of them. They use me and abuse me and then drop me. Can you believe that children whom I taught to read, whose bloody horses broke my leg – I still limp – and who called me Maman Thibaud never visit me? But now they bring their own children here, and they gush over me. They have the instincts of wild animals – they care only for their own. I detest them all. It'll happen to you too, mark my words. *Ah, les officiers russes!*'

Adela, surprisingly at ease among so many, came towards me from the hall once the flow of guests had stopped, and asked abruptly:

'When are you all going to the estancia?'

'After Christmas, I don't know when.'

'We're going for Christmas, for the first time ever. Granmamá is going to decorate the big cedar all the way to the top. She wants to see it covered with candles before she dies. She says she doesn't care if the whole thing burns up.'

'She must be crazy. What if it falls on the house? We were almost flattened by a eucalyptus in a storm once. A branch smashed my grandmother's bedroom window. She said it was the cold, not the noise, that woke her up.'

'My grandmother may be crazy but yours is an idiot. How can she not hear thunder? When there's a storm at Miraflores, Granmamá makes us all huddle in the sitting room in the middle of the house. She lights a candle and has us say the rosary. I must go, Martín, but wait here for me.'

I found Adela warm and indifferent. I could tell she was pleased to see me, but I also knew she'd forget me in an instant. I didn't know how to keep hold of her.

She came back. 'Look at those Poles Granmamá invited because she knew the family in Europe. They're here because the Communists took everything they had. They barely speak Spanish. Do you know what their present was? Flowers. Granmamá says that they haven't got a cent left and they are counts. They congratulated me in French. I said, *merci*, and that was that.'

'Perhaps Miss Judy knows them. She speaks Polish.'

'You can tell her to talk to them. I'm not going to.'

'I feel sorry for them,' I said. 'Imagine having everything taken away, everything burned, and your family killed. Mamá says there'll be no war here, thank goodness.' And then making an effort, I added, 'Will you come to my birthday party, at the end of February?'

'If we're in Miraflores, and the road is good. Wait a moment, Granmamá is calling me.'

She ran off, like the tomboy she was, and almost everyone ran after her. A minute or two later she was back, in a state.

'What a bore,' she said. 'Granmamá wants to have the dining room opened now, and says I can't unwrap my presents until everyone has gone.'

'Why won't you be in Miraflores in February?' 'Papá might take us to Punta del Este in his boat. Martín, where are you going?'

'I left something in my coat.'

'Come back quickly. I want you to sit next to me at tea.'

I want to leave, and want nobody to notice me. Why does she have to go to Punta del Este. Why doesn't she stay in the country until my birthday. She's a fool, and she fancies herself because of her first communion. I've had mine already, it wasn't such a big deal. If she stays in Maipú, perhaps this year they might let me visit her on horseback cutting across the campo, accompanied by el Vejo in case I get lost, because it will take us half a day to reach it, even cantering and with a horse to spare. But this idiot won't be there anyway.

A footman in black livery was opening the dining-room doors. Bebette took Adela by the hand, and called for us to go in. I stayed back, hurt by Adela's bluntness, watching the children's heads in the other room, and the pink, faded head of a boy in the tapestry. He held the reins of his horse in his raised arm. His eyes were pale blue, and his pensive face touched the horse's.

The children's hair shone with oil and hair cream and brushing. Some of them twisted their heads like restless birds, others were tired and stiff with nerves. The boy in the tapestry with his arm holding the horse's head never tired. He seemed old, and yet there was something alive and cheerful about him and the horse. The image made me think of a song that went on and on. In a clearing in the woods behind him, horses were galloping after a falcon. High up in the straw-coloured sky, the bird was about to get its prey.

The children were grouped by the table around a polished silver oval. It flashed, freezing them in chance poses, catching their faces in snapshots that ranged from dead grey to blinding white. Their feet felt tight, their eyes saw their hands far off, the gladioli piled up, the jellies stiff, the water pure ice, and in the centre of the oval a dead silver hare thrown on top of the silver lettuces absorbed all the light of the room.

The arm holding the reins was still, the woods silent. The falcon went on nearing its prey in an empty sky at the top of the empty tapestry. The face brushing the horse's forehead looked at the trees without recognising them.

'Hello, boys and girls, Teresa and Panchito, Malena and Pedrito! Come, lads and lasses, come and drink wine with me. Up the ladder and down the wall, half a jug will serve us all.'

A short clown in tails, his face painted and glaring, bowed to Adela.

'What's he talking about,' Adela whispered. 'We drink tea.'

'Wine, wine and more wine is our prayer,' the clown went on.

'Che, I hope this bore is going to stop these silly rhymes and show us some tricks,' Adela said.

'I like him,' I said. I wanted to annoy her.

'Shut up, you sissy,' she snapped. 'I'm going to tell Granmamá to throw him out.'

'Since you went away, sun of suns, the birds have stopped singing and the river running.'

'If he goes on like this he'll ruin my party.' Adela pinched my arm, which delighted me.

'Let's play a guessing game. I'm going to guess something about each of you.'

The clown raised his arm for silence. Then he said in a bossy falsetto, 'Careful you don't go round the lake too quickly. You'll fall in, victoria and all, and the swans will peck your eyes out and the frogs will lick you.'

Adela looked around the room impatiently. A few children giggled.

'Mamama, don't take me back to the Sociedad de Beneficencia,' said the clown in a different voice. 'I'm the only boy in a row of ladies in black, and I don't know what to do. Well dear, if your grandfather were a cabinet minister and took you to his office you wouldn't complain, would you?'

Adela was trying to catch her grandmother's eye, but the clown continued.

'What can I do if he wants to take me behind the haystack again,' said the clown in a little girl's voice. 'He says he wants to show me his willy so he can play with my thing. What will I do if Miss Wilson finds out?'

I looked at my sister in horror. Mercedes cringed. Where had the clown got this stuff?

'Sacatuseco, mijita, sacatuseco... bugger... sacatuseco, viatuseco! I don't understand, Mamita. Do you want water or do you want me to leave?'

'Che, he's not a clown, he's a mind reader,' I muttered to Adela.

'Don't be an idiot,' Adela said. 'He's mad, and he's ruining my party. Look, some of them are crying. But he just spoke like Mamita did after her stroke. What did he guess about you?'

'Nothing,' I said.

'Liar, I saw you turn bright red.' Adela laughed nastily.

The clown's face became still. 'Now listen to me, all of you, because soon you'll wake up. You will never see yourselves again in these mirrors, you'll have to find yourselves in eyes that will disown you, eyes that will look at you with mistrust and greed, that will laugh in a way you've learnt to despise. When you look around, you'll want to know who owns the street. Your tongue might find your teeth, but you won't know how to use the air or your glottis. Who could bandage your eyes when you are not blind? These sins won't be visited on your children. There will be no children and no flood – just a wind that blows and blows, making a few drawings in the sand.'

The children had fallen asleep, some standing up like horses. The governesses seemed not to have heard the clown. I went back to the dining room, craving something to put in my mouth. The room seemed huge. Frightened, I went up to the table, unable to take my eyes off the screen from behind which the footman might appear. I stuffed my mouth with three chocolate éclairs, one after the other, and with my cheeks bulging reached for some sandwiches. Then I caught myself reflected in the silver urn, a brown pear of a face with fat stained lips and little toad eyes. I don't remember vomiting on the sandwiches.

Carlos had followed me into the dining room. Seeing me being sick, he froze in the same way I did when I knew I must act quickly, saying, 'What's the matter? What's happened?'

I sat down, resting my forehead on the table. Hesitantly, Carlos placed a hand on the back of my neck.

'Martín, Martincito, do you want me to call Miss Judy?'

'I want you to go away.'

'But what if they find you with all this mess?'

'I don't care. Go away, leave me alone.'

Carlos obeyed, but before he left me he kissed his finger-tips and laid them again on the back of my neck.

8

ADELA and I saw each other only in the summer, and even then infrequently. Our estancias were at opposite ends of the sixty-four square Spanish leagues that our ancestor had bought in 1811, both from the Indians and from the country's first independent government. The dirt road between her estancia, Miraflores, and our estancia was often impassable. In my mind, Miraflores stood at the ends of the earth, beyond the horizon, beyond the low hills of Yamoidá. The distance to the sea or to Europe was greater, but more abstract. Miraflores lay at the border of my longings, just as it sat physically at the edge of our vast family lands.

Adela's looks would have found no place in the hierarchy of that arbiter of female beauty, the dwarf at Harrods. He wouldn't have said of Adela, as he opened car doors at the entrance on the Calle Florida in his green livery, top hat and gloves, 'How pretty!' And without these two words, a Buenos Aires woman was finished. Adela's face was too round, her eyes too inexpressive, her colour too muddy. Worse, she had two older sisters, blonde, blue-eyed, who had made a smooth transition from 'How pretty!' to 'How beautiful!' The dwarf never took his eyes off them.

The blonde sisters were a yardstick by which I measured other girls, but it was Adela I fell for. I liked it that she had no outstanding features – like a familiar room you know is there and don't need to look at carefully. Her eyes were big, flat and uninviting like quince jam, and promised nothing, like winter. Her cheeks were like watermelons, you felt that you could swing from them and give them smacking kisses. Then there were her lips, the upper one of which had a cut that I wanted to bite. Adela's big teeth, yellow and with gaps between them, excited me. I wanted to suck toothpaste from the tube and brush them with my tongue. Her features were open, smoothed over by the softness of her skin. She was more intelligent and cutting than her sisters, who were considered bright. Adela had a face and even a body that made her seem like a mature, dim woman. She was nine.

Her aplomb frightened me, but her plainness put me at ease, a plainness only the rest saw because to me she wasn't ugly. When my mother said that poor Adela wasn't pretty, I was quick to point out that at least she had long legs. I decided that I liked the idea of plainness, which seemed to symbolise Adela's attractiveness – something rare and special, like having *chien*. My grandmother had once said of a famous woman that she was the perfect *jolie-laide* and that all Paris died for her. Perhaps I was a male counterpart. Adela and I did have a certain family resemblance.

What I didn't like about Adela were her manners. She wasn't impolite, but used her politeness to exclude. Good manners, when they don't come from the heart, are merely bad manners in disguise. She had a way of copying the mechanical poise of her mother with a supernatural precision that made me feel small. Like so many porteños, I needed another's encouragement to go on. Adela's poise left me dangling, and the worst of it was that I could never ask her what it was she was hiding. If someone had told me I was as cutting as her, I would have defended myself by saying, 'Maybe so, but you can always ask me why.' But then I would fall into that confusion where one's perception is mixed up by memory, and memory is tainted by the weight of the authority of others.

Otropapá was our authority in manners and had a dim view of mine. He was kind, distant, but weak – at least that was Clara's verdict. He was never aggressive, even when I saw him at his most angry, that time when Mamá started to needle him about Otramamá's estancia, Los Derrames, accusing him of selling it too cheaply. 'I had to pay the mortgage for the vineyards of San Juan,' he had told her. 'You should have asked for a loan,' she had insisted. And he suddenly burst out with a voice both angry and pained, 'Bugger – just stop going on ...' and started to walk about the salita – 'Bugger,' as if he couldn't control himself.

My mother went red. I had never seen my grandfather so upset, and his good manners seemed to make him hopelessly so.

As usual with me, in falling for Adela I was following in someone else's footsteps. Otropapá had been keen on Adela's grandmother. My grandfather was tall and handsome, but Bebette didn't care for him. She was a great beauty, and she knew she could afford to turn him down. I don't know that Otropapá ever forgave Bebette. When we ran into her after Mass in the town of Maipú, he would greet her in a friendly way, and ask something like how her delphiniums were doing in the heat wave, but the smile he wore always seemed to me faintly ironic.

Otramamá definitely hadn't forgiven her. 'The woman is an ass,' she would say. 'She goes on about being cultured. She even carries on about me, because she has schoolgirl crushes, even now at her age. Lately she's been ringing at all hours to tell me that she's been reading *Bonjour Tristesse*. She loves the sound of her own voice, and she thinks she's the fount of all knowledge. And she's utterly humourless, which is a common feature of your father's family.'

'My grandfather's,' I corrected her, once again.

I was glad that he had married Otramamá, who was rich, and like Adela, not pretty. Bebette's beauty would have been too much, and at the same time she could never have matched the fairy-tale life that Otramamá had lived before she married. Whenever my grandmother embarked on an account of that life, it was with a self-indulgent abandon that made me wonder if she was doing it to encourage me, or make me feel hopeless. I would mull over my plans for my future life with Adela, and wonder how it could ever match Otramamá's.

'How Papá spoiled me!' Otramamá would gush. 'I was the youngest by many years, my sister was old enough to be my mother. He pandered to me in every possible way. He gave orders to one of the footmen, behind Mamá's back, that I could send him to get me special ice creams at the Confitería del Gas. He bought me a complete set of emeralds – necklace, bracelet and so on – when I was only twelve.' I had heard this quite a few times. 'But my sister was jealous, she made him take them back. As a consolation, Papá had a little carriage made for me in London, which came with two grey ponies. I used it often in Vichy – I've never been back there, or to any of the places which made me so happy. I remember driving in that carriage years later, with one of my Spanish *beaux*, the Duke of Maqueda, cousin of the king. He'd followed me to Paris from San Sebastián. He was much too dim and told the most terrible jokes, again and again, but he was quite handsome, and – why deny it? – I was flattered.'

'Why didn't you marry the Duke, Otramamá?'

'Because then you wouldn't have been born, my darling. I had to choose between you and the Duke.'

'Liar.'

I thought about Adela every day, but beneath my love there was a less innocent purpose. I felt that I must take up the life laid down for me by Otramamá and Tía Teodé and so it seemed the most natural thing in the world that I should do this with Adela. It didn't occur to me to ask her to love me back. When she hurt me, it was by not paying me the attention I was used to at home. What I really liked to do was hold her image in my head, and write her name in ink on my nursery desk, blowing on the letters until the violet ink dried to a metallic sheen on the damp, dirty surface that seemed to accept my scribbles, and felt intimate like the freshness of a pillow. A-D-E-L-A. The letters, barely visible on the dark wood, made me feel nearer to her than I did when I gazed on her inscrutable face.

My love has always mistrusted the other's love, that hunger directed towards me. That's why I fell in love alone. And now when I think of it, how guarded I have always been, how my heart exposed such a small part of tender flesh for that flaming arrow to pierce. How well attuned to the dreamings of its owner my heart was. And if I have wanted to seduce somebody I might have felt attracted to, like anybody would have of course, apart from the saints, I never went so far as to expect that my loving words would be returned. I only wanted words that would answer mine, those words that go round and round, ever more inflamed, without leading anywhere. It would be enough, like Scheherazade, that this story be called off at dawn, with the promise of its continuation. And if at the end of the thousand and one nights, this routine had rendered us inseparable, then good, we would go on being together, and why not? But there would be no urge to become the other.

We'll marry, I thought, and join our two estancias so that all of Maipú is ours, just like in the times of Don Pancho Ramos. We'll have just one son, no more, and he'll inherit it all. I pictured us sitting together, husband and wife, in the courtyard of the estancia, Adela dressed like his wife, Mamita Segurola. I would be dressed like that other Ramos, their young handsome son, who was taken prisoner at the estancia and killed by the Mazorca, who ran a wagon wheel over his neck.

Adela and I sat in the courtyard like Mamita Segurola and her elder son. We were married, cousins, and the land was ours, all the way from the laguna of our estancia to Miraflores, thirty miles to the east and so far away that nothing of its grounds could be seen, even if the Yamoidá hills weren't in between. It was all ours, from the courtyard to the sea, and as the sun set on the laguna and the black-neck swans came back to roost we sat like two burnished quinces, and for once the leaves of the casuarinas stopped their sad rustling. Then the sunless sky filled with that run-away light that darkens towards the sea, and the country-side stretched away, the colour of a hare's eye, and the cows made long shadows. There, I stopped imagining. I couldn't get beyond these scenes that recreated other people's lives. I didn't think of living, and people used to say I had sad eyes.

'What are you doing, with those eyes like a cow stuck in the mud?' Adela threw at me, when she realised I was looking at her without seeing her.

We had met by chance at the Recoleta on the Day of the Dead. Our family tombs were near each other, closer than our estancias. She embraced me abruptly, as if trying to wake me, making me uneasy, as it always did, because I was only used to adult embraces. Adela bared her big, yel-low teeth in a grimace that challenged me to smile back, making me think of her tonsils and then her throat. 'I'll throw myself down her throat to her heart...' – it was the line from a poem. I didn't understand what I felt for her, but I was asking her to swallow me.

'Martín, stop putting on that faraway face. What are you thinking about? For goodness sake, come back.'

'Have you thought about who you'll marry?'

'No, I never think about such things. Have you?'

'I'll marry you, if you want.'

'You must be crazy. I could never fall in love with you, and I'll only marry for love.'

Once more I felt rejected, but I couldn't ask Adela why she didn't love me. I decided to hate her. She might have made the perfect wife, but now she was ugly and stupid. I shrugged her off, and the face I'd liked so much became horrible. I didn't have the astute patience of the unloved and so I would never have known how to court her. I'd believed that she had the same dreams as me, that in choosing her I was doing her a favour. Now I felt like a monster. Only a monster could have got it so wrong.

What did it mean to be in love? What did that little fool know about it? Why couldn't she have fallen for me? Had I thought about it, I would have concluded that I lacked everything. The world for people of my age was arranged as for the two opposing worlds of Gulliver – made for the sizes of its inhabitants. I didn't know whether I was a dwarf or a giant, only that I didn't fit.

'It's my fault, that I've never learned how to play,' I muttered, so that Adela wouldn't hear me.

'Mademoiselle is calling me. I think I must go,' Adela said, retreating behind her good manners.

'I think I won't ever see you again,' I said.

'What's the matter with you? Don't take everything to heart so. You asked, and so I told you the truth. Stop playing the sulky, spoiled brat. I'm the one who's not going to see *you* ever again. You think you're a genius because you read books. Papá says you're a precocious little twit. Look che, reading books isn't such a big deal.'

9

I READ because I didn't know what else to do. But I also felt superior to those who didn't read — and that was everyone, except for Miss Judy and Tía Teodé. And my father — just — who re-read every summer the stories of Maupassant.

While Miss Judy read Grimm and Andersen's fairy tales to us in English, I sat in the corner devouring a French dictionary of mythology. The half-naked gods, engraved in a chaste and sloppy technique, carried me along with their great deeds. Mars and Jupiter were like my father, with broad chests, black curls and a might they were conscious of. They seemed to do anything their strength allowed them — the strongest gods could do everything. I read that they copulated like carefree dogs, and they would stop at nothing, resorting to any fantasy to snare their quarry. I saw Danae opening herself up to the Shower of Gold, and learned that she was a 'magnificent female possessed'. The word 'female' in Spanish is used only for animals. Combined with 'possessed' they became the most obscene words I'd ever heard.

The words reminded me of a disturbing episode, when I was told that the chestnut mare was to be taken and serviced. I didn't understand what this sort of service was. 'The Señora is served!' Casimiro always exclaimed to my grandmother when he flung open the doors of the dining room.

We had just started to spend weekends at the country quinta of Escobar my father had bought north of Buenos Aires. A dozen horses from the estancia had been sent there, including the chestnut, Clara's favourite. I had never seen anything prettier than my mother, lit by the evening sun, dressed in blue, riding the mare side-saddle.

That morning at the quinta, I went with my father and a farmhand who were taking the chestnut to be serviced. We rode at a walk along roads bordered by little fields planted with rows of sweet potatoes and stock flowers. I didn't particularly care for that area of small farms, and was sure that the horses missed the lagunas of Maipú. We arrived at a grocers' store. Behind its red façade and a row of paraíso trees was a dirt courtyard, and there stood a bay horse, strong, shiny and frisky, surrounded by some gauchos. When the bay sensed the mare nearby, he let out a short whinny and began pawing the ground. My tension grew with my confusion. 'Go and wait for me outside,' my father told me in a nervous voice. But before that I saw that the bay had mounted the chestnut, while the mare seemed to slacken and moan. 'Yes, go on, go on. Finish it off,' the gauchos laughed with their flute-like voices. I tried not to understand, but my father's presence there made me feel fear and revulsion.

I read the dictionary in alphabetic order, learning it easily by heart, as the list of Jupiter's couplings and his spawn were no more intricate than the genealogy of Juncal. Beneath the letter P was the story of Eros and Psyche, which seemed to hold the key to the mysterious and incomprehensible love I had never managed to understand.

One evening in the schoolroom, opening and shutting books, trying to calm my anxiety over Adela's rejection, I discovered, in the brown-grey, satiny pages of the *Treasury of Youth*, a picture of Psyche leaning over the sleeping Love. 'Eros came to her only in darkness,' I read, 'and her jealous sisters told her that he was a monster.' Psyche was aware that the price of preserving her love was to stay blind, never to see the face of her lover. The illustration showed both her sin and her happiness. Now, she looked upon Eros and discovered that her lover was not a monster, but a mountain of beauty. But in the book, Love went on sleeping, and Psyche admiring him. Then on bending to kiss him, she spilled the oil of the lamp, and it woke him. Knowing what I did about the drama of parting, I could feel the imminence and the horror of her loss.

I tried to cover Eros's eyelids with my hands to stop the oil from waking him, but I knew that the evil was done. Through the window, the sooty clouds of Buenos Aires were blackening the sunset, and if I looked at it I recognised the fire of Rome. The room had that air of disarray which ushers in the night, drained of its colour, as if life had escaped to fight it out in the battle of the sky, leaving on the little mahogany bookcase the empty skins of the *Treasury of Youth*, Tarzan and the books of Salgari; the wound had sucked the ink from the glass inkwell and the wax of the ink-stained table, but I saw only what was burning in my hands with the fervour of marble, the unknowing youth and the maiden mesmerised, symbolising the unattainability of love.

My brother ran in to ask me something, glanced at me, and disappeared through the other door. Gilda came in with a basket of ironed clothes, then returned with a jug of water and two glasses, switching on the light. The window was solid now, an indifferent yet brilliant black, and the room had returned to itself. Gilda drew the flowered chintz curtains. I heard the glug-glug as water filled the bath, and the other organised sounds of the house closing up for the night. I put the book back on the shelf.

Just as the estancia's laguna releases a great racket of water birds after the tension of dusk, so our floor of Juncal was livelier at bath time than at breakfast. The rooms, given back to themselves, seemed new, the beds just opened, white, the recently ironed clothes, warm. The electric light was more radiant, more intimate. It was the hour of ordered activity, bathing, putting on one's pyjamas and dressing gown before going downstairs to say goodnight, eating supper.

We began the day half-asleep, paying little attention to breakfast, but at bath time we were wide awake, and done up like debutantes for inspection before bed. I sank into the comfort of being like my siblings, trying to smother Carlos with a pillow before climbing into the bath with him. Carlos didn't ask what I'd been reading. He asked so little that his curiosity built up inside him, as if his mute questions went on being filed away next to mute replies, so that his curiosity became indistinguishable from his melancholy.

Matilde's mood improved at this hour, particularly if she could bathe us instead of dressing Mamá. If we begged hard enough she'd scrub our backs with a sponge. She wasn't just a Benita Flores — whom she described as 'that Indian who has everyone eating out of her hand' — but a rather important Spaniard. Sometimes she sang fados to us in her childlike voice, monotonous and cracked. Only *'Pra me'* and *'Meu Amor'* were comprehensible, but we found them irresistible.

'Come on, Matilde, let's have another fado,' we'd chorus, and we never had to ask twice. Miss Judy could be heard singing *'Ochi Chorniye'* as she corrected our compositions in the next room. We quickly learned the Russian words to the song, and the German ones to *'Ach, du lieber Augustin.'* Everything associated with her taught us something.

At some point Clara would burst into the nursery and ask how her children were. Matilde's mood would only have improved so far, and she would respond with a tetchy 'Niña, don't interfere, for heaven's sake.' She had passed the sponge over Clara's body at the same age as us, even in the same bath. Clara would look around quickly and then leave, but this fleeting appearance, usually in a white velvet dressing gown, her face daubed in cream, seemed to set a seal on proceedings, as though the queen had visited her factory.

The nursery, which nobody seemed to pay any attention to, was as indispensable as the Seven Just Men who ignore their own virtue. It was the only part of the house which wasn't decorated, apart from the Mother Goose walls, and the begonias Matilde degraded the windows with set the tone. Slum flowers, Clara called them. All the family rejects wound up there, the expensive and the cheap – rush chairs from the quinta in Olivos, a portrait by Paul Chabas of Otramamá as a child with the feathers of a *bersagliere* on her head, and a grotesque collection of once very valuable ivories. The family's new shoots grew strong amidst the rubbish, like fennel in a waste patch. At that hour, the ordering of new bodies seemed to rejuvenate these old pieces, as if that pile of unwanted old things in front of the open beds had been restored from a discarded heap into something protective and poetic.

The evening ritual in the nursery had the hesitant grace of old ceremonies before the military stuck their noses in, when instead of marching, abbots and brides walked barefoot in ceremonial costumes, escorted by everyday people. The temple is their end, but they don't head straight there, winding this way and that in no great hurry and amidst great excitement, perhaps even returning to retrieve something, and starting again, while the music also undulates, repeating itself, the horses are thin and a child cries, their dresses like pyramids of flowers ready to be set on fire, the ones carrying parasols, barefoot, dressing without ostentation, could well be the brothers of the bride. People approach and people fall back. It could be the most sacred day of the year.

> 'Sana, sana, culito de rana.'
> 'Sana, sana, culito de rana.'
> 'Si no sana hoy, sanará mañana.'

'If not today, for certain tomorrow,' Matilde would sing. 'This boy is coughing again. I'll rub you down with Vicks and wrap your little chest with cotton. Put on your pyjamas and dressing gown, you can be sure it'll pass. This coughing of yours comes when we least expect it, but then when it comes, it goes. It's like a miracle.'

'Caquito's asthma is just a put-on,' I said.

'You can laugh, you're as strong as an ox. Sometimes I think God gave you your brother's health as well as your own. You eat everything, you're like a dustbin, and you don't even get indigestion. It isn't fair!'

'It's not my fault if I'm healthy.'

'And it's not your brother's fault that he's sickly. You win out in the end.'

'But he puts on his asthma. Every time he wants something he doesn't get he has an asthma attack.'

'You've got a big mouth. My little boy is suffering. Do you feel any better, my morriño? Shall I bring you up your soup? You'll breathe better when you've had it.'

'What soup is there today?' I asked.

'What do you care? It's your brother who needs it. But the little angel doesn't ask, poor thing. All he can do is cough. It's the soup you like − Quaker Oats soup. You don't like Quaker soup? I thought it was your favourite. I'll find some broth and make you alphabet soup, and then you can spell out your name, so long as you eat it all up. OK?'

'Why do you spoil niño Carlos so much, Matilde?'

'Because the second born is always the servants' favourite. Your brother may not think it's worth much, but that's his fate. The first-born is loved by his mother and his grandmother, and the little girl is the apple of her father's eye. And then you, morriño, who else will love you but the others and me? Aren't you the favourite at the estancia too? Don't they call you the most gauchito of the family?'

'Guachito, you mean.'

'How dare you speak that way of your mother's honour!'

'What does honour have to do with it? You get more and more stupid as you get older. What does my mother's

honour have to do with Carlos being an orphan or a foundling? Obviously Carlos was a foundling, where else did he
get those blue eyes? Neither Mamá nor Papá has them.'

'Stop playing the scientist. Blue eyes sprout where God
chooses to sow them, and his eyes are bright and pretty,
while yours are brown as bird shit, like mine.'

'I hope birds peck them out of your head, you're so nasty.
Why would I have the cheap dirty eyes of a gallega? I have
Uriburu eyes, like Otramamá says, and that is a great honour. Why don't you shut up, and write a hundred times
with your alphabet letters that Caco is a sissy and Matilde is
an ass.'

'You deserve a good hiding, like you'd get in my village.
That'd put you in your place, you little devil. I'd like to crop
that tongue of yours with my scissors for insulting an old
woman who wiped your mother's bottom.'

'Her bottom would've been wiped by Benita Flores, not
you. And if it was you, you were well paid for it. How else
could you have afforded the house in Villa Urquiza?'

'You'll give me a stroke! You'll kill this poor old woman
with worry, and you're no more than a child. Although why
am I calling you a child? There's nothing of the child about
you. And for your information, I didn't stay on in this house
for money. I could have earned more elsewhere. I stayed
on out of love, and because it's the home of distinguished
people. You've given me a pain in the chest! I can hardly
breathe. You'll pay for this you little monster. I'm going
straight to the Señor to complain.'

'No, not to Papá.'

'Yes, to the Señor. He's the only one you obey.'

Carlos had dozed off. He woke when he heard the fear
in my voice. He always switched off when people discussed
his place in the scale of affections. Once he told Miss Judy
that he wouldn't go down to my grandmother's floor,
because nobody there cared for him. The servants might

have loved him, but that wasn't what Carlos wanted to hear.

What do I remember about that room, that came alive on those nights when I couldn't get to sleep? The weight of the sheets for one, as the heat didn't allow for even the lightest blanket, and which stuck to my skin like green scum on stagnant water. But it was better than nothing, as though the sheet protected us a little from the heat, and if one lay very still one and waited, pools of freshness would form that one could seek out all at once with a knee or a foot, but which were extinguished just as quickly. I associate these hopeless games with that time, though they happened throughout the whole year, the repeated and frustrated attempts to make myself believe I had gone to pee when I hadn't, and after calling shyly to Gilda and realising she wasn't coming, trying to fall asleep calmed by the thought my bladder was empty, and waking up soon after with even more urgency.

Carlos was in the bed next to mine, his presence like a caged animal, pulsating with a dark will opposed to mine, unlike the sleeping bulk of Otramamá, which seemed to communicate with me her thin, spasmodic breathing, exhaling sweet words. What was my brother thinking about? Why wouldn't he talk to me? When we spoke, I could convince him of anything, and he must have been aware of this, because he would suddenly stop talking, abandoning me to a silence which seemed to grow with the sound of his laboured breathing and the brilliance of his open eyes.

'Carlos, listen. Do you hear me? What's the first thing you'll do when we get to the estancia?'

Silence.

'We'll probably arrive at night, and we won't be allowed out, but if it's not too late I'll go to the stables and see if the horses are still tied up.'

'OK, shut up,' he said. 'I don't care. I just want to go to sleep.'

10

'TOMORROW, we're going to the estancia.'
I don't remember anything leading up to this announcement. It came out in the midst of a dreary, unending wasteland of visits to the park, which I accepted as a cross I had to bear. I don't know whether it was the numbing effect of trailing back and forth on those hot December mornings, but even Mamá began to wonder why we came in for lunch with such despondent faces.

I missed Adela, though I tried hard not to think of her. Without her, the city lost its meaning. I couldn't imagine that she might be waiting for me at her house in the Calle Arroyo, where I felt excluded from the outings organised by her mother – tennis, sailing on the Tigre, polo matches – the packed pleasures of a fashionable family. I didn't care for such things, efforts of this kind were not the style of Juncal. But I resented them, because I knew that they helped her to forget me even more.

I had never learned how to play with other children. I would lose myself in that dusty plaza surrounded by benches that was not even a park, where any shade seemed to have been absorbed in the wrinkled faces of the nannies, or in the depths of their blue prams. Those prams, with their big, silvery wheels, were as tall as ships on the high seas, and shrouded in veils through which you might make out the pulsating shadow of a tiny body, bathed, oiled, powdered and pink, cloistered away in its mother-of-pearl cabin, from where it controlled its mini-world of linen and wool with dribbles, belches and sighs, making me feel thirsty and attracting me far more than the other boys of my age, who chased each other over the withered grass.

Each nanny guarded her pram like a watchdog, and there

was nothing else for me to do. Some swings hung from burning hot metal frames, and there was a slide from which one descended into a sandpit filled with paper, rubbish and broken glass. We'd been told that someone had once hidden a razor blade in the groove of the slide. I looked at it and felt my bowels contract as I imagined being sliced right up into my ribcage. A narrow ditch, planted with young willows and full of smelly water, bordered the railway. It was lined with little white paths that opened on to bare patches beneath the trees, as though hordes of people had trampled through on purpose; a secretive, disagreeable place. Every once in a while, dark men stopped behind the wire fence of the railway line and looked through at us.

One day, Carlos pointed something out to Miss Amy, who had returned much to our dismay and full of contrition for her misdeeds when Miss Judy was summoned to Montevideo to assist in the identification of a boatload of refugees. Carlos had found a sticky balloon. Miss Amy blushed, hesitating before the floppy little rubber tube, as if she knew something about it she didn't want to know. She reached out as if to take it, then drew her hand back and ordered Carlos to throw it as far away as he could, and never to go near the ditch again.

Our exhaustion lit up by the heat was increased by the effort of Christmas. We liked neither the crèche, nor the tree, and we couldn't see any reason for all the fuss, apart from the presents, which were waiting for us in the library on the morning of the 25th; we found them immense, out of all proportion to the rest of our lives.

In Buenos Aires, no one knows how to put on a show. Of them all, Mamá probably took the least trouble. There were a few things at the back of some cupboard: a Virgin made of painted cardboard with a blue cape and empty gaze, a porcelain baby Jesus shaped like a Tyrolean salt cellar and some tin cows. They made Miss Amy blench, for she was expected to turn it all into an English Christmas. For weeks she begged for a Christmas tree, without success, until one of the maids won one in a parish raffle and Mamá exchanged it with her for a pair of gloves.

That Christmas, Miss Amy shone like the star of Bethlehem. She hid the Holy Family in a dim corner, because she regarded it as Papist. Only the cows were allowed to be seen, lit by candles. Casimiro, who didn't usually serve our meals, advanced with a tray covered in flames. Miss Amy was terribly excited, and so were we; but Mamá and Papá failed to appear.

Otramamá took me alone to see a Nativity at a convent in the Barrio Sur, of which she was patron.

'Sheñora Mercedes, what a surprise, what an honour!' said a familiar voice through the screen of the torno. It was Otramamá's maid Vicenta, though speaking with an archness I'd never heard from her when she drew the curtains or served us breakfast in my grandmother's bed.

Before I could recover from my confusion, a piece of the black wooden screen was moved back and a thin little old man appeared, dressed as a nun. He ignored me and continued with his breathy flattery of Otramamá in the tones of her maid.

'The Sheñora isn't tired? Wouldn't she like to sit down? I'll go and let Mother Superior know the Sheñora's here, and light the candles of the Nativity. Is this the Sheñora's grandson, the one she loves so much? At last she brings him! I'll have everything ready in just a minute. But while she waits, the Sheñora must sit down. The courtyard is nice and cool, and you can smell my roses from there – the Sheñora knows how carefully I look after them. And it gives me great pleasure to tell the Sheñora that the French rose has flowered – the one she had the kindness to send me from the estancia.'

'Thank you, Sister Benedicta.'

I watched Otramamá's expression with amusement as she managed to haul from her memory the name of the Sister Porter, as she would those of the granddaughters of the retired maids who came to visit us. Pleased by her efforts, she seemed unaware of the effect she was having on her beneficiary. Mention of the estancia roused me from my confusion.

'Otramamá, I'd like to see that rose,' I said. 'When did you send it to them?'

'It's very strange, I only remember writing to Rafaela and asking her to send some rosebushes for poor Mamá's grave. How on earth did they get *here*? Now I think about it, they're not at her tomb.'

'Maybe they're different ones.'

'I don't think so. They must have been put in with the vegetables and chickens I send to the nuns sometimes. I can't believe' − she began to laugh as though she were coughing − 'that they could've taken ...'

Her face turned red and her eyes began to stream as she laughed harder and harder. 'The chickens went to the Recoleta?! Oh how embarrassing! Poor Mamá!'

As she grasped my hands with her white gloves to calm herself, I couldn't help laughing too. Otramamá's mother had remained intact in her shroud for fifty years after her death and when her turn came and the family was present at the opening of her coffin, they found that they were unable to reduce her remains to fit into one of the urns that awaited us all on shelves in the chapel of our tomb, with the surname already forming part of its Victorian curlicues of marble, and the blank, oval, and rather impatient space where the name was to be carved. Her presence had grown since that contretemps, and Otramamá had stopped going to visit her.

That uncontrollable case of the giggles, which she called 'to be tempted', made me nervous. I was obsessed with literal truth, so found it hard to understand my grandmother and those feelings I glimpsed behind her stories, which sometimes obliged her to contradict herself; as if the story that she was telling was not completely true and had been arranged for the benefit of us both, for that pleasure that we were meant to share on Friday nights, and as a tentative effort to keep the world at bay, which would have included perhaps some aspects of 'poor Mamá'. But at the same time I could not break loose from that weft which protected me from the smallness of life and offered me such a privileged position. La Señora de Artayeta and I, the Señora who owned the best that there was in Buenos Aires and in whose stories the whole past was kept imprisoned. If by chance I woke, in those nights when I slept by her side, and glimpsed her sleeping body next to mine, I felt it there like a sheltering mountain. And all this was given to me, not to her children or to her other grandchildren — only to me. I was a part of her; the nanny had orders to give my grandmother's name if someone asked for mine.

The Nativity was waiting for us. The Mother Superior, whom Otramamá treated with the same absent-minded benevolence as the Sister Porter but with an impish light in her eye owing to the mishap in the Recoleta, led us to a chapel next to the high altar. It was a small room, painted white, and its wooden ceiling shone like a freshly polished piece of furniture. The air was thick with the scent of tuberoses. A row of candles burned brightly. The Nativity could not have been more different from Miss Amy's efforts at Juncal. Here, the figures were like glistening jewels, made of a translucent stone that made me think of candied fruit, although a slight cloudiness gave them a soapy feel as though they were melting in bath water, lessening their edible appeal. Everything was housed in a golden box with doors on which two figures were painted — a man dressed in black with a white wig and a lace bib, and a woman with dangling earrings and a tiny lace apron. She held a rose between tense fingers as though it were a spider.

'Who are those two?' I asked.

'Don Pedro de Cabrera and his wife, my great-grandparents,' Otramamá said without lowering her voice. 'They were very religious. Don Pedro built two churches, and then Doña María swore an oath to the Virgin that they would build a third if her child, who was dying, were saved. So that her husband wouldn't forget the promise, she wore only one earring until it was built. To mark its completion they had this Nativity made, and she had herself painted wearing both earrings.'

We knelt down. The Mother Superior had brought in some hassocks from the foot of the high altar so that I could reach the armrest before me, but the scratchy metallic embroidery bearing the initials of Christ hurt my knees, like a cushy substitute for the grains of maize on which my boy saints used to mortify themselves in prayer.

'Padre Nuestro,' Otramamá began, and her voice lost its ironic exhausted tone, and become focused, demanding, emphatic and somehow sorrowful. Her piety was transmitted to me, as usual.

'...el pan nuestro de cada dia,' my voice echoed hers. I asked Jesus, who suddenly seemed to belong to us, since He was reborn each Christmas in a jewelled casket made by my grandmother's grandparents, to let us go to the estancia as soon as possible. 'And I promise You I'll behave and I'll go to the chapel and pray to You twice a day, morning and afternoon, even if it's more difficult for me to fit it in before I go riding, and I'll try to tame myself as Mamá says I must, and let Carlos beat me at gym and not correct his French even though it makes me cross. And I'll try not to mind that the peons prefer him. But You will have to help, Jesus, by letting us go first, please little Jesus, tomorrow or the next day, very soon, because I can't go on like this anymore. And please let me forget Adela once and for all. You who are so good, whom I love so much, though I repent not loving You as much as I should, not as much as I love Mamá. I try to, but You're so far away and it's hard for me to see You, and how can I love You so much if I can't see You? I know You're in the figures of the crèche, and in the Host, but I feel that You're nearer at the estancia, when You die during Holy Week and they shroud You in purple robes and we pray all together, for You to live again, just as it was in the beginning, now and forever, forever and ever more. Amen.'

'Señora, here are some beignets for you,' said the Mother Superior, presenting us with a carefully wrapped package.

'In France they're called *pets de nonnes*,' Otramamá told me in the car on the way home, 'but in Buenos Aires we are less coarse, or more modest. We call them nuns' sighs. They're a great delicacy. You can try one with your tea.'

Evening descended on the city, and it seemed as exhausted as the old men who sat in pyjamas on their front steps. We left the Barrio Sur and entered the financial district, where the façades of the buildings sweated under their cement pilasters and cornices, their windows shuttered. They seemed about to explode. Otramamá, without seeming to notice all this, pulled down the curtain on her side.

There was one day, however, that was special, different from all the others – so different that I found it hard to believe it belonged to those which had come before. It was not even a day. It consisted of the hours before we went to bed on Christmas Eve, when I wanted to stay up later and later, all through the night, and into the next morning, and those moments as I went slowly down the stairs, not running as I usually did, but hesitant, clutching the handrail, a little frightened at what I might discover had happened as I slept. The confused light of dawn was whitening the stone steps and beyond the hall was playing weakly on the parcels in front of the library fireplace. The doors had been left open, something unheard of in Juncal. Perhaps by the saint, in his hurry to deliver so many presents.

Most of all, this difference seemed to be coming from the Christmas stocking. The light paused kindly on that leg covered in net and gave the cotton a mysterious glow, as if beneath the whiteish web something was alive. There were three legs resting against the black marble of the fireplace, enormous, lumpy and orthopaedic, and at their feet were resting the parcels we must open first. Each year I felt the same disappointment, after months of waiting and longing, but it caused me no pain. In those days my curiosity had already started prodding me to open the drawers of my mother's secretaire and read the letters that were kept there, as well as spending hours looking at photo albums of the many childhoods of my family. The same expectation led me to believe that behind the tulle of those Christmas stockings I was going to find something wondrous.

Outside, at an hour when no one else in the house was awake, the cocks of the chicken farm that backed on to our garden were crowing. I heard them beyond the library, a joyful and busy crowing from behind the plane tree that seemed to dot the morning with blue. It was a triumphal sound, as if my confused expectations of the night before had been set at rest by the answering cheer of the song.

11

'TAKE the children with us in the car! Why not put them on the train with the others? The trip will be so long and dreary. I'm fed up with Martín, he's been pestering me about his new saddle since yesterday – he can't bear to think of the servants taking it on the train.'

My mother was eating her breakfast in bed without enjoyment. Her brown hands, short, bony and bare except for her father's too-large signet ring that she moved from finger to finger like worry beads, played with her fork, stabbing slices of apple and then letting them hang in mid air, while she focused on the editorial of *La Prensa* with the intense concentration of the illiterate.

'How well Alfonsito Laferrère writes. He doesn't pander to the government like those cowards at *La Nación*.' She stared at my father, who was reading the paper in a chair by the window. 'You can't just not give me a reason for taking the children with us,' she continued. 'To say "I want to" isn't enough. I have to struggle with a world of whims – yours, the children's, the servants'. Although in *their* case they control themselves much better than you lot.' She laughed, and this made her look younger, and her high cheekbones narrowed her eyes, making them look Indian.

My father would not answer her with the same spontaneity, if he answered her at all. He only spoke to her to calm her, and as much as Clara tried to ignore it, she found herself hating having to answer her own questions. In the end she had learned more or less to control her vehemence, which revealed itself in the gleam trapped inside her eyes, and in the lines of her forehead and frown, which at thirty-three, shone like traces of the violence she inflicted upon herself.

Since her childhood she'd decided she wouldn't feel sorry for herself, which had resulted in her being enveloped in an enormous self-pity, and grew angry with the world. 'She is at odds with everyone' I heard Otropapá say of her, looking apprehensively at the screen of her dark, determined face, against which his own bad temper flickered weakly. 'She is devoured by her pride.'

She had been born into an untidy country, and into a class that was forgetting the manners imposed on a lax culture by two generations of foreign governesses. She had picked up the pieces and made a big show of behaving properly, to the exasperation of her friends, who knew she could also be very funny. But Joan of Arc was bent on her high-minded course and her way of imposing herself. To be with her, most of the time, was to be subjected to constant examinations of conscience, doled out like the pious leaflets you got after Mass. She became unpopular, but she went on with it, moving through the parties of Buenos Aires, butting at her friends, to use one of her criollo expressions, with affection and the service of her innate generosity, all to no avail, because porteños are implacable in the defence of their easy lives.

'Is everything ready? Remember, tomorrow we're leaving at dawn,' my father said.

'Oh, we'll leave at dawn all right. But when we will arrive? How many punctures will we have? You're such a bore Joaquín. I'm not going to spell it all out again, but going to the estancia with the children in the car and sending the chauffeur by train is ridiculous. I feel exhausted at the thought.'

'Don't come by car then,' Papá answered.

'But I can't leave you all alone. I know that's what you'd like, four babies playing truant together. You'll end up staying the night at the hotel in Dolores. You'll be rubbing your hands together with glee, the children will be hysterical

– "Let's stay, Papito, let's stay" – but Martín would like to arrive at the estancia on the same day, wouldn't you my pet?'

My mother turned to me. The women of Juncal never took a stand without first ensuring that they had an ally.

'Stop working yourself up Clara,' said my father, who was getting irritable. 'You can't help but say no to everything. Just see to the luggage. You'll enjoy this unbearable journey, you enjoy things when you stop complaining about them.'

Clara let it go. She'd been raised in the Moorish fashion, and knew she would get her way in other things.

'All right then, fine. What needs to be done? Let's get on with it. Matilde, have a last look in the wardrobes for my summer dresses. And where is the light grey sharkskin? I didn't see it in the trunk.'

'The niña knows I don't forget anything. I was pressing it – if I don't your clothes arrive like rags, and there are only the coal irons there.'

'That's enough, Matilde. I've done all the complaining for today. Those irons are fine, it's only the being alone in the ironing room and not chatting to the others that you don't like.'

'When have you seen me chatting? When? I don't have the time, with everything I do. The ones who do the talking in this house are the criollas. "Maté and gossip" I call them.'

'But they don't complain, Matildita. They might not work very much either, but that's why we have you Europeans here.'

Clara leapt out of bed and went to the bathroom. She didn't look at herself in the mirror. Since childhood, too much tension had prevented her from enjoying an easy beauty. At ten, when she compared her eyes with those of her older sisters, she could already say 'Yours may be bigger, but mine are sadder.' Jealousy streaked the original brown into green and yellow, and there were moments when the colour broke like the glass bits of a kaleidoscope and she seemed to have a thousand pupils full of repressed violence, that went rippling with blood along the whites to the point of dilating the corners. The big mouth, the noble nose, the chin, all set off the eyes. It was a tragic face that invaded my dreams.

On top of this, to put a seal on it, there was the criollo air, accentuated by the matt skin and the high cheekbones: an opaque, tired, greenish tone that settled itself on her during those rare moments she could keep quiet, and set her apart from the other Buenos Aires women of her class and even of her family, of her silk nightgown and of her civilised habits. She was quick to exploit the singularity. 'I'm American, I always have been, you have only to look at me,' she said, and when she got angry she looked at the inhabitants of Buenos Aires as if it were she who had granted them permission to enter the country.

She got in and out of the bath quickly. She never sang in her bath. She put on her makeup with concentration but without care, then dabbed rapidly behind each ear with the stopper of the perfume bottle. She dressed well. She liked berets that framed her face without hiding it in shadow, also turbans and fur collars, and she complained that her legs were not longer, for she would have liked to make an entry into drawing rooms like a ship.

I was obsessed with her. Without meaning to, she showed me her weaknesses every day. I saw her going under, struggling, even when she walked alone, grumbling under her hat, tilted forward as if to meet the world head on. Incapable of the slightest introspection, she declared herself the queen of free souls, while everything filled her with jealousy. With perverse generosity, she gave me the shirt off her back and took away my peace. She had difficulty in sleeping, and I imagined her shut up at the end of the last courtyard, in the room of the idiots of the family, filling the house with a silence louder than any screams.

'Martín, Martín, bring the scrapbook. Today is the anniversary of the day Güemes destroyed the royalist advance in the Quebrada del Toro.' Now she wore the mantle of family historian. 'Bring it here so we can paste the notice straight in. Then go to the green sitting room and look at his portrait — he's the very handsome man with a beard, in a white uniform. A bit like your father, but even better looking.'

'I didn't know he was related to Papá,' I said.

'He isn't, you silly boy. Your father isn't from Salta. Güemes is *our* ancestor.'

'But aren't you and Papá from the same family?'

'Yes, but not completely. We're not even close to being first cousins, as my mother's parents were.'

'Which family is better, then?'

'What a stupid question. We're the same.'

'No, that can't be. Not if you're not even first cousins. One must be better. It's you, isn't it?' I insisted, ever more stubbornly, as I was forced to with all the women of Juncal.

'There you go again with your silly ideas, stop it. Your Papá is perfectly all right. As good as us. Better, even. And this genealogical point-scoring is frightfully common.'

She got up and, ignoring me, began to inspect the trunks Matilde had been packing.

How I hated her and her rigidity in these moments. Here she was, taking advantage of me when I tried to get close to her, and humiliating me, sending me to the corner.

Will you never stop? Last night I dreamt that the three of us were at a ball. Papá and you and me. I was wearing a boy's dinner jacket. Papá went away and left you, and you looked at me with that smile and I asked you to dance and we danced in a corner where we could scarcely hear the music and we couldn't stop dancing because no one came to look for you and you could not be left alone at a ball.

But on those other occasions when she was dressing to go out and the ritual around her beauty seemed to bring all the power of the house to her dressing room, I forgave her everything. I stood as close as I could get to her dressing table and gazed at my mother as she sat completely absorbed in the mirror, her angry face perfected by concentration and cosmetics. The oppressive forms of love were all there for me to see – fear, domination, pride. Her eyebrows were arched, her eyes slanted, her cheekbones heightened. The red of her mouth supported a triangle, accentuated as she pouted, tensely coquettish, and narrowed her nostrils, dilating the corners of her eyes. The tight hair in a bun that covered the back of her neck increased her severity. My nightmares of the desecrators of Otramamá's dressing table came back to me, and I could sense something of that danger stalking my mother.

Her maids approached with her dress, opened it out, and my mother stepped into it as if into a mountain.

'Goodbye, my darling. Do I please you?'

'Of course, you know you do. Mamá, please let me walk down the stairs with you.'

'No, stay here. I'm in a hurry.'

Once, when the lift was broken, I watched her from the second floor balustrade going down the stairs, moving slowly while she held her skirt with both hands. The skirt went down even more slowly with a round and startling fullness, as if it had decided to fall to the next step only at the last moment. My mother's shoulders and the back of her neck were all that were familiar to me, and they emerged from a white contraption which became foam around her arms and started to dry and tighten round her waist, where it shone, foreign and convex, and crackling, in bands both transparent and velvety that breathed and swished as they descended, independent of Clara, and sustaining her, as if she left for the ball carrying her house with her.

My obsession with my mother started to interfere with my religious feelings. They were strong and I wanted to keep them pure.

'Mamá, there's something worrying me,' I said to her one morning when I came into her room after taking the communion of the First Fridays. She was pouring over the political pages, as usual.

'What's worrying you?' she said without looking up. 'In the Catechism it says that you have to love God above all things.'

'Yes, that's true.'

'But I can't love Him above all things, because I can't love Him more than you.'

'Ah.'

'Is this is a sin?'

'No, my darling. It isn't a sin, but God is the utmost goodness in the world. Much more than me.'

'I know that Mamá. But I don't love you because of your goodness. It's not that you're not good, only that sometimes I feel sorry for you, and I never feel that for God.'

'Why would you feel sorry for me?'

'Sometimes when I think of you I feel like crying. I dream that I'm taking care of you.'

She was suddenly angry. 'How very strange,' she said. 'And you don't feel pity for Christ on the cross?'

'Yes, a little.' I was feeling trapped. 'Well, quite a bit. But not as much as I do for you.'

'Well, I hope you don't love your mother out of pity.'

She rummaged for her lipstick and started to paint her mouth with excessive care.

'And why are you sorry for me?' She watched my face in the mirror.

'I don't know, Mamá, I don't know. I must go and get dressed now. Otramamá's taking me to San Isidro.'

'Don't be cheeky. You say these teasing things and then you want to run off. Stand there straight like a little soldier, and tell me where you got the idea that you pity me. You're not stupid, although you look it sometimes. Pity me for what?'

I couldn't bear to go on talking about these things, face to face. I ran out of the room, but she called me back.

'When I was a girl,' she began in a very calm voice, 'Miss Emily and I had our rooms on my grandmother's floor. My parents and sisters were upstairs. One afternoon, Mamá sent word that I was to get dressed, she was taking us shopping and then to tea at Harrods. I spent most of my time on my own, so it was always a treat to go out with them. I dressed quickly in my best new coat and gloves and then waited for the lift. At last it came inching down, but it didn't stop for me, just kept going, and as it passed I saw my sisters, waving a mocking goodbye. I cried terribly. I don't know why, but I still remember that moment.'

12

WE'RE leaving tomorrow. We're all going together in one car. Papá will sing on the journey, in a voice so hoarse it won't seem like he's singing at all, 'I will go searching for you when Lavalle…' and the music will keep coming anyway amid the noise of those churning stones, 'I'll come for you when Buenos Aires… will have got ridden of Juan Manuel….'

We are leaving Buenos Aires very early while the cobblestones are still wet, in that break after the heaviness of the night before the sun begins to threaten behind the loading cranes in the docks. We escape before the doors of Juncal have been opened, before the church doors have been opened, Mamá's straw sandals smell brand new. We are going at the hour of the ships, shrouded in smoke, cut out against the sky treacly like a soup of orange being brought to the boil, they seem to climb the slope of Juncal smelling of tar and mud. But the Oldsmobile smells clean, of leather and straw, and the grass will be hit by the wind. The children go on pestering as usual.

'What time will we arrive?' says Carlos. 'Will it be before the horses are let out? I want them to try out Cómo Llueve with my new saddle.'

'Is it true what they said, that Quico died, Mamá? Who else died?' Mercedes asks.

'What if it's rained and we can't get in? Who knows whether the laguna of Kakel has flooded,' my mother grumbles, still annoyed by the adventure.

I want to arrive at nightfall. I was wearing my new suede jacket and boots, even though I knew I would roast, like Miss Amy said. We are leaving. We pass policemen posted at every intersection, with Foreign Legion white bibs round the back of their caps, the colour of mother of pearl in the sunrise. We overtake empty trams. We are leaving. We abandon the city to its heat, and enter the enormous summer.

We move down the bank with our eyes searching for the outer limits of Buenos Aires which will take more than an hour to reach, the border marked by the woods of San Juan de Pereyra, behind which the plain opens.

The car descended the slope of Juncal and turned into Paseo Colón towards the south. When it crossed in front of the Casa Rosada, my mother looked at it with fury. 'Bastard!' she exclaimed.

I look at that curious monument, that shares a pretentious, run-down air with the other Argentine public buildings, and feel afraid. The statue of the Republic crowning it, smeared in grey atop that pink cake, offering up the harvest with hopeless hands, which the avid men that held power from within would put in little plastic bags the colour of caramels, piled one on top of the other, grain over grain, every time more golden, to take home for the missus to have a quick look at before other men with double-breasted suits and moustaches carried them further away across the ocean, beyond the circle of wheels and cows and swords surrounding the mother of us all, towards the security of the old world at which the Italian Colón gazed with marble eyes, standing on his column at the shore of that red water, giving his back to that immense promised land.

This country is not mine, I thought. Perón could have Papá killed when he wanted, just as Juan Manuel de Rosas had sent our ancestor Don Domingo Cullen to his death. And Perón might take away our estancia, just as Rosas had done. After all they have already taken Tapiales. But that doesn't mean this country belongs to them, this country belongs to nobody.

A policeman signalled us to stop. 'What's wrong, officer?

Why have you stopped us?' my mother asked in a hard voice.

'Señora, you can't pass in front of Government House with your back curtain drawn.'

'Do you think I'd have driven past the Casa Rosada if I had a revolver? I'd have gone straight inside to get at him.'

'Señora, please mind what you say.' The policeman took in the leather upholstery and my mother's legs, and smiled as he saluted. 'Drive on, Señor.' Did he think, what sons of bitches, what a life these oligarchs have, as he saw the little girl wave goodbye to him through the rear window with both hands.

'That policeman was nice, wasn't he? And quite good looking. Did you see his blue eyes? But Joaquín, you should have said something to him,' Clara smiled, in better spirits.

'How about "Lock her up, officer, it'll make our journey easier?"'

'Very funny, you're just covering up your fear. When I remember all those tall stories of your tough bachelor days, when you fought every night at that *boîte* Tabarís, nothing but tall stories.' My mother laughed again, with a trace of anger. She made an effort to take words seriously, and when they came out amusingly, she was the first to laugh at them in surprise.

'Men in this country are cowards. And we are the worst of all, worse even than the military. What are we waiting for? Why doesn't someone topple the bastard?' This last little flame of fury flickered before going out.

We passed an arcade of two arches followed by an empty lot whose walls were plastered with posters praising Evita and Perón and their glorious future, followed again by more arches which looked like large irregular dentures. On top of these were a few little balconies smiling with geraniums. The size of those arches should have sustained three more floors of the Roman order, but some had nothing on top. A few blocks to the south, these grand Italian puddings had been replaced by flimsy walls, once an Andalusian white and now just the colour of dirty cement. This was the Barrio Sur. I liked this part of Buenos Aires, perhaps because it was the road to the estancia, but also because I found something cheerful in its poverty.

Now, as the height of the buildings dropped, the streets widened and opened out into plazas, plains of shining cobbles crisscrossed by glittering tramlines that shone even more, into which the solitary Oldsmobile hurtled as though splashing onto water. The pampa had entered the city.

'How ugly Buenos Aires is!' Clara said. 'And it gets uglier every day. My grandfather Artayeta used to say that God had overdone his punishment making us live here, being born in this country was punishment enough. And if he didn't leave Buenos Aires it's because he wasted inheritance after inheritance in Paris. He even swallowed up all his son's money. Maybe that's why everybody thought he was the most refined man in the city. Of course I don't agree with him. But in times like these I do wonder.' My mother didn't believe in refinement, only in duty. There were always morals to her stories. No, despite her natural wit her head didn't dance, it went against its own grain. But she could laugh thank God, and when she did her mouth stood open, rigid, as if she had lost her senses, and I would slap her on the back: 'Mamá, calm down please, it's not good for you. Mamita, be quiet' — hitting her again to help spit out the stone of her joy.

'Children, lower the window, we're about to cross the Riachuelo,' said my mother pointing. 'I want you to see close up how the poor live.'

'We know very well,' I told her. 'Gilda took us to the Isla Maciel to visit her family, and we had to cross this sewer. I was terrified that the boat would capsize and we'd be sucked into the black liquid, just like those people who disappeared when that tram missed the bridge and went into the water.'

'How you love horror stories!' my mother said. 'It can't be because we put them in your head. Miss Judy says you won't go to bed until she's told you more stories about the war. "*And as you know, Madam, they are painful memories,*" the poor thing tells me.'

'I don't know why the war makes Miss Judy so sad,' I said. 'I think it's the most exciting thing that could happen. Hiding in caves to escape the bombs, dyeing her hair so she could cross borders in disguise, travelling across Europe on foot, working in Rome as an actress. What could be more fun than all that?'

'Oh yes, and seeing the boat your mother was escaping on sunk by a torpedo and your little girl disappear in a burning hospital and ending up as a nanny in the Argentine when you speak seven languages and you're the daughter of a senator?'

'She doesn't seem bitter.'

'That's because she has character, for your information.' Mamá spoke suddenly with the priggish voice of Miss Amy.

I didn't care. I was happy, and I was looking forward to going to Maipú station in the victoria to collect Miss Judy on her return from Montevideo. We were out of the city, and stretching ahead – so vast and endless that they seemed bigger than the pampa itself – were three months of summer.

PART II

THE ESTANCIA

13

W E W E R E woken by the sound of the gravel being raked, and then, when our nanny Gilda opened the window, by the white glow of the maple tree. The sun, already strong, reflected the white of the gravel and the white of the tree, and gave our unassuming country morning the radiance of the sea, or of snow.

Our room was large and tall, with a narrow French window in one corner that didn't manage to fill it with light, and this mica-white, flame-white light, I think, contrasted with the yellow wash of the walls where dark prints, curiously representing children, hung high in ebony frames. There was the usual mahogany wardrobe, but red and mirrorless, and broader than those in the rest of the house. Of the beds, I remember the clanking of their bronze frames, the icy linen sheets and their discomfort.

In the manner of the seventeenth century, the room formed a passage between the landing at the top of the stairs and the rest of that wing of the house. It had been a salita for Otramamá, and had three entrances, one of them double doors that opened into the hall. Compared to our little bedroom in Buenos Aires, perched up on the nursery floor at the top of the Calle Juncal, it seemed enormous. To me it was old and at the same time transitory. It was not ours, and yet it was saturated with a beauty that had possessed me before I was conscious of it; it possessed me, but it did not belong to me, just as the splendour of the Iglesia del Socorro and the laid table in the dining room of the Calle Juncal were not mine. But it was here that I slept, with my brother, for the full three months of summer.

The door which led into my mother's rooms was usually

closed, and it was the third door, smaller, almost hidden, up one step, that led to the new, sunny, young part of the house – the two rooms where my sister and our succession of governesses slept. This difference – important and yet difficult to explain – seemed to depend on the shape and position of the windows. In all the other rooms, even those we children seldom entered, the windows had been set on narrow, diagonal walls that sliced off the right angles of the cubes of the house, an 1880s re-creation of a Palladian villa. Their position made them unexpected, and mysterious like mirrors, but also furtive. Each was tall and narrow and opened with a door-like, wooden part on to a balcony. Their shutters were nearly always closed, and the chinks of light made the rooms dim and cool, and appear larger. Perhaps it also made them sadder.

The window in my sister's room was different. It was the only one that opened straight from the main façade, looking out on the garden. It had no balcony, and was lower and wider and less grand than the others. 'It has the best view,' said Mamá, because it had been her room as a child. And it was true; from that great height I could look out, enamoured and a little giddy, at the arms of the trees joining to enclose the oval lawn, which ended where their hands joined, with the towering and symmetrical cedars. From the wide open window, I looked left to the white maple, here slanted and diminished, rather than straight-on from our window; then the gingko, the golden ash, and the female cedar, shorter than her twin and forking at the top into two hairy branches, where a chajá sometimes perched. And then the great wide opening beyond that green and watery oval, through which the garden became the park, the mouth through which the things of the house might become lost on the pampa. Wild? Brutal? If I think of it now, it seems more menacing than it did then. I am tormented by the gulf between what we had made – our family, there was nobody before us – and what was already there, what is there still, so much more and so many times more beautiful.

The other sentinel of this vista, the male cedar, stood to attention, crowned by a perfect tip like a child's drawing, and festooned with small cones, like so many candles. Beyond it were the black tops of the pines, whose trunks were hidden by pink chestnuts, the only ones on the estancia. Then the branches of the other gingko, the largest in the whole Republic, according to my grandfather. It acted as a parasol for the fat, clipped yew. Our two white dogs, with their black spots that had infiltrated from another breed, sat on the lawn, posing as statues.

As a child, my mother had looked down on the lawn, that oval, green pond like a bowl held by loving arms; and as a child I too imagined resting my head on it. But the clarity and beauty of this window, which filled the only normal room in the house with light and happiness, like a sun-drenched igloo, made it dangerous, like the vertigo produced by its height. If, seduced by those great trees, I fell into that pond of green and welcoming water, I might die.

In the evening, when the sun is setting on the laguna and the low light stretches over the plain as if trying to reach out over the recumbent hills of Yamoidá and touch the sea, the whole casco goes dark. Everything – the walls, the grass, the trees whose crowns are still on fire – holds the heat and yet strains to release it, to relinquish that weight which taints the falling darkness. Beyond this vista, the park flanked by its columns of trees and the last oaks, the pampa is flooded with a yellow light so intense that, as I watch, it seems as if the house has become a throne and the park a great hall besieged by flames. There is no escape. If I mount a horse and open the gate at the end of the Calle de San Francisco, I will be propelled into another world.

Perhaps even then, without fully comprehending it, I was conscious of this distressing fracture, that the casco was a castle defending itself from the plain. But my first memories are of the estancia filled with people. And it was only when the party was over, the grown-ups had left, and the servants were free to dismantle the estancia by shrugging off their servile ways, that the brutal pampa was ready to invade.

* * *

From the top of the stairs, I watched Otramamá as she sat on a velvet sofa the colour of dry leaves. As usual, she was knitting. There she was, surrounded by balls of wool, my birthday present at her side. She was alone, in the middle of the room, like a Christmas stocking. She had made the journey from Buenos Aires to the estancia she disliked, tearing herself away from the smell of her beloved tarmac, especially for me – to celebrate my birthday. It was the 28th of February, the day of the party.

Her long, thin head was waiting for me; behind her glasses she concentrated on the needles, which added stitches while her lips moved in prayer. I watched her through the white banisters. I don't recall seeing my present, instead I remember a large pear, upholstered in grey linen, sitting in her nest of leaves, slashed by the dazzlingly quick and recurrent play of the needles, their beaks kissing like anxious doves, unable to tear themselves apart. Through the light curtains of the big upper window behind me, the sun was already showing its ferocity at seven in the morning, wounding the sky to a fixed, angry blue while it still crouched below the green screen of the trees.

The day of my santo began early in the big house. While the family slept, and the servants were yet to appear through the pantry door, the barbecuers were piling up the wood in the space between the Gruta de la Virgen and the Sala de Sombra. In the stable yard, the horses which that afternoon were to run in the annual race against the neighbouring estancia of San Carlos were being hosed down, clipped, groomed, their hooves trimmed. The day was unfolding between my invisible self behind the banisters and the fine head of my grandmother, turbaned in violet tulle, who for the last hour or so had been adding stitches and prayers on the sofa in the empty hall, and waiting for me. It was my birthday, but this day wasn't for me alone. It was a celebration, a renewal, organised by and for the grown-ups.

Rafaela, our housekeeper, came in first, bearing a packet of dulce de leche sweets bought in Maipú, at La Espiga de Oro bakery.

'Good morning, Sheñora. Happy Birthday, niño Martínsheeto,' she said in her sheeshing Spanish accent.

Each year it was the same, brown sweets that I hated; but I was fond of her wide, Indian, moustachioed face, bred in the most Visigothic Luarca mountains of Asturias, in Spain. Rafaela was the sacristan of the estancia. Rafaela to us. Doña Rafaela to everyone else. Who knows what resentment clouded her shrewd eyes, which I imagined so devoted to our service.

Rafaela had a reputation for intelligence. She spoke French, which she had learned as my great-grandmother's maid at the Hôtel Meurice in Paris. In her dining room was a small bookcase containing some unbound books discarded by the big house, and she had sent her only daughter away to train as a teacher. She treated Otramamá with the respect due to the Lady Dowager, and to a visitor who will soon be leaving.

'The Sheñora Mayor can't help not liking it here,' I once heard her say to her husband, Juan Claro the majordomo, whose family had worked on the estancia for several generations. 'She is not a country person – what do you expect?' Juan Claro replied, closing the subject.

Juan Claro himself was very much a country person. He had the slight body of a laguna bird and the white face of a pampa fox. He had grown up in the cottage that had been part of the coach-inn of Santa Helena, by a log bridge over the stream that joined the two great lagunas of Yamoidá and Kakel. Although he scarcely knew Buenos Aires, he had spent two years of his life in London. He had been taken there because he knew how to handle the kakeleros, the mail-coach horses that were bred strong-headed on the thick grass of the hills of Kakel. He never spoke of this adventure, but sometimes, as if it were enough, he would point to a framed photograph in the dining room they never used. It showed him in profile, sitting on top of what appeared to be one of the wagons of La Porteña, the first Argentine train, a badge on his top hat, his legs covered by a plaid blanket, holding eight reins in his gloved hand, against the Greek screen that marks the entrance to Hyde Park. His other memento from his time in London was a scar, whose origin had become part of the folklore of Maipú. The first time he entered the Savoy Hotel, bringing a message for his master, he met a man walking towards him along the corridor. The man looked him straight in the eye, and as Juan Claro got nearer, seemed less and less inclined to make way. If he doesn't budge, then I won't either, Juan Claro promised himself with criollo toughness, and walked into a mirror, slashing his nose.

I used to imagine that all these people had their memories enriched by our scraps. I would have liked them to tell me how marvellous my family was, how honoured they felt at being allowed to serve us. The most pleasurable of all our family stories, more so even than the deeds of our heroes, was the one of the wet nurse who knew her place so well that she asked that her epitaph be: 'Wet Nurse to Distinguished Babies'. Unlike the English, who so often distance themselves from their parents, and dream of being poor so as to be close to their nannies, I knew which side I was on. The Calle Juncal harboured an excess of love for those of the blood. And when, later, we were sent to the estancia alone, I felt abandoned to that other side, for without the constraining presence of the masters, a sharpness was revealed that terrified me, because my vision of the poor as our despised but loving children was destroyed. It was then that I began to hate them.

But now, I still believed myself happy. Miss Judy had disturbed the droning inertia of those country days, and this birthday began unlike any other. The children greeted me at breakfast with a 'Happy Birthday' rendered with Slavic exuberance, conducted by Miss Judy with a willow baton, on my plate was the most beautiful book I had ever received, Andersen's *Fairy Tales*, wrapped in red paper with green ribbon, and with such an intimate inscription that I was shocked. Miss Judy had written '*Yours, Judy*', as though offering herself to me.

'Miss Judy, you are not mine. And you're not just "Judy." You're Miss.'

I didn't expect to possess a governess who spoke seven languages and was a war refugee. On the contrary, her vitality and distance gave me more air, that air which the reclining idols of the family and their routine-driven servants had made so scarce. The fact was that Miss Judy seemed even more extraordinary on the estancia. To her usual songs, '*Ach, du lieber Augustin*' and '*Ochi chorniye*', she had added the yearnings of '*Surabaia Johnny*' and '*Chrysanthème*'. She even had us perform '*Trois Jeunes Tambours*' to celebrate a visit our grandparents made in January. These interludes marked such a change from our usual summer rituals that it was worth all our effort. And for me, acting – particularly since as the eldest I had the role of king – struck a vein of fantasy in me unfulfilled by merely playing at Statues, and the '*Please Miss Judy, let's act tonight,*' became a nagging almost as tiresome for her, as the famous '*I beg you, Miss Judy, tell us about the war.*'

The estancia had wiped Adela from my memory. The

urgent need to see her that had had me drag Miss Amy up and down the Calle Arroyo, which curved along the river bank reminding my English governess of the winding streets of her country, had been swallowed up by the pampa. Now when I searched for Adela in my mind, I couldn't find her, and I began to think that perhaps I had needed her only to bring the estancia closer to the city. In any case, Miss Judy's adventures occupied all my time. Picnics on the hard clay beach of the laguna of Kakel, fishing for catfish at the lock of Yamoidá, to which we went singing in the brake, boating trips on our laguna to search for chajá and coot eggs. That succession of outings, day after day, was completely absorbing for me, accustomed as I had been to the slow, criollo pace. Apart from the religiously observed daily ride with the majordomo, an outing that had in the past created such havoc that the family needed two weeks of rest before planning another. All this new activity left me free of longing.

'To do' wasn't done in Maipú. For months and months we did nothing. Day succeeded day with the monotony of a dripping tap. But for those few summers, Miss Judy told herself, *Nous allons changer tout cela.*

That morning, after breakfast, she set aside the liturgical ride, and took us to the Bosque de la Virgen. It was early, and the humidity of the laguna hadn't yet filled the air. A freshness hardened the heat, making it invigorating. The acrid smell of the laurels, like a newly washed kitchen, mingled with the sweet, pink perfume of the lilies cut by Rafaela to fill the vases in the Gruta de la Virgen. We entered the wood, which was little more than a cemetery for dead leaves and a dumping ground for the tree trunks that were used for the great barbecues, and dived into the tunnels that the laurels had made under the eucalyptus. The Bosque de la Virgen extended along the steep bank of the laguna, from the causeway through to the chicken yard. Though only two hundred yards from the house, it was a mystery to us – it might well have been inhabited by Saurians. That we were now entering it was another sign of the terrible beauty that Miss Judy was unleashing on the estancia.

'*Didn't I tell you? It's wonderful, almost as good as the pampa.*'

Miss Judy had made it clear that she found the pampa marvellous, and the park, our cherished pride, just about all right.

'*The light, children, the light! It's like Venice. And this arboretum doesn't allow one to enjoy it. Che dolore.*'

Because she had a gift for languages, she couldn't resist perfuming her Spanish, which she had learnt almost without trying, with an Italian lilt. And she mimicked the servants' accents – she didn't allow herself to copy the family's – when she thought we couldn't hear her. She practised the ceremonious sheeshing of Rafaela, the unbuttoned, Galician singsong of Otramamá's maid Vicenta, Gilda's Irish Creole, Casimiro's Polackisms. But it was the gaucho burr that she really fell for.

'*Ces centaurs roucôulent comme des colombes,*' she once said to my grandfather, who didn't speak English.

'*Colombes poignardées,*' he answered, because Juan Claro had told him some days earlier that he'd had to pull his pistol on two peons who were fighting with knives. Miss Judy didn't get the joke, and Otropapá didn't explain.

My grandfather was an exception to the rule that well-born people are polite to their servants, treating them like the gauchos treat their dogs, seldom even bothering to be irritated. He barely acknowledged Miss Judy, whose father was a Latvian senator. And yet, he was renowned for his good manners.

As we collected the laurel branches Miss Judy was cutting, without knowing what they were for, the medicinal smell of eucalyptus made us look up. Rags of smoke were tangled in the shafts of light that pierced the blackness of the undergrowth. The barbecue had begun. They were burning the trunks of the gigantic eucalyptus; those trees that loomed out of the sea of grass as tiny dots of blue when we approached the small town of Guido, thirty kilometres before the estancia. Their minute shapes on the horizon showed us that out there was our beloved island, waiting after a whole year, in its unique but shifting place on that prairie expanded by mirage. Otropapá had ordered that the trees be cut down, lest they fell on the house. Those same trunks, which four peons linking hands could barely encircle, had been lit before dawn, so that hours later, when their entrails were reduced to embers which would take days to go out, they would be ready to roast the birthday meats.

The garrulous twittering of oven birds, parakeets and benteveos pierced the morning with their din, like the chitchat of gaucho women, both likeable and dull. With the cooing of the wood pigeons that swelled out over the lugubrious tunnels of the little wood from all corners of the casco, they created a scaffolding of sound, like the arcs of a cathedral. A cathedral filled with souls in purgatory, perhaps, rehearsing with their mechanical chants a redemptive and triumphant hymn.

Ahead, hidden, lay the laguna. Its voice, so different, brought the harsh notes into harmony. It was a voice made more precious by the intervals of silence, while its damp smell seemed to stick to us like an amphibious tongue. An explosion of hundreds of coots, gurgling in unison like hoarse dowagers, brought to this raucous morning a premonition of evening; and then came the intermittent and disembodied reply of those unknown water birds I sometimes saw roosting when Papá and I returned late from a hunting expedition, and whose calls we thought we recognised from our beds – the song of the night.

The laguna, which seemed the very image of silence, lay like a beast spread out and asleep at the foot of the casco, and never held her tongue. Almost untouched by humans, she was the geological mother of the estancia, for without her there would be no rising bank, and no house. Before our eyes, she displayed a modest, impenetrable, Venetian existence, spent blending the hours and playing games with the light. Before Miss Judy's arrival, on the very few occasions when my father took us boating, I had glimpsed a world apart from the casco or the pampa. But in reality, the laguna was merely a decoration for the willow and poplar-lined causeway, the straight road laid out like a parked train that took a whole kilometre to join our park to its brother, San Carlos. We travelled it on horseback, or sometimes in the carriage with Clara. During his brief visits, our father liked to go shooting at the laguna after the siesta. Then the long carriage would come alive with furtive presences – the prey we watched between the fuzzy blinds of tamarisk. The ducks, varnished like toys, and skittish like my pony, streaked out of the water and cut the air, their wings like quick scissors, saying *ciao-ciao-ciao* until they vanished over the plain. The ripples they left moved out slowly towards the bank, and there was nothing but that dead, transparent water, the colour of horses' eyes. If the dog felt like jumping in the prey was pocketed, if not it was abandoned. We learnt early about criollo waste.

Casimiro and Gomez, the footman, and one or two others, were busy in the Sala de Sombra, a circle of oaks, planes and elms, whose tall trunks were like the columns of a baptistery, or as my grandfather liked to believe, the Temple of Love built by Marie Antoinette. The men were covering trestle tables with vast damask tablecloths.

'Where is the birthday niño going to sit?' Miss Judy asked Casimiro.

'I don't know, Señora Miss, he has no place. The Señores Mayores sit at the head of the table, and everybody else sits around them where they can.'

'*That won't do,*' Miss Judy muttered to herself in English. She seemed to have plans that she wasn't going to divulge.

Further away, in the direction of the Gruta de la Virgen, in a clearing where the bank of the laguna was covered with periwinkle, the barbecuers had built up their pyre. On a circular table around the big oak, the footmen were placing piles of china and cutlery in cold, ordered rows, making a green, white and silver arrangement, fresh like my grandmother's face beneath her parasol, and just as urban. Nearby, a house of embers was consuming itself. Wrapped in a film of fierce heat, it was the grandest of my gifts. It was impossible to get close to it until the smallest of the embers had been spread under the iron crucifixes hung with lambs more tender than the Easter ones. Juan Claro had managed to get a flock of Corriedale sheep to lamb around my birthday, that torrid Easter of the estancia, straddled between Palestine's spring flowers and the first autumn leaves of the Southern Hemisphere. The ribcages of a couple of heifers, stretched out like exhausted accordions, bowed towards the fire, but they weren't sacrificial victims, like those little lambs. Miss Judy, for all her experience of war, had been unable to watch the slaughter that had taken place the evening before at the corral down by the peon's house. Quico had grasped their necks and plunged his knife into the soft wool of their throats, as quickly and gently as he would thrust his needle when sewing up a bag of corn.

'Children, how can you?' she had moaned, walking away. But we knew that another gaucho had cut the throat of a Cullen recently enough for my grandfather to remember.

Quico was our alarm clock. It was he who raked the gravel every morning, and that monotonous combing of the rake, ric…ric…ric…, which would have put an insomniac to sleep, gave me the message that I was awake, and here in the estancia. This herald of happiness looked like a slug. Small, bent and dark, so shy that he seemed to walk sideways, it was painful to see him down there, outlined on the blinding terrace beneath our windows, wounded by light like the caterpillars that writhe when you expose them by tearing away the bark of a eucalyptus tree. It was Quico who swept the pavement for Rafaela, brought in logs for Casimiro when the evening grew cold after a whole day of rain, and from whom the cooks, who remained nameless because they didn't last, ordered fowl and eggs from the chicken yard. He seemed at home only on the edge of things. Bent over further by an enormous bundle of dead leaves, he would enter the Bosque de la Virgen like the bogeyman, and only then did he seem to find his true self — a lone beast called by the wild. And yet he came meekly each day to do his raking, and so we loved him apprehensively, aware that we had caught an animal we could never tame. He didn't speak, he seldom answered, he got ferociously drunk on pay day, and then disappeared for a while so we heard about it only later. He made me think of Jack, the aloof fox terrier who slept under the hydrangeas beneath the dining-room windows and yelped all night at the full moon. Both edged away from you, moving sideways without hurrying.

But they both came back. And finding them there at the estancia, after a whole year of absence, as solid as the house whose façade of leaves was the same dark and humid green each January, the hall door with the same squeak of its diamond-shaped panels of glass, the hall the same smell of damp and newly cut agapanthus, Rafaela's apron the same starchiness, our beds the same cold feel of linen. All of this made me passionately believe the lie: that in the world things don't go to waste or disappear, or at least that I would always find a corner of that enormous summer, more vast than the plain, where dogs that don't lick and peons that don't smile are the guardians, keeping things intact, eternal, and are the price that reveal them as treasures.

14

THE ESTANCIA changed so little during the three
months we spent there that I came to equate fixedness
with happiness. If we didn't move, we wouldn't suffer. So
the joy brought by Miss Judy's changes was to me illicit,
as if we were breaking a taboo. The ironic remarks of the
elders of the Calle Juncal about Miss Judy's energy were
confirmation of this. Only my father could compare with
her, and Papá had never really belonged to the estancia.

'What exotic programme has the Miss devised for today?'
Otramamá would ask, with that disdain that I found irresistible, because it showed her superior to any inventiveness,
the guardian of that natural and beneficial state of boredom.

'*Elle est Slave, Russe,*' my grandfather answered, as if
that were enough.

'She is not Russian, Otropapá, she is Latvian. Her language is not Slavic, it's Fino-Ugric.' Fino-Ugric seemed to
me definitive. No one of the Calle Juncal could know what
it was, and its linguistic detail would save Miss Judy from
the kinship my grandfather sought to establish between her
and Casimiro, whose waywardness was attributed by his
masters to his 'Slav nature'.

'Hungarian – a Hun, if the child finds that better.' And
without changing his tone, he asked my grandmother if
the cook had made a pâté with the hares he and my father
had shot two days before, as he wanted to serve it with the
apéritifs to the San Carlos cousins.

'You might find it rather dry. This cook doesn't have the
last one's knack with game, and he won't take Rafaela's
advice,' Otramamá answered in a bored voice. She made a
feature of her asceticism.

'I can't bear people who coddle themselves,' she was fond

of saying. To be bored was part of that virtue of not taking care of oneself.

Miss Judy had us pile up the laurel branches by the pantry door, then sent us upstairs to change. It was nearly time for Mass. Gilda had laid out our white blouses on a bed, and was sitting by the window, painting a sandal. In the shaft of light that came through the half-open shutter, the little brush ran over the squashed toe, touching it up with a chalky white that dried instantly, losing its sheen, and leaving a dusty surface that stained our ankles. Once they'd lost their pristine newness, our sandals were like Tía Teodé's face after she'd powdered it, quickly revealing their real age. The puffed sleeves of the blouse pinched my arms, and once Gilda had fastened the straps, the pinafore trousers gripped my balls. Because of Mass, our hats were left in the wardrobe. Clara had us dressed with a thirty-year time lag, and in tight clothes so we'd look thinner.

Though we were only going to the Gruta de la Virgen, the grass beyond the gravelled terrace shone with the brightness of ceremony, wet for the party, green, golden, radiant, it seemed to submit to the hesitant tread of our sandals like a carpet leading to an altar. 'Mass grass,' I said to my brother. Like Quico, like Jack, he remained silent.

The day of my santo was the only time in the year that Mass was celebrated in the Gruta de la Virgen. Father Mauro Golé, the parish priest of Maipú, with his mountain boots, close-cropped snow-white hair, dolomite face and legendary virtue, had been brought to the estancia by Juan Claro in his Model-T Ford. He was our Curé d'Ars. My family, slightly insensitive to his sanctity, treated him with ease.

'There he goes again about Austerlitz,' said Otramamá, when the priest, who harboured a Béranger-like nostalgia for Napoleon, wove the Emperor's exploits into his sermons.

'His sermons sound like the inscriptions on the Carrousel: *L'Armée Française vola de l'Océan au Danube, et caetera, et caetera,*' she whispered to my grandfather, who didn't smile. 'And then he starts asking for things, "Could you spare a few logs, Don Juan Claro?"'

Otramamá's irreverence didn't bother me. The priests who visited my grandmother in the Calle Juncal treated me like a hot cross bun – they kissed me, bit me, and Father Echenique loved me so much that he couldn't resist dragging me into a corner and tasting me. After them I found the even-handed greetings of our local saint, scrupulously shared out between me, my siblings, our groom, and the sons of the peons' cook, not so much an indication of his charity, but a sign of his contempt. Without being all that pretty, I suffered the insecurities of any object of desire.

Perched at the top of a ladder, Quico had carried out Rafaela's orders and surrounded the niche of the Virgin of Lourdes with a halo of pink lilies. At the base of the statue, her feet wounded by a gilded rose, two little silver vases had been filled with that February bloom, whose pink flower at the top of its long purple stem spread its infantile, drooping and artificial touch to every corner of the park. Dahlias, heliotropes and roses, each perfectly suitable for the house, were never cut by Rafaela for my birthday Mass.

'*Qué soï era Immaculado Councepcioü,*' the miraculous words of the absent Saint Bernadette were woven on the ribbon around her head. My sister intoned them for Her, kneeling absolutely still on the sharp gravel, her hands crossed on her breast, and a white mantilla on her head. Five eucalyptus trunks, alternating with dining-room chairs, served as prie-dieux for my grandparents, my parents and me. Behind were more trunks for the rest of the family and the guests, but they preferred to kneel on the grass. The staff piled in at the back.

My family had encountered a new enemy in its aesthetic war with the world: the bronze Gothic crucifix that Father Golé was unpacking from his case.

Clara approached him. 'Father, please don't bother. We have already put ours on the altar. It has been blessed by Pius the Ninth.'

The priest had dismantled the high altar of the church of Maipú for the occasion. Now he looked with a mixture of apprehension and disappointment at Otramamá's dressing table, covered with a lace sheet on which the embroidered initials of her many names might be read as an invocation to Mary. He had never understood why these people preferred the squat, naked tapers of criollo silver, mounted on round bases like ashtrays, and their ivory Christ on a background of tatty blue velvet, small as the one he took to be kissed by the dying, to the sumptuous pieces that had been donated by their own forebears.

Ils sont les plus beaux de mes étrangers, he might have said to himself, like Madame de Staël, that bête noire of his beloved Emperor. He prayed for us with a fervour made deeper by his doubts. Otropapá and his cousins, whose estancias surrounded Maipú on three sides, made substantial contributions to the parish, and Father Golé had forced his peasant heart to love them as an act of penance.

Ad introibo ad altare Dei ... To the God who is the joy of my youth. The chimango hawks had congregated over the faithful, flying low, meowing like trampled kittens, and creating a sonorous, plaintive and rather flat dome over our open-air chapel. The birds, the heat, the smell of roasting meat, the impending party, the scratchy trunks, the horseflies heralding autumn, and above all the innate ungodliness of an Argentine morning; all of this combined to rob me of my usual piety. I missed the fervour of those early Masses in the dark temples where Otramamá took me on the first Friday of each month to perform a ritual for which I would receive a good death, and more immediately, the hot croissants of the Confitería París. I found myself longing for the end of this thanksgiving Mass, but I also felt ashamed, because like so many first-born, I was bound by life's ceremonies. I regarded prayer, processions, burials and banquets as exaltations of existence that underlined its frailty, and I had begun to connect these rituals with the desires of love and death.

The priest crossed his huge hands, the colour of his cassock, which commemorated the colour of grass and the penance of Lent, and began his sermon.

'Dearly beloved, Christ has brought us together, among His birds, to celebrate, two months after His immortal birth, that of another child. Each child that is born brings with him the gift of hope. Hope made the pagan world tremble, ignorant and yet at the same time aware of the coming of its Saviour. Idyllic hope, moving in its tragic innocence, shook that invincible captain, Napoleon, when he held the new-born King of Rome in his arms.

'But what remained of all that glory?

'Beware the rich and powerful, those who believe that the pleasures which harden them will last. Christ has shown them the road of relinquishment. Christ has divested Himself of His Earthly Glory to embrace the Cross. They searched for Him to offer Him a throne and He hid in the desert, whence He returned naked to clean us through His Wounds and His Death.

'I want to talk to you all today of death. Death! To celebrate a birthday, this is outrageous, you'll say, the priest is mad. Perhaps you are right. But I have an excuse. Last night I dreamt of death, La Señora Muerte, not the one with the skull and scythe, but the one which left a thousand corpses on the battlefield. I didn't dream this — it was a real battle which happened in Europe, when I was very young and I survived it. But let's bring it here, that scene. Imagine vast herds of cattle being brought down by a terrible storm.

'It is death that puts a stop to everything in this world, that leaves only dead remains, for which we have no words.

'And why do I bring this unspeakable subject to my lips, in this great estancia, before these honourable ladies and gentlemen so distinguished for their ancient history and their virtue? Why, indeed, before this innocent child?

'Because I, poor sinner that I am, I come from Europe where the transiency of everything confronts us every day. I have been thinking for quite some time that this land of yours, this land of milk and honey, seems to laugh at death. What blessed and terrifying ignorance, what barbaric innocence. And just last night my dream, of all those dead left unburied, led me to what I am telling you now.

'Please, please, I beg you, my dear brethren, start looking at death. Don't shy away from confronting her face to face. Prepare yourself to shed this comfortable life. It is all too comfortable. Both for the rich and for the poor, although you might not believe me. A life that is like a sleep, a life that corrodes a soul oblivious of its resurrection.

'What shame to lose one's soul for this rubbish, for these petty little lives, allow me to point them out to you. Forgive me if I scrub your face with them, for am I not your confessor? These lives tired of so much repetition, of so much boredom.

'And you, the masters, can you look at yourselves and find something so different in the mirror? What will remain of these estancias, of these towns founded by your ancestors? Nothing, save the memory of the narrow and arduous path of your spiritual improvement.

'And so, when you find yourselves facing death, inexorable death, I beg you to offer yourselves as an example, as an example of the charitable heart. That is why, at the start of this sermon, I recalled to you the memory of that greatest of great vanities, Napoleon. *Vanitas vanitates*. And the image of the naked Christ.

'You don't have to give up your fortune. You only have to sanctify it through charity, that virtue which Saint Paul prized more highly than either faith or hope, as did the holy poor of Assisi. I beg you, force your imagination to reflect on the smallness, the real nothingness of your present possessions, and of the true abundance which awaits you.

'But before I finish allow me to go back to that weakness of mine, the captain of captains who held in his arms the King of Rome.

'The tragic destiny of the Aiglon will not become, God forbid, that of the boy who was born on this day. We can't control our destinies, which rest in the hands of the Creator of the World, but we can rejoice in births, which are yet another sign of His benevolence towards His creatures. Let us remember Christmas, let us remember that February day in Paris, cold, and yet warmed by the tolling of a thousand bells as the Eaglet was presented to a rapturous people, and let us rejoice that we are here to wish this child, in this place so far from those events but brought close to them by memory and by piety, a very Happy Birthday!'

Otramamá pinched my arm and said quite loudly to my grandfather, 'Didn't I tell you? He can't control himself. Bringing in the Aiglon! He's mad.'

'Very bad luck too,' whispered Tía Pepa from the row behind.

As usual they heard what suited them, but the sermon frightened me. The priest had spoken with a thunderous conviction and had declared us guilty, us and the whole country. And what was it all for? To end with nothing. To lose everything, to lose our immortal soul, and Otramamá didn't care, even if the drawers of her bedside table were overflowing with her little black books of the Good Death.

It seemed more comfortable to enjoy the comparison with my birth-mate. My grandfather could recite Rostand by heart, and once – I always remembered, because normally he didn't pay us much attention – he opened especially for me a huge volume of beige leather, its spine stamped with gold arabesques, one of the most sumptuous books in his library. He had collected copies of the plays he'd admired in Paris during his youth, and he showed me a picture of Madame Sarah Bernhardt, already about a hundred and with a wooden leg, playing the adolescent son of Napoleon.

'*Courage, enfant déchu d'une race divine,*' Otropapá intoned, with *rrr's* almost as tormented as Father Golé's. But the scene I carried to bed with me that night was of another death. That of the Aiglon, painted in the shiny pages of that book, shiny and a bit cheap like a magazine's, not worthy of so much binding, the prince in white and black, naked under his open night-shirt, held in the arms of a fully dressed girl with a high-peak hairdo who was deceiving him in spite of her adoration.

She hadn't told him that his Austrian family were on their knees in the next salon, waiting for the moment when the King of Rome would be brought, reduced to a mere duke, to be given the last rites. Thus another of the ferocities that string together the lives of princes would be accomplished – his death a spectacle before a family with whom he could not and would not live.

Aigle de la Maison d'Autriche, aigle de nuit..., but the French of those facile rhymes on the cheap pages with golden covers made the drama digestible, like Otropapá's recitals, which were neither pompous nor expressive, an Art Nouveau *mise-en-scène* of vaporous faces and spiritual orgasms, deceitful and hard, in the bathroom of Juncal, at tea time in Tía Teodé's sitting room among her infrequent visitors, in her apparitions in my dreams.

'Corpus Domine nostri Jesucristi...' It would be deceitful to receive the Host with my mind elsewhere. 'I can't say the Our Father, I confuse it with the song Valencia' – the words of the mad woman who lived nearby on the Calle Juncal rang in my ears. What should I do? Take the communion without unction and commit a mortal sin on the day of my santo? But it's already too late. What can I do to get overlooked? Just today the only time apart from Easter that Otropapá goes to the bar. He makes this sacrifice, confessing to Father Golé, whom he despises, and then further humiliating himself before him, all because of me.

My mouth was too dry. One cannot bite the Flesh of Jesus, it must fall into our bellies untainted, just as the seed of the Holy Ghost made its way to the Virgin's womb, and so I struggled to push the Host down with my tongue, but it stuck to the roof of my mouth. *Quÿ ÿ era Immaculado Councepcioü.* Afterwards, with my knee gratefully wounded by a knot of wood, I hid my face in my hands in an act of contrition, but I felt nothing, only my forehead growing clammy in my hot fingers.

'Benedicat vos Omnipotens Deus…Patri…et…lii… et Spiritus Sancti'. The priest watched the trajectory of his raised hand as it descended, knifelike, slicing the air, then rose again and deflected halfway in a sharp, horizontal stroke that seemed to say, enough.

'Ite Missa est…' Thanks be to God. Like the spontaneous ceremonies of Antiquity our ceremony dissolved in crumbs.

The chimangos went on hovering above us, forming a wavering baldachino, and Rafaela appeared with the of presents. Now I was to do the rounds of the peones and gauchos and their families, handing out packets of Milán cigarettes, La Hija del Toro tobacco, perfume from the Maipú chemist, Parisi, and rubber balls and dolls from the Ramos store. In those foolish years, I took the shyness of the pampas as another symptom of submission. The leathery hands that I picked up and dropped as if they had no will, and in which I deposited a handle, were less animated than the yielding harness in the tack room. The faces, diaphanous and secret, followed their thanks with a detachment quite different to the demeanour of the servants. The women were inclined to be garrulous, but never in company, and even less so at the estancia. If one caught them alone, by the low doors of their cottages, they would embark on crystalline, unceasing, monotonous and yet enchanting monologues, whose candour, had I been more aware, would have revealed to me the true nature of our relationship. The children, with the wary eyes of wild game, wouldn't put out their hands to accept my gifts. Their mothers piled them in their laps of faded flower print, watery like the purple *macachíne*, that modest wildflower which dissolved in my eager hand before I could pick a bunch for Otramamá, in payment for all her troubles. '*Voici des fruits, des fleurs, des feuilles et des branches…*'

15

'AH, TESORO! These "violets" which aren't from my estancia, come with the *souhaits* of your old aunt, with her black eye, bandaged wrist and rotting tooth. And the money is in the ribbon, in its silver thread.' It was difficult to decipher Tía Teodé's handwriting in the damp, dark salita, but that was where they'd put the presents brought from Buenos Aires.

I undid her mocking ribbon, tore off the tissue paper, and found what I had feared – one of the bottles of Eau de Cologne that my aunt had been given over the years, and which she kept stacked in her wardrobe, each labelled with the donor's name. I knew her tricks. Still, I felt moved to think of her spending her own birthday alone the week before, with only courting couples for company, clammy like their nests of thunbergia bushes, that she watched from her sitting room overlooking the Plaza San Martín.

Cajoled by my mother, Otramamá had taken the trouble of going by tram to MacKern's in the Calle Cangallo, to buy me two English books with attractive and expensive-looking hardcovers, particularly *Master Skylark*, emblazoned with its sworded and beruffled hero. But they had no illustrations, and even their smell couldn't compare with Miss Judy's fairy stories, so candied and dense. Otropapá presented me with the cufflinks he'd worn for his first communion – gold lentils with such thick, long chains that I dubbed them 'ankle-links', which didn't amuse him. My family were used to my offhand manner, which they regarded as ingratitude. 'Don't give me presents, you know I won't like them,' I would say each year before my santo. But they persisted, moved by conflicting emotions: zeal for my education, nostalgia for their own childhood, a sense of obligation; and – as with the chocolates filled with dulce de leche given each year by Tía Pepa – vicarious greed. Their actions weren't guided in the way that would have suited me best, by asking themselves what I might like. What I liked was too obscure. Papá, as always, was the exception. My father's presents surprised me each year with their extravagance, as if their unexpected value pushed open a door, each gift seemed to me to contain a message, they were from him, who never spoke, they pleased me, and they were useful. This year I had received a saddle with leather-covered stirrups on which horses' heads were beautifully embossed, with long manes quite unlike the rigorously clipped ones of the estancia. The present was proportionate to his silence. It was like a huge envelope that contained only blank pages although it was addressed to me, and the last page bore the reassuring flourish of his signature.

It wasn't that I suffered from living, like so many shy hopeless people. I just suffered from being me. I was like the umbrella stand in the entrance hall of the Calle Juncal, where everybody stuck their umbrella, but also where a collection of the canes and parasols of the dead grew old, their bejewelled handles sticking out like the turbans of Oriental deities, and were only rescued occasionally, to complete someone's fancy dress. And so I tried hard to read the signals that my father sent me, with a mixture of hope and fear. His gifts seemed designed to take me out of myself – hadn't he given me my first collection of books, when I was recovering from appendicitis? *The Adventures of Tarzan* and the *Tesoro de la Juventud*.

I got lost in the African jungle with such hope that I finished all seven volumes in a week. I came out exhausted. In those pages I had found no door through which I might escape to the depths of the wood, and hide with that other boy, who was free. When I closed the last volume, I was still in the same bed. But I had made a discovery. Tarzan mentioned people and places without bothering to explain them, and with a candour that shocked me. They existed simply because he was familiar with them. That Kerchak, that clearing, that hut, what were they? It seemed to mean there was no need to place them within a rigid diagram of life like my own, in which every cousin, every house, was labelled and pinned down in the catalogue like creatures according to the velvet of their wings. The days of the son of a monkey required no such structure. They were there because they were, without the scaffolding of a story. And they seemed much happier than mine.

Papá was the son of a monkey. And he told me stories in a language I didn't understand, with the secrecy of the jungle. His were petty stories – fights with the grocer's son, characters with untidy names that didn't merit an explanation and which he mixed confusingly with the posh names of his Buenos Aires' family, who had appeared at weekends in their big black cars to visit those orphans. Papapín, Pichín, María Ayerza, Bolita, Pepe the idiot, Victoria Aguirre. What tumbled out was a salpicón, shy and clumsy, intimate but insignificant, an intimacy that lay not in its heart but in its detail. To know what was left unsaid I would have had to read between the lines, like when I went on about what I had for lunch at school, mentioning the menu and not that my new friend, Fernando Braun, had sat with someone else.

My father might have been free, like Tarzan, but he was a beggar, and timid to boot, while his son was a captive prince. The only language I understood was that of the fairies, good and bad, who guarded the tower they had built for me. And fairies don't play cops and robbers in the streets of San Isidro with the children of immigrants.

If my father couldn't save me, then perhaps there was another beggar out there who could. He needn't be strong, or even free. I began to dream or perhaps fantasise about a wounded child, just a bit older than me, whose head

I bandaged. The tenderness I felt as I wrapped the white rags around his temple was akin to that intimate warmth I had felt when my father rubbed my chest with Vick's, doing it himself rather than Gilda, because he was afraid I'd catch pneumonia. It was a warmth that he enclosed in my chest, protecting it with cotton wool and stiff bandages. I told no one about this.

The gravel awoke to the sound of wheels. Midday had come and gone, and now they were arriving, along the laguna causeway, the Calle de Chacabuco, the Calle de San Francisco and the Calle de Kakel, the two-dozen sons of our cousin estancias, scattered over the sixty square miles which our common ancestor had marked out on the deserted pampa a century and a half before. Now, it occupied most of the county of Maipú. From tall, box-like cars, the slamming of their doors reverberating in the heat and anticipating the charm of the visit and the thrill of the party far better than those discreet criollo embraces, smart ladies emerged dressed in white linen, with tennis hats or Biarritz berets, and older ones in black silk and city shoes. They were accompanied by men rather less fresh and poised, and less comfortable in their finery. Some had squeezed themselves into the garb of the English squire, and sweated in their tweeds; most of them wore light-coloured suits, or jackets with bombachas and high-cut, beautifully polished riding boots. The older generation sported correspondent shoes. They all had colonial names and were descended from the Conquistadors, but they didn't look very criollo. Captured in the albums which I pored over so passionately, they looked more Northern Italian than Spanish. Many of them were blue-eyed, some had intelligent faces, but they had no air of command. Their families had let the Republic slip through their fingers with the 1916 vote of universal suffrage, and though they had snatched it back in the Uriburu coup of 1930, they found their old mistress devious and disillusioned. From being owners they had sunk to administrators. And now a new seducer, whose strength they had yet to recognise, would soon carry her away for good.

As for the flood of the poor from the fringes of town which had filled the Plaza de Mayo in 1945, they chose to see it as one of the recurrent floods on our marshy lands, which used to burst every decade and one had simply to put up with them. Being criollos they knew in their bones that after long periods of calm they could be suddenly slain, for the sake of it, by those poor orilleros. That fool, that easy-going America, was dangerous.

It wasn't political control this time that was draining away; it was the rents. The estancias were filling up with the lean and ugly cows, and they didn't seem that bothered. They tightened their belts and cut down on servants. So much the better. My grandfather's cousins had been born in the Argentine of the 'seven dishes of rice pudding' and their present impoverishment must have seemed a return to the puchero-smelling bosoms of their childhood.

'Mecha, everything is looking marvellous,' the women exclaimed, without looking.

'Che, Jorge, what a good idea to put box around the agapanthus. At Horacio Acevedo's they planted them along the cypress alley, and I've copied it at San Francisco, but I like this,' said Tío Sebastián to my grandfather, in a voice whose hurried jokiness softened some of its arrogance.

'Are you going to copy me too?' Otropapá asked, looking at his cousin *de haut-en-bas*. Sebastián was younger, and like him had married money, but instead of losing his wife's fortune he'd increased it. Since he hadn't inherited land of his own in Maipú, he had bought San Francisco from some other cousins and was doing it up with an energy and expense that irritated my grandfather.

'No, don't worry, che, I'm not into Italian gardens.'

Tío Sebastián was intelligent but insensitive, one could hear the coins clinking in his pocket, they made him feel rather too good. After forty years he had come back to this land which swallowed up every effort, he who had been born in that enchanting pigsty of Santa Marta, and had returned to build. And how. Everything was white and shiny and perfect, like the last of the parvenus. But he resented the tacit superiority of my grandfather in matters of elegance, so that he — who was 'not elegant, just well turned out' as Otropapá put him in his place for my benefit when I admired his luxury — wasted no opportunity in firing little poison darts, the vengeance of the younger cousin who had done better. Otropapá had suffered the humiliation of being forced by gambling debts to sell him the thousand hectares that joined Kakel to Yamoidá.

The fortunes of the cousins had changed since my grandfather's far-off childhood. 'In those days we could ride from our estancia to Miraflores without going through a single gate, hunting venado with bolas,' Otropapá liked to say, referring to the deer of the pampa, now extinct. Back then, the family had yet to sell even one of the fifty square leagues returned to them after the battle of Caseros, which had put an end to the spoliations of Rosas. Otropapá could look out at the horizon from our terrace, secure in the knowledge that his inheritance stretched leagues beyond it. Whereas I, sitting on that terrace sixty years later, had to fantasize in order to experience the same sensation. What had we lost? Yamoidá had gone, along with Marihuincul, La Atalía, El Galpón, Pichimán, El Arazá, Las Lisas; and during the time of the tyrant Rosas, San Simón, El Chajá and the hills of Machado. We were enriched by intruders and resentment, and by our dreams, which inhabit lost estancias better than blood can.

But dreams were not Otropapá's inheritance, they were mine. For him, the land was a cake that had been pared away in slices before his eyes. Poor Otropapá, impoverished by reality, forever crossing properties off maps. For me, so many years later, the little of what was left was the magical whole. The same properties that I traced with my finger and ringed with a blue pencil on the 1865 map of Buenos Aires – the fifty leagues of Ramos Mejía in El Tuyú, and Tapiales, with its two leagues at the gates of the city, by the river of La Matanza; the ten thousand hectares of Castex in Baradero, squandered by the Artayetas – all hanging in the safety of the hall, immured from the heat of the summer and the title deeds of the intruders, they weren't the delusions of a boy gone mad, because it was still possible as the sun fell – no longer from the terrace whose view had been narrowed by the years, but sitting on the wood fence two hundred metres towards the campo – to survey the faithful cascos that remained. Purple with waiting, the grazing light had pushed them like dogs into corners. They huddled before my eyes, that had absorbed the light of the setting sun, while I went slowly over them with a sad and triumphant smile. With my back to the ivy covered house, which the arms of the park enclosed like a box holding a darkened emerald, alone, sitting on the plank mottled with little explosions of lichen, I took possession of those sapphires that had belonged to me in the past, and were impossible to lose again. I couldn't lose them because they had already been lost, but here I was looking at them, holding them, me and no one else.

In the reality of my birthday the cousins eyed one another with distrust. All of them, even those who had had to give up the key to the gate of their estancia, shared the same passion, a tie whose strength seemed independent of their character, their position, their name, a mad and uncriollo obsession with that modest geography of vast featureless fields, of lagunas and low hills. And it was not greed, this longing and the disillusionment felt by each of the cousins, occupying their hearts, making them eye one another like rival lovers eager to kiss the same mouth. Such an empty and enormous mouth. Apart from those great hills of Kakel and Yamoidá – the first ones after the frontier of the Salado river, the hills that persuaded Don Francisco to settle here – it was almost impossible to single out one marsh from another, the laguna of Santa Helena from that of Pichimán, the hill of Marihuincul from that of El Arazá. We all belonged, we each had a place in those empty spaces, which had tricked us into believing that they were one great and special loneliness, *mine, mine only*, so much so that even a brother would be too much.

'*This pampa sucks away the soul*. Especially at sunset,' Miss Judy liked to say. Perched on the fence of the Potrero de las Lecheras, I felt that the appearance of anyone on the plain, apart from a horseman so distant that he might only be a bird, would trample those folds, unknown but alive, of my soul, that went on draining away as I watched the setting sun push the horizon out towards the sea. The bruised lilac impregnating the sky over the hills of Yamoidá darkened so softly, so slowly and so calmly, that my soul expanded to meet it, reaching out to lose itself in that dying beauty. The vast landscape was deaf to the beating of my heart, and still it urged me to follow, to disappear within it. What do they know, those who speak of stillness? I stood there with the flat vista stretching out before me, the locked door of the casco at my back, and behind it the sunset burned, its light spreading out like a semi-circular fan before me. I watched the light move on, with the pace of an eye that closes. Eye, eyes. Although the horizon was receding, the smells of the pampa, revived as the heat exhausted itself, returned; mint, grass, dung, the dust of the corrals. But my trapped eyes ignored them. There was no smell, no temperature, no sound, only the silent fire at my back that enlarged that empty world that was me. And people complain that gauchos don't plant flowers.

* * *

'I like the trees best of all, and these are unique. Look at this maple, it doesn't have a single green leaf,' someone said.

The old criollo manner, which drew on forgotten reserves of Arab courtesy, praised the host's possessions as a matter of course; but one had to watch one's step, in case one was then presented with the object of one's praise. It was best to limit one's comments to the immoveable.

'That's because it's been pruned mercilessly,' my grandfather answered. 'In order to keep it white one has to cut off the green branches. It's a graft, like the best roses.'

'And how old it looks — a hundred years?' asked an in-law who wasn't au fait with the ages of the estancias.

'I am not a hundred, although I may look it,' said Otropapá with the hint of a smile, so urbane and youthful that it was charming. 'I remember well the first time I was brought to Maipú. I was four and Mamá was still alive. The train stopped at Dolores, and we were met by the estancia coach. I fell asleep, and woke at a cottage by a laguna. "El puesto de Rivero," my mother said. There was a willow tree, nothing else. That was here. Three years later, Mamá died, and her sister Niñita named the new estancia after her.'

'Poor Jorge,' said Cuca, Tío Sebastián's wife.

Not so poor, some of them were probably thinking. Here he is, the owner of everything, and thanks to her death. If Tía Niñita hadn't brought him up he wouldn't have inherited the estancia, or anything. His father squandered his own inheritance, and then his children's.

'Mamá was the eldest daughter of my grandfather Madero,' said Otropapá, as if answering their thoughts. 'Her own mother died when Niñita was a child. She became the mother and mistress of the house. And when my mother died, her sister wished to repay the debt. So after we returned from Paris, where my father spent the first years of widowhood, she took Bebé and me to live with her.'

'How just, and how beautiful.' Cuca added her own words of commiseration. She was childless, besotted with a spoilt dog, and hid an indifferent heart behind the most tender manner.

'But the gingkos, Jorge! The gingkos are even more beautiful than the maple!' Chita, Adela's mother, gushed. She combined an exaggerated beauty − enormous blue eyes which I couldn't look into, blonde curls − with an exaggerated manner. She had German blood and more colour than all the criollos put together; they treated her with apprehension. Chita looked around her, a bit silly and a bit strong, like a pineapple in a fruit bowl, her shine upheld by a Teutonic thoroughness.

'She's always so frightfully thorough, it opens every door, and I end up hiding in the bathroom,' said Otramamá, confusing one persecution, real according to her, that of Chita's mother-in-law, for this one, perhaps more flattering but inexistent. Bebette did actually find my grandmother irresistible. Bebette's own extraordinary beauty had bewitched my grandfather more than forty years before, but Otramamá, who had never felt pretty, was getting her revenge in old age.

'I don't know what's hit her, but honestly, it's gone beyond a *faible*, it's become a *béguin*. She tortures me with phone calls. Even here, where the line is terrible, when there's nothing to say and it's dangerous to use the phone. The other day she rang for the fifth time, wanting to know if I liked fig jam. There was a storm coming, the thunder seemed to be right inside the phone, so I hold it away to protect my ears, and just then a tongue of fire shoots out of the receiver. God, who reads all hearts, should know that I am innocent!'

'Your tongue isn't innocent. That's what He wanted to burn.'

'Jorge, you certainly haven't got over your crush. This

family suffers from eternal love, m'hijito,' she said to me. 'Don't let yourself be a slave to it, there's no better recipe for suffering.'

'To suffer for being loved? Who wouldn't long to suffer for that?' I answered, as if someone was speaking for me.

'It will happen to you, because we loved you before you were born, and the love that brands itself on a child is more aphrodisiacal than beauty. But you will come to see it as a mixed blessing, as Mrs Fiddlecroner used to say.'

'Mamá,' Tía Pepa said, 'that's just like your favourite saying of Saint Teresa, "Save us, oh Lord, from wishes fulfilled." But surely it only applies to the ones who have everything, to the eternally dissatisfied. As far as I'm concerned I just want to be loved, and get the four little wishes I have left.'

'Hoping for nothing, anything makes you happy,' answered my grandmother, with a detachment with little malice in it.

The cousins were all interrelated, some of them had mixed their blood two or three times, but one could discern class differences. Those of Santa Marta had the curious position of being poor and intellectually alert, educated in the criollo way, spending summers on the estancia with only a fold of sheep and sweet corn for sustenance. They had never been to Europe, and spoke no languages. Their humour, the sharpest in the family, was honed by their envy, but also by their objectivity, for poverty had made them the natural allies of the landscape. And the way that they flaunted their lack of pretension was an indication that ultimately they would triumph.

They embraced no causes, and they didn't even care about their gaucho customs. Once we rode over to visit them, arriving sweaty and dust-covered in the late afternoon, after a six-hour canter. They greeted us warmly but without effusion, sent us to unsaddle, and then offered us a jug of rainwater with one glass to share, on hard benches out on the veranda as wide as a drawing room, where they spent their days.

'What luxury is showered on our cousins. English saddles and silver bridles!' the elder son said.

'What do you use — a recado, a gaucho saddle?'

'A recado, for what? A sheepskin and a stirrup. Aren't we descended from Chacabuco like you? You know what they say:

> The Chacabuqueros
> you know them everywhere
> by a grubby white sheepskin
> and one stirrup of a pair.'

I didn't know this, and I didn't find it funny. We were also descended from Don Francisco, the first criollo to use an English saddle, in the midst of the Indians, at the time of the May Revolution.

It was easier to give in to barbarism — but wasn't barbarism the *genius loci*? I could compare the ease and nonchalance of the men of Santa Marta with the rest of the family: my grandfather's decaying elegance, Chita's precision, the 'class' of the three Madero sisters, the Biarritz chic of the Marquise de Mailly, Tío Sebastián's improvements that avenged a childhood spent at Santa Marta, Bebette's youthful association with Ansermet and Stravinsky, the cultured Urquiza cousin of Kakel who read Plato during the siesta in a wire-mesh cage to ward off the mosquitoes. And then the operatic epilogue of the Countess Adda de Merenberg, whose arrival brought Maipú's history to a crescendo in which the voices of the princes of Nassau-Luxembourg, the great Pushkin, Doña Encarnación, wife of the dictator Rosas, all faded *pianissimo* as her ashes were scattered from a small plane over the hills of Kakel — 'Her dust enamoured of this hole,' Otramamá said, quoting Quevedo. Viewed alongside the naturalness of Santa Marta, the civilising impulses of our ten generations might seem affected, useless. But not for me. I was the most diligent pupil of those criollos, who remained so determined to polish themselves.

Madame de Mailly was wearing pink canvas espadrilles with cork soles and laces that coiled around her legs like asps, and a pale grey sharkskin suit that revealed its true colour only in the shade, as she approached the barbecue to ask for a slice of the meats. One of her self-imposed roles was to teach the family the right taste in clothes and in furniture, and she took her task seriously, without ever intending to patronise. Beneath her straw boater, chosen to be amusing because it was going out of fashion in France, her half-closed, smiling eyes showed how thrilled she was to be home. Her branch of the family were rich, refined, and had the energy – as was said among the cousins with raised eyebrows – to have married into the European nobility. But they lacked humour. They strove constantly to improve themselves. Was it because they spent the best part of the year on that continent from which we had so much to learn? There is no doubt that she was less at ease than the Santa Marta clan. But perhaps this was the price to be paid for being compared with Cleopatra by Proust, at a lunch at the Ritz with the Aga Khan.

Does it need to be said that I would've died for Madame de Mailly? Above all else for her lack of humour, which I saw as her sorrowful mystery, a sign of secrets that couldn't be shared. Apart from her little lessons on taste, for which nobody thanked her, she never boasted of her life in Europe. And no one referred to it. Even the Santa Marta cousins believed that we were Europeans, and to ask what was happening in Europe would be as absurd as to question our belonging to Maipú. But while all of the cousins relished the memory of Don Francisco, as soon as Madame de Mailly arrived for one of her dutiful visits, their cherished recollections of Paris disappeared. Even Otropapá became more criollo. He had ordered wines from Caucete to be served with the barbecue.

'Tasty and sharp, like the sun of the Andes, that never stops shining.' Chita's radiant smile gyrated, as if her tremendous goodwill had freed her vertebrae, making her head swivel like an owl's. Madame de Mailly's answering smile was cooler, and yet more tender. I felt jealous. Chita was only an in-law, and German too. But the intense training which Madame de Mailly had undergone in the Rue de Varenne, by a mother-in-law who had changed her 'At Home' days so they wouldn't clash with those of her Argentine daughter-in-law, had honed her snobbery. Chita was rich and fashionable; she was part of the set that had abandoned Mar del Plata for Punta del Este. My eyes should have been opened by the fact that my adored marquise had shored up her position with bricks and mortar, adding to her inheritance properties at Biarritz and Punta del Este.

My snobbery and hers were not related. Hers was real, fed on parties and connections, undimmed by disappointment, mine was imaginary. Mine thrived on absence, and on names whose appeal was proportionate to their improbability, like that *Boudroulboudour*, Princess of China, whose lovely syllables I intoned to myself, and whose image I searched for in vain, in the pages of *Vogue, París en América* or *The Tatler*, making do instead with the faces of the friends of my aunt Mailly, who so often appeared. The great void of the plain, so receptive to my readings of mythology and Miss Judy's fairy tales, not only made a place for princesses and gods, but even seemed to call for them, provided that they didn't cross their legs and gossip inanely.

My infatuation with Madame de Mailly had a thick crust, and she had too gentle a touch to break it. And I also had my little way with ladies. I don't know if it was because of my calf eyes, her pleasure at finding that the birthday boy, rather than playing hide-and-seek wouldn't leave her alone, or my having kissed her hand when we met, but she said to my grandfather, 'This child has the prettiest natural manners of any I know.'

'But Clara has brought her children up with no manners,' Tina interrupted, because she was always apologising to the world for us.

'That's why I said natural,' the Señora said, rolling her rrs like my grandfather. Both pronounced the famous *mejoorr* with the throat, opening and elongating the *o* in the way that the French pronounce *Vogue* and offering to the *r* a rubric, like a gargle.

'Tina! You remind me of what Adda said about me, when I was sent to live with her,' shouted Estelita Elía from another group, her mouth full of empanada, '"It is not, my dear, that you have been brought up badly, you haven't been brought up at all."'

'The trouble with Adda Merenberg was that she was *morganatische*.' My grandmother slurped her German like Juan Claro slurped his soup. 'That made her more popish than the Pope. What a cheek, criticising your manners. Her whole life was a contradiction, half princess of Luxembourg, half spa adventuress. When her sister managed to hook her Grand Duke, he was forbidden from returning to Russia by the Tsar. And why do you think Máximo Elía didn't tell his family he was married? He received them at the Savoy and never breathed a word about her. When Adda appeared out of the blue in Buenos Aires to claim Máximo's inheritance she didn't have the papers to prove it. She was fun though; I adored her obsession with looks. You know she used to make her ugly lawyer sit in the next room. But she was mad, too. She believed she was the reincarnation of Doña Encarnación Ezcurra, the wife of her husband's family assassin. I can't think what she learned from the Court of

Luxembourg. It wasn't exactly the hoo-ha of Rosas' Court of Palermo, that would've been far bloodier.'

Otramamá never tired of saying how bored she was by her husband's family, but she wasn't going to pass on an opportunity to show off her wit.

Bebette was delighted. She fixed her famous, orange-green cat's eyes on my grandmother, and projected her soprano laugh up to mingle with the smoke rings. 'Hoo-ha, how very funny, Mecha.'

'What a pintora,' Otramamá whispered to her husband, giving Bebette the unconcerned smile that accompanied her jokes. With this, a Maipú word describing someone with affected artistic airs, Otramamá put both her husband and the love of his youth in their places. 'She's nothing more than a pretentious ass, and those are your own words.'

My grandmother's sharp, arbitrary criticisms kept the world at bay; they allayed my fears, but not my imagination, which thrived on Bebette's estancia.

16

EVERYTHING began with Miraflores. It was there that Don Francisco Ramos Mejía settled, allowing the Indians to go on occupying the higher hills, at the time when the Viceroyalty was deposing its king. It was named Miraflores after the hacienda in Alto Perú sold by his wife, Doña María Antonia de Segurola, Mamita, when she was brought down to the River Plate, because the hour of Buenos Aires had come, and with it the end of three hundred years of Indian serfdom and patios de honor. *Parturient montes*, for our Miraflores was begotten by the Andes, by the silver of Potosí, like the Armada and the Italian Wars. But perhaps rather than a birth it might be described as a slide, a timely escape downhill towards the open sea.

Mamita Segurola, we named our benefactress. It was sad – for she seemed to keep guard over us, born in that unique hole of a city, La Paz, under the merciless peaks of the Illimani mountain – that she should have disliked so much the plains she was brought to live on by her husband. It was she who saved us from her unbreathable altiplano. However it was the instinct of Don Francisco – his face survives in photographs of a portrait I never saw, as the face of a poet – which won the love of this orphan, heiress of half of her grandfather's thirteen hundred Aymara serfs and four hundred thousand silver coins, and which extracted her from the colonial treadmill in Alto Perú where the masters had become prisoners of their slaves, where Castillian cruelty was so intricately overlaid with Indian hatred that any of those spicy concoctions tasted amidst the suffocating perfume of tuberoses and served with the most twittering of courtesies could be your last.

Mamita's father, governor of La Paz, had to defend his

city during the six-month siege of 1781, laid by Tupac Amaru and his forty thousand Indians. It carved the bitter frown of command visible in the portraits of his two daughters – the other one was my father's ancestress – and perhaps justified an escape. Our hero Don Pancho, as Francisco was known, seduced this captive princess and carried her away to the iconoclastic port of his birth. But then he went further, taking her south, to the uncharted desert, to the true freedom invoked by the revolutionary chants of the Cabildo of Buenos Aires, singing of the break with their King.

'I don't know where I'm going, corazón,' he wrote to his favourite cousin, the mother of that other starcrossed hero, Lavalle. 'But you at least won't think I'm mad, like everyone else.'

This was no mere criollo pronouncement. Even then he knew the price he would have to pay for this private bid for independence. Like the convex mirror on the wall of a Flemish painting which reproduces the scene before us, making it mysterious, the act that saved Mamita from the mestizo patio of La Paz was merely a reflection of the convulsion rocking the Spanish ruled viceroyalties. He ended his short life imprisoned in the tower of Tapiales, his other estancia on the outskirts of Buenos Aires, and as he was dying, scribbling invocations to God and to America on its whitewashed walls, , while the Indians whom he had befriended stole his body and buried it in a grave known only to themselves, and were decimated by the jealousy of the dictator Rosas. By then, everyone had decided that he was mad.

It was the sense of having inherited a myth, rather than having paid for their land like the other family owners of entire counties, that cast its halo around the cousins, the clever and the dim. And Bebette had inherited Miraflores, the place Don Pancho had founded, where the sword had cut the grass three times and where the first pole had been hammered into the earth.

Even two hundred years later, Miraflores still keeps its distance. Forty kilometres from the nearest town, it is as if the expulsion of its founder has girded it with a no-man's land. But this was the Argentine, so forgetful of its own past, and the house revealed no trace of its heroic beginnings. Miraflores, rebuilt, was an estancia of the Belle Époque, and had come to resemble its granddaughters, among them our estancia. Its daughters, Kakel, Marihuincul, Chacabuco, which were products of the first land divisions of the 1850s, and enhanced by abandonment, didn't just seem older, they really were.

Once, on one of my rare visits to Miraflores, Adela, who was as indifferent as Tina to the family legend, took me for a ride around the edges of the park in her *tonneau.*

The afternoon was heavy with the threat of rain which burst at nightfall. Again I felt that awe, stronger than any other, without understanding it. The low hills are dotted with scrubby talas like a landscape by Piero della Francesca, not as tall as Kakel and Yamoidá, or even Marihuincul, but they were chosen by Don Pancho. The park that contains the big white house keeps its distance, because we might have been inside it four times in ten years, if that, and its occupants, apart from Adela, would hardly know me. They were the most distant of the cousins, both in the remoteness of their estancia and their indifference, and when they deigned to appear at my birthday lunch I felt both thankful and afraid.

I remember a party celebrating I don't know what nuptials of Bebette and her husband, with mass and the ribs of five bullocks roasting, and dancing on the pelota court, but I remember more the apparition of Adela's elder brother. In that casco crammed full of people, he came walking by himself along one of the avenues that sloped down from the house to the barns, in long beige trousers and espadrilles, a green hat on his blonde curls, with a haughty and nonchalant sway, alone like a fifteen year old angel, so extravagantly beautiful that he seemed pursued by a sun ray which ran after him through the leaves, while I, just ten and in short trousers, standing under a tree as though behind a curtain, was the only acolyte of the ceremony.

Afterwards, to reinstate myself, and also because I had travelled without the protection of the family, only the servants and the majordomo, and felt obliged to sit with them, I went into the house and kissed the hands of the ladies, one by one. They were having their coffee and welcomed me with charmed surprise.

Ah, Miraflores! Those towers of myth of the family, so beautifully placed in castle-like isolation in the depths of the pampa. They should have been exchanged for the real towers of Tapiales, which had been humiliated by the modern world, by the motorway to the airport, and the lorries ferrying tomatoes to the vegetable market of Buenos Aires, in one of the flights of the fairy Mélusine who would carry castles in her apron, or like the gifts of those saintly queens, donors of churches, which they held in their hands and offered up to God, minute, meticulous and golden, with a gesture of complete abandonment, as though surrendering their heart; those towers embody for me, and I felt it once more in the trotting *tonneau* of Adela, that quality of treasure that the horizon hides behind the hills of Yamoidá, which I searched for every evening from the same place, the wooden fence of the Potrero de las Lecheras; and yet it didn't hide or escape from me, because after an hour, or even less, taking the dirt road towards the sea, past Chacabuco, past the white pyramid-topped gates of San Francisco, turning towards Segurola and leaving behind the concealing hills of Yamoidá to the right, and with it the great basin of my evening longings, leaving behind La Magdalena, La Paz, and El Yeruá and El Carmen, the road like a slippery causeway amidst a chain of lagunas and lowlands where only the snail-eating falcon hovered, crossing a corner of the other Santa Marta, my eye would at last catch the long blue casco, dishevelled, enlarged, shaken-up and re-assembled by its two centuries of habitation, the mother of all but not ours, its white gate closed.

The European park gave way gradually to clumps of talas. We went down towards the laguna where Don Francisco had erected his tents...

The smell, it's always the smell, locked into the hippocampus like an immutable virus, immortal while we live, immortal like a stone, not like inconstant memory. That smell, wet, muddy, reedy, rotten and fresh, the smell of the stagnant water of Maipú must have been the same for Don Pancho, making him laugh with joy when his horse sunk to its belly in the limitless swamps whose borders he was determined to settle.

The horse jumped and shook itself, in a desperate effort to escape the clamping of weeds and mud which opened our senses to wafts of decomposing stench, that seem to contain the mystery of the land better than its circular sunsets and the din of its birds, while the rider, seated on his mount's elastic back like a skiff on a dangerous wave, kidneys creaking as though tied to kidneys: a blissful and improbable union, a centaur. Sweaty, gleaming, drenched, the centaur rediscovers its triumph in the voluptuous knot of every jump. Water snapping, legs tight, stirrup loose, hand to mane, arse up and balls caught, but still down there the strength of bones and muscles, and the desperate machine striving to get free.

Bodies delight in bodies; that's why our mouths laughed, with the pleasure of fighting together against the swamp. The back arched against my pelvis, the forge of the great convex carcass like the ribs of the ship sang beneath me, with the contraction of muscles and the trembling of skin, but it was the tight-knit mass which vibrated from the legs battling in the mud to my hair ends; from the hooves to my brain it was just one nerve, recognizing the quarrel and the victory. The marsh reveals the horse to his rider. There's no walk, no trot, no gallop on dry land that joins them better.

Ah, my criollo pony of the tight short canter...No, he wasn't criollo, my mate, but a mestizo, a product of the complex crossbreeding of Maipú. And me? So European, so French...

But the *bañado* has to be taken slowly. That's why I ask now how Don Pancho could have managed to cover more than sixty square leagues in one day, stuck up to his horse's flanks in those quagmires of El Tuyú and Vecino. Still, he bequeathed to me that perfume more corrupt than any in Baudelaire's imagination, which one can only taste on horseback, and not on the banks of the swamp but deep inside it, lost with one's horse among the reeds and the paja brava, taut with pressure and fatigue. That smell of nest, of feather, of ophidian transformed into bird, of mud that sprouts useless and beautiful weeds, hot but cracked by cold shivers; the swamp where life was born, disgusting, and yet saved by the air, like an opening and closing fan, because its secret reveals nothing of its mystery, like the hide and seek winking of the reeds in the luminous water. Instead, it incites the eye to more searching, straining, searching, while the smell just sits there, and possesses us. Until that moment when, choked by a message the memory will never decipher but will go on repeating to itself, identical, with the same heat, the same splash, the fright of the hidden heron's sudden croak, Don Pancho's same joyful laugh repeated in my mouth, the horse's hooves tread the dry edge of the first slope and one breathes at last the clean, dumb fragrance of grass.

And it was on that low hill, as he emerged from his confrontation with the bañado, leaving behind the heights of Kakel and Yamoidá occupied by the Indians he never thought of evicting, with the blue bulk of the Montes Grandes closing the sea's horizon, on a little pampa of rough grass by the white shore of a laguna of 'white' water, that Don Pancho started something of such importance, that it would take two centuries to be understood, and not fully even then.

He might have been vaguely conscious of his exploit, but deceived by the sweetness of the country. It was one of those embalmed days, of a death-like beatitude. The water was like glass, the scent of vanilla that filled the air must have come from the pampa grass lining the shore, although it faded if one got near, a benteveo dived without hurry, two or three straggler swallows flew around to fill the space. The pampa grass was opening its first flowers which sprout like a fox's tail, plumed, pink and silky out of a green cornet, and he was touched by the contradiction between the hard sharp green blades where Indians on the warpath hid, and its soft flowers which made him think of the shy vicuñas of Alto Perú.

He was consumed by nostalgia, so intense that he could not feel it, as usual, as something voluptuous. It was without edge or depth, it was still like the evening and the water. It seemed like death, because it filled everything, had no object and missed nothing. But he felt full of an emptiness that was also a longing, and though this word implies an object, there was none, just a consciousness of overflowing, of a complete calmness that seemed about to spill itself, that only the borders of the body still breathing could contain. Perhaps the image of death, then.

And beyond, that immensity which gave itself to him. From one end of the horizon to the other, tame but impregnable, sixty four square leagues extending beyond the reach of the eye seemed but a dot in the desert he had ridden through. How did he measure his estancia then? Were they enough, those leagues, to feel oneself stationed at last in that boundless plain? What did it matter anyway.

There was water for cattle, hills against floods, which the Indians had named, Kakel, the solitary one, Yamoidá, the Seven Hills, Marihuincul, the Ten; there was wood in the Montes Grandes, and there were the Indians, whom he was determined to befriend. It was a plan of grandiose invention; and it was ploughing the sea. Because what blurred his eyes and scuppered his plans was the sadness, the immense and paralyzing sadness of those horizons that escape even as one moves towards them, those confines of ours which run away for the sake of running away, so that we learn to stare at them without love or hate, with no pain, unconscious, with the soulless eyes of birds. Birds that must feel something, perhaps their minute size in that vastness, as they scream with the fear of death in their voices.

Don Francisco Ramos Mejía y Ross y del Pozo y Silva was descended from a line with a hunger for lost land. His grandfather was the Scot Captain William Ross of Tarrel, employed by the English Royal Asiento, which covered up its commercial spying in the River Plate with some activity in the slave trade. In 1738 he signed a power of attorney to reacquire his mother's land in the County of Ross, in a peninsula battered by the North Sea.

It is possible that Don Pancho was never aware of this touching wish, written in a document in an enemy tongue, in a hot city next to a river of thick waters, thousands of miles away from the stone towers of Tarrel with its fresh fields and its cold sea, because the heretical grandfather had secretly married a Catholic criolla, had begotten and disappeared.

The grandson inherited the narrow face, clear eyes and hunting nose, and the adventurous uprooted spirit of this young Scot who had chosen not to live with his colleagues in the luxurious headquarters of El Retiro, but alone in a little house that he shared with a servant by the river, at the foot of the cliff of Santo Domingo. It was from here that the authorities suspected he was contacting the smuggling ships. He paid for it with four months in prison when Spain broke with Britain.

After that Ross left for Alto Perú and only returned to Buenos Aires for fleeting visits, fathering another child whom he hardly knew, until he ended dying in Charcas when Don Pancho's mother was only a girl.

A hunted devil, possibly a demigod, and who impregnated a mortal in her sleep: such were the stories and lullabies that rocked Don Pancho's cradle, and which inspired him, fair like his grandfather, to seduce another nubile nymph. This one came clothed in silver scales. She was an Andean nymph, born amid peaks similar to those his grandfather could see from his Scottish tower on its flat peninsula, the romantic highlands beyond the water, refuge of the persecuted.

But there was another more urgent claim. The hundred square leagues settled in 1650 by the captain Juan del Pozo y Silva, Don Pancho's maternal ancestor, in the Rincón de Todos los Santos, between the river Samborombón and the Plate, plus one or two estancias on the Arrecifes river, had obsessed María Cristina Ross y del Pozo's family ever since they were sold by a villainous uncle, twenty years before Don Pancho's birth. Don Pancho's mother inherited the law suit but not the estancias, and she died when her son had still to replace the lost tala woods of the Samborombón for the treeless land of Miraflores.

It was always the women who fought to regain the land. María Rosa del Pozo − who wrote to the Viceroy Olaguer of a *delicado* dish, an expression nobody used in the twentieth century outside the house of Juncal − and her niece, María Cristina Ross de Ramos Mejía, and their descendants whom I had the bad luck to know; in each generation they branded their mandates with fire. In the end, Don Pancho was just manipulated like any of us.

And then what was so unique about his achievement, to plant an estancia amid the Indians two hundred years after his ancestors had founded cities amid the Indians? It was charity, that most precious of the cardinal virtues, the attribute of saints.

The poetic imagination of Francisco Ramos came from the North of Europe. It was the voice of a chieftain of equals who pulled the clans to action. And as the mythical hero tends to come from afar, the irruption of Ramos among the tribes, including them in his vision, was one more mission, like that of the Irish saints who brought Christ to his woad-painted ancestors, the Brendan who decided to become San Borombón on purpose, to show him the way.

Those eyes, so clear, must have been blind. He who sets his sight on heaven sees nothing around him. But the vision drove him beyond his will and brought him down from the Andes and across the Salado river, sleepwalking. The Indians couldn't resist him; one form of innocence recognized another.

It was too much to deal with: the adolescent idealism of a man of thirty which went directly against the Spanish instinct of dominion over the natives, a foundation in the desert among scattered tribes whom he would represent against a ruling power greedy for land and cattle belonging to no one. It was an impossible quest, which ended costing him eight years of prison and his life. It could be read as one of those late vocations which change lives, to be suffered in solitude.

He was aware that he was considered mad, as he wrote to his Lavalle cousin, because he saw what nobody else did, a pampa with enough space for everybody. He drew up a plan of coexistence between Indians and Christians, written with hallucinatory bombast, and sent it off to the government in Buenos Aires where it was filed without an answer. His implied recognition of aboriginal rights only increased the bile of officialdom, and of those who felt curtailed in their stealing of anything that moved on the pampas.

The plain was a space without walls, where that explosive mind could only multiply and lose itself. His plan began: 'We have a continent so vast that not even in the Map its surface extension can be known and dinuminated; to populate it is at first sight the work of the life of the centuries…', and then, the 28 of America of 1820, in Miraflores, 'the year of the universal deluge of 4777', he draws up the 'Evangelio with which the citizen Francisco Ramos Mexía responds before the Nation', starting with the Proclamation of the Fatherland, Rom.2.4. '1. Our Father by the power of your Father. 2. Blessed be thy Name. 3. Thy Kingdom come. 4. Fill with your mission the earth, as it fills the heavens. 5. Give us this day wisdom. 6. Untie the councils of iniquity, because we, as patriots, do what we must. 7. Do not allow that we shall fall back into slavery, but deliver us from it. Amen.'

He died of a fever, just over fifty, in his room in the tallest tower of Tapiales, obsessed 'because the world is falling down, the edifice of the world is collapsing completely, there is no remedy to the art of its architecture…it is completely useless to undertake the labour of its reparation…' And even if he believed 'in the virtuous second coming of Christ, in glory and majesty,' he was alone. Who could he communicate with, who would understand him, when he walked down from the tower to give refuge to four Indians escaped from their forced labour in the Cathedral of Buenos Aires where they were plastering in shackles? The church accused him of heresy, the government of treason. Mamita must have looked at him with fear. She re-married soon enough her brother-in-law, Ildefonso, who had been governor of Buenos Aires for a day, the Day of the Three Governors. Long live the law of Ramos! It might have lasted less than ten years but its determination carries on.

Misunderstandings between master and peons...for all his idealism Don Pancho became the highest tax payer in Buenos Aires...how many squaws were pushed into the rancho as a gift, how much mare's lung, raw and still warm from the trembling carcass, had he to swallow? And the stench, which must have made Mamita gag, Mamita so grand and ladylike, accustomed to treat her altiplano coya Indians with pleasant condescension.

But in the end it becomes a boring intercourse. It is easier to point with a finger than to tell them go and kill me a duck. Even if orders are expressed with care they don't get them, and everyone contradicts the other's version. It would be fine to give orders if it wasn't so pointless. One shouldn't expect perfectionism, not with our gauchos, but at least they are mild. The effort to keep themselves awake in the emptiness they live in doesn't allow for more. There is such abundance around them: wind, heat, dampness, the big heavenly sun, tons of green grass, cows and birds, and yet it is an abundance of nothing. An excess of space where nothing reveals itself exultantly alive, because cow and horse and sun all shrink within it; you see nothing but mud huts similar to those tents of cow hides which welcomed Don Pancho, from which women and children still emerge brown and half asleep, mouth open and eyes glassy like dried fish. Indians were even lazier, their habits were war and sleep, but they fell in love with the unknown, a chief different from their own with his snout flat like a catfish: a chief with the head of a heron and the tame eyes of a spring sky.

In the end, compared with the three and a half centuries of Miraflores, those ten years that finished in disgrace were nothing but a drop, but that drop swelled into a perfect fountain, which multiplied in the air and not on earth, a Pentecost without ears or disciples, the Estancia of God.

I jumped out of the *tonneau* and opened the tiny door for the niña, whose weight on the step raised the green barrel's front so high that the pony could hardly press it down. If Adela had been any heavier it would have shot up, pony and all.

We walked on the gray gravel beach, that neat band like a silver carpet between grass and reeds, and I found out that Adela lived in a Maipú landscape different to mine. The view from Miraflores was the opposite to ours. The long hills of Yamoidá, instead of being laid out facing our casco like a stranded whale far away in the distance with two or three pink humps, appeared from Miraflores to one side, close, short and mountainous. Kakel, to the north of us, towards Buenos Aires, its extended hills marking the beginning of that amphitheatre of ours which emptied itself into the sea towards the south east, Kakel, the doorway, could hardly be seen, and the estancia had been swallowed by the horizon.

I felt lost, I started to speak. 'You know, of course, that it was here where the wagons stopped. But they couldn't be unloaded because the vermin would have devoured all the food stores, and until they built the ranchos Mamita and her children could hardly have come down at all, though I suppose they wouldn't have minded sitting on such a clean little beach, with the water lapping...' Adela was tracing grooves on the gravel with her whip. I assumed that she was listening.

'Everything happened here. The Indians of Ancafilú and Pichimán arrived from east, west, south and north! To be preached at by Don Francisco. And from here he was taken prisoner to Tapiales, and his sons returned here, after the defeat of Chascomús and the triumph of Caseros, all but Panchito, the one who buried his silver in Chacabuco and had his throat slit in Córdoba, to restock the despoiled estancia' – I liked fancy words. 'You know that we lost forty thousand hectares, fifty thousand cows and ten thousand mares!'

I felt so moved by my story that I gasped with shock. 'Enough! Enough with the past! You know that I don't care a fig for it, even less for all this moaning about what we lost. At Miraflores we haven't lost anything, on the contrary,' and she focused her eyes on me, hard and contemptuous.

I forced myself not to show anything. I held the reins as she climbed into the tonneau, though I felt tempted to make the pony bolt and drag her behind, caught in the step ring by one of those fat ankles she had inherited from Chita.

'*Qué mierda*, what a fool,' I thought in the long silence that followed, as the victory lines of returning ducks filled the vast sky with their whistling and the lowing of a solitary cow announced another melancholic evening. 'Why does she need to be so awful? What am I doing here? But I like it. I like it because she pushes me out. I belong here, anyway. And she makes me feel guilty, just because I insist on what I like, stuff she doesn't care for. I know, I am different. My likes are not the likes of the others, and that makes me feel guilty. But only when they find out and I'm put on the spot. Then I feel alone and guilty. I'm neither a boy nor a grown up. But I am not a monster. I'm quite popular at school. The sporty boys, they like me because I'm clever. That's fine, I much prefer them to the swots, but then I hardly tell them what I think. And just now, when I'm talking to Adela about things I might have thought would bring us close, when I was feeling close to her and at home, as in this bloody place, she glares at me with those eyes of an angry cow and pushes me away. Why do I ever speak to her? Why do I bother? I suppose I must find her a bit like me. But smarter, of course. And then she lives near.'

Adela whipped the pony, which like all ponies behaved like a mongrel dog, like Jack, shy and bad-tempered. She had remembered about her croquet match, typical of her idiotic smartness, like the San Carlos boys who couldn't just be bored as one should, like us in the estancia.

'Let's hurry, so we'll be in time for tea. Today there'll be sponge cake because you're a visitor. And then croquet before you go back. The Maipú road is not as bad as your grandmother likes to say. Your grandmother is funny, I won't say she isn't, perhaps funnier than mine, who can be such a bore sometimes: no Elbows on the Table, Don't Speak until you are Spoken to, she can be more German than the Fraülein, and much more than Mamá even, but then you know as Granmamá likes to say: "You have to tie Mecha up to get her down to the country".'

My relationship with Adela had been corrupted by my apprenticeship with the niñas of the bathroom of Juncal. It is possible that to feel more at home with her I reinvented her as older and more powerful. But still I didn't trust her. I had learned to use those weapons which blooded but never killed, as a kind of healthy and ugly gymnastics, an unhappy readiness to go to war. And yet I was a child. Sometimes I felt the welling up of a love I couldn't contain, which astounded me. Like with Finita Bullrich in the dark car flashed by passing lights, or with one or two faces at my First Communion party, and later, on that sad beach, with Carmencita Lezica, that very young version of her aunt Tía Teodé, my heart was seared by a longing so overflowing that it could drown me with its pain. But they were shooting pains, like the car lights which grazed the cheeks of Finita Bullrich, they shone and disappeared.

Adela was more permanent. I was finding her out. The newness was wearing off, and if there was any shine left it was of the flash of her cutting knives, different from those of the bathroom. They were more constant, the struggle didn't tire her, and she never forgot. She was too Teutonic, like her Fraülein. As I saw her like another version of myself, and I didn't love myself anyway half as much as I was always told I was loved by the bathroom niñas, I ended up finding her disgusting.

Still, I was attracted by her bad points. She was both ugly and hard. Whereas her brother, glimpsed in a shaft of sun in the darkened allée, was the most far away thing in the world, beyond any longing or stupor, beyond anything in my life.

Her grandmother Bebette, who was 'so musical,' according to the townie Mecha – she meant genteel, for Bebette's famous voice and even more her beauty that had enamoured Stravinsky was dismissed by my grandmother, I suppose, because she was jealous – Bebette, then, had kept Miraflores in an embalmed lyricism. Borders of pale flowers made the pines seem darker. The house, a crenellated Italian villa with Gothic arches and Spanish tiles, protruded from the eucalyptus like a white amnesic tongue. It had much to forget, for it had risen from the ashes of a murderous fire. The young and rich wife of the third Ramos Mejía, Don Pancho's grandson, carrying on the tradition, perhaps, of Mamita Segurola's disenchantment, had set fire to the ancestral ranchos, which she found wanting. She made it seem the result of lighting and then insisted that her husband use her money to build this lavish new Belle Époque villa. She decorated and lived in it charmingly enough to appear in a book written by a pretentious Frenchman who couldn't believe that the Revue des Deux Mondes could be found in that desert.

But her punishment was to be barren. The Miraflores line suffered another of those sleights of hand with which our history covers its tracks: the extinction of the male line. The fact is that the Miraflores of Bebette, whose name was no longer Ramos, with its statues half-hidden with ivy, its oleo fragans, its Italian cypresses, its fountain of a heron gulping a carp, avenues of plane trees, marble lions slumbering, Jugendstil interiors, bore no traces of Don Francisco Ramos. There was a portrait of him by Pellegrini, which was not him. Mummified by a conflagration that bore no fruit, the charm of Miraflores made me think of those Art-Nouveau ladies on the walls of our estancia's salita.

Ramos had ceased to be our name. It had diverted from the great river some time earlier, and was cascading gradually into a social cul-de-sac. There were some Ramoses who visited us from time to time, who in losing their land had lost everything, and on whom I looked down upon as impostors. How could they use that name when they were not us? Not that our own names counted, the ten or so attached to the remaining estancias. What counted was possession. We were still the sole owners of Don Pancho's dream, inherited by mothers who didn't take on their husbands' names, so that the severing of the paternal link put each estancia and its children in a world apart, the haloed figures in an icon. These women left us their own icons, in the dark rooms of the estancias. There, hanging over the fireplaces, were the benefactresses whose wombs bore our geographical fruit, looking unconcerned and a little out of place in their feathers and tiaras. Were they true likenesses? Some had been painted from photographs after death; but they continued to watch over us, awesomely alive, accumulating life with the years, even though the sitters had long since gone to sleep for ever.

To found an estancia, to sit for one's portrait: these seem like acts of a different order, but their simultaneous irruption into the cycle of Indian raids and cattle poaching heralded a new world. A world of weak and complex forms that could never be nurtured to maturity, like children who never grow.

17

'LA SEÑORA está servida.' Casimiro bowed to Otramamá. The scattered groups left their half-eaten sweetcorn empanadas and their canapés of hare pâté and moved towards the table, covered in its white damask, with the hesitant and wondering steps that showed how improbable the family found lunches in the open air. Shafts of light, filtered by the leaves of oak and plane, fell over the red dahlias arranged in silver tureens, fixing them like a painting under a halogen light, and at the same time softening the dazzling silver with pink shadows. The family wine of Caucete betrayed its cheap purple tint in old crystal decanters worthy of more; it was better matched to the asado's smoke than was the green and white china, embossed in gold with the estancia's cattle brand. The china was from Goodes of London, difficult to replace, and was brought down from the high pantry shelves only for these occasions.

The head of the table had been transferred to the centre. My grandfather was punctilious, and preferred to have his wife near, so they could keep a close eye on the service.

'Twenty-four at the main table is going to be quite a thing,' he had declared the night before. 'Particularly with the Elía, they haven't been to the estancia for ages.'

The Elía guests were the branch of Madame de Mailly, Otropapás cousins, it was only by chance that they were here in Maipú. The car taking the Señora de Elía to Mar del Plata had crashed at Guido, resulting in a fractured pelvis, a rallying of the family from their respective holidays, and a rush to the hospital at Maipú. They had been lodged at the Hotel de la Luna, in San Carlos, in the luxurious San Francisco, anywhere but with us, because the birthday party had filled the house, and they were surrendering themselves to the melancholy thrill of revisiting a land lost to them fifty years before.

Though they had ended up with the best hectares at the other end of the province, the Elía went on mourning for Maipú. Otropapá must have understood their loss, as he himself had lost so much, but he probably felt it more keenly when they were there, since these rich cousins had come in order to covet the one jewel they lacked. They couldn't exchange it for cattle or shares because it was like a spiritual principality. Like some of those poor but scarce lands that the Holy Roman Empire had invested with the *Ebenwürtigkeit*, it was precisely this jewel, which suited so well my grandfather's elegance built on rejection and which had fallen to him almost by chance, that they so desired. And although he was discreet, he recognised this unspoken triumph.

'I don't want corn mousse for the first course tomorrow. I want eggs. Scrambled egg with asparagus,' Otropapá had announced the day before my santo.

'Asparagus? In February? You must be mad. Why not Jerusalem artichokes or funghi porcini or some other non-sense? And how will the kitchen make scrambled eggs for forty that aren't all dry?' Otramamá answered with the ironic testiness she considered her best weapon.

'Calm down, I spoke to Sabelio this morning, and he says that with all the rain the asparagus has come up again. I asked him to send some to the kitchen, and I'll try them. If they're too watery, we won't have them. And the new cook is good with eggs, Henri will be impressed.'

'It's up to you. It's more natural to serve sweetcorn in the country than to be mimicking the Rothschilds. But they're your cousins. You know I think Henri Mailly's an ass. As for the wife, she's perfectly nice, but she's a bore. When she comes to pay her visit, straight off the boat, in that little blue suit and a bunch of gardenias, I don't have the nerve to say I'm not at home. What an idea of Carmen to break her pelvis just at this time. And those sons, with their Eton education. Frightful bores.

Otramamá didn't understand how much she needed those people she loved to mock. She was driven by the family wit to use the world as a target. And the bores, educated in the English manner, hid their feelings, something that the Uriburu nature didn't allow. Otramamá would go to bed quite pleased with herself, savouring another of her Pyrrhic victories.

'Not really that boring, your cousins,' I heard her saying to her husband, as the light went out on the night of my santo in that room where no one had been born, and no one had died.

I looked around the table and again felt irritated by those guests – I couldn't call them cousins – who bore the name of which we were so proud. It seemed vaguely threatening, like a mask, that every day of their lives they should use this mythological name, which linked the owners of Maipú with their land. One of them even bore the name Francisco Ramos – Paquito, he was called – and yet they looked as if they had lost everything. I found it impossible to comprehend. They were the blot on the long, festive table, owing their places to their connection to the irreverent cousins of Santa Marta. Yet these intruders looked very staid. Stiff, serious, lawyers, they probably ate soup in their house in the Calle Azcuénaga prepared by a cook they called 'de estancia' to justify the watery mess of the broth. But there they sat, taking for granted a name that we, its real owners, hardly dared utter.

This jarring note was made worse for me because we were at Maipú, at the annual ritual which, on the pretext of my birthday, brought all the heirs together to celebrate the founding; and the presence of those dapper mice – 'Paquito' with his pearly tie pin – put a check on my fantasies. If those overdressed *notaires* were Ramoses, then who were we? They are as much Ramos Mejía as I am Cullen, I thought. In other words, not.

For me, those six letters, with their tight little vowels, nailed me just where I wasn't. What could Paquito have felt, then, with only his bare name, surrounded by the trees, the cows, the lagunas, that belonged to the rest of us? Possibly he felt what I had felt, when I was taken to visit my father's uncle on the day of my first communion.

I was with my mother, who made a point of cultivating her orphaned husband's family. We arrived at an ugly house in the Buenos Aires suburb of Belgrano, and entered by the side door, through French doors that opened to reveal some red-haired women who shared our name. They smiled in a friendly way and took us in to their father's study. He was a small, fierce man with a white moustache, whose untidy clothes annoyed me in a way that was different from my reaction to Paquito's dapper ones. He was my father's only surviving uncle, since Cullens die young, but he made no great fuss over me, offered me nothing, and as he inspected me with his bloodshot blue eyes – I was still wearing my Eton suit from the communion – he seemed to realise what I had expected him to: that this boy was not at all a Cullen.

To accept that I was a Cullen would have been like surrendering to another identity, alien to the aura of the bathroom of the Calle Juncal. The thing that anchored me was my connection to Maipú. I bore the name of my estancia, in the same way as Adela was miraflorera and others kakeleros, chacabuqueros.

My various mother figures wanted me to adopt their own names. Otramamá had even bribed the nanny who took me to the park to call me the Uriburu boy. Tía Teodé, who couldn't force her name on me, since it wasn't in the blood, took her revenge by putting down her in-laws' ancestors and praising her own. I was so excited by her tales that

I began to speak of 'Papá Alvear' and 'Mamita Mendeville', mimicking her special family voice. And as for Artayeta, for all that it wasn't the name of Maipú, it fitted perfectly with the jealous, exclusive atmosphere of that bathroom. Even Otramamá was submerged there in the Artayeta steam.

We didn't have to share this name with anyone. My grandfather was the last shoot of a bare old tree. And its intimate, masticatory sound, in which the loose vowels were hit by the two 't's but survived in the last syllable, just as the women of the Calle Juncal ended an argument with the last word, was a sign of its feminine nature. But that the name had been carried perversely down to us through the male line also indicated its status as hostage: five generations of weak, handsome men, seduced by the daughters of powerful fathers, who then sat down to eat them at their leisure. Artayeta was ours alone, because those women, even if they gave birth frequently, left only one son.

Each was limited in her power by the presence of the others. When I was born, the Calle Juncal was crammed with three generations of these young ladies of indeterminate age, all of them eager for a doll with a willy. Every floor of the house was an enemy fortress, bristling with schemes for my kidnap. I remember, or think I do, my pram rolling at full speed along a dark corridor, and Otramamá whispering to Vicenta, her maid, not to wake up Gilda; and then the lift, and Tina on the floor above seeing me off with a furtive kiss as I flashed by, before Otramamá pulled me out of the pram, and dived with her trophy, triumphant and alone, into her massive bed. Antonia, maid of my great-aunt Niñita, ran back down two floors to report that I was missing, but Gilda was still snoring.

'Antonia, stop your Spanish yacking, it's going to wake poor Clara – now go and check with the night nurse if she's still asleep.'

'But Sheñora, I went in and saw to that conceited nurse

only ten minutes ago, I don't believe a word she says and so I pushed her aside and went to the Niña's bed, she's sleeping like an angel, though she sighs like a lost soul, pobrecita, it's so sad…'

Artayeta was the name of that possession, and of the fear of disappointing the hearts beating behind each of the closed doors. What must Otropapá have felt, he who had been dispossessed of so much, when he came home from his club and found the women squabbling over my cradle? Like my father, he was orphaned in childhood. Who knows what pangs he must have felt when he discovered his grandson, ringed with salaams, where he least expected him to be? His own grandson, who, once more, bore an alien name. For in the Calle Juncal, Cullen was anathema. Fifteen years before my parents' wedding, that untidy uncle had acted as receiver in the bankruptcy that sucked them dry.

'Look how the marquis is gobbling up your eggs,' said the tilt of my grandmother's chin as her sidelong glance met her husband's; at the same moment, with unconscious intuition, Mailly wiped his lips and opened his mouth.

'*Délicieux, Mecha. Ça c'est délicieux. Ça me rappelle Ferrières, le château des Rothschilds. Je dirais même plus, ça me rappelle d'un déjeuner à Mar del Plata chez Josefiná Unzué. C'est tout dire.*'

The aplomb of these Gallic clichés had the rumbling accompaniment of a bumblebee, attracted to the table by the red dahlias, and made my grandfather smile. But Otramamá's look was one of disapproval of both her husband's culinary pretensions and the silliness of Mailly, and so Otropapá remained silent.

'How curious,' said Otramamá, 'is this passion of your people which destroys not only their livers but also their humour. Of course, I'm not referring to you, Henri, you are so English'. (The marquis believed that he was the natural son of Edward VII.) 'It makes them bilious, as the word suggests, and *je dirais même plus*, ha! That famous *nétteté* of yours, it's a way of coping with indigestion – *Une nétteté résignée.*'

Otramamá had the bit between her teeth, but Mailly, with a pale British smile that seems really to be its opposite, and hurts more than it irritates, murmured simply, '*Plutôt renfrognée.*'

'You can smile Henri, because you have the advantage of seeing your country from the outside. You can look at it and smile, because you've been bred with that British ability to make your bed anywhere. Your marriage to Teresa is a sign of that ease: *An imaginative leap,*' she said in English. 'You could boast about it if you weren't so modest. It is also a sign of laziness. Here you are, sitting at this table of *métèques*, who watch you to see how to use their forks. Here we are, at the bottom of the world, open to every experience, just as much as your proud people are closed. And on top of this you take us all for granted.'

Bebette couldn't believe her ears. She gaped at my grandmother. Her shaky soprano laugh dissolved into a cavernous sigh. Otropapá, who was bending his high shoulders towards Madame de Mailly as if to protect her from these impertinences, thought she was choking, and turned suddenly back to Bebette, a napkin in his hand.

Otramamá was now in full flow. She hollowed her voice to mimic the velvety tones of Bebette, and intoned, '*J'entends l'écho de ma grandeur interne*, as your friend Victoria would say. She has made us all sick of Valéry, who in the end isn't a poet, but a mere purveyor of pretty lines. Some are useful though. I recite this one to hurry the effect of my Inca brew.'

All my grandmother knew of Valéry was the lengthy quotations of his work by Victoria Ocampo in the literary pages of *La Nación*. But when her mind became heated she seemed able to jump between opposites, as though inspired by the Holy Ghost, or better still by the genie which hovered over the Uriburus when they abandoned themselves before an audience; a magical bird that connected distant voices and sang them with an insolent truth. Now this jealous bird, who inspired only his own children, floated for a while over the flowers at the centre of the table, its shadow drawing around it a pool of silence.

As Monsieur de Mailly sucked impassively on his last asparagus, Otramamá laughed, full of the things she had yet to say, which the bird would soon carry away with it. Bebette opened her eyes even wider within those great sockets that had enamoured Buenos Aires long before Garbo. Frozen between astonishment and confusion, she forgot to be angry.

Madame de Mailly concentrated like the good pupil she was, anxious not to miss anything of 'the best', and closed her eyes in order to memorise. A studious smile played on her long, thin lips, beneath her great nose of Cleopatra.

My grandfather was furious. But the precepts inculcated by Mademoiselle Maillard ensured that in his round, mild face, only sadness showed.

The bird departed. The loud Argentine voices washed like a wave over the silver tureens. Otrapapá told Casimiro to start serving the asado.

Tía Juana had been watching Otramamá. How clever Mecha is, she always has something to say, she seemed to be thinking, as she tried to close off the captive ear into which Tío Sebastián had been pouring the full catalogue of his refurbishments for the past half hour. She was trying to hone the other one, which had brought the bird's song to her. For the Unzués, who were obsessed with boredom – they had coined the phrase 'How boring to amuse oneself' – to have something to say, and a lot of it, was a sign of the highest intelligence.

Clara used to say that Tía Juana was the least Unzué of the three sisters, which was praise indeed, but she still spoke in that half idiotic way of theirs. Four long summer months at San Carlos, and during the rest of the year the chore of a daily visit to the Calle Juncal had made the Madero girls the elder sisters of the Juncal girls. And Otropapá took on the role of the brother they didn't have, although distant, and twenty years older. Those ties, close and yet free from fraternal rivalry, strengthened a love that thrived on the others' fortunes. Which was lucky for the Unzué girls, since the Alvenida Alvear was so much richer than the Calle Juncal.

'Quite right of Mecha to put that frog in his place,' Tía Juana whispered to her cousin. Tía Juana was tall and shy. A masculine streak from the Maderos had crossed with the overpowering, feminine gene of her Unzué mother, and made her appear like an English criolla, who rode beautifully and dressed without conviction. Madame de Mailly, with her didactic urge, had once tried to give her advice about her hats – Juana favoured berets in winter and white cotton hats in summer. Tía Juana had never forgiven her, but her manners, also honed by Mademoiselle Maillard, made her ashamed of this; and so she greeted her Parisian cousin with a meek and smiling kiss, encouraging more unwelcome advice.

'Juana is nice, but she's very gáucha.' To behave like a gaucho is to be kind and helpful, but my mother meant that she was not social, not smart. And in this way, this daughter of San Carlos, the most opulent of our estancias, was more akin to the Santamarteños.

To say that she looked like an hidalgo is to belittle her femininity, or perhaps rather that absence of female asperity so typical in her branch and unknown in mine. But watching her in winter, alone under the black trees of the Recoleta, hurrying home for lunch, with her long, rhythmic stride, her gloved hand holding the collar of her *loutre* coat that was cinched with a rather military belt, a beret framing her heart-shaped face and wide-set grey blue eyes, I recognised the lonely, vulnerable, stubborn dignity of the hidalgo. Or perhaps simply of her father. Her hard-soft eyes reflected him, a feminine and authoritarian man who had engendered three nymphs in a dryad, and was left to search for the remnants of his masculinity in corners.

His daughter had transformed herself into an Amazon, to keep him company. She had his same distant eyes. He was a remote father, who like my own father and grandfather had lost his mother as a child. At least one daughter of the motherless boys found her life mapped out for her; and Tía Juana, perhaps even like my own Tía Pepa, seemed to march along the yellow pavements of that wintry Recoleta, with her determined step moulded to his, thinking not of her lunch but of her dead father's fears.

Tía Juana's Unzué humour was both sly and silly.

'The Unzués play the fool to perfection. It gives them a reputation for stupidity, but I see it as a sign of intelligence,' said Tía China, owner of Santa Marta, to her neighbour Paquito, as they watched Tía Juana whispering to Sebastián.

'Think of it Juana, what a business,' Tío Sebastián continued with his *idée fixe*. 'You know we bought quite a few things in London for San Francisco. Everything arrived, thank God, but we've lost the cheese knives that we found at the Silver Vaults. Remember, they're in the City, Nena Salamanca suggested we try there. Basilio can't find them, though he's turned the trunks inside out. A bother, che, a real bother.'

The small, squeezed voice of a naughty doll answered Sebastián's coot-like volubility. 'Could the mice have eaten them?'

Next to Paquito sat Lola María, a fervent participant in the festivities. She couldn't cope with the Unzués, she was confused by the admiring awe with which they welcomed her on her annual descent from her bat-reeking house in the middle of the sombre woods on the hills of Kakel. She never missed a year, but she came bristling with defensiveness. The sight of her excited the San Carlos girls, who had never seen anything so ugly. They approached her tentatively, shyly, but with a glee in their eyes that Lola María, who had long ago undergone the trauma of the mirror, registered with her thick lips drawn tightly together.

'Lola María! How lovely to see you! How are you, ratóna?'

'Ratóna' — little mouse — which they used for everybody, cut her to the quick, because she believed it was directed exclusively at her. It may have been patronising, ratóna, but it wasn't cruel. She felt that that unconscious ease was aimed at her moustache, her snout, her Chinese eyes with their white turned yellow, the whole year spent buried in Kakel, the dogs that had given her tapeworm, her handsome but hopeless husband. *Lola María! Ratóna!* sang in her ears on her birthday, in the winter, at the asado they shared with their farm worker.

Now Lola María picked up on Tía China's praise of the Unzué charm. 'I'm surprised at you, China, that you should be taken in. If they seem so stupid, no smoke without fire...'

Like the Old Vizcacha in the Martín Fierro epic, Lola María was keen on proverbs. Her loud, cracked voice reached Otramamá. The bird stirred, and my grandmother closed her eyes and intoned, in a singing falsetto, *'Where there is no remedeee...it's already been remedeeed...'*

Like so many others, Lola María responded to Tía Juana's forlorn quality, apparent in the way Juana greeted her cousin, tilting the right side of her face which fell, dragged down by the sudden weight of her shy smile and drooping eyes, so that her chin rested on her sternum. It seemed to beg for a helping hand. 'I don't want beauty all the time,' the hoarse, macho voice of the owner of Kakel seemed to say in response. 'Just let it touch me for a moment, let it clothe me, even fleetingly.' And I was touched by the doglike gaze of her heavy-lashed eyes, and the prayer addressed to Tía Juana by her ardent and afflicted heart. But then her pride would be attacked from so many angles, and her intelligent curiosity so taxed, that she hardened once again. Angrily? Thankfully? Lola María was suddenly in a hurry, her long nights ahead of her, and so she, who was greedy of her dreams, let Tía Juana's sad little smile sink into her memory, and moved on to studying the almost Sevillian angle made by Madame de Mailly's straw boater as it sat on the net covering her auburn hair.

18

Now the asadores were approaching with the asado on wheelbarrows, and having spread the grass with embers, they nailed onto spits by the table the ribs of the heifers and the four crucified lambs. The parrillada, overflowing with chorizos, black pudding, and contorted offal, lay on the bigger wheelbarrow. The effect wasn't as dazzling as the evening asado; then the dining-room door would be flung open to the night and the tall, black rectangle pierced with the brilliance of torches, knives, embers and roasted flesh. But even at midday, an asado is a spectacle, and the hesitancy with which the guests had sat down for the first course grew greater as they stood up from the table to be confronted by the second. Two courtesies, one carrying a china plate, the other a horn-handled knife, approached one another.

'Julio, how nice to see you, how are you?' Tía Juana's head tilted sideways, but this time the chin didn't reach the sternum, and there was no ratón.

The hedge-trimmer, Julio Quiroga, Quico's brother and husband of the turbulent cook of the peons, bared his black teeth shyly, and pushed up the brim of his hat with his long knife.

'I'm fine, thank you, Señora Juana. And you? On your holidays?' Since we didn't seem to work, the gauchos assumed that our lives were an endless outing. 'What would you like? I've got a nice juicy piece of fillet here.'

'Oh Julio, just a little rib. You know I'll chew it like a dog.'

'Ha, niña, you girls from San Carlos, always joking. You never change – a little older, perhaps, but slim as ever. Never a good eater, were you, Niña Juana.'

They were united for a moment by their shared memories, made stronger by their shared blood. Juana found him waiting whenever she returned home; he who had never seen the sea had travelled with her over the years, and now here they were, face to face. Perhaps Juana felt herself to be the sister of the peon, whose huge hands she'd used as a stirrup when they were children. Perhaps, just for a moment, she saw herself in Julio, the blue-eyed teenager, tamer of horses, her bastard cousin according to Maipú gossip, the son her father never had; someone who perhaps she thought she might become, on those afternoons when she'd slipped away from the siesta, riding pillion behind him to the laguna in search of duck eggs. On those afternoons her normal life disappeared, Miss Midwinter, the gossip of boyfriends with her sisters, the preparations for Mar del Plata, the ceremony of riding in a side-saddle habit, all of it was left behind.

Until he married, Julio had kept a picture of her. He stole a society magazine, *Plus Ultra*, which had been lent to the peons' cook by someone in the big house, and cut out Tía Juana's photo with his knife. He didn't pin it to the walls of the room he shared with Quico and two other farmhands, which were decorated with cuttings of Gardel, women in underwear and some Spanish cards. Instead, he hid it under his bed, between the pages of *El Alma que Canta*. It never occurred to him that he was in love.

The Argentine noon drew on gaudily and innocently, sizzling like the grease that fell on the embers. The smoke, the heat, the voices of people and birds, young, loud, acid, the smell of the roast, of the flowers, of the still fresh grass, all floated up towards the canopy of oaks and beyond, towards that yellowish blue, both neutral and menacing, and then vanished. Nothing was returned; the sky of my birthday was vast and indifferent.

Miss Judy's European sensibility was pained. She looked

around the abandoned table and saw me at the far end, on the throne she had built from the laurel branches we'd collected, imprisoned by the tall bower, but placid, even a little proud to be deserted, and felt an urge to pick me up and carry me to her bedroom.

'*Darling, come with me. Let's go and choose you a juicy piece of meat. It's your birthday, after all.*'

'*Thank you, Miss Judy, but I don't like meat. I only like the ribs, and I'd rather not move. Would you be so kind as to bring me some, please?*'

Miss Judy, disappointed, began to hum the song she'd heard sung on the ship by a cocotte who was on her way back to Buenos Aires to rekindle her pre-war career.

'*J'aime les marrons parçe qu'ils n'ont pas de saveur,*
les camélias parçe qu'elles n'ont pas d'odeur,
et les hommes riches… parçe qu'ils n'ont pas de coeur.'

Then she began to speak to herself, as if in a dream. 'No it's not that, cynicism is born of disillusionment. In order to dismantle, one has first to build. What is it about this clarity that is so oppressive? This hope, that seems like sleep? *Que dolore…*'

'Let's see, Quico, cut some kidneys for the Señor.' Otropapá took Monsieur de Mailly's arm, worried that his son-in-law would get there first. My father regarded it as his right to eat the kidneys. He would sulk if somebody pipped him to the post, and I had seen him stalk away from the table on more than one occasion.

Mailly's arm tensed. He had never got used to the criollo pawing. And he found the famous Argentine beef too greasy; the cold plates didn't help, and nor did the dusty road, the terrible sun, his indigestion, the damp sheets of the Hotel de la Luna.

'*Tres peu, Jorge, je vous en prie. Je viens de sortir d'une crise de foie.*'

Otropapá, who detested asados, was offended, both as gourmet and host. He cast aside his characteristic mildness, and borrowed a weapon from his wife. '*Vous avez tout à fait raison, mon cher Henri. Mais quand à Rome...*' He asked for sweetbreads to be added to the kidneys.

At the foot of the table, Mr Overington, our summer tutor, felt included and happy, as he always did when he was invited to attend a party of his employers.

'If Mother could see me sitting here,' he muttered to the smoke and the leaves. He had the same thought on every such occasion. Given the polite indifference of those around the table, of which he was well aware, his snobbery must have been all-embracing, like the love of a saint.

He was English, anti-Semitic, and hopeless. The Misti, as the peons called him, rode with his bottom up, and used the deer antler on his whip to open the gates. To expose your arse is taboo on the pampa. But Leonard G. Overington's phlegmatic nature kept both mockery and indifference at bay. I never saw his round, brand new face, pink like an embalmed baby, change expression. Behind their gold-rimmed glasses, his eyes were of an indistinct colour, and not hard. And although he seemed moveable, like a chair, that inertia clad in green tweeds radiated a certain power.

He was protected by a national defect, the English lack of imagination, that rejection of contact with the outside world in order to protect one's identity, even if as we know this was not Otromamá's opinion. He moved along the streets of Buenos Aires or the parks of Maipú, immune and smug. But English snobbery is also canonical, and we were included in his devotions, but only when we took the trouble to organise a ceremony.

Along with Lola María, Mr Overington was the most assiduous of the faithful. Since the death of Toribio, Tía Juana's eldest son and the life tenant of San Francisco before its sale to Tío Sebastián, whom the Misti had cared for as tutor-nurse for twenty years, he had agreed to come down in the world and spend the summer in our estancia, where he played hide-and-seek, and let my sister plait his wispy hair, with its white leopard spots amidst the ginger. Maybe he did so only because of the party at the end of February. In losing Toribio, he had lost his position as the manager of a flawed treasure – and with it the satisfaction of giving orders to the San Francisco staff, teas surrounded by the opulence of the Avenida Alvear in the winter, dinners with Sebastián's smart set of Lake Nahuel Huapí, who summered there before he settled in Maipú. There, seated at the foot of the table among the teenagers who ignored his attempts at conversation, he would let his little eyes wander over the naked shoulders of Tío Sebastián's guests, on their throats encircled with 1940s necklaces of retractile gold, outlined against the darkening lake, and see his mother in her Stockwell kitchen – 'If only she could see me sitting here.' But what was left of all of that now, to impress his snooker pals at the British Club on the Calle Cangallo?

Like love, his snobbery took him out of himself. And like all Englishmen, he was keen on disguises. But the criollos wouldn't respond to him, for they are terrified of fancy dress. And so we didn't please him much.

Time moves, and even then there weren't many left who marked the day's ceremonies with a change of attire, as my grandfather still did. Tío Sebastián appeared one day after tea, in his dazzling Americana trap, and draped in a new tweed cape which, with the Hermès harnesses that he had cannibalised from San Carlos, was another symptom of the new extravagance of San Francisco. 'Here he comes in his fancy dress,' Otropapá remarked, to the chagrin of the Misti. Nuance is everything: Otropapá went down the terrace steps to welcome the be-costumed Sebastián encased in suede breeches of an orange-brown hue, cut with the fullness of a startled elephant's ear, and the mustard waistcoat of an *incroyable*, but he did so with the grace of a reed bent by the weight of a laguna yellow-breast. I longed to be as svelte as my grandfather. The Bengolea boys of San Carlos, who thrived on coining unkind nicknames for their friends, had christened my sister The Scourge for her eager affection; I was The Tank. 'Here comes *Tanke Schön*,' they would giggle, Unzué style.

Tïa Juana quickened her step, so as to avoid the Misti. She could see him out of the corner of her eye, trotting towards her with his Delft doll gait, weighed down by a plate of offal. He brought her sad memories.

'This family thing of passing our staff around is a bad idea,' she whispered to Lola María, who was following her like a dog. 'He would've retired after Toribio's death, if it hadn't been for Clara. It's partly my fault, I should have given him a better present. But it's really the gossip he comes for.' She managed to sit down just in time. 'Ah, thank God,' she said, then turned her face towards the plate borne by the Misti, laden with convoluted forms that would have delighted Archimboldo. 'Oh Mr Overington, you are always so kind. But I can't, I just can't. It would kill me.'

'There is nothing so lethal as entrails. The man who wrote that bolero, "My Adored Torment," was just a lover who had swallowed some offal,' Otramamá sang out to Tía Juana. When we had an asado, she ordered a boiled chicken for herself, and shared it with Tía Justita.

19

I N   O R D E R to introduce Tía Justita I must first describe San Carlos, her estancia. For one contained the other.

As I have said, to reach Miraflores, we had to penetrate the horizon, going beyond the hills of Yamoidá. But if we took the San Carlos route, we could avoid the town of Maipú, and with it the main road to Mar del Plata, which to travel along was to be plunged, disagreeably, into another world – the world of everyone else. By going via San Carlos we could go directly on to the Camino Real, the dirt highway, by the gate of Chacabuco.

At four in the afternoon, after proceeding along the dark and odorous tunnel of the causeway, the longest corridor of the house, dank and reeking of water-birds' feathers, and which had to be traversed as part of waking up from the siesta, we emerged into the clearings of the other park, perfumed by hot pines and tired grass, contained in vaster spaces than our estancia, and which announced in my recently awakened nose, in the procession along the gravel drive, gusts of jasmine, magnolia and oleo fragrans, still baking hot, before the relief of the cold tiles of the interior of the house. But no, we must turn right, behind the chapel, and skirt the eucalyptus wood surrounding San Carlos, whose sad, summery, Argentine smell seemed to envelope all others; we would pass by the palm tree, enthroned in its tracery of box hedge, and leave the park by the road which crossed the wood and ended with two white pillars crowned by French lanterns.

Now the sun hit us in earnest, as though falling onto the open sea. It was as if the lanterns of San Carlos were the twin Venetian columns of the Piazzetta, and the blinding brilliance of the field would beg for the mercy of some shade – not the bulk of the island of San Giorgio but that of the woods of La Sarita. There were still forty kilometres to go before we reached Miraflores, and so we must leave our urban, marshy, awning-covered, Venetian refuge at the worst hour, and confront that wasteland, navigating a canal of loose, slippery, runaway dust, which could swallow us like water: a Camino Real. The open country would hit me with its clear, dry smell, so different from that of our estancia's islands. Despite the glaring heat the light pounded joyfully on my breast, erasing the memory of the refuge it had seemed so hard to leave.

The cluster of eucalyptus woods that encircled the casco of San Carlos was another sign of its opulence. But from a distance they appeared tight and severe, and seemed to me to narrow the vista, turning the five kilometres that separated it from Maipú into a vast park, into which the last allotments of the town encroached on the lodges, creating the sense of a suburb. Our own estancia, built on the eastern bank of the laguna, looked out onto the open plain, with San Carlos behind it for protection.

The only one of the estancias to look more like an archipelago than an island, San Carlos was built with money from outside, and because the spending continued until the arrival of Perón, its Belle Époque opulence was cooled in the thirties by chrome, parchment, and pale wood, and obliged me to confront the anguish of what is very near and offers itself but resists. Just as the dispersed woods hid the casco, so the excess of gardeners and servants concealed the heart of its owners.

Neither Tía Justita, nor her sons – ten years older and idolised by us – nor even less her husband, who ran racehorses at Palermo and like Otropapá spent idle evenings at the Círculo de Armas, seemed to be in any way responsible for that impressive creation, planted overnight on the spills of our laguna, while its owners travelled around Europe.

The girl who became our Tía Justita must have walked up those steps of newly cut marble and smelled the potted palms and straw furniture of the veranda with the same mild surprise experienced in any of the grand hotels they frequented. Fifty years later, she continued to occupy the place with a worrying air of detachment.

San Carlos was a machine that cost a lot and ran itself. It was the employees who kept the key, and the family who paid for and received its services, like guests in a hotel. Because of this, because it had no heart, I loved and yet was pained by San Carlos. I was fascinated by its luxury and hurt by its silence, by its emptiness. It was so near, and yet not actually at hand, and its seductive aroma seemed like a distillation of the perfume of Tía Justita's pink and bronze bedroom, an absent fragrance which made me push the door open stealthily, afraid of being caught by Petra, the old maid who had also served in the Calle Juncal, and who seemed to conceal all the family's secrets in her rat-like eyes. It was a smell I associated with the well-born heroines of Paul Bourget and Guy de Chantepleure, whose lives I explored eagerly in books taken from Tío Bebé's bookshelves. At the same time, I had begun to suffer at the dwindling visits of my grandparents, which made me feel that our estancia was losing something that San Carlos was retaining splendidly, while its engines rumbled on at full steam. Even more so, perhaps, because there was nobody who embodied that opulence; there was no one there to whom I could reach out, to tell me stories, memories, secrets, no one to bring me closer to their mysterious archipelago.

San Carlos had become a house inhabited by beautiful shadows; they weren't allowed to be bored and so they carried on, as in the forgotten books that I read, with their rituals of five o'clock tea, carriage drives, absent minded purchases in Maipú, the same rituals that were fading from our estancia through the absence of my grandparents. But

I wouldn't have been so affected by this if the seed hadn't been planted at home, in Buenos Aires, in the restless abandon of the bathroom of the Calle Juncal. Love, in my childhood, was something that came wrapped in parcels of tissue paper, and I spent my time seeking it out, my sweaty fingers tangling with the ribbons, only to find it within an old, pretty box, already open. It was something waxed, darkened, furnished, hedged, well-ordered and soft; it was a house, a park, an estancia, cared for faithfully and obsessively by others while I slept, kept empty and free just for me, so that when I woke and had tired of reading, I could roam around it, without disturbing the pillows, or the gravel, or the flowers, lodging the people of my books among my own things.

Two bronze dogs sat on grey stone plinths, beneath the grey lacy shadow of some elms, not so much on guard as resting from the chase. There was a chain across the drive, offering better protection than these indifferent hounds. Even more effective was the invisible barrier, the hot, lemony fragrance of the tiny flower of the oleo fragans, which stopped the visitor in his tracks on the uneven stones, warning him to tread carefully. This barrier came from a dark, scaly and metallic clump of bushes sheltering a fountain, in which a boy embraced a dolphin. The leaves, interlocked and dazzling, of camellia and magnolia and gardenia seemed to deny the softness of the treasure held at their centre.

On the other side of the drive was the entrance to 'the pines', an open-air room carpeted with needles the colour of dulce de leche and furnished with white lacquer tables and armchairs, through which a sea breeze seemed to blow. The dark heavily fragrant tumulus and the Atlantic grotto smelling of resin faced each other, like the dogs, creating a tight-rope that led the visitor to the marble steps of the entrance, which was concealed by marble urns and lagerstroemia bushes, and remained hidden. In the estancias, where no one uses the front door, and the bell is always broken, the entrances are furtive. And as the drive was short and the house big, but placed side on, the visitor was confronted by a mass that seemed to be watching his approach out of the corner of its eye.

Square, white, with a simple Italian roof, a fringe of Virginia creeper running under it, and above a cornice of turquoise tiles printed with Art-Nouveau lilies that softened the sheer white drop, to one side a tower, which from the ground seemed to peer vaguely down from the façade like a massive and inattentive head, the house of San Carlos had a festive if not welcoming air. The blackness of the pines made it appear paler, like a villa on the shore of a blue sea. The visitor climbed the curved stairs, and pushed on the wire-mesh door.

Nobody in the gallery, nobody in the salita, but the smell! Never has there been such a smell. An accumulation of expensive artefacts: finely tressed whips with silver handles, fly swats of black horsehair, Panama hats, cork helmets, all hung from the antlers of a stand by the door of the gallery. The pinkish hides of criollo cows picked up the blush of the tiled floor, scaly like Jonah's whale. The arches, which at the beginning, before the foreign design was digested, had been open to the elements and covered by canvas curtains, were now filled with diamond-paned glass, creating a constant, tender green light, the light of an ideal conservatory, for the brutal sun was halted outside by the dripping leaves of an acacia wood. Straw armchairs, cushions of bay colt hide. On the walls hung charming views of early nineteenth century Buenos Aires by Emeric Essex Vidal, framed in silver, and in pride of place a map of San Carlos in 1930, all fifteen thousand acres of it, with slick, sporty lettering and little red buildings and green woods, like a thirties' plan of a golf course. On the tables, photographs of the three daughters of the house, the Madero sisters, twenties-style, flat-chested and with heavily-lacquered hair, dressed in expensive crystal rags; and those crystal paperweights with blind eyes swimming in their depths.

Two great Art-Deco chandeliers of frosted glass hung from the high ceiling. The cushions of the long Spanish refectory bench were striped white and yellow, and the effect, in that simple, whitewashed gallery, was of something light and sharp, breathless with longing, like the music of Debussy. Drops of music, erect, disconnected and insistent, that lost rhythm, like that rain, green, sunlit; the sunlit diamond glass, in the empty room as vast as the empty day, where the only music that came from the gramophone, whose handle would spin back suddenly with a lethal machine-gun noise and hit your fingers, were fifties songs.

There it was that they sat after lunch, leafing through *El Hogar, París en América, Atlántida*, commenting on the photographs of parties they'd been to in that glandular voice of theirs, deliberately slurred, while in the background the gramophone sang '*Rain falling from the sky ... like lonely tears through misty eyes*' or '*I wanna kiss ... aaa kiss ... but you donwanna ... you donwanna...*' And outside, the mesh of tiny leaves that protected our shade fought with the sun.

Drops of music losing step, my heart that waits the next drop, slanted, hidden, the hand is held suspended above the keys and then tears out two more notes; and the heart stumbles, searching in that indifferent room, in the fixed light that no wind moves and which is blurred by its screen of weak green drops, for a memory that has nothing to do with time. In my oldest memories, it has always seemed as though those first visits, of which I could hold no memories, had already happened in the past, like the music of Debussy.

20

Tía juana's eldest sister, heir of San Carlos, was blonde, and took advantage of her reputation for silliness in order to suit herself in most things. I had never seen legs like Tía Justita's. Nervous like a stallion's nostrils, they spent hours sleeping by the pale emerald water of the pool, indicating a life absent from their owner's eyes. They were useless, but with them Daphne might have broken free. Her sons inherited them, but not as a whole. Dionisio got the shape and elegance; Fernán, who was chunky, the nerviness of his mother's tense and supple ankles.

This voluptuousness, with its counterpart of emptiness and secrecy, was very much alien to Maipú, and Tía Justita displayed it without making real use of it. She was frightened of everything, even the setting sun, and yet I found her dangerous. The way she poured tea, which was the only thing she ever did, tilting the silver pot over white china cups painted with pink rosebuds, and offering them around with a shaking hand, turned her actions into something unexpected and abrupt. She was *gentille*, like a French girl; but her eyes, of a more intense blue and yet without the severity of her sister's, seemed to brood, like active, hidden, hostile insects imprisoned within her good-natured body. They seemed to contain a hidden plan, which she was too lazy to carry out, but which floated in her blue gaze like an invisible cloud.

Like so many of us there she was constantly bored, and her boredom was total, because she didn't even bother with gossip. Such a world-weary Infanta required her jesters though, and in February these sprouted in San Carlos, along with the pink lilies and the horseflies. They were a multi-coloured pack with a common blessing, poverty, and an impossible task, because too much amusement tired her. There were her nieces, a Spanish marquesa with a mad daughter, her Buenos Aires masseuse, a slightly retarded spinster cousin and Paco, a mural painter with the mannerisms of a hairdresser, who ended his jokes with 'Ah loro!' a reference to the din of the parrots which pierced our ears from their nests in the eucalyptus trees. He was the mascot of many summers.

'You must listen to Paco, he gets funnier every day. Ah loro! Isn't he divine, Paco? Ah loro!' And Tía Justita laughed in that way of hers that had been inherited by her sons, and which surprised Gilda, in her Irish innocence: 'Señora Justita's laugh sounds like me when I'm trying to shit.'

I had asked for her to be seated next to me, but Tía Justita, who had brought her masseuse without permission, called to her, 'Come here Hortensia, sit next to me so you can amuse the birthday boy.'

And before Otropapá could intervene, the seat reserved for Jimmy Elía, a son of the victim of the ruta 2 accident, was occupied by an intruder to whom not even Mr Overington deigned to speak. I was mortified. Hortensia was smarmy, her smooth masseuse's face wore the fragile and false friendliness of my aunt's followers, although in spite of myself I rather liked it, tired as I was of the simplicity of our estancia.

'Oh, Señora Justita, look at the throne they've made for the Nene. Isn't it lovely! If he wasn't a bit dark he'd look just like Shirley Temple, sitting there among all those leaves.'

'Don't be so common, Hortensia. How many times have I told you, one doesn't say Nene.' Tía Justita winked at me. 'She is wonderful, Hortensia, she never learns. Ratóna, I'm going to make you write every evening a hundred times: I mustn't be common, or Señora Justita, who is so good, will have to spank me. You're right, though, the arrangement is pretty. The new governess has taste. It reminds me of being a child in Nice, when Miss Midwinter took us to the Promenade des Anglais to look for palm branches to decorate my chair at my birthday party. I gave all my pocket money to one of the Negresco's bellboys so he'd climb the tree for me. Well, ratóna, there was a terrible to-do, because the bell boy fell and broke his leg, and Papá had to pay for the operation, and they tried to get me to visit him in hospital. I was dying with embarrassment. Miss Midwinter gave notice – "Madam, I am too ashamed to stay, all the other governesses in the hotel are laughing at me because of Justita's behaviour. With respect, Madam, if I was the Señor, I'd whip her." But my father would never have hit me. I was sick all night long, but I wouldn't go.'

'Sheñora Justita, what courage!' Hortensia's sss and rrs turned messy in her mouth.

'Why wasn't your Miss allowed to hit you? I read somewhere that the English Misses always hit their children.'

'How divine, Martincito – he's always reading. Here's something for you to learn, Hortensia, you only read the gossip columns, and then you get the names wrong.'

'But, Sheñora Justita, I'm not the only one who doesn't read.'

'So, we're answering back. Just imagine, ratón, this clever lady tells me that Señora Beba or Señora Someone, clients she likes to boast about to make me jealous, are reading Françoise Sagan. I'm curious, so I send her to buy it for me. Novels give me a headache, I can't get interested in other people's lives. Then she charges me to massage the pain away. When I think of how you treat me, ratóna, I wonder why I like you so much. But be careful, suddenly, when I'm least expecting it, I'll take against you, and that'll be it. It's terrible, but there's nothing to be done. You, Martincito, you're such a clever little thing, explain it to me. Why do I turn against people?'

The masseuse gave a mad, full-throated laugh. I could see

her grey tonsils dancing. I laughed hard in return, thinking I was safe, but behind the bubbles of saliva that framed those wormy tonsils, Hortensia's eyes watched me.

'Don't you think, Sheñora Justita, that this Nene is a bit precocious?' Hortensia toyed with her chorizo.

'But that's exactly his *charme*, you moron. I've never known a child with more to say for himself. Pepito Demaría was like that, but he was pompous. Martincito is more amusing, more gossipy.'

'That's what I was getting at Sheñora Justita, she pursued, ominously. 'He might turn out a bit sissy.'

My reaction to danger was to embrace it, as if I'd rather bury the knife in my chest than feel the horror of it slicing me from behind as I tried to escape. This way it would be over more quickly.

'Hortensia!' I cried. 'What a pretty new lipstick you've chosen for Tía Justita. It makes her look younger.'

I was trying to kill two birds with one stone; not to fight against an insult but embellish it, and at the same time dodge it with flattery. I seemed to respond to love and hate in the same way, throwing myself at them, in order to suffocate them, since I found it hard to believe in either. I tried to smother them with what I had at hand – presents, words, sweets, suicidal dancing – anything that would clear the room of their desperate presence.

Time stood still. In my ears the voices fell silent, though the chorus of the laguna sang on, as if offering refuge. My eye framed each of the mute guests.

In the shadows, dappled with light, I saw them as hard and soft: the pretty and foreign Elía, with their English features and dark hair, placed carefully by my grandfather so as to add colour to the table, were hard, their mouths opening and closing, munching, smiling; the light-eyed Santamarteños, fine bones and hooked noses, their skin pink, red, raspberry, their mouth knowing, were soft. Then

Chita, like a bowl of fruit, Lola María's extraordinary features, the big straw hat of the *jeune fille en fleur* that was Madame de Mailly, the pebble glasses of Paquito, the net and tennis racket of Tía Juana, the Boldini grey of Monsieur de Mailly, the velvet down on Bebette's temples and those great, Garbo-trumping sockets, the unprepossessing plumpness of Estelita Elía, the handsome noble nose of Otropapá with his courtly smile, Tita, Tío Sebastián sweating in his tweeds like an English print; the ones in black, Otramamá, Tía China, the ones in white, Pepa, Tina, Tía Lula; my father who had got up from the table and looked like Clark Gable in his grey bombachas, Tía Justita winking at her chicken wing, and to crown it all Hortensia's triumphant dentures, and far away, but fixed on me, Clara's dilated pupils.

They're mine, I thought. All of them. I must carry them with me because they will vanish. And they haven't made an impression on anyone but me. I must remember them, describe them, do something they'd refuse to take seriously. They don't care about memory. They care about sleeping. They'd laugh — what's the point? How tiresome, we want for nothing, and in the end there'll be room for us all in the Recoleta, in the faithful tombs we seldom visit that await us with their sickly smell. To live on? Who cares. *Schlafen, schlafen, ohne zu erwachen*, as Otramamá might say, without really believing it, but because it sounded pretty. Like children, they gave no thought to their happiness, ignoring it was a game they played. Why had I chosen this role of mirror, if none of them really wanted it? I imagined that they were asking me to remember, and yet I had never seen a finger raised to mark a particular moment. Perhaps they couldn't ask me directly to remember certain things, but I would do so, at my own cost. And so I looked at them, aware of Hortensia's revelation, excluded because I was chosen.

'Here's the *sablé*. Yum yum!' Estelita Elía shouted from the other end of the table.

And with the *sablé* of dulce de leche came the torrejas, the quimbo eggs, the *poires Belle Hélène*, and the *compotes*. Tía Justita waited for the fruit course. She followed a strict regime, always bending to collect ping-pong balls, exposing her thighs for ten minutes to the icy jet of the swimming pool, and asking for fruit when she had to choose between too many deserts.

Now everyone was shouting. Otropapá, his complexities sharpened by Mailly's manners, gave orders for the rough wine of Caucete to be followed by the pearl of our cellar, a Château d'Yquem 28, which battled with the dulce de leche in the marquis's throat. The chimangos moaned more and more loudly, but failed to overwhelm the din of the party. The laguna sang on, voluble yet unheard.

'Come on, I'm not going to believe that!' 'Shut up! You don't know what happened next.' 'I told you a thousand times!' 'Nothing can be done, nothing can be done.' 'Listen to me' 'I hear you all right, my dear, I hear you!' '*Quel pays!*'

The *pays* was so green, the light so yellow, the sky so blue, and still these infants didn't realise their good luck. There they were, their feet immersed in Roman grass as black as a yak wool rug, patches of light staining their faces, the fruit, china, silver, and thickening the honey of the Château d'Yquem that was being passed to and fro in Casimiro's butterfly-gloved fingers. The smoke of the asado hung from the dome of tattered oak leaves, like Spanish moss; and fifty yards away, against the black wood, the asadores squatted together, eating the meats, their backs to us, like dark, indifferent beasts.

'We must toast the birthday boy!' I froze at Tía China's suggestion.

'Yes, the boy of the santo, who brings us all together for

this wonderful *gathering*,' said Madame de Mailly, stressing her use of the English word.

'*Hear Hear!*' The Elía took up the refrain.

Miss Judy placed herself next to me, with her willow baton, protecting me from Hortensia. Her Valkyrean breast launched an inflamed G to begin the Happy Birthday, with a force that alarmed the self-conscious criollos. But they were in good humour, and joined in happily enough.

The Miss had to be halted, though, she was thinking of Breughel and we were in Maipú. When my grandfather saw that my brother and sister had been pushed forward to recite '*Lorsque l'enfant paraît*,' he rose, and Otramamá followed, and the scintillating cousins began walking towards the house, to take refuge in the cool of the hall and drink their coffee.

PART III

THE JOURNEY

21

OUR JOURNEY was prefaced by a lie. We couldn't tell Otramamá that we were leaving for Europe – 'She can't bear goodbyes.' I can't imagine where we were supposed to be going, since my grandmother never allowed closed doors, and the Calle Juncal was crammed with trunks and suitcases. It was another of those criollo white lies, of which Tina was mistress, but I still wonder how they managed it. We were all going, or nearly all – my parents, Pepa, Tina and I. And Tía Teodé, who made herself conspicuous by her arrival at Juncal each afternoon at four o'clock sharp. And our cousins, Isabel and Eloísa, and their husbands. Now, I realise that perhaps we were supposed only to be crossing into Uruguay – although with all the accoutrements of exile. The dictator was tightening his grip, and one needed a certificate of good conduct to travel, but it was some years before the men of Juncal would be thrown in jail.

Otramamá saw us off with that smile of pained incredulity that waits upon disasters. From my jump seat in the car I saw her come out on the drawing room balcony, accompanied by Vicenta, who was doing the sobbing for her. On display was the other side of my grandmother's verbal bravura – a nervous disposition, which her husband called her sensitivity, and Tía Teodé called spoiledness. Whatever it was, it cast a shadow over our departure. Not so much for me, even though I experienced any journey as a wrench or a loss rather than a liberation. That day was so extraordinary – To Europe! By sea! – and I was so buoyed up, that for once Otramamá's sorrow didn't achieve its objective, usually so easily won, of making me sad. It was early January, the time when we always left for the estancia. Only it wasn't the dark dawn, but a fierce four in the afternoon.

Lunch had unfolded with its usual rhythm in the gloom of the uncarpeted dining room, on chairs already shrouded in white dust sheets, the smell of food mixed with the tang of mothballs, the sun pushing at the shutters; while we, the travellers, were about to set out over the ever more chilly sea, towards the snow-covered coast of France.

Only those born in Buenos Aires can know what it is to take the boat for Europe. Nine years I had waited, all the years I yet had, my yearning first recorded in a photograph of me on the South promenade in my grandmother's arms, in a pale woollen bonnet, like a buoy bobbing between river and sky. That promenade was a balcony open to the limbo-coloured waters that cut us off from Europe, a separation measured in days rather than leagues — twenty in our case — and which, like Purgatory, might be shortened through good deeds. We called it El Charco, the Puddle, we porteños, even those who would never cross it. For me, it was a great open plain, without even the respite of the hills of Yamoidá. I devoured it with my eyes on my weekly car rides with Tía Teodé, focusing obsessively on the river from one end of the South promenade to the other without ever glancing back towards the city. It was as if I knew that one clear day, instead of the woods of Uruguay beyond that caramel-coloured sea, I would be able to make out the silhouettes — over the dark and indecisive line of the horizon, condensed to purple in the sunset just like in Maipú — of the towers and domes of Paris.

'*Ah! la charmante chose,*' Otramamá would intone, and I, well-trained, replied, '*Quitter un pays morose.*' And then together, '*Pour Paris ... Paris joli.*' Then Otramamá, '*Qu'un jour,*' and me, '*Dût créer l'amour.*' And then both of us together, with ineffably silly smiles, '*Ah! la charmante chose, quitter un pays morose ... Pour Paris!*' Otramamá ended Poulenc's song with a Paris!! much shriller than Jeanne Duval's.

And it was all the sillier because Otramamá hadn't been back to Paris since she was married, forty years earlier, and I had never been. Now I was off. An ocean liner awaited us at the North Dock, a ship with two funnels and four or five rows of windows and portholes that would weigh anchor before nightfall and bear us away. But not her. And now that I know that my grandmother would never again set foot in Paris, I can't look at her unblinking eyes in that portrait painted of her facing the Tuileries, at that time she described as the best of her life, without sensing her reproach. Those eyes of hers would disappear behind the smile of her wrinkles when she recalled her youth, but Monsieur Albert Lynch captured them differently – in the portrait they are the eyes of an expectant yet already disappointed girl. I tried to swallow the whole world through my eyes, but she stood back, her eyes fixed and naked of lashes, taking refuge in an uncultivated inner life, the idle, spoilt dreams of an intelligent younger daughter. She lived as a prisoner of Juncal and the estancia under the Moorish jealousy of her husband's great-aunt, taking charge of the household only at the age of sixty, when it was too late, when I had just been born.

The boat was French. Our cabin had beds encased in red mahogany, with dark-blue covers – *Bleu de Roi* according to Tía Teodé – on which the embroidered white anchor seemed perfumed with the all-pervading smell of tar soap, which remains in my memory as the symbol of that flight and that intimacy. A hole to escape to and to hide in, but with someone, remains my idea of heaven on earth. Tía Teodé was my accomplice. It was a happiness gained through treachery, someone always had to be left behind, and still I felt blissful and treacherous and free of guilt, as if I were a prisoner and it was my duty to flee. There were roses and hydrangeas, and cards wishing us – or her – *Bon*

Voyage. There was a yellow bathroom, and a tiny salon with a pretty desk fixed beneath the porthole. On it my aunt placed my first present.

'Here you will keep your travel diary.' She pointed with a regal wave of her crooked fingers in the direction of the desk and a black leather book bearing my initials tooled in gold.

Tía Teodé had organised our elopement with a zeal of which Otramamá, who was far too criolla, was incapable. Teodé travelled each year – to Europe, of course – 'Without a maid,' she boasted, making a virtue out of necessity. She had spent most of her married life in hotels; when she finally moved out of the Plaza to a house in the Calle Rodriguez Peña her husband died, and now all her world was crammed into trunks. From one of them, a battered Vuitton catafalque the colour of tortoiseshell, she carefully extracted the things she felt were essential for my journey.

'Here is Pancho's jewel box,' she said. 'You will need it.'

'Totola, it's lovely. But I don't have any jewels.'

'Don't answer back. Open it, silly.'

I opened it, trembling, and those precious stones that have always killed me winked up at me from their nest of brown velvet – the leftovers of a rich Edwardian, offered to a Peronist boy: shirt-front pearls, round and tapered at the top in a refinement of aggression as spikes defending the rich man's heart under its starched and sparkling armour, like those stones that held poison, cufflinks of cabochon amethysts at the end of a thick linked chain of the most sumptuous gold, vulgar like a royal present, a platinum ring with a rectangular sapphire of art-deco chastity with its blue clouded by grey, an evening waistcoat watch as thin as a gold wafer, and chains and more cufflinks, everything marked by that excess of the Uriburu inheritance; which made me think, owing to the duplication of pieces in principle unique, that in those days, when Tía Teodé was marrying, even Villa

Elisa must have come with a spare of Villa Elisa. What a prize for a righteous desertion.

Because Tía Teode was so alone, alone in her salita waiting for me, alone in the street walking in the afternoon towards Juncal, the street so full of people, alone at tea surrounded by her sister's family, alone like me though I looked at myself from the inside, it was as if two thieves had managed to escape together.

'Totola, Totola!' I cried gasping for air, as if to say, I'm dying, I'm dying! I was choking as when I filled my mouth with sandwiches at Adela's party. I already knew that when faced with any display of abundance, it didn't matter what, I was grabbed by the vertigo of swallowing. I had to fill myself with what was there, instantly, with eyes shut and dislocated mouth, and the fury was such that I felt nauseous almost at the same time, without having had my fill, even without getting to touch whatever made me so hungry. It happened in patisseries, bookshops, parties, first day classrooms, and now, in front of this undreamt-of jewellery shop.

I want to make it clear that beyond this illness of greed, covetousness was not my main emotion. Yes, there was the value of the jewels, and even more their brilliance, but above all I was seduced by the aura of those hard beauties, and their coming from a dead man, someone of my family. My aunt's frown — she was constantly irritated by the world's lack of distinction — softened into a charming smile.

'What a silly boy you are! If I'd known you had such a passion for jewellery, I'd have given them to you before now.'

Lies! Tía Teodé planned her attacks carefully, in advance, like Louis XI.

I got dressed to go up for dinner. I had never been allowed to dine with the grown ups before, and as my aunt cut holes in my cuffs in order to display the marvellous amethysts, I looked out through the porthole.

'We are leaving!' I shouted, suddenly uncertain.

'Go up on deck so you can say goodbye to Buenos Aires. It's pretty to watch the sun go down behind the smoke,' Tía Teode said calmly. 'And don't get lost. You're far too excited.'

The passages, stairs and hallways with display cases lit like streets had been swarming with passengers when we boarded. Now they were empty. I ran, got lost, they've left me, opened a door, tripped on the coaming and fell flat on the soft planks of the deck, with their already familiar smell of tar. My father picked me up.

'Come quickly,' he said. 'Somebody's had the bright idea of bringing your grandmother.'

How high we were. The crowd, writhing with goodbyes down there on the square paving stones of the quay, looked like an egg smashed on a patio. I couldn't find Otramamá, and then at last I thought I recognised her, the only figure who wasn't waving.

'Look, it would be that idiot Negra Gorostiaga who brought her. Just to embarrass us,' said Tía Pepa.

'Where?' said everyone at once.

'There, on the right, at the edge of the crowd. She's in white, with dark glasses, holding Mamá's arm. Mamá's standing very still, and she's wearing her drama face.'

'*Where?*' said Tina, with exhausted severity. 'You and your eagle eyes. I can't see anyone. Never mind, I'm already miserable enough, with the lies I've had to invent for you all.'

'Vieja! Vieja!' my father bellowed, with the voice of Chaliapin. I was mortified, my grandmother wouldn't hear, but half the ship turned to listen.

Clara, who took his side as a matter of course, began to shriek, 'Mamá!' Her voice rose with a feminine hysteria that reminded me, horribly, of the radio broadcasts of Eva Perón.

Yet at the same time I was safe. Neither my grandmother's

sadness, nor my parents' bungling could touch me. I was leaving. It didn't matter that half the family was leaving too. I was conscious of that slick of mucky water widening every second, between the boat and the land, between that thing, the journey, and Buenos Aires. I was breathing a new air, my own, which revealed through the damp thickness of the sunset the freshness of a delicious impunity.

My first escape was my first betrayal. I escaped from the others, though Otramamá was the only one left behind, when we locked ourselves in our cabin. I escaped because I had made my choice at last. I had allowed myself to be chosen, really, by an outsider. Tía Teodé was a world away from that vertiginous, incestuous birthday in the estancia. Her vast family were the dead, illustrious but silent, her days were silent and from that silence came her voice of a sphinx, which needed no questioning. To reach her, for she was always older and more distant than the others, one had to go through a door unlocked by a silent butler and along unending corridors past the reception rooms, and find her in her chair, always, no telephone or radio or walking about like Otramamá, seated at the foot of her adolescent sister painted like a life size ghost against a misty lake where consumptives went to die. That she should have extracted herself from that stillness to take me on an adventure – it was as if my guardian angel had descended to carry me away.

I went back below to put on my new cufflinks and find my ally, who had proposed a walk on the deck to steady my nerves for my first dinner in public. At first I had eyes only for my jewels, but then I felt the excitement of escape as I looked back at the three skyscrapers of Buenos Aires – the Comega, the Safico and the Kavanagh – tied to the receding coastline like tree trunks supporting the scratched, smoking and curling amethyst, the crown of the great ombú of the sunset. I thought of the song, 'It's leaving, the boat is leaving … the steamer's going too…' that I'd sung on those endless afternoons at the estancia, clutching a postcard of a clumsily drawn waif in her orphan's uniform waving her hanky as the boat headed out towards the horizon. Her face said *Bon Voyage*, the boat said To Europe, and Tía Teodé was President of the Sociedad de Beneficencia orphanage. None of these left-behind moments could affect me now. Never again. This time it was me who was leaving them behind. I don't mind one bit, I thought, remembering my brother and sister, and how we'd spent the last afternoon locked in the most unexpected of embraces and caresses and goodbyes before I'd boarded the train for Buenos Aires, leaving them to the dogs and horses and servants, with whom they — unlike me — got on so well.

I leaned on the rail, which was sticky with new varnish. The ship ploughed forward, parting the brown water that was turning purple, and throwing it aside.

'Totola, we don't have to go back, do we?'

'No. But we have to drown first.'

22

LIKE somebody brought up in a house where parties were never given, and the chandeliers never lit, I was impressed most of all by the light in the dining room. It radiated from the ceiling, from its edges, without a visible source, and bathed the whole room. It also seemed to enhance our differences, and I was conscious that my aunt had taken my arm as we entered the room. I felt up to it in my grey suit and blue silk tie, and my amethysts, although for once my shirtsleeves were too short, and I had to pull them down to show off my cufflinks. There was something in that insolent clarity of light that made me conspicuous.

You could see everything, the captain's long table beneath a modern tapestry with yellow crabs and purple mermaids, the big round table where the eight members of my family were already seated, the Argentine hair gel, the exuberant hairdos of the ladies with their naked shoulders, the jewels, the black and white waiters coming and going. But no other child.

The *maître d'hôtel* approached us. '*Madame de Uriburu? Suivez-moi, je vous en prie.*' The little satin shoes with their diamond buckles began to waddle over the carpet, in their eternal first position.

As we passed my parents' table, Tía Teodé didn't stop, but bowed an amiable and distant greeting, which I felt I must copy. The men made to get up, and behind us I heard my father's laugh.

'What a couple!' he snorted to the vast dining room, with the brashness of an unloved adolescent.

And like an unwelcome echo, Clara's voice, 'Tía Teodé, you don't know what you've got yourself into.'

A table for two awaited us, set apart against the wall,

gleaming white and with a linen dove at each setting. I locked with the *maître* over the chairs, in a fight to pull out my great-aunt's. I sat, unfolded the dove on my knees, and with a trust never again to be repeated, abandoned myself to my first lesson in refinement.

Lonely people, when they offer themselves, can be stronger than a whole family. Tía Teodé had had time enough to concentrate her powers, since she had spent forty years dedicating herself to her husband, and the last two to his memory. She had also reached that age where the first years, those years I was living, become the most important; and perhaps in that elephant's memory of hers they now offered up sweeter and clearer images than those of her life with Otramamá's brother. And so she was like a pedantic girl, with a strong need to talk in that scolding and delighted tone of hers, humourless but full of giggling conspiracy against that table of grown ups who knew nothing. We sat there, she with an air of conscientious and chaste triumph at her kidnapping, and she inspected the way I placed my hands next to the plate and then changed glasses to read the menu, her tongue poking out between her thin, pursed lips.

'Ah! The *Soupe de la Grande Tante*, that's a good start. No consommé, Martinete, but a lot of literature. It was the favourite soup of Châteaubriand, the cauliflower cream that Madame Récamier served him when he dined with her, almost every night. And don't make faces, the cauliflower is mixed with milk, cream and the yolk of an egg, and it tastes of heaven. I remember it very well because I gave the recipe to the chef at Paillard's, who didn't know it. Pepita Errázuriz, who would snub us when we first called on her in Paris – she was mixed up in the intellectual set of her Aunt Eugenia, who was a friend of Picasso and Apollinaire – anyway, in the end she accepted all our invitations, and how she licked her lips when this was served. And after that we'll have the *poularde* with truffles. You must have a proper meal, even though it's hot tonight. Otherwise you won't sleep, you're too excited. And you must have wine, one doesn't eat without a glass of wine.' Her nose twitched.

This wasn't greed, it was the schoolmarm in her. The red wrinkle between her brows, which could have been a broken vein, but expressed mortification better than her eyes, had vanished.

'Look, it says *Poularde du Mans* – Mademoiselle Maillard, you know, Otropapá's governess, she came ...'

'Forget your grandfather's passion for France, forget Maipú, that family of loose women and stupid men. *Il y a une belle différence entre Paris et l'estance!* You're going to see that for yourself. There's nothing worse than an armchair traveller – your grandparents are a good example. It's so Argentine. Le Mans is where the best chickens are bred, there and La Bresse, and this dish should be called Chicken in Half Mourning. Poor love, you'll never taste the real thing, because the Mère Fillioux is dead, and her successors aren't up to it. Pancho and I used to make a pilgrimage every year from Vichy to Lyon. The Mère was on her last legs by then, but she came to the table herself and carved the *poularde*, and the truffles gave off a fragrance that made you dizzy.'

'The *Petit Duc* at the estancia was made in Vichy. It has rubber tyres, and they used to harness it for Otramamá ...'

'Don't interrupt me, and shut up about the estancia. Now I've forgotten what I was going to tell you.'

'But you never forget anything!'

'Ah yes, *la Volaille Truffée Demi-Deuil*. Poor Pancho, he was so greedy and spoilt, like every son of a criollo mother. Just like you, Martinete, and you're cheeky with it. But this trip will cure you. We girls of the family were treated quite differently. Once my mother decided that we should make our brother's beds, like Martha of Bethany. I refused –

I was very rebellious – but now I think she was right, at least about women's education. While our husbands have been throwing the Republic to the dogs, we've been running the Sociedad de Beneficencia, practically Buenos Aires' only public welfare service for women and children, as if we were Prussians. For a hundred and twenty years. Anyway, when I try to understand what went wrong, why we have fallen into this hole, I get very confused. It's our fault, that at least I know well. We opened the door, and it never occurred to us to defend ourselves, and these thugs jumped into our beds.'

Her words combined with the food and the wine, and although the story wasn't new to me like they were, I was thrilled. This was the way to live. The best things of the past, linked to adventures I would seek out. This idea made me terribly happy. At some point in my life, very early on, I had been admitted to The Very Ancient and Noble Order of the Name. Names heralded stories, and were the only things that took root in my head. I couldn't really concentrate on a story unless it came with a name attached. Stories without names weren't really stories, just as people without names were insignificant. There were two exceptions to this rule of mine, and they were connected to God, and to the beating of my heart. If God appeared in a story, names weren't necessary because I knew and never doubted this truth, which sometimes made me weep with awe and gratitude – that God loved all of his children equally. And as for the beating of my heart, it was enough for the story to feature a lost boy.

Our small table seemed to sit within a dome of silence. It didn't occur to me to look around, or focus on the din, which scarcely reached us. I felt as though we were in one of those interiors, captured with a fine, hard line at the end of the Middle Ages, in which there are two or three objects and a lot of space, and within it a monk sitting at a table appearing to study, but actually he is waiting.

'This bird can't compare with the Mère's, but it's not bad, although the truffles are really there just for show. Eat slowly, savour the different tastes. *Les nuances*, my darling, those shades we are so in need of, they are only there when the tide of coarseness recedes, and since we are drowning in coarseness, we must escape to Europe every six months. Let's have *coeurs à la crème* for pudding. I want you to try everything. Ignorance isn't just a flaw, it's an illness. There's so much to teach you! And don't ask what for, please, you'll remind me of that salteño cousin of your grandmother; a rich, spoilt only son, when his mother told him to get out of bed, he'd answer in that funny sing-song voice of his, "What for Máama, just to be stáanding up?" I'd have liked to know them better, those salteños, but Pancho never took me to Salta, though we often went for cures at the spa at Rosario de la Frontera, just round the corner. The few I met were terribly chippy, I think Pancho was a little ashamed of them. I remember one time at Villa Elisa a little boy, one of the ten thousand cousins, marched up to me at breakfast and told me his dream about the Devil. "Do you know, Señora, who the Devil was? He was porteño." The Uriburus liked to romanticise Salta, but they kept it at a distance. Your grandmother talks all the time about her Señor de los Milagros and the mountains covered with spring flowers, but she only went there once. I started going after Pancho died, and I've found that I have to keep the candle burning. The last time I went they'd plastered over Don Francisco Uriburu's name on the façade of the children's hospital, which he paid for. It cost me quite a bit to have it put back. In our country everything gets lost, everything is forgotten. And none of us can escape from that huge sense of inferiority. The salteños tried to cover it up with their terrible pride of blood. For them, no porteño was well-born, what with Don Francisco de Aguirre and the caste of Saint Teresa of Avila. But for all their Conquistador blood, they still felt provincial in the capital. And they couldn't forgive us Alvears for being so grand. Mind you, who could! They went on about how General Alvear was jealous of San Martín, but they just didn't want to face the truth — that the two men were brothers. It's well known that San Martín was an Alvear bastard.'

I was spellbound. Tía Teodé was pulling the Father of the Country down to an unseemly role in her family saga.

Her commanding voice dropped to a genteel murmur. 'It all happened when Don Diego de Alvear, Governor of the Jesuit Missions, was sailing down the Uruguay. He fell for a lovely Guaraní Indian bathing at sunset, naked I suppose. The child was sent to be brought up in Spain.'

Then, her voice rising again, 'But San Martín was lucky, he didn't have descendants to dim his glory. Instead there's us — we are the dead weight in the General's ship of fame. The people of the Argentine are consumed with envy, just like in Spain, where the tourist guides make it clear they resent the fact that one can travel, and they can't.'

What did it matter whether this solemn blend of luxury and madness was the truth? The women of my house had crammed my imagination with their visions, with family epics in which the main characters, like in Homer, were always well born. They had tricorns, tiaras, capes, ponchos faded by their trials, gloves and staffs of office; they were Dons of *de* and *y*, they were not good but powerful; and their defeat, which on one side of the family seemed constant, had earned them their statues. The enemies closed the shutters of their houses in the face of such radiance, paid for by the people, as always without name. The Recoleta wasn't big enough for them, nor the principal churches, and their corpses hissed with rage on being thrown into the sea. Their shrouds were the flag and the habit of St Francis, a rough leather saddlebag on the Andes, and a silver urn in the Cathedral of Buenos Aires. As wives they took first the

Ñustas, the sisters of Atahualpa, and only later their own cousins. They didn't stoop to identifying with the Republic, it was the Republic that fed on them, and the history of the Republic ends where the family ceased to lead it. It went on breathing, all right, just like Venice after Napoleon, but senselessly, exhausted.

I would dress like Tía Teodé, I thought as I looked across at her, not like she is now, but as she did when she was young, when she married. She didn't even marry in white, the beast, but in apricot – what next! How disappointing, a bride who wore apricot, but all of Buenos Aires was there, and she must have convinced them that apricot was *the* elegant colour for a bride, that to dress in the colour of a fruit which always looks better than it tastes was the thing. She tells me that flowers were hung from the ceilings in baskets on that great day, and that the flowers told emblematic stories of felicity and fertility and the cornucopia of untold riches; but the poor girl didn't have children, which of course is why I'm here. And then a train was waiting for them at the Casa Amarilla, that station at the foot of Lezama Park, and the coach was filled with more flowers and it took them all alone to Villa Elisa, the copy of Chambord which had just been finished, to start their honeymoon.

And if I dressed like her, and dropped that long, deep curtsy when they sing 'Les Roses d'Hispahan', and swoon with love and sadness, then perhaps I'd be left alone, and I'd feel at peace somehow, so that I could go and play rugby, because when I do play I get carried away and I'm not bad at it, and I like being with the other boys, but then when I'm alone I can't stop reliving those memories that only I know, and that I prefer to the prattle of the boys. Who can I tell them to? Did she look like a statue as she came into the church? Her fingers were already bent, but she was the eldest like me, and she was marrying the eldest, and she was the first granddaughter of Papá Alvear, who had hundreds of thousands of hectares. I'm sure she was like a statue, and that she didn't look at anything, not even when she reached the altar and her bridegroom, she looked beyond the altar, beyond the Crucifix, she was always so proud.

'I've always been so disgusting.' But she meant that everything disgusted her. Who would she marry, when she walked on her wedding day up the aisle of the Iglesia de la Merced, fixed on that point beyond her groom, beyond the bishop, beyond the altar heavy with lilies and arums? 'God will punish me for being so disgusting.' And she couldn't stop looking at her finger. 'Put on the big diamond,' I said to her. 'Very well, just for you.' 'Put it on and I'll kiss your hand, I'll kiss all your fingers, one by one.' 'What a silly boy, what a great big silly idiot.' And she laughed and pointed at me with her crooked finger. I knew that she liked it, and yet why did she put me in the wrong, as though I wanted things I shouldn't, as though it were bad to want. And her, with her astonishments, her stop-its, her look-but-don't-touch-me's, she sought to convince me that it wasn't her, that it was me who desired what one shouldn't, confusing me, making me feel bad. Or maybe she was right after all, and it was all my fault.

'Everything seems to be going very nicely with my little turtledoves.'

I was woken from my reverie by my mother's aggressive tone. Her bronzed, modern look imposed itself on Tía Teodé's pale features. As usual, I admired the brightness that her beauty took on at night, but this time I noticed a vulgar edge to her. She seemed older than her aunt. I was aware of her jealousy, but this was such a common emotion that nobody in the Calle Juncal took it seriously. Still, as my father always said, Clara could be unstoppable.

'I really can't see, Totola, how you'll cope for months on

end with this child, who thinks that nothing and nobody is up to his standards.'

'Well my dear, for the time being, I'm pleased to say, everything seems to suit him just fine. I've given him Pancho's jewellery, and he's as pleased as Punch. He's even gobbled up his cauliflower soup. Leave it to me, my dear, and I'll return him to you transformed.'

Astonishment didn't soften my mother's face; it hardened it. Her long eyebrows dived together and locked in the V of Snow White's stepmother. Her brown eyes turned green with rage.

'Tío Pancho's jewels! All of them! But Totola, you must be mad. Now I see how you'll send him back. Even more common, a second-rate little Maharajah. This child shouldn't be decorated. He hasn't the looks. And those amethysts would look much better on me. I've just had some Charvet shirts of my grandfather Artayeta altered, divine, in crêpe de Chine, and I don't know how to button the cuffs.'

The Señora's powdered double chin trembled a little. She was accustomed to the feminine wars of Juncal, but tended not to be their target. And her position as kidnapper was a delicate one.

'I think it's much more common to ask for something you haven't been offered. Since when is it the fashion to dress like men? It must be the war. The last war hacked off our hair, this one disguises us as soldiers.'

She managed to keep her features calm, that soft moon face so sparing of signals and so benign, with its round eyes behind round glasses, a granny in her riding hood, so free, thank God, from the porteño *chien* which was storming our little corner table.

'I have some garnet buttons which might do as cufflinks. And they'll look more feminine, too,' she added, in the same coy voice which had revealed to me the riverbank conception of the Father of the Country.

'And now we are going to our cabin, Martinete. You have to start your diary.'

Clara left, grumbling to herself, looking at the floor, and clacking her heels, her usual way of walking on this earth. When I approached the big table to say goodnight, I was glad my cuffs were hidden.

23

BEYOND the horizon – my eyes bored holes in as we glided along the esplanade in our tall car, across which Tía Teodé had been forced to trot to reach her seat, giving me a full view of the black dome of her widow's bum – was not Paris, but Montevideo.

Montevideo didn't disappoint me because I didn't see it. A grey cone of a hill and a port of clear waters, from which the body of my salteña great-grandmother had set off back to Buenos Aires in a black-sailed ship. In order for me to see something properly an image of it had to have been handed down, tablets of the texts of the world, seen through the steam of the bathroom of Juncal by eight hands entwined in a Shiva dance, or by those two with crooked fingers in the sitting room facing the Plaza San Martín. It meant that I formed two different perceptions, one heralded by the imagination, the other real, and this created a double nostalgia, for the memory of the longed-for encounter and for that of the experience itself. Every city would acquire two faces, every parting a double regret. It was as if I clung stubbornly to what I had been told I would see, and then what was before me had to struggle to dislodge the official version, as if it arrived late and a bit soiled. Those hands, if they picked up Montevideo, did so with the fingertips and then let her drop without a second glance.

María Carmen Mendizábal was there to meet us; she would take us to lunch at her house in Carrasco. She was Tía Teodé's Uruguayan sister-in-law, a relationship my great-aunt seemed determined to resist even after thirty years. 'In the River Plate there are three cities that are common,' Tía Teodé used to say, 'Rosario, La Plata and Montevideo. And look what that ass Toto got himself into. That María Carmen is not only common, she's stupid.'

I rather liked María Carmen's pretty, over-painted face, and her efforts, and the frightened volubility with which she treated the eldest sister of her dead husband. But I sensed somehow that her pirouettes were also for my benefit, and so I adopted my aunt's disdainful manner.

'So now it's your turn to be taken to Europe. My boy Ramontchu will be really jealous. Before you came along, he was Teodé's favourite.' María Carmen smiled with a sympathy I didn't deserve.

'I've never had favourites. I take all my nieces and nephews to Europe for their education. Only you, María Carmen, who spends all day reading about kings' mistresses, would say something so silly. One shouldn't have a *faible* for a son, nor should one for a nephew.' My aunt was clearly upset by María Carmen's tactless intuition. The plumes on her hat trembled. 'Though it is difficult to get the idea out of this child's head that everybody dotes on him. And that's his grandmother's fault,' she added, defending herself by shifting the target, 'she has no qualms in proclaiming her weakness to the four winds!'

María Carmen's toffee-coloured make-up turned orange. 'Oh Teodé,' she exclaimed in fright. 'It was only a joke! Your nieces and nephews adore you.' She launched into a list that Tía Teodé cut short with a stare. 'Of course,' she corrected herself. 'Now, Carmencita is waiting for us, just last night she was saying how much she's looking forward to seeing you. As for me, there's no need for me to say ... I'm terrified that you won't like the new house. It's small, but it's free of memories of Toto.'

'Lovely,' said Tía Teodé graciously. 'But to return to your silliness, I must repeat what I said when Toto had the singular idea of bringing you into the family, and you began straight away with your smarminess: It's years since I've cared about being liked, and since Pancho died, I live as I can, and as I should, completely indifferent to this Anglo-mania for "feedback." As Sarmiento used to say, "The lonely bullock licks himself well enough."'

Tía Teodé wouldn't have chosen, as I might, *The Book of Marvellous Stories* from the *Treasure of Youth* series. Instead, pencil in hand, she would have poured over *The Book of Interesting Facts*. Her mind was like a cabinet of curiosities, packed with modern gadgets. Though she only talked to me about the past, she loved anything new, and loved to be *up-to-date*, an English term the smart criollos pronounced with a French accent. Before the débâcle of Perón, who put an end to the great welfare charities of the patricians, she had sought to impose these novelties and inventions on the doctors of the Sociedad de Beneficencia hospitals. This had made her unpopular, much to her own amusement.

Uruguay seemed to me an insipid version of the Argentine. The grand, French, sad Hotel Carrasco, the esplanade of Pocitos, the suburbs of Punta Gorda, where María Carmen really lived, using Carrasco as a better address, seemed off-season even in the middle of January, and the empty suburban wastes stretched away into the sluggish river that was already the sea. Even María Carmen's accent, although the same as ours, sounded flatter and rather twee, with its unexpected *tu* instead of our *vos*.

Still, it was all new, and I fell in love with Carmencita. She was twenty-four. She treated me as an equal and took me to the beach before lunch, fixing me with her aunt's button eyes, which on her were young and deep black, and confided in me that she couldn't make head nor tail of the shorthand typing classes which Teodé was trying to impose on this side of the Plata, having failed for twenty years to make them acceptable in Buenos Aires.

She appeared to me as friendly and calm and neutral, and seemed to expect nothing of me. Perhaps it was our differences that made her appealing – that slight maladjustment between the two shores of the Plata. Her face was pleasant rather than beautiful, she was a tiny bit taller than me, and the skin on her naked legs was very smooth. As we walked on the beach, she threw a stick into the small grey waves, and her spaniel dashed in to retrieve it. Carmencita pulled the stick from his jaws with that natural feminine grace I already found slightly oppressive, like a gift without a donor that sometimes seemed more exclusive than beauty, and threw it back into the placid water.

'When Tía Teodé took me to Europe she was wonderful to me, but I felt smothered. How are you managing?'

I felt trapped. I was managing beautifully, but her question seemed to require a particular answer, and I didn't feel safe in telling her the truth. But my new friend was also offering me an escape route.

'Do you remember how bossy she was?' I said. 'But she gave me Tío Pancho's jewel box, with everything in it. I'd like to show it to you, but I've left it in the cabin.'

I had to defend myself to myself. I wasn't feeling disloyal, but confused — a trap was opening somewhere, and it seemed best to accept Carmencita's opinions.

'Well, she's promised me the big diamond,' she said, 'but only after her death.'

'How can that be so, she always says it's for Toti, her eldest niece?'

'So much the better. We'll see who runs to cut off her finger first.' She looked at me with a calm smile. 'Before it gets cold.'

'Don't be so silly. I know where she keeps it. I'll tell you.'

We were walking quickly over the wet sand, and she appeared to concentrate on the dog, she didn't speak into the wind as people usually do on beaches. Without slowing her pace, she turned her head and fixed her opaque eyes on mine. She had a rolled silk scarf tied around her hair and knotted at the nape.

'It was just a bad joke. I don't need jewels. I'm going to be a nun.'

The surf fanned out on the sand. The sea was very quiet, the only noise was the splashing of the dog. There was nowhere in those runaway mirrors to hide. But that was where I wanted to disappear. Carmencita, unaware she had hurt me, announced that it was time for lunch. The dog shook off the water, and for a second he looked like a glass sunflower. Then he shot off towards the house. Carmencita followed, and I fell back as though I were looking for something. I watched her from behind, fixing her in my memory, feeling abandoned. It was a voluptuous feeling tinged with sorrow, more controllable than love.

As our ship sailed on towards Europe, faithful as always to that which wasn't there, I went on reliving an idealised Uruguay, walking on the beach with my new friend. I strained each day to recapture it, in the sleepy early hours of morning, at bedtime, and in the middle of the day when Tía Teodé locked herself away for the siesta, and there was nothing for me to do. I walked the decks alone and went to the children's games room, which had seemed marvellous when they'd opened it just for me. Now I found I didn't know what to do there, but I went on going, just in case. I wandered up and down, through the library, the saloons, the honey-coloured halls … No, it wasn't then, it was later, Carmencita didn't speak to me first at the door, it was when María Carmen took Totola upstairs, she asked me if I wanted to come and walk the dog, it was hot but the day was white, the beach almost empty. I hated my bathing suit, it was woollen and old-fashioned and made me look fat, but she said it was just the thing for the big waves of Mar del Plata, she didn't seem to be paying me attention, but really she was, she didn't have a boyfriend – obviously not, if she's going to enter a convent, or was that a joke? Why didn't

I ask her if it was a joke? Totola says that she never heard such rubbish, that she's not particularly religious and anyway convents have become quite déclassé these days, but Carmencita is deep just when you least expect her to be, the Uruguayan side has won out and she still doesn't marry — if poor Toto were still alive.

How lovely she was, with her smooth skin, like those older girls who asked me to lunch once at the Ocean Club in Mar del Plata, and called me Artagalleta, full of biscuits, which I thought charming, I like grown up girls, not little beasts like Adela, especially Finita Bullrich whom I saw only once, but will never forget. I've never felt so happy as I did then, we were driving back from the country at night and I was sitting in the back seat next to her and we had been talking, I don't remember what about, and I asked if I could put my head on her lap and she said yes and then everyone fell silent and every now and then a lamp lit her green-checked skirt, and my chest and head were lit too but with an inner light, and I felt something I'd never felt before, as if my chest was being pushed from within by my heart, which was beating calmly in there, but it wasn't pushing for me to kiss her, no, but to prostrate myself before her, as if that door which had started to yield were the door of the tabernacle, and her own heart the host.

24

Now we entered the real sea. An enormous and boring thing, which changed colour with the sun, now and then sprinkled by flying fish.

To find out where we were we had to seek out a little red flag stuck to a pin, which moved forward day by day across a map of blue water that hung on the wall in the top hall, as inscrutable as its liquid prototype. The cloying and impassive eyes of Femme, Ma Griffe, Je Reviens, gleaming inside their glass cases, seemed to punctuate my loneliness, and although I was used to being bored, I began to wonder what I was doing there, walking aimlessly among grown ups who read, chatted, played cards and drank, paying me little attention.

I was Tía Teodé's partner, and both my parents and the rest of the family had abandoned us to what they conveniently imagined to be our honeymoon. When they saw us coming slowly along the deck, me carrying my great-aunt's rugs and papers, they vanished in the most scrupulously discreet way, as though in respect for our great passion. And Tía Teodé, surfeited with the little lessons she limited to mealtimes, relaxed into reading, embroidery; and although she urged me to follow suit, leaving me *Eulalie ou Le Grec sans Larmes* open on the cabin desk, my concentration didn't go that far.

I got to the point where I didn't know what to do with our love. The boat was like a palace without secrets. The opulent saloons welcomed me, but if I opened a drawer in the way I always did at Juncal, I discovered clean and empty spaces, at most a matchbox or notepaper embossed with that ship I had so recently thought marvellous, instead of all those letters, opera glasses, parasol handles, photos, Easter candles, aspirins, *souvenirs pieux* and First Communion stamps, each embalmed in its own, tormenting perfume.

Ping … pong … ping … pong … the small, light ball sang on the deck with the tension of two cousins who would kill to win. My mother and Tía Isabel were making these arching, clicking sounds over the silence of the siesta, although really it was first broken fathoms below by the scream of the ocean as it was sliced by a keel of thirty thousand tonnes. Ping … pong … ping … pong, my arrival made no impact on their silent duel. Mamá, her cork sandals adding ten centimetres to her height, her shark-skin shorts even smoother than her cheeks, was immune, indifferent, because she was facing that witch Isabel, armed with her superior serve.

'Why have you left Totola on her own? You should keep her company, instead of running after me,' she snapped angrily, without glancing at me, consuming the jumpy ball with her frown. 'And stop mooing Mamá, Mamá like a calf, specially when that nice Monsieur Couturier is around.' She trounced her cousin with a smash.

Everyone had paired off. And the rules of Juncal had changed, there were no mothers to hand, the Niñas who'd spent most of their days on shore waiting for me had opened the door and slipped away, each with her partner, or in search of one, while I was stuck with my choice, which I still liked to think was the best, except that it was turning out so suffocating, so exclusive, that my prize was becoming a prison.

But I lie, because it's only now that I get it wrong composing these misunderstandings à la Marivaux to add salt to the writing. Whereas in those first days I didn't see anything beyond Totola's lashless eyes and dead silk cheeks, lashes that had fallen with age but were once there, not like Otramamá's which didn't grow at all, and which only shows that children have no taste, and that they love without the need for beauty, blindly, but with the desperation of those who choose, those who believe they choose.

When the boat docked at the port of Santos, I heard of an expedition to São Paulo. By mid-morning I could no longer bear to gaze at the tropics from afar, and so I went to my parents' cabin to ask them to take me ashore with them. Tía Teodé, after her visit to Punta Gorda, had made it clear she wasn't leaving the ship until we reached France.

The heat was strong, the hills very green, the earth very red and the wharfs seemed oiled, like the slow blacks carrying bananas and pineapples. I didn't like it, one doesn't travel to find that, but to disembark was to break the monotony.

The maid handed me a note in that big, back-slanting writing my mother had copied from Dolores del Río: Martín, We've gone to São Paulo. I'll bring you something. Kisses, Clara.

I felt an urge to sing, full-throated, '*J'attendrai, le jour et la nuit ... j'attendrai toujours ... ton retour ...*' feeling only the senseless voluptuousness of the song. That's what they were for, those love melodies which opened up in my memory like the scent of the datura flower at nightfall. When, dizzy with dejection and a disappointment I was struggling to make triumphant, I reached our cabin, Tía Teodé was waiting for me with my costume.

'Why should we care whether we were invited, Martinete, we're much too busy. You'll see, they'll fall flat on their faces when they see you at the Crossing of the Line, dressed as a *pescatore napolitano*. I've already cut out more than twenty fishes in crêpe paper.'

I had begun to dread the empty days ahead. But that same evening, on the screen of the ship's cinema, Bertrand du Guesclin appeared. He was an eldest son, and he was ugly − but to me clumsy rather than ugly, and that clumsiness borne of sheer passion. He had the passionate eyes of the unloved, and the disconnected gaze of an animal, and his forehead was wet with blood. The blood would never be washed away, because the King dipped his finger in the wound and crossed it over the spread eagle on the boy's shield, so that it would remain as a mark of his heroism.

I was sitting on the floor before the first row, and Bertrand was there only for me. Like me, he wore disguise; and like me, his family had failed to create a proper place for him. But the attraction I felt for this lonely boy who fought for recognition extended beyond his deeds. His keen, bruised face, his eyes that couldn't hide, the strength he was unaware of, like an agonising beauty that didn't exclude me; all this seemed in perfect accord with the soft grey images of the film, a bit damp and lumpy, like much-washed felt toys, and with the language we would hear when we reached France. And best of all, he didn't weigh on me, because he couldn't see me, and yet I could devour him complete, as naked as the Sacred Heart. Dressed in chain mail, his hands on the hilt of the sword that reached his breast as he drove it into the ground, this boy without a den, forced to fight, seemed to me to embrace the Cross, the cross of his solitude. I begged my great-aunt to dress me for the ball as a medieval knight instead of a fisherman, but she refused to squander her twenty little sky-blue fishes.

Later, I realised my position was different to Bertrand's. His achievements had made him chief of a fighting band, mine had reduced me to the position of Tía Teodé's walker. But he couldn't see me, he couldn't see me, and the fine grey light of the film was a relief after the tropical sun. I imagined that light as smelling like the damp books of the estancia, which also held the sun at bay, even if they described the dreams of prim young French girls, rather than heroic adventures. The grey which Europe held. Bertrand's determined gaze would help me see my father's furtive adventures in São Paulo. Determined and aloof. But the band? Would there be anyone to sign up in Second Class?

25

AMONG Tía Teodé's papers which survived the purge she had effected in the last years of her life – in that little sitting room made even smaller by its large plumed portraits, where she sat hour after hour next to the waste paper basket reading letters with a magnifying glass and tearing them up, looking back upon her life as she dismantled it, all alone, childless, another diminutive survivor, a version in negative of those painted goddesses, her clothes increasingly dirty and out of fashion, her maid María even more blind than herself, at least that was her excuse – I found the beginning of a memoir and some letters she had decided to save from the basket. Did she leave them behind on purpose for me to read?

In it was the Uriburu account of her engagement and how pleased her fiancé, mother and sister-in-law were to have appropriated her, but covered up with their usual wit, and more letters from her to her own mother written from the Hotel Pupp in Karlsbad where she was taking the waters with Tío Pancho, in which she revealed a rather innocent filial garrulity. Although nothing in those letters points towards it, I still think she married to protect her family from her father's debacle.

Other loose ends I tie together consist of Otramamá smiling ironically at Tía Teodé cleaning out Lavalle to furnish her mother's house in Avenida Alvear, the bronze dogs of Villa Elisa guarding her sister's estancia, and her will in which she leaves us nothing. Not much to go on really, apart from a faded photo of all the Lezicas together in Villa Elisa in which Tía Teodé, standing next to her seated family – lodged, or perhaps even given asylum by Don Pancho Uriburu in his quinta – reveals a smile of protection and triumph. And then another little story pops up told by Clara, in which Tía Teodé is revealed as an opportunistic Levantine, persuading Otramamá to exchange her inherited silver canteen and its five hundred pieces for an ivory hunting scene I remember as a ponderous copy of a XVII century original, German and clogged with horses, dogs and prey, armours and plumes, overframed in ebony and ghastly which, immune as she was to the goods of this world, Otromamá accepted, much to the merriment of her brother who disclosed to Clara the manoeuvres of his wife, in the presence of the imperturbable wife, at one of the weekly lunches at the Plaza.

So she was avid for things, but above all for the things of others, having allowed her brother to trick her and keep the vast Alvear lands in Santa Fé which in the end they had inherited, in exchange for two or three houses in Buenos Aires; and because she never spoke of money not a word of this was ever uttered.

But this doesn't seem enough, on such flimsy evidence, to justify my suspicion. This woman who hoarded everything, had it photographed and listed, and when the time came to say goodbye to it all, destroyed it, still somehow allowed small traces to slip through.

Of the house of the Calle Lavalle on its slope by the river, demolished and rebuilt as a garage, there is no photograph left, nothing of the pink marble columned façade, or of the hall with its imperial staircase splitting into two branches either side of a wall where the Bouguereau of Abel's death towered over dozens of mismatched paintings, from Christ in the Garden by El Greco, to Beethoven composing the Pastoral Symphony by who knows who. But Tía Teodé had kept a photo of the dining room, if only because something of hers had once been there. Squeezed in between the Louis XIV boiseries hung the great tapestries of Saint Cloud under a ceiling painted with a Venetian carnival, and the largest was written over in yellowed ink by my aunt's French handwriting: 'This is my gobelin, which I had to take down when Enrique Uriburu moved into Lavalle with his ten children and forced us and the Castells to vacate the premises.'

I read in these words a sort of triumphant aftertaste. 'It was I, Teodé Lezica, the eldest great-grandchild of General Alvear and Madame Sanchez de Mendeville, who saved my family from the consequences of my father's death by marrying the Uriburu son of some provincial parvenus with whom, fortunately, I was in love.'

But how would I know this, except by my inventing it. It was my revenge for those stories which diminished my things, because the Señora de Uriburu would never have acknowledged let alone accepted these interpretations, in the unlikely event that they had been true. Of the slyness common to all women, the wound of the serpent's tooth, Tía Teodé carried a higher dose than any Levantine whore. There was no one more determinedly comme-il-faut, no one more tricky. Particularly on the delicate subject of her family. She abused my ignorance with her calculated good manners and I was more than happy to accept whatever she wanted to tell me, much better packaged than the loose and contradictory stories of Clara and Otramamá. All these stories of make-believe. Why is the ground we walk on such a minefield, unbreachable to those who come too close? What is the true name of the secret at the bottom of the well? Perhaps if they could get near they might help us decipher it, the name of that secret we hide so remorselessly and cover over with flashes of glitter.

As I have said Tía Teodé was porteña, a city dweller, never a countrywoman, and so thoroughly travelled that her conversation, endlessly comparing Paris, the villes d'eaux and the great transatlantic ships to the soi-disant modesty of Buenos Aires, had deprived me of the innocence with which any other boy accepts his lot. She couldn't have cared less about my loves, the estancia and the sons of Maipú. With that hardness she treated everything that wasn't hers, the only connection she found with Maipú was the lameness of Tío Pancho. During one electoral campaign the conservative MP Uriburu, driven by his porteño chauffeur, had been thrown out from an open car which had skidded typically on the loose sand of one of our dirt roads and broken his leg. To paraphrase Lady Bracknell, that was all that could be said of Maipú.

I don't remember any mention of the bounteous plains which had enabled her Papá Alvear to offer for her wedding the great house with its river view and terraces with marble fountains, and which had allowed her mother to live in the palace at the corner of Alvear and Rodriguez Peña, inherited and sold by Tía Teodé before I was born.

Perhaps because her brother had dispossessed her of their land, but of fields and of what they produced and of their moving memories, silence. Nor did it ever occur to me to mention it. Porteña, Lezica, international traders, controllers of the Cabildo, you name it. Her mind looked beyond the sea like the eyes of Columbus on top of his column, offering his back to the world he had discovered, focusing outwards beyond the lion-coloured river to that space crossed by storks carrying Parisian babies and by the soaps English invaders used to seduce Madama Mendeville, another emblematic Porteña, whose love of land stopped at the suburb of San Isidro. For her great-granddaughter land went a little further, to the church of our Argentine mother, the Virgen de Luján, founded by Don Juan de Lezica y Torrezuri, reached by its pilgrims after walking through a day and a night.

Faithful to her silent mandate, to be recognized as the living, much travelled, suffering, solemn and rather better built version of our Pyramid of May, I will use my aunt as an emblem and group around at her feet, perhaps, the other women, I knew to embolden her profile. Just like as the Pyramid, with its neoclassical simplicity amidst the poverty of the young Republic, needed the exuberance of the May Revolution Centenary and the glorious Argentine at the top of the Monumento de los Españoles, to be more true to her and her choir of disdained criollas. The shabby Pyramid, then, and the big-boobed Monument, with its garlands of rounded and ephemeral triumphs.

As for Otramamá, we know that she pined for the smell of asphalt melted by the Christmas heat. Pepa and Tina had always detested the estancia. Only Clara loved it, and with a devotion that aroused suspicion like a rebel's rosette. But still she only mentioned it priggishly, harping on about her imposed confinement with her great-aunt in that heat, and of all times at the start of the dancing season. I too was confined there, but for the whole of the summer. Could it be for that reason that I loved it so, that castle of mine, of worse heat and worse abandon, that prison from which Tía Teodé rescued me.

The happy see nothing, not even their happiness. The thousand eyes are those of the suffering. And the hungry heart. It is the framework of all that our memory cherishes. Prisons, from Fabrice del Dongo's, Albertine's, Dostoevsky's gulag, have been described with more care than houses. And of the houses how many of these were not prisons?

Those porteñas who were meant to like the countryside, they didn't seem to recognize it. They knew nothing of birds, or trees, of Hudson, Sarmiento, or the gaucho epic *Martín Fierro*, let alone flowers. They repeated the same stories, like terminus stones limiting and defining the life of the family, not with the head of a bearded god but with light, funny anecdotes, a small drama, trips of a bygone luxury between the estancias with cars and chauffeurs and grooms in which the only fun lay in something not working, and the most fun of all was to get stuck in the mud, but with no particular emphasis, no obsessions, no *route barrée*.

They spoke without depth, but also without concealing. And the bankruptcies, and the suicides? Because the scars are there. They must be. Or is it that in that society of pumice stones one can live, survive, eat, sleep and laugh, and finally die, completely immune to disaster. So then, my work is not so much one of archaeology, but of imagination.

To find them I have to scratch my own scars. Just as one paints the portrait of another with one's own, not the face but the expression of that face. Literature doesn't make use of archeological findings, it is made up by the imagination. The lives of the house of calle Juncal are not the lives of the niñas de Artayeta; I have to trace a replica of their shadow.

'Niña Clara, the majordomo is waiting for you with the horse. He sent the new peoncito to let you know.'

'I'm coming Anselmo, I'm coming. Could you bring me some more coffee, please.'

'Clara, look at everything carefully and when you come back you tell me all about it. You and Bebé are my eyes, but you more, because Bebé has a weakness for that majordomo, and I don't trust him.'

The Señora de Lynch spent four months at the estancia but never went out beyond the park. This apparently was in expiation for the death of her husband after thirty years of marriage. A tall and good-natured estanciero, great-nephew of San Martín, several times mayor of Maipú, a glutton whose popular portrait was in every rancho, much more loved than the heirs of the blood, and who had fostered his wife's orphan nephews, Otropapá, and his elder brother, Tío Bebé.

Tío Bebé ran the estate although there was little to do, its ten thousand acres being let. The majordomo, Juan Claro, was crafty enough to rent one or two thousand and juggle the figures, but my uncle loved to drink maté with him, seated on two short-legged benches by the coach-house door looking towards Kakel and chatting about horses. Tío Bebé took horses seriously, he bred them tall and strong, and rode them in the estancia with recado and bombacha, an old fashioned recado long and flat and not the tight little boat favoured by the peons. On his rides at Palermo he changed into breeches and rode on an English saddle.

Clara went walking to the stables under the tall planes of the Calle Verde, in the yellow light of the morning filtered by the still fresh leaves of December, without looking beyond her shiny boots stomping on the shaved grass. She had her blue riding skirt on, and a jacket and a tie and a hat. She liked Juan Claro, who had a way with ladies, but she didn't like his relationship with the Señora de Lynch, and was even more bothered by her own role as a spy.

But the grandmother and the youngest of the house protected each other and Clara felt the pride of her loyalty. On top of that the estancia was there for the two of them, and nobody else, apart from Tío Bebé, so terribly lonely. The others, the townies of the Calle Juncal, particularly her sisters, had disappeared. She might be missing out on the summer dances but her reward was the eclipse of those two. At last she was the only one, the favourite of the owner of everything. Because though isolated on her second floor, and very quiet, surrounded by her silent maids who sewed as she prayed, the Señora de Lynch was also the undisputed queen of the house of the Calle Juncal.

Waiting for her under the great oak that shadowed the façade of the coach-house, Juan Claro Ledesma pulled off his hat and smiled at her with his cunning eyes.

'Good morning, niña, how are you, ready for our ride? Today we are going quite far, to the end of the estancia, I want to check the laguna of Yamoidá, how swampy it is. If it's too heavy we'll have to move the cattle.' He pronounced it Yamuidá and the cows were his. He wore a light cotton jacket and grey bombachas, a scarf of green and pink silk around his neck, held a silver braided whip in his hand, and if his boots lacked the polish of Clara's, cut out of a colt's rump by the famous boot-maker Fagliano, he looked quite elegant.

Juan Claro was the son, grandson and great-grandson of puesteros of Miraflores going back more than a hundred years. His narrow face had the paleness of rainy weather, not of the hard sun of those lands, the same with his colourless eyes which contrasted with the round black buttons of his wife in the middle of her wide and flat Indian face cooked in the Asturias of Spain, the only corner of the peninsula untainted by Moorish blood. The descendant of our puesteros and the old maid of Juncal controlled together the paradise missed by Madame Lynch during the rest of the year and it had fallen to Clara to be the uneasy witness of that power.

But like Tío Bebé she found the majordomo agreeable, with his good humour and his compliments: 'The Niña Clara sits nice and straight on her horse, just like the Señor, both really good riders, the only ones.'

'Niña, I had the Alazán saddled for you. Orders from the Señor. He wanted you to try him. He said you'll like him. He's a bit hard on the mouth but tame enough, anyway you don't want them that tame, do you? And also he's too big for you, but then he who commands...' Juan Claro's irony annoyed her. Clara felt that he was up to something, and using her for it. But what?

The Alazán was a shiny monument, with the curved head of a ram, a defect as unforgivable as the thick ankle, but more than enough presence. With his finely braided reins, great silver disks on his bridle, and English black saddle, the horse appeared distinguished and discreet, like Otropapá. Brown and black. The majordomo made a stirrup with his hands and arranged her skirt around the pommel. The horse snorted and pranced a few dislocated paces. Up there Clara smelled the stable dung, the horse's hide, the fresh and bitter kerosene from the brick floor of the coach house, the heat on the grass and the leaves, she felt the unquiet trembling under her, and realized that she was happy.

They made their way under the poplars of the curved Calle de Kakel, even taller than the planes of the Calle Verde with its black and cracked columns and sticky leaves, towards a gate that had been swallowed by the light.

Juan Claro was riding his grey mare harnessed with the modest luxury of his position, but something, the smaller size of his mount or the weight of centuries or whatever, had reduced him to the place of a groom whom the niña up there, both joyful and distrustful, was deigning to let him accompany her in order to open the gates and tighten her girth when necessary.

Clara was aware of that, but instead of ignoring it as usual, she decided to pair it with the majordomo's sarcastic tone, which she picked up on now after Madame Lynch's recommendations. So that's what it is, me higher than him, me the daughter of the house? And so what? It's true, any-way – but what a bore, the weight imposed on us by the resentment of those who control us by their service, who are meant to be there to love us, am I not fond of them? – though it's not easy, obviously, it's a real bore, particularly in the estancia with its independent life, that seems to function alone, and everybody free and so happy to see us after a year of absence, not like at the house of Juncal where servants were servants and served us without talking, the estancia more valued, more dreamt about, but far away and mysterious, and all of a sudden with a resentful majordomo. This upset the bliss of the radiant morning.

But the Alazán danced of its own accord. The moment

they reached the fields he started to pull on the bit and Clara felt the deliciousness of driving an enormous and well oiled engine. Tío Bebé knew about these things and had offered her a finely matched opponent, she with her instinct to fight and win. What did she care about Juan Claro's prickliness when she was mounted on that flower of a horse?

'Let's canter.'

'Steady, niña, steady. One goes out to the fields at a walk. What kind of horsewoman are you?'

'Juan Claro, this horse is dying to start, and I want to try his canter.'

'Fine, if you say so. But only until the corral, no more. You know it's getting hot and we have more than two hours to reach Yamuidá.'

'Two hours if we just walk. And it's not at all hot, it's just lovely,' and Clara sent him a smile that made him shake his head.

The canter of the Alazán was short and easy, a rocking chair. It was strange that he could rest those big hoofs so softly. It was true that the spring had been rainy and the Potrero of the Lecheras had grown a mattress of thick juicy grass, but still. Clara felt a wave of love for her grumpy old Tío Bebé. What did she care now about her sisters dancing at the Alvear, on a horse they were just sacks of potatoes. Why be bored by her great-aunt's old stories over tea with scones and brown and yellow cake, when she had come to know them by heart and love them. On top of the Alazán, who pulled her gloved hand but whom she knew how to stop because she wasn't afraid of him and the horse sensed it, nobody could match her.

Clara didn't pay any attention to the landscape, though the small lagunas were boiling with birds. The ducks whose brown-grey plumage the colour of burnt winter grass looked much too poor between blue water and green shore took flight instantly, frightened and bashful, but the teros reales allowed themselves to be admired in their black and white gala robes, slowly and elegantly lifting their long red legs one after the other amidst the musical swirls of the grey plovers and the ear-piercing din of our tiresome lapwings, their vulgar and raucous cousins, called just teros. The cows, red and fat, let their overgrown calves go on suckling and looked at you with their shiny, dark and empty eyes. All around the plain offered itself with placid desolation.

Without hurrying they crossed enormous fields which all seemed alike, La Manga, The Stream, The Sluicegate, Trinidad, La Niñita. Juan Claro had his way, there was not much cantering. Every now and then a larger laguna broke the general indifference with the mystery of its reed beds. They got wet crossing the stream of Santa Helena with the water up to the horses' flanks. At last, after the prescribed two hours, they arrived at the wide white beach of Yamoidá.

There was no muddy swamp to be seen, only a great sheet of luminous water where the cows were drinking happily without having to move too far in. What was this story cooked up by the majordomo?

'Juan Claro, why did you bring me here? So far, and now it really is hot. What's this all about?'

'Just to make sure... but as we are here there's something I would like you to let the Señora know. I could have spoken to the Señor Bebé, but then you know, the Señor... Anyway, it is you, niña, who has the Señora's ear.'

'Where did you get that from? The Señora de Lynch doesn't listen to anybody, least of all to me.'

'Nóo, nóo... Young and tiny as you are you are her favourite, Rafáela and I talk about it. Serve the quince jam which the niña Clara likes, and that chocolate pudding, and so on. She doesn't know how to spoil you enough. Didn't she send to England just for a crop that you admired in San Carlos?'

'Oh, really? But enough of your flattery. What do you want?'

'Well, since you ask. We are having problems with the puesteros, they're too old, they were taken by Don Julián years ago and they just do whatever they like. The Señora doesn't want to hear of changing them. What Don Julián decided once is sacred, as you know.'

'But, what does Tío Bebé have to say?'

'He loves them even more than the Señora. Eustaquio Lara taught him how to ride, you know...'

'We are not going to get rid of Lara when he is on his death bed. It is you, Juan Claro, who wants to throw out the old puesteros to put in your own people. I've already heard that you want to take over the fields that Fontana is giving up. What more do you want?' Prickled by the tension that had been building since her great-aunt had set her the task of opening her eyes and finding out the majordomo's intentions, she said at last in anger, 'Is that it? Do you want control of everything?'

Her nerves transmitted themselves to the Alazán, who started walking sideways. Juan Claro might have been crafty but he had a short fuse. He exploded.

'Cará...cho! I haven't worked for this family all my life to end up insulted by a girl. A girl...a ff...,' there he bit his tongue, 'even is she is granddaughter of the patrona. Caracho! You're so accustomed to rule that whatever suits you becomes the law. The law for everybody. You even believe that all the gauchos of Maipú were born to serve you.'

The Alazán leapt. 'Careful!' – Clara shouted, not knowing if to the horse or the majordomo.

The jump unseated her and she lost the reins. A loud Oh! was heard, she grabbed the saddle with both her hands, and the horse bolted into an unstoppable gallop.

He rushed back towards the estancia, a long blue wood to the west seated on the waters of the mirage, leaving behind the laguna and the majordomo who whipped up his grey pony furiously without any hope of reaching that thoroughbred which had been oat fed for the Christmas races. Even in the throes of her worry Clara recognized the vertigo of the rush, the noise of the air, the successive odours of the field made stronger by the heat, and on top of all that, and with more fear and vertigo still, the beat of the Alazán's hooves which at last had recovered their dimensions.

It was very dangerous, but then it was her, *sans peur et sans reproche,* and the urgent thing was to recover the reins which had slipped towards the ears of the beast. The moment Clara bent over his neck, which seemed terribly long, the horse, remembering the races, accelerated. The field was so large that she couldn't yet see the wire fence that would have stopped them, but then so much the better, because as he stopped sharp her mount would have dispatched her flying over his head to be cut into pieces by the barbed wire. At last, crawling like Jackie Kennedy over the presidential limo but with none of that cowardice which went uncriticized, or like a blue caterpillar on the horse's neck black with sweat, she got hold of the reins and managed to resettle herself on the saddle. She pulled, but the Alazán had bitten the bit. Fine, at least she had the reins in her hand and her legs gripping his sides. She started to saw with the bit, to push the wet neck with her right hand to turn him back towards the laguna. Slowly he started to veer, but he never stopped galloping.

Now she was in control. They passed the majordomo like a flash and Clara sent him a smile of triumph. The Alazán approached the beach of Yamoidá without faltering, as if he had gone blind. Clara had lost her hat and her long hair was falling over her eyes, but the rocket beneath her and the exhilarating smell of dead water and the screaming of the frightened swans and the imminence of the plunge made her shout: 'Go!'

Horse and Amazon were lost in a sun lit geyser of

yellow water. The Alazán went on jumping heavily until he stopped, and Clara feeling her feet swimming in her boots burst into a loud laugh.

It was midday.

26

BUT THE other criollas that I had come to know,
living elegantly and pale in Buenos Aires, in their vast
and ugly apartments furnished with presidential leftovers,
seemed like jumped-up porteñas, their lack of French taste
a sign of the patio where they were born. I found them
enchanting. There was something weightier, older and
more mysterious in the bones, bleached bones it seemed, of
these tiny women bred in those locked-in valleys, isolated
by leagues of desert even a hundred years after the publi-
cation of *Facundo*.

Otramamá treated all this with pious and false respect.
She wouldn't have touched Salta with a barge pole, never
saw her salteño family, but shared with the other heiresses
of the Casa Rosada: her sister-in-law Copeta Roca and her
cousins Juarez Celman, all of them products of the need to
balance the power of Buenos Aires with imported chiefs of
state, a passion for the capital that Tía Teodé would have
found excessive. For a start genealogy, that demon of the
provinces, sounded Chinese to her.

'You can't imagine, greedy-guts, when one of those chat-
terbox cordobesas Copeta Roca likes to invite, started listing
all her thousand aunts. They're not just limited to Córdoba,
God no, they cover Santiago del Estero, Tucumán, all of
that back-of-beyond middle of the country, although curiously not Salta, I wonder why. Well, it's like being trapped
by the obsessions of a specialist, the mania of a turf man
or a doctor, I thought I'd left those horrors behind when
your grandfather lost his money and I stopped working for
the Beneficencia.' I was surprised by her truculence usually
vented on her husband's family.

'And once there was something more, though not at

Copeta's but at the Juarez', one of those cousins of Santa Catalina got going and couldn't be stopped. Rather refined and clever, you know, with that simplicity which I love and I can't help feeling proud of, still it was quite hard to unravel her meaning as her words were pouring out like a torrent, anyway she was saying that the provincial aporteñados were the worst, because it was bad enough with the porteños calling the rest of the country the Thirteen Ranchos, but God help us with those neophytes who despise what they have left behind.

'"I understand that they should find us poor", and she looked around admiring the junk the Juarez Celman's had rescued from their big house in the Paseo de Julio, "but that they should look down at our blood, it's too much. They should know that the Jesuit estancia of Santa Catalina was the grandest in the republic before the civil wars and the growth of Buenos Aires, and as for La Paz" − the magnificent property of President Roca, paid with government grants − "was nothing but a puesto his wife had inherited from Santa Catalina," she said, addressing herself to Copeta. Copeta smiled back with that sly smile of hers. She is funny, Copeta, you never know what she is thinking, just like Roca.'

Otramamá paused, she seemed to want to put some order into her words by looking at the portrait of Wellington by Lawrence hanging on a wall of her sitting-room.

'That well coiffed dwarf started to become agitated. The cordobés' singsong became more pronounced as it occurred to that salteño boy upset by the luxury of Villa Elisa. But don't think it was because of the Juarez' *croutes*. No, not at all.

'So she went on − "The problem is that these displacements can have terrible consequences. Appalling consequences. The excessive vanity, the pride, that first and worst of all sins, the sin that stained the angels, makes them deny their brethrens. How they hurt them... But no, I can't go on. If only you knew..."

'She burst out sobbing, which upset us, particularly after her bishop's sermon. You know how they all have nuns and priests in the family whom they visit daily. You can't imagine the faces of the Juarez; they can be quite silly and looked as if they were expecting a murder. Even Copeta's expression changed, well, no, that would be too much, but her smile went. Me, I was impassive. These provincial convulsions leave me cold. Quite simply because I don't understand where they come from. They seem from another country. Though my poor Mamá came from up there, she never took the trouble to teach me its language, but I've learned something that applies to us all: There's nothing more common than someone poor and well born. Look at Paula Albarracín, Sarmiento's mother, who couldn't accept her best friend's hospitality, and always arrived for lunch with a little bag of provisions. This ridiculous chip was praised by her son in Recuerdos de Provincia. Proud till death do us part, my foot.'

At last the Cordobesa did tell her story; according to my grandmother it wasn't so dreadful after all. In fact, Otramamá had shared all that suffering, although she had never learned or been told of the price paid in bankruptcies and suicides for the sudden transfer of her own family to the capital.

It was the story of a shy and plain girl, whom nobody noticed in Buenos Aires, who woke up to love on a holiday in the provinces. A cousin, a country bumpkin, illiterate and beautiful, looked at her. Perhaps he was also shy, perhaps imaginative, perhaps avid. What the new porteña saw was a centaur covered in leather and dust, svelte and well seated on his mule, he had just crossed the Andes, his eyes as he took off his hat were the colour of forget-me-nots under a mother of pearl forehead and a mane so black that it seemed blue; the eagle nose a sign of his conquistador blood. But her father wouldn't have him. 'Don't bring another beggar to my house. Just when we managed to get out in time. A rover, like Sarmiento's father, with a woman at every cross-road. No, darling, no and no. I don't want another Paula Albarracín.'

The plain daughter ended by dying of tuberculosis and the centaur, who resembled a black headed Achilles, although he must have left offspring in the ranchos, never married.

'She was my half sister. We were the ones who were left behind.' But by the end her eloquence and the sadness of the story had dried her tears.

This quality of the people of *tierra adentro*, as I am try-ing to say, was enriched by a life shackled to the enormous family, the colonial towns, the haciendas of Tacuil, of Maza-sacate, the infinite and confusing cousins of Luracatao and Santa Catalina, and even – though they covered it up and it was hardly noticeable – by the jealous Faulknerian love of a father with a wife and a string of daughters he doesn't want to marry, 'where are they going to be better than at home?' told by the eldest like an old tune first hummed so long ago that it seems to be cherished like an heirloom, the virginal hopeful tune, so modest that when on the edge of eighty she is asked about some boyfriend, and in her criollo openness starts to describe the Hoyos cousin, or better still that other one, a bit short but so clever and funny whom she preferred, and then stops, 'I feel embarrassed,' whilst every so often within the clever, unstoppable, humorous, obses-sive and singsong babble, a line will be picked up that is a hint of the sadness of a hope cut short, 'perhaps we stayed on too long at Tacuil,' a sweet and melancholic beat, 'of course, I'm quite ignorant about love and couples,' which never allows the shadow of a word about the selfishness that kept her caught until the very end. 'One hundred years and seven months, Papá was when he died,' she mumbles with a proud precision that hurts.

What about their moral shape, both peasant-like and aristocratic? The sagas of conquistadors and cattle rustling, family stories and the depredations of jaguars and the song of birds, these they knew well, all equally repetitive and monotonous, the calm of the sleepy chat of the unchanging days, but then what weight there was in this liquor, distilled over so many days, feeding the babble, each word going on beating and repeating itself, every time denser and more hermetic. And what energy wasted in embroidery: they knitted and made lace and embroidered for empty cradles, fit only for those listeners captive to their lullabies.

They were solid, these provincial criollas, fed on corn like in the Mississippi and the Veneto, older than the heroines of Faulkner and Henry James, marked by four centuries of Catholicism, of the tradition of land tenure, of orders to the resentful Indian peons, and of rituals in the patio, which before the ravages of the civil wars would be paved once a year with silver coins brought up from the cellar to be ventilated. They were as bright cheeked and delighted as Isabel Archer, but they were saved from Isabel's Puritanism and guilt, those chimeras alien to the Latin races, by their all-knowing indolence.

Their cousins of the port seemed freer and didn't care about the stories they remembered of their country days. They didn't mention them because they didn't think them important. They had been bred on a boat on the sea.

No, they were not poetical, the porteñas. If anything, those men who disrupted their lives had more imagination. They would never have allowed themselves to follow the wanton path of Isabel, but then they didn't fool themselves in believing that they were capable of choosing it. They were neither independent, nor poetical; they had learned intuitively how to position themselves.

These were positions which hardly budged. When their lives were ending, one could hear a rough noise around their opulent beds where they lay like those saints of wax lying adorned with lace at the step of altars they were meant to shoulder with their sacrifice, a noise of the rusty machine of those early choices, the blinded lighthouse tired of having to show the right course day in day out, sphinxes weighed down by their errors. How few of those well bred smiles were joyful.

The wrinkle of disappointment can be traced from the last daguerreotype of Madama Mendeville, founder of the Society of Beneficence, to the hurt lips of Teodé Lezica twenty years after the Society had been dismantled by a vindictive Eva Perón.

Commanding women who died aware that they had failed to straighten up their husbands and the Republic, and yet there was something moving in the persistence of that affiliation. In their last years they spoke less of their loves than of the country. Perhaps it was more comfortable to project oneself on the vast and shapeless homeland, but it is still surprising that these keepers of houses and moustaches should murmur in the throes of dying: 'Argentina, sweet name,' the password of Rosas' sentries at the Campaign of the Desert.

It was a discouraging homeland, for those porteñas so imbued with Europe. But if the puritanical innocence of Isabel Archer is corrupted by the complexity of a culture she barely understood, the porteñas with less energy and even less curiosity felt easy with the Mediterranean and very much at home in the hotels of Paris where they were protected from the natives by Latin waiters and swarms of Argentine locusts, chewers of velvet and silk. But even more so, more than Achilles and Siegfried, they had been steeped and made immune in the mud of the Plate; deep down they were insensitive to the Parisian chic which had at first caught their attention, fixed for ever on our things, impervious, with their 'what's the need for that?' – 'Ah, another pain in the neck!' – 'Don't all these complications just kill you?' They were branded at birth, like the salmon by the stream of its eggs, with the smell of puchero and patio.

They didn't know that they were saved by their indifference to culture, that of their mother Eve before the fall. Who gives a fuck about Worth, when you are swallowed by the horizon? The same need to simplify which inspired Eugenia Errázuriz to cut down on the furnishings of her house and on Stravinsky's compositions – '*Assez, Igor, arrêtez-vous* là,' was simply the apotheosis of this rejection.

It was not so much a rejection as a withdrawal, a kind of forgetting. They had been born into this enormity, and nothing else seemed to matter. And the disappointed mouth was the scar left by life, just when it was ending and there was room for peace, the bliss without space and without time dreamt by all theogonies, revealed to us, the blessed ones, at birth.

But their instinct forced them to organize as best they could a kind of life to populate that emptiness; the days, so many days because they lived forever, could not be filled with contemplation. Anyway the temper of the race is hardly mystic, so they were obliged to postpone until the very last that encounter which they had always known was waiting for them. Although they didn't appear joyful; they suggested a rather placid exhaustion. Their mothers had obliged them as girls to make their brothers' beds, their husbands offended them with confidences of their escapades, their sons who preferred them to their wives babbled away without listening and only about their worries. At last came the time of rest. They hadn't got it wrong in the end, for what else was there left to do? But still one could sense something heroic or inconsolable as they awaited the arrival of eternity, which they knew to be well-intentioned, with that little grimace of distaste.

27

'.... APART FROM the fact that I fancy Jorge Artayeta, when
he enters the room his height seems to fill it, and when I feel
his bulk near me it accompanies me and even protects me,
though it's not a bulk but a shape, a shadow, while Mariano
Castex is cleverer maybe and with a good career in front of
him as Mama says, though he might amuse me and laughs
and goes along with my jokes like that night at the Hofburg
when my Argentine pride couldn't take it that we had been
stuck in a room so far from Franz Joseph and I forced him
to follow me sliding through doors behind servants with
trays until we'd almost reached the Emperor and Mariano purple with embarrassment and giggling let me pull
him by the hand, that's something Jorge so courteous and
stiff and well brought up would never have allowed, well,
Mariano, he feels easy because of my friendship with his
sister, Enriqueta, and my mother's with his, that fat Susana
Torres. He's too easy, too comfortable, short and blond, he
leaves me cold. He lacks that distance, that unknown land
of a family only interested in itself, which Jorge disguises
under his charming mock-humble good manners, not like
his aunt, I was going to say his mother, no, not like his aunt
Niñita, that huge *énergumène*, with the legs and hands of
an elephant which they themselves think of as a rather
pretty defect, the Madero hands, and she looks down her
nose at you, so thin and straight one can't help admiring
it, it makes me hide my hooked nose, so common for a girl
I think, and so big, under my hat, and of course she doesn't
get my humour or my references, she's so thick and ignorant, though she has a lot of presence, she always seems to
be putting you in your place.

'This having a body next to mine, just there, no need

to touch it, much better not to, I think, or kisses or never ending embraces, or petting, as they call it, horrible word, I wouldn't like any of that, not that it ever happened to me but I imagine that it would all be over in a flash, without me noticing, *entre chien et loup*, and leaving almost nothing, only some memory of a storm, of something exaggerated. Whereas the shadow, would it be the trembling of it? No, it's more that I feel shaken by the presence of the other, it's a warmth, no, an air, a draught, a wind that blows around inside but doesn't leave, doesn't go — like some lover's imaginings of the Guardian Angel?'

Otramamá, seated in her little blue armchair, picked up the book of poems of Marceline Desbordes Valmore she had let drop during her reverie from the hollow between cushion and arm-rest. The ivory chimney of her sitting room with its gilded caryatids smoked. The May evening was getting darker. In the mirror over the mantelpiece she saw her olive face, and over it, like some grotesque crown, the chandelier of Vieux Saxe flowers. She winked at herself half mocking, half discouraged. She often suspected that the faces she pulled in her mirror were just a sign of hopelessness. '... A beauty like Lita Moreno would let herself be reflected without bothering to look. But then what a bore they were, those beauties.'

Otramamá's rooms looked over the garden with the palm tree, which secluded them from the noise of the Calle Lavalle. The city was stirred up by the Centenary, and the house by the visit of the Infanta. The jingoism in the streets got on her nerves and she laughed at the efforts of her elder sister, almost her mother in age difference had it not been that Misia Dolores was still very much alive. How she insisted in trotting after that royal tomboy who spoke like their Spanish maids, just because she had been appointed her Argentine lady-in-waiting! There was even to be a ball in her honour at the Calle Lavalle. How idiotic.

She no longer cared for her country's glory since her father's death four years ago. When she was born he was already an old man. He had occupied so much space in her life; when he abandoned her at the gates of adulthood he had left her hanging in thin air. Was that why she didn't bother looking at things? She hardly saw her own rooms, and the grandeur of the house beyond them. She swallowed it all without even thinking. On the rare occasions she mentioned the years spent in the paternal house, it was to recall the man who had died too early. Papá who spoke French with a Salteño accent, Papá who grew orchids, Papá the Senate, Papá Villa Elisa, who stopped counting expenses when he topped a million, Papá who was asked by President Juarez Celman to save the country from the 1890 crisis, Papá who gave me endless presents, Papá who adored me, Papá, Papá, calling his name after so many years like a widowed swan. And, still grieving for her father, it was as a widow that she ended marrying Otropapá.

But she went on calling for him. Some time after her death, a niece of Madame Lynch told me that on Otramamá's first visit to the estancia she used to be heard calling in a loud voice, Jorge, Jorge, lost in the alien garden.

That famous father, despite his money and power, was always a provincial in the capital. He was an austere criollo, and couldn't get accustomed to the promiscuous extravagance of the port. But still he filled his houses with opulence; as a sort of defiance, the surge of the heir of the old provinces which would leave Buenos Aires down there and reach Europe, a leap-frog of the imagination that would force the porteños to look up, those upstarts who made a triumph of their ignorance.

But chippiness tends to leave us with our arse exposed, and Don Pancho Uriburu was enchanted when a respected porteña like his consuegra Teodelina Alvear treated him with deference. Meanwhile the cousins spent lavishly on adornment. God knows they had eaten cheap matambre in their mutual grandparents' house in Salta. He had the dining room ceiling of the mansion of Lavalle painted with a Venetian carnival, and then he decided that his fat chatelaine at the top of the table needed some proper pearls. Misia Dolores wasn't tall and the pigeon's egg necklace reached the floor. She looked around and in her turn decided that this room which seated thirty guests needed some good silver more than a mistress from Sheba.

Otramamá was born when all that had found its place, but she was marked by its tensions. She was the flower which her father cradled in the biggest tureen, the *doppelgänger* of the Llullaillaco mummy enthroned in ten kilos of silver wrought in Birmingham. So much doting had left her tired. That's why her eyes look so detached in the portrait at the estancia.

'... But Jorge's family is not like that. They are stupid, and happy with it. La Niñita prays and eats, Bebé Artayeta rides, Carlos Madero is building himself a great English house but he doesn't buy good pictures or cultivate orchids like Papá. Jorge is Jorge, who manages to shelter me with his gentleness like the Guardian Angel. Anyway, what am I doing, thinking of allying myself with a family of such idiots whose world is limited to visiting their endless relations? I have none.

'And they look at no one outside their clan, and they certainly admire no one. There is something apostolic about their contentment, as if they had been branded by the epiphany of their precious genes. Ignorant of it, of course, as they know nothing, but active in their bones. Jorge, though, he seems to know things he talks about, Peruvians, or Alto Peruvians or potosinas, paceñas, arequipeñas, cuzqueñas, *et tralalá et tralal*á − *j'en passe et des meilleurs*, like in *Hernani* − which his Mamita brought down to the port. Mind you, Papá also came down to the port with his silver Mestizo kettle and his portraits of morose grandmothers, Papá and Mamá, with blood as ancient as those peruleros, but incapable of their aplomb.

'Jorge's people changed their haciendas of La Paz for their famous desert and they collapsed like a meteorite, crater and all. And there they stayed, stone-like, blind, deaf and dumb. Because if you ask them about their family they don't wax eloquent, like Teodé, who can be tiresome, they don't even bother to answer, as if it was something too obvious to be mentioned.

'At the same time if you pull them out of their hole they lose their footing, like those proud Spaniards I met at San Sebastián, you couldn't talk to them about Europe, they just changed the subject. When La Niñita entered the Calle Lavalle for the first time her face shrunk. The Alvears can be very affected but they are more worldly.

We princes have to woo...'

Otramamá had few illusions about her looks, but she had the instincts of a spoiled princess and it was she who cornered Otropapá with her vivacity. She could run rings around her cavalier, eight years older than her, who had been taken to France as an orphan to be consoled, although the rolling of his rs made her uncomfortable. Jorge Artayeta could be ironic but never lost his composure and his gentleness. Otramamá was accustomed to her brother's cuttingness – 'Pancho is so sharp that you find out too late' – and the put-downs of her sister Elisa, who was jealous of the paternal pampering. From that to the measured, though never pompous, elocution of her prey, his sad and welcoming smile, and immutable good manners... no! definitely, he was not to be trusted.

But then those silences which she covered up with her verve betrayed her. Alone, facing the mirror under her Saxe contraption, she felt pushy and gross.

'... In the end, I only remember my *boutades*, and him

smiling politely. There's nothing like the stupidity of those who trust their cleverness and can't stop talking. And what about the silent strength of the weak? You want to shake them, you stuff words in their mouths, and they swallow them. They go away with their stuttering smiles and leave you as if they had raped you. While it was only me, Mecha Uriburu, I who stripped and displayed myself so shamefully....'

Otramamá was exaggerating. Like anybody who hasn't been met halfway she felt exposed. And her father had always guessed her thoughts. As she had never had to fight with anybody for her first loves she didn't see beyond her nose. Her youngest daughter Clara could have taught her a thing or two about managing men. She was spoilt like Mathilde de la Mole and as blind as her. But nobody less like Julien Sorel than Jorge Artayeta, nobody less seething with revenge, although he was hardly immune, either, to the advantages of an heiress. He would be the fourth Artayeta to marry well, and to ally himself with this rich and vigorous family had its amusing side, and he had managed to push the beauty of her cousin Bebette to the back of his mind.

Otropapá was an orphan. Helena Madero saw her two eldest children die of diphtheria, one after the other: Mariano, named after the colonel of Lavalle, and Marta, after the munificent, child bearing, and I don't know why I imagine melancholic, grandmother Ramos Mejía, who also left her two younger children as orphans. Helena Madero became the mother of these last siblings, La Niñita and Carlos. She was twenty-three when she married the handsome Artayeta and when Mariano and Marta died she sought her lost children in two more, giving birth to Tío Bebé and Otropapá. But when Otropapá wasn't yet seven she allowed herself to be defeated by tuberculosis.

Twice I found out Otrapapá touched by this tragedy.

'I don't want to go back to Tapiales, it makes me feel sad,' he said to me on one of those nights after dinner in the estancia, next to the big stone fireplace of the dining room where we sat alone with our coffee.

'We had gone with Mamá from the quinta Madero to visit Tía Magdalena Ramos at Tapiales. Mamá had a malaise. She spat blood, I think, she was put to bed in the corner room by the front gallery. It was evening, I was left alone in the garden. I could hear the lowing of the cattle being driven to be slaughtered in Mataderos. That mooing that increased my sadness, I always associate it with Tapiales.'

The other time was worse. It still fills me with shame. It was a summer midday in the salita of the estancia. I, who never stopped searching in the deep camphor trunk of family archives, old papers as it read on the heavy key, had found something I wanted to show my grandfather.

'Look at this, Otropapá, a letter from your mother.'

It was a small piece of white paper, foxed, with wide edges fretted like a lace handkerchief, folded with an oval centre smooth like hard silk, where with a childish hand, Helena Madero, as she had signed at the bottom, expressed her kind sweet wishes to her father. But there was something more.

Otropapá unfolded the brittle little paper and found a lock of blond red hair. The wail that shook this tall and measured gentleman froze us. I don't know who else might have been in the room but now I can only see myself and him. My reaction was the one I had learnt in the white bathroom of the Calle Juncal, when faced with any show of intense emotion.

'Otropapá! What is this? Please, control yourself!' It came out automatically like the retchless vomit of a cerebral tumour. I would have been twelve. I note it down with a guilty shame, when I was only repeating my conditioning. But we have never been innocent and baptism is not enough to clean the taint of our original sin.

'… He is not empressé. No, he is not at all empressé. Not with me, anyway. While he is so amiable with everybody else, he does the rounds of all of them sitting next to every each as if he was a crowned head, smiling and asking and bowing, and not at all cold or stiff or genteel, as if he was terribly interested, but I feel that with me he turns opaque.

'If it wasn't so anguishing I could even take it as a sign of attraction, of rejection, of confusion, of fear, of exhaustion, of torment – enough! enough of trying to be funny. What an imbecile, with his flat Chinese face and his long legs and ugly hands, with his mannequin suits and his English shoes, and that accent from neither here nor there nor anywhere, it seems French and is shared by his cousins who were all bred together in Paris with that Mademoiselle Maillard with more tits than the Diana of Ephesus, as they all hung from them, all ages, a herd of Argentine pigs, thirsty for *comme-il-faut*, yes, because though he's not at all affected, not a sissy, he doesn't move an inch from the *comme-il-faut*.

'I don't know why I like him so much, when really he is a bore. It's all the fault of that damned shadow…'

The shadow overflowing with gentleness which Otramamá called on for protection seemed solid, but I wonder if it carried enough strength. What had happened to him in Paris? There, from the beginning, to console him, he was surrounded by the cousins from Kakel headed by its owner, his great-aunt Magdalena Ramos Mejía. Why did he never go back? What wound was hidden under the balm of his affable manners? Because sometimes something ugly would flare up, a sudden temper which would break the skin of his usual meekness, but then the shout would be just as quickly drowned by a snort of discouragement.

And then he lost so much. It was a weakness perceived early on by Misia Dolores, and she left the famous fifth part of her inheritance to Otramamá to staunch the leakage, at least for a while. But those material contractions seemed to be happening far away, or very much beneath the mask of placidity which had nothing foolish about it as he opened himself to the world, a world filtered by the Círculo de Armas but even so crueler than the patio of his Jesuit Colegio del Salvador, with his smile of ironic good humour.

I have seen other faces which didn't reflect failure: Argentine faces, they are quite different from those Parisian ones worked by the anxiety of competition, their grey looks curiously disagreeable, framed as they tend to be by the uniform grey scarf.

The shadow might have accompanied Otramamá during the rest of her life but I wonder if it supported her. And yet who can ever know? How can I discover the smallest trace of truth in those fifty years of mysterious life shared by my grandparents?

I think of those last months of Otramamá's life when she lacked the strength even to utter those horrible neverending sacatuseco-viastuseco-sacatuseco phrases, and Otropapá who became delirious because of a cerebral metastasis of his prostate cancer which his great age had kept dormant. He would look out of his bedroom window and smile with pleasure because he was so rich, as all the buildings of the streets of Arroyo and Esmeralda belonged to him, a pleasure that seemed to contradict his habitual indifference to his relative poverty, while Otramamá seated by the bed held his hand in hers and cried, tranquil and silent, her face still, she wept, without letting go of his hand and without Otrapapá noticing, while he smiled happily with his head supported by the square cushions of stiff linen, feeling expansive because of the revelation of his sudden fortune.

'... Bore? What bore? How do you measure charm when what makes you fall in love is a shadow? As if the solemn height of this thirty-year old gentleman with his useless lawyer's title and his lost lands which his father, a famous spendthrift, had sold remorselessly, this gentleman whom nobody seems to appreciate at home, a marquess of Carabas with neither cat nor boots, who has read some classics out of convention, and with less care than the giving of orders to his tailor about the cut of his sleeves, without wit, without real solemnity, thank God, with something tender and young in his formality, can he be shy? Well everyone's shy, I'm horribly shy but then I look horrible. In the end it is the bulk that kills me, that tall and silent door neither open nor shut, with its shadow that changes with the day but never moves when I get near, as if it were the door itself that follows me.

'"How Metaphysical," my brother Enrique would say, he's the serious one, the philosopher, who hasn't got Pancho's wit. Metaphysical or not, it is not physical, it is not a physical crush, and it's not that I don't find him handsome, he's ten times better than poor Mariano Castex, but he is too elegant and lithe, and at home, except for Enrique, we are *trapus*.

'Ay! Mira que el amor es una mar muy ancha. Here I am, I've spent all that time reading *Madame Bovary* and *Le Rouge et le Noir* and my head is so jumbled up, I don't know where I'm standing. All because of a *coup de foudre*, never, nothing of the sort! It is the invisibly growing shadow of this marionette of the Châtelet which has come creeping up under my feet. Invisible? Growing? How? Just on tiptoe, with no intervention from the marionette. Yo? Argentino! meaning I have nothing to do with anything, a new expression. The idiot would be the first to look surprised.

'Oh God, I feel I'm going mad. The blindness of this bloody love, it's so urgent and blind that it masks any feelings that Jorge might have for me. I can't stop covering them, such as they are, with my own obsessions. They drown me, but if only the puppet would at last say yes, me too, me always, ever since I saw you at the foot of the stairs of Lavalle – I was in white, with white orchids from Villa Elisa on my corsage, and looked ghastly, he must have liked the stairs – anyway, he never said anything, don't you see that I'm raving, I'm dragged along by my words not by my thoughts, words that burst out carrying away prudence, intelligence, imagination, they seem to be sucked in by the vacuum of that shadow, they need to fill it, no, not to fill the shadow with my words when what I crave most is its protection, but the protective shadow has to be Jorge, and it shouldn't abandon me, it shouldn't grow apart, the shadow, Jorge, perfectly signed and sealed, offered by those short fingered hands and the courtly smile, sealed, signed and stamped.

'How thick, how dim, how witless! Where, in any of my novels, have I read that there is even the most minimal security in any pledge, however binding and solemn? Only in incest, like Papá and Mamá who were born and grew up together and it would never have occurred to them to separate. Even Papá who loved me so much had no qualms in dying and leaving me alone.

'Can Jorge's shadow really be the shadow of Papá, Papá's ever-caring ghost who wouldn't abandon me for the world? No, that's an idiotic fantasy, when the charm of this shadow is that it is so long, it stretches from the floor to the ceiling, long and thin, like an angel's I insist, while my saintly Papá was just like the Rey Petiso, the short king with his moustaches and top hats and his short man's dignity, the same as Pancho, which makes them swell up, into even more of a cube and a dwarf, but Jorge bends inwards as if his shoulders which are so much higher than my head would bow to push back the sun from me and his shadow becomes so hollow and sinuous and lilac and deep deep grey but this is an invention of my passion, of course.

'To win it I must stop. I must be mute and quiet, to get him to walk up the famous stairs and have him shown into my sitting room, and me sitting nonchalantly in this blue armchair offering him a seat with my pretty hand, the hand at least is not bad, and dismissing the footman with an air of *princesse lointaine* as if I found it easy, but mainly I have to stitch up this mouth which never learnt to control itself. Anyway, he would never agree to stay alone with me. He is just like a Viennese lady, my angel.

'In the end, this is my last excuse, to pray that his reticence is nothing more than good breeding. Luckily I manage to look at myself from a distance and laugh, a nervous laugh, of course, it doesn't flow from sheer good spirits. But nerves or not it relaxes me, even if the tightness comes back only too soon.

'How long will the shadow last? Will it last a whole lifetime? That double presence which seems to heighten and sometimes even take the place of the real body, and leaves me peaceful in a way the real body never does, and is silent and wholesome which of course suits him beautifully, the mannequin who swallowed his tongue.

'I suppose my own shadow, if only I had one, would drown under the torrent of my chatter, and if Jorge spoke he would disappoint me, as usual with words, and then, couldn't the shadow be the equivalent of his silence, like the condensation of everything that his body can't or won't voice? If that is the case, the dark, the solemn mystery, the mystery of the ghost of the man I love can accompany me always. The best of him, of everything that seduces me and protects me, is his other hidden face that could very well last for ever. Although the shadow of a young handsome man is not that of an old crotchety one. But Jorge doesn't even have any eccentricities, and I don't think he will with the years. He seems as polished as a shiny bobbin and all flying fluff will slide off him. My love, I feel modest about that name, it's too definite, has been concocted in Paris with his air of an Annamite prince just to slide. Yes, the air is Oriental, come to think of it, and the Orient...*Il est partout. Au Nil je le retrouve encore. L'Égypte resplendit des feux de son aurore...*

'No, poor love, no, he is not Napoleon. Nor has he been made for this coarse country. Once, Mama let slip that Jorge Artayeta seemed to live in one of those autumnal evenings of a *f*ête *galante*, though not like a leading actor but hidden behind a tree or walking away along an avenue, how strange, how little like Mama, but something in Jorge must have aroused the studious provincial in her. And it is true that Jorge likes to quote Verlaine, *et la mandoline jase parmi les frissons de brise*, with the rolling of the Maillard rs which make me nervous...'

Clara always used to go on about her father sleeping until midday during her childhood. If she was conscious of that defect she must have heard it criticized in the Calle Juncal and her need to jump on the other's hump to get noticed went on putting the moan in her mouth so many years later, for my benefit.

Papá was lazy. While most men of his class without *occupation accordée*, as Montaigne describes himself, got out of bed when they felt like it, what made him different? Was it his insistence on self adornment, with a single-mindedness that a society weary of variety would find aggressive? That photograph of a hunt where two dozen men dressed identically in brown set off a tall svelte lily standing under the parasol of a dry chañar, plumb in the middle of little more than a line of nondescript beaters. White as white, from the cap to the tall boots that shone amidst the forty hunting shoes like a clarion call. That photograph of my grandfather like a maharaja surrounded by his people was like a declaration of war.

At the same time he was balancing on a thin edge.

The pink shirts, the deer suede breeches with the flare of elephants' ears, the white chain stitch polo neck sweater, all could have been the flourish of the most consummate poofter, whereas Otropapá, like Aramis of the perfumed gloves, was the best shot out hunting, both of women and beasts. No wonder Otramamá couldn't make him out.

'... All this is exhausting, and I'm going straight to bed to dream of nothing. Good God, I never dream of the things that torture me awake. Last night I dreamt of the stuffed crocodile in the grotto in Villa Elisa. He moved his jaws to say something but I couldn't hear. Perhaps he was trying to give me the clue to this mess. But I'd be lucky, as the most disagreeable of my English governesses used to say.

'In his African patois the crocodile could have recited my favorite lines of my favorite Hélène Vacaresco: *Fouettée par le vent froid des intimes angoisses.* I do like them. But though I'm moved by the lines, and I have a musical ear, I only half understand them. I haven't got a lyrical voice, it's more like a brass band that can make people laugh with its pirouettes. But from Jorge it only gets a pained smile. How can we have been born so incompatible?...'

Six French years: puberty had washed the mourning from Jorge's face and made him unrecognizable to his old fellow pupils at the Colegio del Salvador of the Calle Callao. They found a well brought up boy of thirteen, well spoken like a foreign señorita, who confronted their taunts with a smile of incomprehension.

Otropapá spent his life disarming obstacles with his courtesy and on the way he lost ten thousand hectares, a few houses and properties, etc, but over forty years he kept a sinuous and authoritarian grip on the most exclusive of men's clubs, the Jockey of the Jockey, the Círculo de Armas of Buenos Aires. And to achieve that he escaped, like all the men of the Calle Juncal, from the anxious hands of its women.

'... No, I'm my own worst enemy loaded with this torment which turns me into the proverbial bull. And the curious thing is that I start my advances quite shyly but the moment I get the minimal response I jump on the victim, like I used to climb up onto Papá's knees in front of ministers and presidents, expecting applause. My antics don't deserve God's pardon. A scarecrow with the aplomb of the Duchess of Malfi.

'... But stop, who knows, Jorge is shy and snobbish, it would be such a coup, such fun, if I could take him by assault, like the Duchess did Antony, no, that's not the Malfi one, it's Cleopatra, with her silken sails and her pearl in escabeche. By assault, like a black rat which starts by tickling his ankles and crawls up under his clothes to make her rat's nest by his heart.

'I will infect him, I'll infect him with my disease. What in the end is love but a disease, but sadly it doesn't necessarily stick. If only I could graft the infection on him with my Indian fangs sharpened with so much munching of maize ...'

Otramamá spent two months in bed with a fever and ended marrying the shadow of her life after the Centenary flags had been gathered up, dirty with soot and piles of confetti. But she didn't keep a single photograph of the occasion.

28

B UT THERE was another country, another space, which
floated half seen, hardly reachable and wonderfully
impermanent, over this laboured opposition between Buenos Aires and the historic provinces. It was occupied, as an
exception to all the rest of the Republic, by the nymph
granddaughters of Mariano Unzué.

These magnificent cousins, modest and forgetful, mean-
dered along like butterflies doubled into praying mantises
with no respect for the husbands of others or the rules of
the rest. They were impelled by a good will impressed on
them by the luck of their birth. They were so obviously the
best, because of their beauty, their money, their elegance,
and their idiocy which they deployed to dazzle at night so
next morning they would be forgiven both for their triumph and their indifference.

They seemed to float hanging by their hair like Mélisande
and moaned on street corners of the Barrio Norte a contradictory '*ne me touchez pas, ne me touchez pas,*' whilst the
hilarity with which they confronted the outside world as
they waited for everything to be brought to them, 'only at
home we are safe from the giggles,' was so unexpected, irresistible and childish, that it was seen more like an opening
than a rejection.

Even Tía Teodé forgave the mothers of the cousins, their
descent from a henchman of Rosas whose fortune started
in a grocery of La Boca was centuplicated by his sons with
leagues of desert won with the financing of Roca's campaign. 'They were so pretty and sweet and generous, and so
many, and then they married half of Buenos Aires.' If they
had managed to escape her censure, why was anybody to
keep bothering.

But it was the voice, which I have tried to describe when I brought in Tía Justita Madero, which was unforgettable. A bumblebee stuck in the throat, disoriented, hitting against the vellum stubbornly and ticklish, an excuse for the giggles to cough it out. The contortions of a parthenogenous chrysalis struggling to burst into a jewelled butterfly, blindingly colourful, the price one had to pay, as a clear voice would trivialize it, for such luxury.

The first sounds seemed without direction like the confused thoughts of waking and didn't match the focussed smile, but this was so tender, almost cloying, that it was as if the voice just followed the smile, after a hesitation of baas, to add an aural welcoming with the stuttering of passion or of the newborn, the bumblebee filled with all the best intentions but lost. 'Hooww aare you, hooww aare you, little mouuuse?' and the voice went mute. The wavering of silence that one didn't know how to fill in was a section, as important as words, of the impromptu. Which at times seemed to have given up words and was reduced to a string of favourable epithets: gorgeous, colossal, splendid, marvellous, to be crowned by cuété – porteño for rocket, and the sign of the finest of sensitivities and the quickest intelligence. Cuété was the door to their hearts. If one was considered a cuété one was unbeatable. But the little value that they seem to give to all other words only magnified the presence of their magnificent forms, like Garbo, with whom they shared the need to be left alone.

That instant aristocracy, manifest in the finest *attachés* in the world, found its equivalent in an instant decadence, and the daughters of the 'quinta' as they called their house, the presidential mansion where Eva Perón died, immune to any genealogical justification, drooled like an Infanta of the House of Austria.

One of them, Clara Lenoir, perhaps the most beautiful apart from my dear Tía Lula who will appear later, found me agreeable. She chose me, extricating me from the soup where my own Clara insisted I should stew with her other offspring, and took me for drives in Mar del Plata, as that arbiter of taste, Matías Errázuriz, had done along the Costanera of Buenos Aires.

It was so strong, the contrast between her darkroom voice and the blue yellow light of Mar del Plata, the shine of the mica incrusted stones on the green of the cliff lawns, the abyss that plunged into the sea, the battered jetties and the rushing waves, that I find it difficult to piece together those drunken displacements. The famous voice had found its natural tone, that of intimacy; these sought after women were not sociable, they were intimate, and what bliss to be sitting there next to her in the blue turmoil of summer at the Cabo Corrientes en route to the port, 'to the smell of salt and rotten fish that I love. And Martincito, little Ratty, do tell me, don't you love it too? Say yes so that we feel more comfortable. Don't you think that if one is going to take the trouble of going out with somebody they should have the same tastes? You do? That's perfect. Then you can't imagine how you're going to like the surprise I have arranged for you.'

God, she was lovely. That wide face which I like because it allows room for more things but held tight by its cheekbones, the fresh, soft love-slide cheeks, the brown eyes that looked violet, that scarlet mouth of those days, the scent, the perfectly tanned arms, the red nails and the white dress, but above all the hair, the crown of thick, enormous, chestnut hair which pushed out the sun and was under the sun like a burning parasol, the sitting close as if we were the same age, the furtiveness of a pleasure controlled by her and allowing a kind of space for me, cleaned of dangerous sinful bodies, made more innocuous still by her elegance and beauty which she treated as nothing.

For me, who fell in love with Carmencita at Punta Gorda

only because she was a younger version of Tía Teodé, without bothering much about her beauty, the dazzle I experienced for Clara Lenoir was fresh of my usual associations, it was innocent, hopeful and very curious, of pendant tongue and bulgy eye, and if it hadn't been that I only saw her two or three times, as our sojourns in Villa Unzué were short – invited by Tía Justita when its owner Madame Cobo moved in February to her nearby estancia of La Armonía – that house on the hill so simple for such a rich family, with its little hall at the foot of the stairs and its vast dining-room and the signs which struck me because they proclaimed in big black letters SILENCE as one entered the servants quarters, Clara Lenoir's beauty and her ease would have freed me earlier of my ties.

Luxury loosens, like destitution. The poor and the very rich marry on a whim. In that the Unzués were modern. Clara was more or less separated from a polo champion, handsome and coarse as they tend to be. Anyway, nobody seemed to have had children. Ignorant and impervious to any rule, beyond good or evil, they knew nothing, nothing held their attention for long. They ended seeing no one, robbed by their maids, caring for stray cats, finding dogs too affectionate. One of them took to her bed in a room transformed into a cage, an aviary to which the bronze bars of the four poster served as swings, wiping bird shit from her eyes with an embroidered handkerchief.

If they had been reminded of the country that kept my grandmothers awake they would have answered that they didn't know what one was talking about. So when I heard my cousin Fina alluding to her difficult sons, 'to each one his cross,' the expression seemed to have come from another mouth, the diminished Madero voice, ancient and catholic, the cliché of a long-suffering history, something unimaginable coming from the most splendid and evanescent of our fungi.

Imaginative fungi. Those bodies with the undulations of an amoeba were blessed with imagination. The great imaginatives, Keats, Proust, were frightened of finding nothing in the mirror. They could express the most complete reflection of this world, but had no face. They were the invisible lilacs and the unstoppable nightingale, and as for our nymphs, if they abounded in a collective personality, they were too chameleonic to recognize themselves.

'Though of course I find him unreadable, like that bore Borges, but I've been told that Proust was a great flatterer, just like me, I go so far in praising my maid that in the end I'm not so sure if she hasn't become the Señora and me, well I wouldn't go so far as to believe I had turned into my maid, there are limits, but I swear there are moments when I get confused. What a bore the servants are. If one wasn't so lazy. But patience, little mouse, patience. Monsignor Devoto used to say that it was one of the capital sins. No, not sins, God I am stupid. No, wait a minute, let me remember, yes, I think he said it was one of the capital virtues, or was it cardinal, Oh God, what a muddle, I should call Juana Madero, she's the only well read one of all the cousins. But then she looks at you with those cold eyes of hers that seem to judge you, and frightens me a bit. What a need to judge. To judge what? As if one knew the difference.'

If I could push the metaphorical finger into somebody's body to measure the degree of acceptance and understanding, the finger would melt in the Unzué's viscosities, or rather it would go loose, while the rigid breast of Tía Teodé would send the blunted finger back to its starting point. My darling Totola had too much personality and too little imagination. And from that faithfulness to herself, which had decided from the first bawling to be Teodé Lezica and nobody else, sprung the consistent balm of her love.

One could count on her as one never could with Tía Justita. But even in Tía Justita, behind those blue and wearied eyes always searching with no illusion for a respite from boredom, there lived a poetical pep, the glimpse of an explosion which might alter something. A hidden love, the abrupt sale of San Carlos, something unexpected and seductive that added to the glamour, which made her attractive despite the disappointments, but never happened.

The chauffeur parked at the quay. Clara was tall and used cork platforms. She was just what my own mother Clara would have given her life to be, though she sometimes mentioned that the eldest and darkest of the Lenoir sisters, Tita, had done her the honour of finding that she looked like her. 'I wonder if she wasn't the most beautiful, but of course I couldn't hold a candle to her. She said it just to be nice.'

'Now we are going to have a good time, little Rat. I hope you will like filth as much as I do! Mmmm, how delicious filth is. No, don't get frightened, darling, there's nothing wrong with filth. What's wrong is people disapproving of one's taste and criticizing. What need to criticise people have! I wouldn't think of it, I don't know, but then I hardly notice people. No, no, I only like people like you, all the time ogling at things, so fond of having a good time, so nice. You're colossal, little Rat, you remind me of papa who was so cute, a bit cuter perhaps? But no, not more cute, more pretty, but not cuter, anyway he was an old man and you are a boy, though he kept himself young like a deb, Papá, with those eyes slanting upwards like Scarlett O'Hara's which I wouldn't have minded inheriting, but they were black, because he was the handsomest of blacks. I don't know what's got me going on about Papá. I know, because I think he also loved filth.'

Yes, I was frightened. Clara Lenoir deployed a beauty so complete, so inaccessible, and yet intimate, but deceptively intimate as if it couldn't be any other way, that it caught me by the throat, dragged me after her, as the instant slave of her divinity, as it is written, like others have left fathers and sons, and my first illuminations of love – the surrender that night in the darkness of the car going towards Buenos Aires in the night with my head on the lap of Finita Bullrich, of my heart to a heart which had transformed itself into the host of the tabernacle, or the crush on Carmencita Lezica of a boy excited by his trip, and not even to mention that little cow Adela – revealed themselves quite clearly as of another world. This was not the world of the child stringing love garlands for his grandmothers, no, it was a new one, unimaginable but mysteriously familiar, filthy because of the fear of what attracted me so vertiginously and of which I thought myself so ignorant, poor idiot.

That big, smooth face, so radiant against our chaste sky and our turbid sea, which I looked up at from her waist, seemed to hold the enigma of the golden masks, the ones that hide a deformity like the leprous features of the last king of Jerusalem, but it had nothing of the rigidity of a mask. On the contrary, it murmured and smiled, because it was her beauty, a quality I had always felt as both terrible and sad, long before Clara Lenoir, ever since that night in the Calle Juncal, of the beauty of Psyche in the nursery, which overrode all the babble and the light touches and massages on the shoulder or on the hand, with that hand which made her bracelets tinkle like a leper's rattle; it was still clear that neither my own Clara nor I could do anything about it, it was so obviously beyond our reach, that it reduced this Clara's excitement to about what we would find in the port of Mar del Plata to sheer idiocy.

No, Clara Lenoir was incapable of showing me the way through that world dislocated by her beauty. But I didn't know it, I only knew that it frightened me. It made me aware for the first time of what a coward I was.

'Come here, and smell,' she murmured. She took my hand in hers, narrow and fresh, that seemed to shrink in mine, and took me to the water. A mess of orange boats were knocking against the wharf. Orange-skinned men, hard faced and battered, with clear tame eyes, their hair faded to orange, were unloading live fish. The smell was new to me, and disgusting. In mud colour baskets a writhing pandemonium of fine gray forms were turned silver by the sun as they slowly died. Pink crabs still muddy gray in colour, of a slow and obsessive turpitude, moved their claws with the begging intention of the blind who should be innocent but whose murky gelatinous eyes are menacing. One or two small sharks, or something similar, deployed wide mouths of useless teeth and thrashed their tails slower and slower.

'Don't bother about the fish, look at those hands, those nails all broken and black. Aren't they gorgeous? And the smell of rot. There's nothing like the smell of rotten fish. Some people find it disgusting, but I would put it in a perfume bottle and take it home. Of course I couldn't use it. But who knows, if somebody would like it... In the end it's the sea, che, and these fishermen so natural, so handsome, and the sea, the whole thing. La mar en coche!' She laughed, because a good part of the Unzué imagination was to find language so extraordinary that it was always surprising them, and they savoured it carefully like a new fruit, particularly people's names they had never heard of, which were most of them, and pronounced them with a stuttering admiration, as if they were using their tongues to spell out the ruggedness of Hungarian. Their favourites were the sonorous Italian names of the immigrants: 'Fa-to-che-tto, how divine, darling mouse, Fa-to-che-tto. What fun to be called Fa-to-che-tto. Clarita Fatochetto, isn't it just colossal?' A blond fisherman with a hairy naked chest jumped from his boat with the silent elasticity of a cat, and approached us. 'Ah, Rubén, what a surprise,' said Clara, without seeming surprised at all. 'I would like you to meet Martincito Cullen, one of my cousin's nephews. No, you don't know her. How are you doing, Rat? Such a long time! I was wondering if you could get me the surprise I've been thinking up for this dear boy. You wouldn't have one of those shells that sing?'

Clara Lenoir spoke to the young acrobat as if he were me. Worse, with an insinuation that I guessed but didn't understand, as if she were more interested and concerned about him than was necessary, as if that fisherman had something to do with her life. As if from those muddy baskets, from the contortions of the beasts in agony, a filthy angel had sprouted who attracted her even more than the stench of dead fish.

Why had she taken me to the port to show me this? She went on smiling at me, but with such composure, I don't know if it was me who imagined it but it hurt. In the ship later on my father was going to force me to discover much more distressing things, to learn about the blindness of certain attractions. But then I hardly knew my father. He was a man. And neither he, nor anybody in the bathroom of the Calle Juncal, had taught me how men managed. But I thought I knew reasonably well how women managed. The hands which had interfered with me from the beginning were chaste. Those hands dealt with love, never sex, with not a bit of blindness. They loved gentlemen and marmalade with equal measure. That was why they used French, where the verb is ubiquitous. And suddenly this goddess who seemed impermeable to desire, if it wasn't for the thrill of the toy room with its little obscenities, Baudelaire, and *patatí* and *patatá*, gets all nervous when she's approached by a hunk with his hairy chest bleached by the sun of the Pearl of the Atlantic.

But here comes the Unzué play, a notion that I unfurl to protect myself. They were human, the hunk wasn't bad looking, but it wasn't easy to distinguish in all that confusing interest in filth who or what ends up prevailing. Clara Lenoir could have messed herself at the bottom of the mud coloured baskets with stud, crab, shark and assorted fishes silvery and dying, and then emerge, enchanted, smelling of rot, but, like Aphrodite from the Cytherean sea, unpolluted. Because what did she lose, what was it that stained her, with those desires? No matter what she did she'd irradiate innocence, or even better goodness, which seemed the price to make her loveliness more approachable.

Clara could die of love for Rubén, allow Rubén to abuse her, to abandon her, but even though she could believe that she lived every minute of the day, without rest, under the motto which she shared with the Lady of the Unicorn: '*À mon seul désir*,' she also was, like the Lady of the Unicorn, imprisoned by her beauty within the white fenced corral of the untouchable. Where, by the way, again like the Lady, she sat quite placidly at its centre surrounded by daisies and rabbits. Knowingly, unknowingly? It was she who didn't need to understand anything. It was me, the prying boy, who got things wrong, the arrogant and rapacious creep frightened by his own desires, desperate to be protected by a circle of pretty virgins, needy, angular, fastidious and Botticellian.

When the shell arrived, nacreous and hard, washed to a purity of bone by the swing of the sea, and Clara put it to my ear, I heard a murmur that went on repeating itself like the sad memory of the waves that never tire of breaking. I still have it, and sometimes now I put it to my ear, and with that capacity of objects to conserve a life that has vanished, a life we thought forgotten, which we changed deliberately even if perhaps we never wanted it to change — like I who for so long stopped visiting Tía Teodé but would still do anything to be able to sleep again in the blue and mahogany cabin of that ship heading for Paris, immune to the still inscrutable seductions of Clara Lenoir, because that awful need for things to go on being what they were tricks us into believing that we haven't changed, a belief that would sound false if it wasn't so persistent – goes on singing in my ear.

29

THE MOST imaginative of the Madero sisters was Tía Lula. '*Elle est habitée par la fée,*' was the verdict of Otramamá. She did everything differently from anybody else and not very well, as if the fairy had been both bold and hesitant. She liked the sound of the harp of the romantic ballads of Paraguay, the colour purple, diamonds when the fashion was for pearls, a good investment; coming up to eighty she took a liking to jeans. Her houses were built below ground with windows that didn't open into the landscape but into the sky. She didn't have taste, she had strong preferences. In her wavering voice she uttered banalities which resonated like oracles. They had to be untangled from the slow disconnected drivel, only for her listeners to realize afterwards how wise she had been.

She used to send unexpected presents that resembled her, like a silver mapuche necklace to thank for a hospitality that didn't warrant it; she would suddenly appear on the phone out of the blue, and after silences and mumblings announce that she didn't know why she was calling; once, in a daydream, when she was being dressed by her maid, she discovered a cocktail suit in the mirror, and asked, 'wasn't I meant to go riding?' The maid was domineering and masculine, as in all the Unzué households, and spoke in whispers like a duchess.

Like her sisters, she was immune to boastfulness; it didn't seem to come from being born rich, like Otramamá, who had been given so much as a child, and enjoyed remembering it. But then they hadn't gone broke.

I don't know how many fairies are genealogically minded, like Mélusine, who fiercely guarded the destinies of her offspring, but it would have seemed that the Unzué fairy

— as there are no fairies of the Madero name, or anything approaching a fairy to speak of -didn't carry the colours of Lusignan on their distracted and transparent wings, rather the pollen of the flowers which had cradled her daughters. The result was Tía Lula. She carried things lightly, she seemed to disdain nothing, but she placed on her forehead a storm-coloured headband, on the band an aigrette, under the band shone two dark beautiful eyes which could have been Oriental if they hadn't been detoxed by the River Plate, and then she would make her oblique entry into a room, tall, both apprehensive and absent-minded, dressed as the Queen of the Night with some loose rags, haloed by her bold preferences like the bold words of a poem by the negative capability of the poet. All that accumulation of pauses, presenting itself clear like a work of art.

In those days Buenos Aires could allow such leaps. Although to call them evolutionary wouldn't apply, because they turned backwards with the same haste, which is easy. But what seems inexplicable was the urgency with which the chrysalis refined itself to allow the granddaughter of a Mazorca thug to open its wings, morphed into a Levantine princess with a humility more regal than any criollo manner. As if Buenos Aires, like those civilizations of the borders, Petra, Palmyra, or those cities of the Silk Road that built monuments and incrusted mosaics on domes and disappeared, had had the strength, thanks to a favourable conjunction of stars between the Centenary and the rise of Perón, to squander on some disproportionate fires which lit the night. One of those transient flares was Tía Lula.

She seemed to be made from the remnants of some forgotten excess, dulled like the gold rubbed off a statue that goes on shining on the wrinkles of the neck, so extraordinary were her byzantine courtesies in the dust of the corral on a January morning.

But watch out. If the Unzué swiftly acquired blue blood

and riches had merged with the austerity of Maipú to finish her with a master's varnish, it had also unleashed a capricious alloy. Because that cut of the gloved hand, like that of her sister Tía Justita, with which she underlined her few assertions, short, definitive, in a horizontal diagonal from the chest outwards, seemed to have soldered her gentleness, her incongruous visit as mistress to the corral on branding day which could have drawn a smile, with an unexpected hardness. And despite the disorder of the Argentine paradise she lost fewer hectares than most landowners.

Was this a trace of sudden riches? Tía Lula's humility turned into an arbitrary toughness that asserted: 'One has always to come back, as Camilo said,' the voice and the glove and the cut turned dangerous, with the inflexible impatience of the parvenu grandfather who had appropriated land the size of Provence thirty years before the imaginative fungi were born. That implacability, like Tía Justita's abrupt changes of mood, was never shown by the easy hearts of Santa Marta, or even the spiky and tender one of Tía Teodé, their soft criollo swing inured to the seesaw of fortune. 'Camilo said,' which expressed a subject that worried everybody, how to survive in our infuriating paradise, could defile anything with its tacit violence and made me think that some imaginations demand too high a price.

Camilo was Camilo Aldao, an acclaimed *bel homme* in his day, one of those old bachelors who travelled constantly to Europe, who accompanied the ladies without bothering them with love, or, in principle, with the jealousies and rivalries of the other ladies, one of those solitary men who had been reared amid the cruelties of their provincial society and had put up with a false position; neither pets, nor machos, nor mates, they were needed by those ladies who took care of them in a way, and mistreated them and didn't want to hear about their sorrowful hearts, who manipulated them, in short, for pure gain. They listened to their feminine worries, decorated their houses and even chose their clothes, and were appreciated as purveyors of international news, like the bombshell that shook not only the Unzués but the rest of society: 'In Paris nobody plays canasta.'

Tía Teodé wasn't part of that society, even if she was sensitive to its glamour and could claim quite a few blood connections. She was old and austere, surrounded by that solitude which touched me without knowing why. To see her with a card in her hand was as strange as to think of her flirting with a gentleman, things that Otramamá didn't do without, and the only man who ever visited her was her cousin París Lezica, a widower with descendants, with whom she talked about their ancestors. The truths that merited my aunt's attention had been stipulated by Rivadavia, the founder of the Sociedad de Beneficencia, and all the others left her unmoved. But then to each its own Solon.

My laws, my truths, I heard those for the first time in the bathroom of the Calle Juncal. It is only because of their indefensible triviality that I feel forced now to unravel them, as though to straighten up the crooked steps of the child I once was.

It is a curious belief, that of the healing effect of literature, because whether we read it or we write it it seems to straighten up the world, to cure it. But really, it's all made up by us, it is just a poor relation of the world, its fire doesn't burn, its knives don't draw blood, at most it could pretend to frighten like the howl of a wolf during a game of sardines, or perhaps like beauty, but less, much less, as the beauty of Clara Lenoir is the world from behind which lurks the terrible. Both are doors, but dear literature is a door that yields blandly into a room of counterfeits.

Whether Proust likes it or not Albertine dies prettily for us even if he wails every four lines that he will die because she is dead, and if Wilde said that the greatest sorrow of his life was the death of Lucien de Rubempré it must have been because he couldn't bear to imagine the death of Lord Alfred Douglas.

What counts is the voice of the Solon of the moment, branding itself on the clay of the child. And how I still long to be twisted again in the steam of the bathroom by those false truths. Just to hear the inflection of those loved voices which went silent, let them come back and decree whatever they please, let them sound again just once more in the empty room, those voices of mine, dry and ironic, unconcerned, untouched and indefensibly inviting, heavy with the irresponsibility of love, the voice of my flowering girls of so many different ages and all so much older than me, speaking at random in the vertigo of the dizzying steam.

But then who cared about the lies, when the truth that tied me to them was their bodies? Those loved voices couldn't lie in the end because they came from a body that I loved. How could I care what they lied about, or really what they hid, when they couldn't remove their bodies, as there was nothing less of the sleight of hand of the fairy in those women of perennial routines: bath, chat, gossip, massage. The steam was the only thing that could confuse their features but could not turn them invisible, make them disappear, like Eros before Psyche.

Mere mortals, they abandoned to me their crooked fingers and their short legs, their eyes without eyelashes and their furious eyes, their smells always sweet, so that I would feel sated without even knowing where to start. All the veins and the varicosities and the wounds and the sorrowful flesh were shown to me right there.

There are those sad idealists who never have touched anything properly and despise a corpse because the soul has left it. They don't know that they are missing the ultimate delight, of spending the night of the wake, when everybody has gone to bed, kissing the cheeks turning every hour colder but still identical, until they are covered by the tomb, of those whom, since for the first time I opened my eyes, I loved.

30

ONE MORNING, when I drew back the short curtains from my porthole I didn't find the endless sea, but a city. The ship had reached Rio at dawn, and parked, like a car, at the bottom of the Avenida Rio Branco. And this time my outing was assured, thanks to Pepa, who had spent her honeymoon in Rio with that-monster-Caró, and decided she'd stay in her cabin. There were odd numbers in their group, and I was fitted in. Even so I discovered my presence was affecting the party.

There was a limousine, and the French secretary of an absent old friend of Tina's to show us around. So we let ourselves be embraced by the tropics and its army of termites, which devour time. If the public buildings of Buenos Aires had seemed improbable to me in the summer heat on the road going out to the estancia, in Rio they had gone mad. The Art Museum and the Municipal Theatre wore an orange halo of heat like electricity when it was promoted for the first time: a classical nymph refulgent in her crown of light bulbs, printed on a flaking poster. The buildings seemed to blister before our eyes while all around them a damp, stifling force sprouting from the sea, the streets, the thick oily trees, the sky, ate into them, laughed at them, and laid them to waste.

The Frenchwoman spoke without drawing breath. She pointed out the mongrel multitudes, the black beggars, the mulatto women with swaying hips. *'Regardez quelle intensité de vie!'* she said, in her tight, low, suffocated voice. *'Ça c'est la vraie vie.* A life that has been lost, in those countries that call themselves civilised. Europe is dead. I'll never go back. I will die here.' She looked fine and old, like a Sèvres *trembleuse*, and Brazil had made her overly familiar.

Worse, it had fried her brain. I wasn't the only who felt uncomfortable.

She had the chauffeur take us through the poor districts. Houses painted pink, sky-blue, yellow, all such malleable colours that they seemed to move with the changing light, seeking out different parts of the day, as if for comfort. Through open doors and windows we saw rooms painted dark red; the façades became faces, the rooms their throats. Tiny and quiet, they were filled with a sofa overflowing with black children, or a double bed. The red was purplish, like tonsils. Old black men sat in the doorways, smelling the day. We stopped at a covered market, where the world of these people was bought and sold. Coconuts sliced by the blow of a machete, dropsical bulls' tongues, blood-encrusted hoofs, a myriad of fruits that smelled of honey and shit, black gods and Virgins and Sacred Hearts, shrieking bails of nylon, tunnels of dried meat and sacks of cassava flour, the meat hanging from the low roofs like curtains of dead skin, beige and pink, flour like white wells, covering everything with dust. The tunnels were like roads to the past, to the Orient of Simbad the Sailor, through which half-naked black men, splashed with white, trotted in and out of the darkness, like messengers sent by somebody.

No, not the Orient, the America of Vespuccio. That murky tumult, which no story could tell, wasn't this the key to our continent? This great landmass, so empty of people and loaded with the rest of creation – I imagined it as a writhing knot of green bodies, that bread and killed in areas the size of empires, hedged by rivers as wide as seas, beneath worlds of clouds that rained down interminable deluges. That place where the earth boils and smokes and the sun, when the clouds part, seems small. Those vast rivers, reflecting the light in their pampas of mud, enclose its flatness with a merciless indifference, neither flowing nor stagnating, but repeating themselves. How could it be that Buenos Aires had existed for four hundred years at the mouth of those horrible rivers?

'*Chère* Madame Blot, don't you think we might visit Copacabana, or the Portuguese houses on the Largo del Boticario that are said to be so pretty?' Tina's good manners made her better than the others at dealing with certain insults.

'But that is for tourists. And I understand that you are travellers, not tourists,' answered the implacable secretary. 'What Brazil has to offer is life. And by that I mean life lived with the utmost spontaneity, the utmost crudity, what has been steadily lost in Europe since the Middle Ages. Here, the poor can teach us a lesson about poetry and reality – one and the same thing, though they may seem to be opposites. That is what I have shown you. Art. Art, *tout court*, which can be understood at a glance, and is open to everyone, like all great art.'

Madame Blot went silent, and her face switched off like her words. She seemed to have repeated this harangue many times. Little bubbles seeped from her dejected mouth.

There was no answer. I looked at Tía Eloísa, who had studied literature at the Sorbonne, and her face showed the annoyance of incomprehension. The others stared out of the window, while Tina smiled bravely at the Frenchwoman, who had shut her eyes. Then, without opening them, she ordered the chauffeur to turn towards Copacabana.

Tía Pepa wasn't the only one for whom Rio brought bad memories. Next morning, as the ship was sailing away from that beautiful and confusing bay, on a celadon coloured sea, I found my mother, alone for once, leaning over the railing at the stern. I went to her, with that instinctive desire to get close to people she and I shared.

'Oh, there you are. I was thinking about you,' she said. 'About when you were born. I don't like to think of it. But

Rio brought everything flooding back. I've never talked about my first labour before – or what happened afterwards.'

She didn't look at me. She stood, her chin pressed on her fists, following the turquoise trail the ship was leaving across the green of the sea. She wore a new expression, one of discouragement. I felt desperately curious, and instinctively feline, which was not at all me.

'You must know that your birth went on for ever,' she said at last. 'Instead of pushing from top to bottom as it should have done, my womb contracted in reverse, at its mouth, as if I didn't want to let you go. Madness – if I'd known then what a monster I wanted to keep! After I don't know how many hours, they decided to operate. And then in all the fuss they forgot you, and if your father hadn't found you turning blue in the corner and started hitting you so you'd breathe, you wouldn't be here.'

As always, her mood lifted with the drama of the tale. But then she sighed deeply.

'Anyway, that all ended, but then the *danse macabre* started the next day.'

She turned and looked at me, and those brilliant, proud eyes were clouded with fear. She looked like a little girl caught out, as if she'd wet her pants, but to the shame of her guilt was added the panic of confusion.

'It was then that I started to lose my mind.'

I had heard something, but very little, for though Otramamá and Tía Teodé delighted in describing how I'd been thrown into their arms, they grew vague when asked for a reason.

'You were brought to live with me before you were a year old,' Tía Teodé told me. 'I made a charming nursery for you in my dressing room. How you loved to crawl out on the balcony and look over the Calle Rodriguez Peña! I had it scrubbed, but you always came back covered in soot. Why what? Ah. Well, because your parents were travelling and your grandmother had her hands full with Tina's illness, and I wasn't going to miss out on you …'

Otramamá, who had passed on her love of drama to my mother, would say ominously, 'The sorrows that fell on our house at the time you were born…' But she would never be drawn further.

Mamá fell silent, and I didn't push her. My curiosity had evaporated. The barriers were going down, what was about to be revealed was mixed up with my own feelings, and I felt the shame that I had recognised in my mother's eyes. There was something obscene in the disparity between her tone, that combination of beauty and pride, and her failure, which I didn't understand, didn't know how to escape. But one thing I was sure of: the shame was not only hers. It seemed as if we shared it. How revolting. I didn't feel the slightest compassion.

31

A FTER THIS incident I was more appreciative of Tía
Teodé's placid routines, which arranged those long days
into identical parts, through which the ship floated without
making any advance, over the quiet, luminous and sad sea.
Their triviality worked as a remedy. We would seek out
the furthermost corner of the promenade deck to take our
mid-morning consommé, reclining on canvas deck chairs.
Tía Teodé would study the hundred-year-old statutes of the
Sociedad de Beneficencia, seeking some legal loophole with
which to wrest it back from Eva Perón's grasp, and I would
write in my diary. We did our constitutional one hundred
paces without talking, leant on the railings and gazed at the
soup of the water, where there was nothing.

Lunch offered the relief of going down to the fresh,
artificially lit dining room, the smell of bread, the butter,
the starch of the tablecloth, the thrill of the new dish each
day, and then the sleepy stroll afterwards. All this seemed
wonderfully restorative. Then we went back to our cabin.
Tía Teodé, after much chivvying from me, had begun her
memoirs on the ship's notepaper, while I was struggling
with a book about the French Revolution, bought in the
bookshop, which I didn't understand.

Even Bertrand had disappeared. I didn't have the energy
to find him. He wasn't on board, he was within the cinema, and now it pained me to imagine him. Like Tarzan, he
didn't know how to turn up on cue, those models on which
I had based my longings seemed to be lost to me. They were
wrong, unwieldy, unusable. I didn't want to do anything,
least of all to move, but the ship went on imperceptibly,
and now we were approaching the Equator. I had to prepare myself for the Crossing of the Line – for the rituals

of baptism, for being dunked in flour and drowned – and I would have to disguise myself for the grown up party and face it all alone, because Tía Teodé had crossed the line so many times that after Tío Pancho's death she had decided never to cross it again.

Absorbed in our listless routines, we paid no attention to the preparations. This mattered little, since my great-aunt took it upon herself to cram me with all the details that counted, the crossings of those first steamships before the great war, the *Cap Arcona*, the *Cap Vilano* and the *Principessa Mafalda*, in the days when one travelled properly, with cow and valet. And so, when the day arrived, I turned up on the afterdeck, by the swimming pool, where I assumed the ritual would be performed, and when a steward plonked a tricorn on my head and hung a musket from my shoulder, transforming me into one of the guards of Neptune, God of the Sea, I asked him, 'Who is going to be Neptune?'

'Don't you know? *Mais voyons*, it's your father.'

The prospect of this new form of contact with my father threw me. My father as the world saw him, out and abroad from morning to night, out there where his needs were melodies so very different from the pressing whistles we imagined we heard as we threw ourselves at his neck when he returned to Juncal, or the happy, indolent, gaucho and Flamenco songs he sang on the long summer afternoons on the road to the estancia. Now he was coming towards me, heading a procession across the starboard deck, with crown and trident and a turnip face created by a white woollen wig surrounding his narrow temples and wide cheeks. His fatuous expression irritated me more than I can say.

Another procession advanced from the port side, at its centre a pretty young woman with a vulgar expression, also wearing a crown. My father winked at me. The steward pushed me into line behind him, and I watched with mounting disgust as he directed an even more fatuous smile at the crowned girl as they bowed to each other and mounted the steps by the pool. The girl was Amphitrite, Neptune's wife, and though she beamed at me, I knew she was an enemy. She wore a silver bathing suit, attached to one shoulder by a diagonal band of rather dubious charm. She was evidently a passenger from Second Class, dark, with a straight nose and green eyes. If she hadn't been usurping my mother's place, I might have liked her, she seemed so pleased to be there. But this usurper was making me see a new father, a fat-cheeked boor with greedy eyes, drunk on success, and worst of all, who excluded me. I had always regarded myself as surfeited with love, but now I felt a strange and unexpected jealousy.

My father's new face seemed marked by this mysterious and repellent sense of exclusion. I had never before seen such eyes. They looked far beyond the worlds of Juncal and the estancia, they seemed to dismiss, to scorn, to forget them. There was no place for us in those eyes. And there was nobody to witness this but me.

The afterdeck was packed with people I'd never seen before, noisier, more animated, and worse dressed than those I'd seen each day strolling from bar to pool. I was excited to discover some boys, older than me, who stared at me impassively from time to time. Once more I was surprised that the world should harbour so many people. My family had disappeared. Apart from my father and me everyone else, the court of the Kings of the Sea, the bishop, *gendarmes*, dunkers with their buckets of flour, this whole rabble before me seemed to have risen from the depths like the crowned goddess at whom Neptune and his erectile snout leered. But then I got carried away. And after the baptised ones had been immersed in the pool, which quickly became a semolina soup, and there was no one left to take part in the ritual, I started to shout, possessed, that there were still the gods and the bishop, and though the stewards tried to stop me, my *sans-culotte* fervour quelled the suspicions of the older boys. I gave them my tricorn and musket to incite them to follow me; my father allowed himself to be dunked, but Amphitrite shrieked in a common voice that they would ruin her special swimsuit, she was the Queen and deserved respect, she'd spent a fortune at the First Class hairdressers'. But I enjoyed my revenge. I caught one of her ankles and before the semolina swallowed them I saw that her little round toenails were painted silver, to match the slinky swimsuit.

32

THE PUMA-OGRE was distant, and as such incrusted with all that was good. He had given me Tarzan, he embraced me with his suede jacket, he never spoke or criticized, to get close to him would redeem me, he was my father.

Who was he? I just saw him at a distance on the ship, where everyone was distant. But then they didn't reveal new faces, just their well known defects magnified by a new scenario. He did, though. This caused me fear, and then disgust. Because of its furtiveness and suddenness, and not making any place for me. On the contrary, in pushing me towards the scaly old arms of Tía Teodé he made me feel that I wasn't up to him, that satyr expert in abominations which I would have to learn, which I would inherit as his elder son. No, we were from opposite worlds. His indecencies didn't touch me of course, or even less excite me; they drew us into hostile camps. What I was discovering of him, what I had never even suspected, was branding me as someone alien to himself. Of this, you'll have nothing. Nothing of this is yours; just as well.

And still, the woolly wig which made his face idiotic with its narrowed temples, and the awfulness of his chubby cheeks, ridiculously streaked with red paint, but it was no good laughing, since Neptune couldn't take a joke. It was a nightmare with no little cracks of solace, there was no shared wink that could open doors, the wink would have meant look at me – not come and play with me, it was nothing but the god's enamoured drool winking at itself in the mirror. My father, who had washed his hands of me. It's not just that I don't recognize you, I am annoyed that you're here, the stupid potato face was opening its mouth to say.

I accepted that first cut with the calm with which a child confronts horror. I threw myself into the struggles of the semolina pool, the costume for that night's ball, my disdain for the Second Class Queen of the Sea, so that I wouldn't feel the wound which one day would cut me off from my father. The wound went on growing with an accumulation of slashes as time went on; some quite soon, like his coolness on the return ship to Buenos Aires, but most would sink in silently, over time, when the pain had stopped, to make me realize at last that we had become strangers.

My father only made room for me when he felt like it. He approached his family on his own terms and watch out if you caught him unawares, for the puma would bare his fangs. So there was his outside life; and the absences, which Clara's seductive efforts were unable to conceal. Because I wasn't the only unwanted one. Clara's abandonment made more noise, Clara, abandoned when she didn't feel him near, covered up her helplessness by flirting with Monsieur Couturier, which I didn't mind because I knew it was pointless, but it saddened me. And in those satyr's eyes of Neptune as he savoured Amphitrite, I felt the strength of a youth out of control, so much the opposite of the slow ceremonies of Tía Teodé. It was as if a child old beyond his years and beyond desire were to measure an adolescent father, blind, incandescent, dangerous, incomprehensible and hostile, and to discard him.

The puma had been silent and welcoming; the avid little eyes of Neptune betrayed a ridiculous greed. Desire has few organs to express it, perhaps better to underline the vanity of desire. And my father became Pepa, her wet eyes and trembling lips in front of a chocolate éclair.

I also felt the shiftiness of Neptune. If Clara, in her abandonment, had confronted him, his eyes would have folded, white, and his cheeks would have flushed like a scarlet turnip. My father's dissipations were secretive. He would have died rather than parade his desires in front of the Calle Juncal, as my great-grandfather had done, and a bit, although very carefully, Otropapá. But the counterpart of shyness is revenge. And then there was another complication, the instinct to copy. It drives one to dress like one's father, but it made me shudder when I thought of Joaquín's clothes. Even the famous suede jacket could only take life from his own torso, to wear it myself would have been as lethal as the poisonous robes of Medea.

Instead I chose to wear Otropapá's coats and gloves, which on me seemed like fancy dress. Children tend to carry clothes unsuited to them with charm, but not me. 'Poor thing, he tries so hard to play the dandy, but he can't pull it off,' was yet another verdict from the white bathroom of the Calle Juncal.

Sometimes I see sons who fit their fathers like a glove, the young face and the old one smiling at each other with idiotic complacency, the younger trapped and content hanging on the selfish approval of the older, and I think of my struggle to escape from the charm of the puma, who locked the bit of his ways between my teeth, without softening my mouth with caresses. The shovings of shy people. What an idiot.

But how ugly the twisted body which doesn't find clothes that fit. How ugly the discarded heap of clothes on the floor. Is that why I dislike actors, who change their faces as they change their shirts?

And the puma? Could he be a real one, or a Chinaman disguised as a puma? Or lots of Chinamen dancing wildly inside the loose costume of a dragon? From the welcoming skirts of Tía Teodé, Otropapá's well-cut and outsized coats, to the jacket which could poison or incinerate me. Crooked or not, the body goes on straightening itself as best it can.

It takes time though. But they could never be for me, those clothes stolen innocently by the son who wants to resemble his father, to get a bit closer, just a bit, but always tentatively. Because the jacket that almost made me faint with its smell of my father when he appeared so suddenly, without notice, in the damaged summer, still poisons me with its secrets. It's the secret which shows that the jacket is not for me to use, with a clarity that confuses me and has nothing secret about it, it tells me there are no clothes for me to arm myself like him, but in the end it conceals one other secret, that coils around the wand of that seduction which flattens me, so dangerous that it makes me feel that the jacket is lethal, that it is the forbidden chamber, the ark of the arcanum of the Minotaur.

In the end, the puma was nothing but the just bearable face of Joaquín. Beyond it was the entrance to the cave that leads to the labyrinth, and deeper still the bull with the thick black curls on its head and on the scruff of its neck, on its wet torso, and on the worms of its gut which mask the sex like the giants of Goya.

And what if sex were more independent of the personality that we know? And if there wasn't just a timid creature disguised as a puma but both puma and the timid one walking side by side? Or a nocturnal puma like Mr. Hyde, and the Minotaur only in the voluptuous nightmares of the victim. It would be the same, because the effect is the same.

It is a great part of our ignorance of life not to recognize the passionate vulnerability of childhood. The child who runs naked and disconsolate, as in that photograph of the Vietnamese girl escaping napalm. The child so confused by his desires, trapped in the paternal bedroom, that he forces himself to forget them like a secret he will be unable to forget, who wants to swallow something he will be unable to hold down, that the breast he loves and hates is a pillow both delicious and impervious, capable of what is both good and horrible, and so big.

We were born too small. That is why the iron gods and

the perfection of Adam and Eve emerged grown-up from their fathers, until at last Jesus took pity on us. Too small for that big chest, wide as a wall, which we hit with all our hate and love, until we go mad with contradiction and can only sleep, and then pass the rest of our childhood sleepwalking, so that we won't envy that squalor, the squalor that oozes out of them, the grown-ups.

33

L IKE a guardian angel, whose stitched up holes were saving me from the disgusting humours – 'I've always been very disgusting,' was her talisman, blotting out the confusions of filth; as if by inverting its meaning, and calling herself disgusting because everything disgusted her, she dismissed it. The rice powder spread on the wounded nose and the wobbly cheeks with such affected ceremony made us neutral, angelic, and protected.

What attraction could the Señora have offered me, that I, who in the end was a more or less normal boy, happy with school, with sport and so on, would dive into her faded skirts with such trust? The mystery of love. The first of all loves, chaste love.

Years of hide-and-seek, both adoring and pitiless, in the bathroom of the Calle Juncal, had kept me dormant. It was the journey, like the downpour which makes the indiscernible button flower on the cactus, that woke me up to the didactic tenderness of my great-aunt, the counterpart of the asperities of Juncal. And as I climbed the steps of the ship and discovered our cabin with the Bleu de Roi bedspreads and the desk and on it the diary opened for me, presided over by that tame and mitigated figure, I couldn't not fall in love.

It was my own trip, organized by my aunt for me as nothing had ever been organized before. And there was no room there at all for the satyr's snout and the screams of the jealous fairy, my parents with their dirty instincts.

I'm sure that this intimacy was the detonator. Pulled this way and that by the others I had never experienced the relief of having to say yes to only one. And if love reveals itself by altering one's life altogether, for me, who had always felt the urge to disappear and hide, the escapade with Totola fulfilled that unattainable dream of exclusion, but with somebody, but together.

It was my first disappearance, and the price was to be left alone with the kindest and most distant of mothers. She was not of the blood, but her stories fooled me by making me believe that I had a share of their glory. She was the only one who still kept the key of Paris. Yes, it was the best prize. And she was shielded by her widowhood, her snobbery and her barrenness from the dirty secrets that soiled Clara and Joaquín.

Virgin and Angel, always dressed, even her nakedness of nightgown and let-down hair didn't reveal anything but a pair of rounded shoulders and the tiny feet of an altar image. She was a sacred doll to hold in awe and to play with, for even with all her grandeur there was nobody softer. But even better, she didn't want to take anything in. Whatever might have thrilled the rest of the family seemed to resonate on a parallel boat, noisy and confused, and didn't reach her ears. We were alone, in a park of statuesque and voiceless couples; we mounted the stairs to sit on the morning deck and descended the stairs to enter into the evening dining room, bathed in an enchanted silence.

I don't know. What I do know is that I never felt happier. Now that my girlfriend is dust in the neoclassical tomb of Mariquita Sanchez and I don't have much time to wait till I join my dead mothers, when I compare this escapade with the other adventures of my life, I don't find any one of them so full, so happy or so innocent. Perhaps it wasn't love, though, as it didn't hurt. But I have spent a whole life missing it.

She wasn't of the blood; that was the gap through which Cupid could direct his arrow. I was too cloyed by the incestuous bathroom, and fascinated by it, not to run towards her. She was the nearest of the others, and she made this otherness clear. In all the feuding in the steam between the interchanging lines of my ancestry, there was nothing which matched her own. The first crooner of the national anthem and the liberator of Montevideo and the courtier who moved the Infanta towards Louis XIV were hers, not mine. In this contest her love for me went cold. Even her adored husband came in for her disdain.

My father could disgust me all right, but it was he, not the old aunt, who kept the key that would straighten me out. He, so splendid and so thick, who traded his son's respect for the dish of lentils of Amphitrite's silver bum.

Some years later, full of filial fervour, I ran to score a try on the rugby field of the Athletics Club of San Isidro, the only try of my life, only because the white wigged satyr had morphed into the rugby champion that he was; my father, in the club founded by his father, inciting me with his stentorian voice of success to follow him, a voice which pulled me up that one and only time from my usual mediocre game, to crown the finishing line. He didn't come again.

Poor babies both of them, father and son missing each other, what a waste. And yet, perhaps not that much, as the warps tend to leave their mark. That brand burnt on the rump of every son, copycat monkey of him who carried that child in his arms at birth, and in the case of my father in the indelible car of his visits to his CHADE patients of which the thankful baby carries forever the memory of that early embrace: which holds the man's hand, like the Angel to the Evangelist, and moves it to write what he is annotating now.

Order was restored that night. At the ball were all the well-known faces, and the sense of *déja vu* created by the conscientious costumes of the French ladies. Some were dressed as famous paintings — like the 'best' which Tina worshipped, everything had a brand. Madame Kesselman was a tube of Inca pink cut by Schiaparelli, Paupiette de

Langres had herself cut the dress and hat of Jeanne Avril from crêpe paper, using Fauve colours rather than Lautrec's, in homage to the Tropics. The Belgian Ambassadors, sailing home to retirement, had produced velvets in an attempt to impersonate the Archdukes, but being fat and blonde, they seemed in the leaden night more like victims of the 'Spanish fury' than its agents. Time had made them identical, and the Flemish *bonhomie* in their rabbity faces gave them an air of joy in the midst of torture.

But the triumph was my mother's. As if to create a stir, she arrived late — so unlike her — and everyone turned to look. She'd enlisted the help of a Spanish painter, who kept repeating himself, as Peninsulars tend to, 'Listen guapa, I've never seen an Indian with more style — Guapísima!' She was dressed as a Hindustani, in shawls of emerald silk. The Spaniard had painted a black star on her forehead and arranged a mantle of blue satin on her head.

'Really, he's made you look better than the Maharanee of Jaipur,' said Tina, impressed more by the effort than the result. She had done little more than take her favourite Dior dress from the wardrobe.

My mother smiled as she went by her, self-conscious but proud, and took my hand to receive the adulation of the crowd in its disguises. 'So you put that common little tart in her place,' she said to me. 'Well done. I didn't go. I didn't want to see your father making a fool of himself. It was enough to see him heading off puffed up like a peacock. I hear you made quite a fracas, and even got a gang together. Just like your hero, that ugly French boy who was always fighting. *Bon soir. Vous avez bonne mine, Monsieur l'Ambassadeur.*'

'*Madame, il n'y a que vous qui soit ravissante ce soir,*' was the answer of the velveteen rabbit. Sweaty and courteous, he bent almost double in an Escorialesque bow, with the unexpected grace of the fat.

So Bertrand had helped after all. I let go of my mother's hand and gave her my arm, piloting her through the throng like a proud father. Clara allowed herself to be taken, partly because she hated to move alone through these dangerous alleyways, fraught with pitfalls, and her terror of being a wallflower made her latch on to anyone's arm. She always had at her fingertips the excuses of the chaste spouse. 'Only fast women have any success at balls. The serious ones must walk and keep moving so as not to be seen to be alone. One might end up dead, but at least with one's honour intact.'

I led her around the groups, each parting to make a place for her, each appreciating her beauty, her fidelity, her class, her wit. And it was me who repaid the compliments, to which my mother responded with a confused silence. I was able to name the sad *chanteuse* Lautrec had portrayed in four brush strokes, easy since I had seen Madame de Langres copying her on one of my journeys to the library, and this won me an enchanted smile and the accolade of being the first Argentine to recognise her costume. I asked the Ambassadress if her costume as the Infanta Isabel Clara Eugenia was designed by Bérard, praise so excessive that it made her blush; I was unstoppable, in my glory as knight errant I appealed to everyone.

Dazzled by my mother's costume, I saw the emerald and the blue-black as a symbol of her abandonment, which had triumphed at last with such ostentation. I had forgotten my own disguise. Beside my dusky mother, a Hindustani widow painted by Gustave Moreau, I was a fine sketch of a Neapolitan fisherman. I had a cap made out of Tía Teodé's shoe bag, of green felt with a red fringe. From my shoulder hung my net, a white string bag filled with the little crêpe fishes. Of my attire my great-aunt could have said, as Satie said of Bach, 'My stuff is shorter and less pretentious.'

But the murmurs of *charmant!* were enough for me, especially alongside those which rained upon my captive queen.

Those Franchutes were fair: after spending a week cutting and stitching their own elaborate costumes, they were now being ecstatic about tat assembled in half an hour, with murmurs of *exotisme*, and '*regardez cette dame...un oiseau des îles...les Américaines du Nord par contre sont des bicyclettes...*' And Mélisande smiled at the Comtesse de Castiglione, while Pelléas, who was on honeymoon, couldn't take his eyes off us, and tried to push past the broad back of Philip II's daughter, who was pressing Clara to play bridge, a game she knew nothing about. In one corner were my aunts Eloísa and Isabel, who had lived in Europe so long they'd forgotten to play to their charms, and were dressed as two *petites-filles-modèles* – they were the evening's wallflowers.

A child's taste inclines to an exaggeration of reality. My fishes, with their black-lined eyes and black scales, which Tía Teodé had drawn with Chinese minuteness, seemed fine until I came across a girl who had got hold of a sailor's oilskins and a bag of real fish from the cook's freezer. Her version of myself was so true that it knocked me flat. The cute little cut-outs, which had earned the praise of Madame de Langres – if she'd known my aunt drew so finely, she'd have had her do her make-up for the ball, '*C'est tout à fait le trait Lautrec,*' – dissolved in the face of their originals. These were wet, shiny, more hyper-real than in Chardin, while mine were flat and abstract. I wanted to get at them, but couldn't think how, so instead I pushed myself at the Breton fishergirl, trying to grab the pipe from her mouth. I only wanted to be like her, but the pipe was wedged between her teeth, and I pulled until it hurt. She hadn't noticed me until then; she was pretty, and was enjoying a rustic version of my mother's success, pleased and impervious in her disguise when her teeth came under attack. She looked down to find a cartoon version of herself, and instead of acknowledging me as such, she stripped me naked with the fury of her grey eyes.

34

B ECAUSE of the narrow Artayeta line, the girls of Juncal
had very few close relations. That was why the Castells cousins Eloísa and Isabel were embraced like sisters,
they were the daughters of that nephew of Otramamá who
was four years older than her. They were also closer by
being the only girls of the house of the Calle Lavalle, which
they shared with Tío Pancho and Tía Teodé, in those days
when different branches of the family went on living
together in the big houses, but their long stay in Europe
had altered them.

Paris had made them discreet. They spoke in low voices,
they used irony not sarcasm, they were distant, a bit inscrutable. For them this journey was a return.

From what I gathered they had had problems in Paris.
The father, another spoilt criollo, according to Tía Teodé,
had squandered his Uriburu inheritance – the house that
ended as the archbishop's palace in the Calle Suipacha, the
desolate beauty of the Italian villa of Punta Lara, which
still shows off its glade of marble columns and balustrades
in a bare field by the river surrounded by chorizo stands –
and a great part of the Roca fortune of his wife. In the end
he had to accept a consulate in some French town obtained
for him by Tío Pancho. There is a photograph of his daughter Isabel as a teenager, with a dark coat and hat pushed
down over her ears, with the sad pale features of a Balkan
exile, standing next to a black car. 'This car is ours,' she
wrote underneath, a caption which wouldn't have occurred
to the niñas of the Calle Juncal.

In the end they came back, and Tía Teodé took Clara to
welcome them at Montevideo. Clara put on make-up and
high heels to meet her cousin of the same age, sixteen, who

was still in white socks, and rushed to hug her. But they resumed their intimacy and Isabel became for my mother the understanding sister she never had.

She opened her shy arms to Clara, hesitantly at first, she made her cousin wait, her cousin with that porteño vehemence she had almost forgotten, the Uriburu wit overlaid with Clara's madness, but then Isabel also found a heart worn on its sleeve. Still, it was one of those hearts of ours, pushy and slightly false; she would have come to terms with it slowly, after the effusions of the reunion.

Clara had a natural exuberance that Isabel must have admired and envied, and must have felt the need to appropriate, to copy the porteño poise, the flowering of rouge and high heels, which Clara was determined to bestow in her unexpected role of older sister. The little one seemed to suffer her lot quietly, like the expression of that photo by the big car suggested. Clara reckoned she had paid with blood for her own right of passage, but decided to hand it on for free to this *petite fille modèle*. Everybody happy then, but Isabel must have had to swallow a little disloyalty. Not only that her insecure cousin was looking around, perhaps unconsciously, for a more brilliant friend who would better match her older sister's standards, but she suspected that her own lack of smartness could embarrass Clara. I wonder if she ever realized that underneath these little treasons common to society, Clara's fidelity was iron clad.

But another thing: Clara had to win, all the time, regardless; it would have felt like another betrayal, were it not so innocent and unstoppable, so typical of the porteño rice-pudding, so quickly forgotten by Clara's generosity. But as in the end she would never emerge from her little girl knot of fury and competitiveness, the most energetic little girl in the world, very few of the visitors to her sisters' fourth floor ever forgave her, the new friends seduced by her charm didn't last, she would be tied up until the very end to the Sysiphean treadmill of the house of the Calle Juncal, the perennially closed doors of her sisters' rooms, because no amount of understanding Isabels could match its fatal attraction.

Now, on the ship, the calm behaviour of the Castells offered a rather pale backdrop to the Artayeta racket. They were, for better or worse, accustomed to be shunted around. They didn't do witty fancy dresses for the Crossing of the Line, they didn't quarrel. Tía Isabel's voice sounded so low in the high sea wind that she seemed to be hiding something. To me, it felt like a criticism of my mother's jealous tantrums. But I read her affection for me, though not at all affectionate in the demonstrative style of Buenos Aires, as a kind of secret consolation.

Tía Eloísa liked to talk. She had a slight accent, or really an accent contaminated by foreign 'll's which was pleasant to hear, like the cautious inflections of her sister. She spoke to her frivolous cousins about France, and books, but there was a sort of respect for their social poise, because though it was Tina who was the sociable one, while Pepa wouldn't venture out to even the smallest cocktail party, to Clara's dismay they appeared yet again inseparable, in the claustrophobic ship. It seemed as if Eloísa's chatter was needed to keep them close, like those lovers who babble unstoppably to each other about nothing to delay separation. Tina with her fashionable chic was a stronger draw than the paintings of the Louvre and the poems of Ronsard, and such was the voraciousness of our snobbery that it too affected the Parisian Castells, with their curious lack of elegance.

The objects of Eloísa's attraction didn't listen, one was obsessed with recipes and the other with dresses; apart from Clara who believed in culture, but Eloísa didn't give her the time of day.

Eloísa, and most of the habituées of the fourth floor of Juncal, didn't bother to acknowledge the youngest one. She loved Tina, who returned the devotion absentmindedly, criticized her clothes and raised her brows when she talked about books. People like people who don't overshadow them and Eloísa didn't care about clothes, she was attracted by that curious mixture of indifference and constancy, that absence of criticism which was distracted rather than benevolent, the offered and deaf ear, and a rigour which didn't pretend to morals but aimed at fashion and good manners. All this offered Eloísa a tepid and perhaps European comfort. And every time that she came up to the centro from San Isidro – where she had organized a family of girls around her stiff and pretty husband, whom she called 'my Mont Blanc', in a modest house at the corner of the abandoned palace where he had grown up, which had been donated to the Curia – she rushed to the fourth floor to feel restored.

Tina was so different, so removed from the swings of heat and cold that suffocated and touched Isabel. She had perfected her distant tone and Clara had given up trying to resemble her. Everything so measured and incisive. It might have been easier to approach Pepa who had some pull with women, although not much, with her discouraged heart; Clara thought she was hopeless.

I found the Castells more agreeable than the only other cousins, the Uriburus who were aggressive and raucous, and still carried the stigma after twenty years of our common bankruptcy, of having ended up in that apartment block of the fashionable poor, the Palacio de los Patos.

Paris was all very well, but what really singled out the Castells was the malleability of Cordoba. Not for nothing they were the granddaughters of President Roca, the Fox. One could feel the compromises and sacrifices of old cities, of provincial strictures which they might not have suffered but had inherited in their bones, bones with less fat and more humour than the porteños. It was as if the insecurity of their lives in Paris had been added to ancient resignations, and marked them with a stoic irony. I felt that these women educated in France were more criollas than my mothers. They seemed older. They showed that simple and immutable face, expressed by the bald stone façade of the Jesuit Church of Cordoba.

'Why don't you let in a bit of air?'

'What do you mean?' asks Clara aggressively. As always she confronts what is facing her but doesn't get it straight away.

'Well, I was just thinking... thinking in general... Joaquín, perhaps. I'm not at all sure, but then I don't think it's a bad method. You know, men. Always running away.' Isabel, who had let herself be beaten yet again at ping-pong, answered in a neutral and distant voice.

'What's got into your head? What have you been looking at? Who have you been listening to? My sisters... M'hija, if I can't trust even you...,' filling her fear with words as usual, as the serve with smash expects the counter smash of her sisters that doesn't arrive, and makes her doubt for a moment.

'Never mind, Clarucha, forget it. I don't know why I said it, you're the first to know I'm hopeless about men. But I saw you were a bit worried. No, don't listen to me, silly idea of mine,' Isabel murmured not changing her detached tone.

The boat has levelled them all in a field without shadows. Each of their lives is exposed to the others. There was nothing left to disguise, as Clara used to do on the phone to her cousin, not so much to hide as to suit herself. She liked to put new words to her life. Who knows how the other craftier ones managed, but my mother had never gone to school, and had emerged from her solitary nursery determined to cloak herself with noise, like Pallas in the clouds of battle, and in those windy decks where bodies were exposed as in the Trojan plain, there wasn't enough noise to cover up these deceits.

Isabel loved her though, 'te quiero...', something tricky for us who use 'want' as a word for love, but more, she wanted to help her. It was an impossible task. Only when asleep in the estancia, when she didn't expect a thing, not even our useless love, would Clara have left a half open crack for the colourless voice of her cousin offering her help. What danger. To mount a tiger when he is having his nap.

'Anyway. Don't you think it's more fun to play a bit? You like to boast of how you ensnare your beaux, or you ensnared them...'

'Oh, that's very true. I was always much more able than my friends. And not to speak of my sisters! I don't boast because it's a fact, and you know it very well. You were at that costume ball at Dulce Martínez de Hoz where I had Joaquín invited because poor boy he wouldn't have been on the list. Anyway, the idiot arrives dressed as a sailor, with that little medal of the Virgin which I used to give to my suitors hanging in the middle of his hairy chest! I had to ask you to get it back because I was stuck in a corner with Marcelo Sanchez Sorondo, another one with the medal.'

'And now as his wife, you don't go on charming him?'

'What? But that would only flatter his vanity. Of course one does it all the time, but there's a limit. No, you must be mad. If it is to ensnare, only Monsieur Couturier.'

'But listen, don't you like to flirt with men?'

'Yes, che, but not with the husband. One needs a rest.'

'Oh, Clara, rest is for me. I keep Eduardo a bit anxious with my coolness. Which doesn't cost me much as I'm always tired. But you would tire out a regiment. That's why I mentioned the air before.'

'Isabel, I don't understand you. You're too franchuta, and cordobesa on top. Your mother is more cunning than mine, though she's as little cordobesa as mine is salteña. No, she is more, because you still have La Paz, and Tía Copeta goes for holidays in Ascochinga, while we have nothing left up there, but that's fine as my mother would have to be tied up to move her to Salta.' And she went on thinking. 'But I love you because I don't get you. You talk to me about Joaquín, and though I won't tell you anything you must have heard that something's brewing. But it's funny, you don't make me angry, like the others do. No, you don't make me angry. On the contrary.'

She planted a quick kiss on her cousin's pale cheek and went to her cabin, heels clicking and head bowed.

In these various branches of the same trunk, the ancient criollo trunk of the young republic, there sprouted leaves of different greens, of various shapes and skins, and a thousand flowers, everything, like life: modest prairy macachines, simple roses, and roses of a hundred red petals, odourless arums and fragrant wallflowers, camellias with their distant and insipid look, jasmines, heliotropes, and sometimes even a silk orchid. They were variations that had taken shape within the absorbent strength of Buenos Aires, through the sucking-in of her people, as she defended herself from the void of her foundation, that didn't allow her children to escape, and if so where to? the claustrophobic ship, beached between the sea-wide pampa and the sea-wide river, variations that took their shape from the mixing of Spain and the criollo provinces, the sudden riches, incest, the countryside, the negro slave, the doing nothing, the years in Europe.

That's why the Santa Marta cousins were like a grove of talas with hard and tiny leaves, which in its Franciscan freshness housed humble macachines and daisies of an Andean innocence; of the Madero sisters, Tía Justita, under the parasol of the catalpa, was a congested and lazy rose, Tía Juana like a white carnation amid the serious leaves of an oak, and then the hothouse orchid of Tía Lula trembled with its liquid shades; Tina was a rosa gallica on a maclura hedge, Otropapá a leafless camellia on a buttonhole, Tía

Teodé a heliotrope that perfumes a drawer, and Clara, many young branches together, willow, eucalyptus, ombú, and some thorny tala; but for Tía Isabel it was the jasmine. Not the jasmine of the Cape with its dizzying velvet, filling the rooms of November with a perfume which refreshes or exacerbates the heat, and sets one yearning for a summer that never comes, no, the diminutive jasmine in its nest of black and pointed leaves, that quiet firefly in the dusk which shines less than it smells, whose whiteness seems to be in hiding and in need of warmth to permeate the night.

There is no doubt that we were all porteños, that jumble of ignorance and melancholy. And if most of us were dry, something that the Argentines have now lost, we inherited the austerity and the meagre imagination from American poverty. For it is a fabrication that America was ever rich, it was Europe who got rich on American silver. Our dryness came seasoned, like the sing-song voices of the Interior, with quechua herbs, the monotonous plain, and was corrupted by the profligacy of Paris.

It wasn't that we were versatile, only that we responded with as much guile as we could manage to the chaos of the River Plate.

Ignorance and melancholy? It pushed us to embrace what we didn't know but imagined we had lost. As we are Europe's heirs and we dive with arms outstretched, eyes, torso and legs apart to be carried away with her. Orphans on the butt of the world but at the Plate's mouth, that mouth which opens more than two hundred kilometres wide. It was not for nothing Darwin and his company found the porteñas more lively than English girls, those criollas who in their ignorance thought that the angelic invaders of 1806, so pretty, so blonde and so feminine, with their Scottish skirts, were Muslims.

Still there was a price to pay; something dark behind the silly innocence. And in that ship's sleek dining room under the diffused yellow light, around the table of the eight cousins, there stood the ghosts of Papá's brother, Papá's Paunero uncle, the grandfather of Eloísa and Isabel, the father of Eloísa's husband, and by the intimate small table, isolated against the wall, the ghosts of Tía Teodé's father and brother, and of her brother-in-law, Enrique Uriburu, Otramamá's brother, all dead by suicide.

Cullen, Paunero, Castells, Alvear, Lezica, Uriburu, every branch was loaded with its pathetic death. Just there, some steps behind every one of the travellers. Wives, sons, fathers, brothers, branded for the rest of their lives by the impulses of a spoilt upbringing, by those unrestrained subconscious knots which burst into calamity.

It's not that I knew anything about the circumstances that pushed these criollos to throw in the towel with such abandon, but the apparent reason was the sudden loss of the fortunes which had fallen from the sky like the fattest of lotteries, and in the case of my father's family, there was a streak of madness which had started with the hanging of a young lover from a lamp-post at the Presidential Palace of La Paz.

The branches that came down to me were short. While Buenos Aires was full of hundreds of people of the same name, those who brought me up were the last of their line. With the names of the suicides. As if we had been the survivors of Venice after the fall of the Republic. Perón was our Bonaparte.

But the women, immune to these excesses, had to pick up the pieces. First, doggedly, with silence, total and unending silence; and after many years with lies, to confuse everything, and cover with a pall of silence things on their way to being forgotten, and which flowed at last like everything, into oblivion. At any rate this was the plan that got them out of bed in the morning.

These branches were not rotten, it was just that the sap

was flowing lazily, and its leaves sprouted with their usual shape but yellowing. Little flowers, little twigs, little leaves, and sometimes the exquisiteness of an autumn rose.

Most of the branches were proud of their rather humdrum chastity, that is why the improbable corruption of the Unzués was hardly believed, with its brothel-like flowering, tropical Venus flesh-traps of laughable avidity, devouring policemen on the street corners of the Barrio Norte or adolescent cabecitas negras from the provinces, just off the train in Retiro station, who would be stalked by an Amazon with a chalk white face, scarlet mouth and carbon bandeaux, reclining naked under a silver mink coat on the red leather cushions of a white limousine, and would be led to her by the hand of her chauffeur.

Tía Teodé disapproved of fornication, but as a social disorder, not a sin. A story that she liked to tell was of a visit with her mother-in-law to the house of the cultivated and nouveau-riches Luros, where a butler showed them into a drawing room to present them with an enormous cabbage of black satin shaking on the knees of a footman. Before the patrona managed to disengage herself, they turned on their heels and left. But it was Clara who suffered illicit sex as an affront.

I never understood why she flared up with such a spinsterish fury. Unless she associated the sexual awakening of her sisters with her jealousy like Cinderella abandoned in the nursery with Miss Emily; she would unleash that total rejection which came out naked like a scream: 'What filth, what a whore,' without curiosity, without a trace of humour, or the itch to revisit the scene of the crime, even from the corner of her eye. It went deeper than the anger of the moment. She forgave nobody.

I don't know if my mother told Isabel her worries about Susi Bosch, the flirtatious divorcee who had latched herself onto our group, as she didn't like to show herself vulnerable in front of her less attractive cousin. But she had to confide in somebody, and wasn't used to controlling her nerves. Tía Isabel always seemed happy to listen, she spoke so little. She must have calmed her as they trounced each other at ping-pong.

Such a contrast: one pale and slight, hopping like a chingolo sparrow as she sent back the little white ball with cunning shots, the other swarthy, furious and broad, crashing her serve against the net, losing by sheer excess despite one or two triumphant smashes. But they shared something: the unspoken determination to win. Though generally Isabel gave up in the end, out of breathlessness and a sense of proportion.

Sometimes she kept enough breath after a match to invite me to an orange juice at the bar, the only drink I liked on the ship because it wasn't free. No, she wasn't indestructible, under her pretty caution she hid a fragility more dangerous than Tina's tuberculosis, which revealed itself when she died suddenly three years after our trip, from a brain lesion she had carried since her birth. After her there were almost no Rocas left of the blood of the great president.

I have known, but from some distance, relations who were sheltered by a name they shared with many others, indifferent to the trifles I describe here, apart from the comfortable and coarse pride in their own things, sometimes inexplicable, like the pride of being Argentine, which divides us into two bands, the insensitive and the nervous.

I think the short branches such as ours paid the price of culture. It's not the same as saying that the insensitive were stupid or even uncultured, but compared with the other's refinement, the thousand Figueroas – to use a name both illustrious and widespread – didn't just seem to be but were of another class, though their vanity in numbers made them blind. Just as with Tina's elegance, when she complained how her careful choices would go unnoticed.

Porteño jealousy cuts down three quarters of perception. Of course the male line was broken, that line so honoured in Europe where the king of Spain is the direct descendant of the thousand-year male line of Hugues Capet, or in England, where, incredibly, people deny the female name, but still our own disparaged women somehow managed to keep the party going, although neither the music nor the dancers were discernible. There was no Hapsburg chin nor Bourbon nose to place them, no pavane or cielito. They were fast flowing currents or slow streams, all sinuous and some invisible, which seemed to sweep along what wasn't theirs, or got lost in remote lagunas and emerged unexpectedly somewhere else to carry on its indifferent flow.

Since Mendoza, who founded Buenos Aires nine years after the sack of Rome by Charles V, our porteño bloodline had mingled with Indian captives and some pretty black slaves, and had been whitened every two generations or so by a Spanish macho. Thanks to the anarchy of the port, the blood of Centurión, Barragán, Hurtado de Mendoza, Gaete, all without portraits until the XIX century, had passed on to us their capricious features: a Guinea snout and the tiny pompon of Shirley Temple, first cousins barely recognisable to each other. But we were one of the few streams which run down from the Andes, the union of arribeños and abajeños – highlanders and lowlanders – and in Perú they had been painted since the XVI century, showing their proud and empty faces, all fraudulently pale; and we produced some notable combinations, like that cousin of Clara who died a countess in Austria and who, two metres high, as stylized as a Hindu idol, as green as an avocado, had become an emblem of America, like those marble river gods which represent the continents.

The classification of these kaleidoscopic features is as inept as Borges' 'Chinese inventory'; and it would have been a relief to give it up and sit at a café in Buenos Aires and just register absentmindedly the passing faces. But the Jesuits resolved to catalogue America the moment they set foot in it, and after five centuries we are still enlightened by their errors. The Buenos Aires strollers have no idea to whom they owe their noses, but we are meant to know. The Republic might suffer from an excess of errors but it lacks catalogues.

There is an urgency for words. So I beseech you to populate my madness, fill it with words, so that to our China of the future, to those indolent Pampean streams, we may add the mercury courses of the tomb of Shi Huangdi.

35

'WHERE's your father?' Clara had got rid of Pelléas and was searching for him. Her success lacked one witness. She hadn't decked herself out for him – in Juncal they dressed only for other women, which was why they took such care – but she needed him to witness her triumph.

'I've got to show him I'm still attractive.' It was something I'd never heard her say before the trip – like the rest of us, she was unaccustomed to living each day with her husband in public. The faces that peopled the Calle Juncal had become as ritualised as the Liturgical Year, and brought no surprises. Nor were many afforded by outings in a society in which the couples were bound and sealed on their wedding day, the husbands got their thrills during office hours, and the tiniest deviations of the women were dissected without mercy or disgust over lunch.

Now, in those days at sea, if Clara had considered her married life in any detail, which she probably never did, it must have seemed transparent, like life in the countryside, so crammed with domestic routine that its panache seemed superfluous. I knew by heart the letters she wrote from the estancia during the early years of her marriage – they were scattered through her dressing-table drawers, where I rummaged when I was feeling sad – and they were little more than lists of forgotten clothes, dressmaker's orders, anxieties about the improvement or otherwise in her children's looks. Nothing beyond the contents of her dolls' house seemed to interest her.

But she had married an orphan, and in her orphaned subconscious a plant of the most urgent feelings began to sprout its confusing leaves. My father came naked to Juncal, his world peopled only by those vague siblings, and the Mamapola who took care of them all with the equanimity of a school matron. A stronger yearning took hold in my mother. She dedicated herself to the task of nursing and admiring him with a narcissism so innocent and intense that any life outside her role of mother-lover was reduced to playing with dolls. He was the answer to her impossible longings, those dreams of a last-born confined to the third floor with a nanny or to the estancia with her great-aunt while her sisters were dancing and flirting and sunbathing in Mar del Plata, and he arrived from nowhere, choking her. She had grown up feeling short and abandoned, and then at the age of fifteen, she'd hurried, head down as usual, straight into the glass door of the estancia dining room, and torn half her face off, leaving her with a terrible scar down the left-hand side of her face, which instead of healing normally left keloids of white dead flesh branding her cheek with an infamous wound. And then suddenly she had this man, a man without ties, full of beauty and vitality and the mystery of his rough manners, free of the sterile elegance of her father, young, new, poor, intelligent – he got his medical degree at twenty-one – and to top everything, and because one didn't expect to find Clark Gable in a drawing room, he was well-born. All for her – it must have felt like robbery. She paid for it by disappearing, effacing her own vanity in his. To his soft, macho and boastful frame she clasped an iron shadow.

She felt free and sated. If they hadn't been so poor, she might even have run away from Juncal. She stopped trying to find herself in books, she handed me over to the other women as if I wasn't hers with an absent-minded gesture of abundance. As though in a dream, for her life had overflowed, she wrote detailed instructions to Aurea, dressmaker of Juncal, ordering lace and velvet and tweed from Harrods for the decoration of us dolls, who would advertise the triumph of her trickery in the Plaza San Martín or at the parties of the Barrio Norte.

It was here that she pulled off the most serious of her disguises. More than the enchanting Inca Cupid with its bamboo bow and its heron wings which survives in our album of carnival photos as her posing on a stone bench in the estancia, more than the thrifty housewife who saved toothpaste on the brush, more even than the young and virtuous matron given to sexual censorship: the costume of 'doctor's wife' excited her like no other.

With her ignorance of a niña of the barrio of the Cinco Esquinas, who jumped straight from the nursery to the ballroom with no school in between, she dressed herself in an apparel of ridiculous rhetoric. Doctor's Wife, just like 'science,' when much later she set up the Foundation for Child Endocrinology, in order to force herself completely into Joaquín's life and which ended up sinking him; these were the mantras that carried the *beau idéal* of herself. Doctor's Wife encompassed everything and revealed nothing, certainly nothing of her scarred face or her short legs, or even less of her plight as the youngest sister knocking at a closed door.

Professional titles had no currency at the house of the Calle Juncal. If any of her men folk had managed a lawyer's degree in a past as remote as that of their schooldays, they had forgotten it. Nobody had a profession. One founded newspapers, planned enterprises, inspected estancias, accepted a ministry from time to time, and certainly the presidency of the great clubs, and in all of this one lost money, but to work steadily and industriously, no.

That was why the arrival of Joaquín was such a boon for Clara's imagination, so hungry was she to transform herself into something new. He was so different. His grandfathers had owned important law firms, thank God they were traceable because of the family connection, his poverty was compensated by his title, he needed to earn his living like Charles Bovary, 'what will Papa say?' 'but then Papa, who stays in bed until lunch time, the shame of it,' – expostulations she would never have allowed herself before the arrival of this new husband that forced her to take a new position, no! She was never forced, she was blessed, although she wouldn't have thought of it like this, she never thought she acted, that's why, I say, that the role was inspired, and the moment that she found a name for it she embraced it with her usual fury, so irritating to her docile and lazy father, and proclaimed its heroism without realizing that it fitted her like a glove.

How necessary they must have been for Clara, those roles she assigned to her dolls in her isolated floor of the house of Juncal. According to her sister Pepa they were performances which filled her days. At least the naming of their roles did. It seemed as if she named them in order to perform them. A *bourgeois gentilhomme à rebours*.

My mother used to describe herself as lazy, and she contrasted her achievements against that exaggerated sense of sloth. But as the normal calmness of people eluded her, those disordered efforts detracted from their serious purpose with their adolescent noise, and forced her to hold up her title like a shield, the shield of her protective and repetitive mantras.

If she had remembered her early readings she could have said with Montaigne: 'I prefer to be pleased by my stupid behaviour than behave properly and rage.' But there was nobody less philosophical than Clara in her prime, and she would never have applied Montaigne's doubt to herself.

And yet, when she was carried away by her humour, she laughed at her own foibles as if Otramamá's Uriburu bird had veiled them with its wings and taken her in its flight high up over fields and hollows where she herself on horseback, very small and far away, would be watched over by a neutral eye, both sharp and affectionate.

What suited her most in her new role were the medical

congresses, where she dressed with a chic that seduced the Nobel prize winner, Dr Houssay, and chatted him up shamelessly, 'to help Joaquín,' with a poise the other wives were unable to match. These prizes were now reserved for her, the prizes she had felt robbed of at the balls by society ladies just as elegant, but less tense.

She planned her appearances at the medical dinners and awards as though protected by an invulnerable mask, free from any anxiety, as she didn't recognise herself in those institutional mirrors, nor the learned company. She might have kept the respect of the illiterate for 'science', but she measured the social level of the scientists like an altimetre.

God, how she loved the titles of these lies. Hidden behind them she could eye the smart women who ignored her and scatter them with a nod, like she did to the Bad Fairy in her play room. Because though we all repeat the gestures of childhood, in Clara they seemed to have condensed for ever, as if her angry energy had kicked in from the start, full throttle, as if she had been born ready-made and perfected as a girl, and that girl went on walking side by side with my adult mother, who behaved so grown up and serious, who seemed to have kept nothing of the girl she once was, at least to me, who always looked at her spellbound and was so ready to pardon her with my love. She was like an invisible double, which made her both impossible and adorable.

But there were two, not just her, who laid on the seduction with a trowel. There was the duo of the ideal couple, whose performances I must have watched without noticing, perhaps applauding, but of which I remember so little that I wonder how they organized their effects.

It must have been Clara who gave in. She wasn't going to outperform somebody she already possessed. She would manage him.

She surprised herself. So much so that she boasted about something that any other woman would have taken for

granted and which confirmed that she had grown up isolated, like a kind of *princesse lointaine* with a lot of *peau
d'âne*, and that she was unique. As though she had learnt
human speech and custom like a child suckled by beasts.
Clara, bred among the conventions of the house of Juncal, her unitarian grandmother, her clubman father, with a
mother who complained wittily of her imprisonment, with
excessively frivolous sisters, discovered herself so different
from all of them that to say good morning in everyday
Spanish made her laugh with wonder.

Something similar happened in her manipulations of the
macho. Play had been her first refuge, and she seemed to
marvel that playing with her dolls in the nursery had found
currency in adult life. It was another trigger for her glee.

'I learnt quite early to give rein to your father, what a
baby. Men have to believe that they get their way. Everything else is a piece of cake.'

She savoured these ladylike clichés like delicacies. But
her uniqueness was in the Quijote expressions which she
squandered with a bounty unconscious of their beauty, or
even their strangeness, and which I, confusedly, recognized
with a feeling of pride. But then, who doesn't like to see
oneself as the son of a fairy?

And as I grow older, driven by that love that Clara never
learned to accept – 'how you did love me in those days,
when you used to run after me on the boat to Europe and I
couldn't think how to push you back into Tía Teodé's arms,
and just when I felt you'd fallen in love with her, you'd
jump on me suddenly with those eyes of *merlan frit*, as Papá
would say, or better, of a strangled calf, just when I didn't
have a minute for you, what with your father's philandering
with that Susi Bosch and Tina's smarminess, because that
beast was always up to something, there was never a minute, as I say, to breathe, to calm down, because in the end
you never stopped being a baby, precocious or not, making

all those demands on me out of the blue, because ever since you were born you've always, I repeat always, been a pain in the neck' – I find it increasingly urgent to scratch down into that tight and confused pit, the result of the isolation of an imaginative girl whose desperate but stubborn knocks at her sister's door, like the necessary pressure for the crystallization of a gem, that there should've burst out such a twisted, inventive and poetic tongue.

Only at the poetical instant of the jump; for it wasn't the expression of a poetical mind. All of Clara's imaginative effort was spent in finding her place: the few times when she was given it, exhausted, like a boa that had swallowed too much, she would fall asleep.

But who can measure poetry? Doesn't its language burst anywhere? From the Irish navvy who gets drunk in a pub of the English foe and takes revenge by making his English flash with the sinuousness of his Celtic wit, or the complaining and meticulous letters of a porteño majordomo written to the patron with such verb, that the patron, a writer, can only envy. There is no doubt that Clara was one of them. Like that time, when with that mental crack to which Cervantes' tongue seemed to cling, she addressed the chauffeur who was parking the car at night at the end of the casuarina avenue with its sound of a darkened wind, and said, with the gesture of pulling down a curtain over the still lit headlights: 'Close its eyes'.

But she couldn't be left alone. Particularly without Joaquín, she couldn't be without him. At the estancia, after a tense lunch where we were forced to speak in two foreign languages, we dolls had to massage her through the siesta, trace love messages on her wide, brown Inca back which smelt deliciously of *Femme* and rub cream very slowly on her angry face, urged on by panic at seeing her so depressed and lonely. Because, though she was surrounded by her children, by Matilde, Miss Judy, Gilda, Rafaela and the cousins of San Carlos, San Francisco and Santa Marta, and at the place she claimed to love best of all, Joaquín was working in Buenos Aires, and so Clara was dying.

Only the night revived her. Then she dressed for dinner, as she did throughout the year in preparation for his coming home, and we would go into the dining room to be kissed goodnight, and her cheeks shone in the darkness, reflecting the candles, as she sat alone at the end of the dark table, against the fireplace, close to the telephone, and if it rang while we were with her she jumped up like a girl as we watched her, feeling maternal understanding, because our father's voice brought us relief and happiness too. And perhaps the weight the estancia has imposed on each of us children began in those empty and impossibly long days, when Clara seemed to burden us with her abandonment.

Now, this Atlantic crossing had altered ten years of routine, as if my parents had chosen unconsciously the public life of the ship against which to weigh their marriage. They faced each other in the scenery of the tropical night, against the backdrop of the overwhelming sea and the dusty stars, surrounded by strangers who made riddles of love. Hadn't the Spanish painter said that she was lovely? And that Monsieur Couturier, the banker who sported a quiff like Jean-Henri Aumont — a little common, but tall and tanned with forget-me-not blue eyes — hadn't he stared at her constantly, and struck up a conversation at the bar about the disastrous economic policies of Perón? This flattered her anti-Peronism, although it also made her doubt his amorous intentions. And Pelléas, who was cute but just a baby, hadn't he escaped his bride in order to follow her to the upper deck? Like a good daughter of Juncal she thought and spoke of love as it were described by Delly, the novelist we had both read at the estancia. Of sex, she spoke in a brutal and masculine way, in infrequent outbursts of the Uriburu tongue, as if she didn't know what she was saying and was using a borrowed language, like the gaucho speech used by the ladies of Maipú to describe the couplings of animals. And always, and like me, she was driven by her urge to run towards danger rather than avoid it.

'Where the hell is that cretin?' This time Clara addressed the entire room, her eyes narrowed. She charged forward like a bull, fending off obstacles with her sari, the black star on her forehead seeking out her prey like a headlamp. She hunted with an animal instinct, without any human indecision. Her charge was a bull's, but her nostrils flared like a cow sniffing out her offspring in the corral, her nape dipped to follow the trail, yet without the innocence, the pathetic uncertainty of all creatures. Clara was possessed by a divine wrath. I laughed with horror, and felt again that disgust I was learning to associate with my mother.

Stop it, I begged her silently. Control yourself, don't shame me, why must you show your jealousy, this terrible anger, don't show it, get into bed and cover yourself with your sari and go to sleep. Wasn't it enough to receive everyone's praise? Didn't I help you? Not that I don't want him to be caught, but someone other than you should stop him in his tracks, someone who couldn't care less. One of those people who don't really see, don't need others, Tía Isabel, or Pepa, who seems to accept the world as if she were mute, or even Tía Teodé who can keep secrets, not someone like Otramamá, who exaggerates, and above all not you, you who brings the house down with your fear. Don't think I wouldn't love to see you whack him with your shoe, not those cork ones, the stilettos you get Matilde to bring when you want to hit me. I'd love to see him shrivelling in a corner, the punctured macho, giggling but impotent under your rage, that fury of yours which diffuses as you scream and scream, until its spent and next minute you've forgotten it, while we tremble for days.

Tina tackled her.

'Stop worrying, just stay quiet.' Her voice was hard and calm. 'He'll be up on the bridge. You know what he's like when he drinks – he'll be pretending he's a sailor in control.' She was brave, with the silent composure of those who would resist to the end, and she offered Clara an invention so improbable that it was possible it would work. Her *idée fixe* was the social order, and Clara was on the verge of creating a scandal. She had to be stopped.

But the younger sister wouldn't listen. She pushed on, still looking downwards, both Hathor and the Minotaur. Tina changed tack.

'Don't be so mawkish. You're too old for these little jealous tantrums. Let him go where he likes, you don't have to trot after him. I've told you he's on the bridge, and you're not going up there dressed as a Maharanee and foaming at the mouth. There's nothing more common than running after one's husband as if you were on your honeymoon, especially with that big brown calf of a son mooing after you. Dónde se ha visto?' Tina's thin, dry voice accumulated authority as she spoke.

'And what would you know about that?' The retort was *de bas en haut*, and the ascending scale drew its weight from the Calle Juncal. Feeling foolish, Clara turned her fury on the blonde stiffness, enhanced by the New Look, of her unmarried older sister. She arched her back like an enraged mongrel. 'Like I said, what would *you* know about honeymoons? How would you dare to give *me* a lesson on how to deal with men?' Now she rounded on Pepa. 'One of you offers herself up as the slave of a lazy pretentious bastard, a thief to boot, who cuckolds her before everyone, forces her to organise his girlfriend's abortions, and when she can't take any more she crawls home with only the clothes on her back. Then when she finally manages to get herself a lover, she gets left again. Why? Because she's a bore. So she's turned herself into a tart for nothing. And as for the other …'

The glove and the thin arm that executed it muffled the slap, but its force was sufficient. The rows between the niñas of Juncal were aerobic – they emerged sweaty and calm, and more fraternal than ever, having tested once more their impregnable hides.

If it was indeed the water of the Styx that sprang from the white bathroom, it served only the bathers in their knifing spars, who emerged unscathed and convinced, wrongly, that everyone in Juncal shared their invulnerability. Not Otropapá, our drone king, certainly not the other absent macho, and not our final trio, of whom my sister, arriving last, was denied that ritual immersion – not even I, who was included – none of us were possessed of that armour plating. The rites and ceremonies of the Guerra Florida, the thrill of believing themselves wounded, the simulacrum of damage and revenge, were for the niñas alone. And Clara had exposed to them her Achilles heel, that which tied her to my father.

She had become mortal, and so she could no longer go to war as she had in the old days. And like the family bird, which inspired the Uriburus to eloquence only before an audience, the Stygian bath water made the Artayetas invulnerable only between themselves – most of the time Otramamá was witty but not that interesting, and out in society Clara couldn't shake off her Cinderella fate. But each retained the memory of their triumphs, and this made them deaf to the language of mere mortals.

'*Ses ailes géantes l'empêchent de marcher*,' the bird might have whispered to my grandmother, to the delight of Cousin Bebette; and Clara would have aimed blindly for someone's weak spot, without concern or even awareness of the wound she caused.

36

CLARA would have given anything to penetrate the bond between her elder sisters. She never tired of trumpeting her own achievements, of counting them with her fingers, of talking of them to herself in the mirror. They were real enough: it was only she, in the end, who had brought new life to the house. But nothing could staunch the wound of her exclusion. 'I am the cleverest but the ugliest. My *sisters,*' – she couldn't stop mouthing it, it tasted both hopeful and bitter – '... are tall. My sisters are smart. My *sisters* don't even notice me when I come into the room. It is their fault that I hate women, but I don't care, anyway I always preferred men. And haven't I had more success than *them*?'

Joaquín was her crowning success. It made her sisters' lack more obvious as they came down alone to the ship's dining room, Tina with her new-look, a bit over designed, a bit too precise, modelled on her father's dryness, and Pepa dressed in Tina's cast-offs. And for me, looking from the little table by the wall, they were the shadows, the negative, of the radiance of the plain one, with more glow on her cheekbones than Dior's satins, with the insolence, false? true? that she shared or copied from her husband, the real reason for my irritation and rejection. Whereas in Tina's mannequin dryness I found a kind of neutral acquiescence, like the aloofness of the furniture of the Calle Juncal. She just smiled and went past, although without leaving me alone; she would always make a place for me undemonstratevly, and welcome me around her bed.

Around her body martyred by the tuberculosis, which had robbed her of one breast, eaten two or three ribs, lowering her shoulder, and left her with a scar with its stitches on one leg, because they had to repair the torso with the tibia. But Tina with elegance managed to turn these injuries to advantage. The scar on the leg seemed like a scale on the silk of the stocking, the higher shoulder suggested her disdain, and as she dressed with such luxurious care her clothes seemed like a suit of armour protecting some heroic wounds.

I don't know how she might have been before I knew her. She was thirty when I was born. Clara offered me up as a godchild to console her in her illness. I called her Manina, god-mummy, until I was twenty.

The photographs show a young girl too adorned for a long face, thick lips and small eyes. But soon enough, as she sheds the ugly duckling plumes of puberty, one glimpses the determined swan. A beret, a cinched mackintosh, a search for form which would correct the defects of the cradle. Shoes bought too small which would exact the price of hammer toes, the long face free from the brim of the hat, the hair up, the big mouth in fashion at last, and the thinness, the irredeemable Artayeta thinness, which according to Otramamá almost killed her.

If I don't mention her inner life it is because she didn't consider it. As I said before this asceticism had its reward, in the mirror. Tina never bothered to impress people who didn't dress as carefully as her, among them, Borges. Once in a while she would sigh: 'What a waste. If only someone, just once, would take some notice.'

Her long illness left her quite alone. She got out of bed without her fiancé and with a crippled body, which she would have inspected without the affection with which I accepted it. But then children take the loved body whole, and I loved Tina's crooked shoulder as much as Otramamá's varicose veins. And she had become scarred, hardened; I couldn't help noticing on the boat, in the way she treated my mother. They still carried on the nursery courtesies, just about, and they gave each other presents, which Clara accepted with more pleasure than her sister but kept quiet about, because although presumably they loved each other they expressed it grimly. Moved by her heart or her anxiety and all too aware of how much she had suffered, Clara gave me to Tina. She complained, of course, about her generosity, but without repenting of it. It wasn't so much a present as an offering.

Tina might have loved her putative son but she disappeared on the boat like the others. I only remember being with her once, one afternoon at the bar, when she bought me one of those twenty franc orange juices and told me that she had always dreamt of having two beautifully dressed sons. She didn't need to look at me.

But there they were now, she and Pepa, like Joaquín and Clara, on a creaking island, burnished and driven on its course, between the immense sea and the immense sky, loosened from the heavy habits of Juncal and quite lost.

The bodies one knew so well changed size on the ship. Their constant presence, or worse, the way they were perceived by others, deformed them like in a dream, when the face on your pillow gets up and puts on John Barrymore's teeth to eat Claudette Colbert. Everything got confused, the unending French, the fall-back English, the complicated and not at all criollo courtesies, the distant good manners that leave one standing, the hard women and the effeminate men.

Luckily the Artayetas could use each other to complain and also could ask advice from their Parisian cousins, but not too much, because it would have shown their ignorance. And there went Eloísa Castells embarking on some long discussions with the Belgian ambassadress over the difference between the culture of oil and the culture of butter which it had never occured to her to ventilate in the Calle Juncal, and left them gaping.

Feeling at a loss they plunged into flirting. I couldn't

believe that the disdainful icons of the white bathroom had transformed themselves into these prevaricating clowns. The only one who kept her manner was Clara, who had so many. Pepa and Tina, each in her own way, had changed personas.

Pepa, very nervous, very false, so diminished that even I felt sorry for her, made use of the weapons at hand, the twee talk of the genteel canasta players of the Hotel California, and spread them very thinly, with a lot of stuttering. 'That's enough, Pepa, twittering like the Cacha and the Titina! You're pathetic, always copying exactly whatever you hear. You're an embarrassment,' Tina would slam at her on their short walks on the deck after lunch, before the eldest rushed to bury herself in bed until the nine o'clock dinner.

And as for Tina, who was so cagey, the most I could discover was a redoubled version of her usual services offered to the two ambassadresses – the Belgian and the Uruguayan one in Paris, a handsome, dark skinned lady with the name of the painter Figari and with a loose pupil which danced in her eye like a broken kaleidoscope – and also to some titled French women. Even so, I detected more pirouetting than was noticed by the unfocused jealousy of Clara.

But I was just looking in from the outside. It was amongst themselves, looking at each other and searching their faces on the mirror, that they failed to recognize the familiar. It was amongst themselves that confusion revealed its contradictory colours. That overworked phrase: 'Sos otra!' 'You are another person!' if a dress suited or two kilos were lost, didn't come to their lips, because for once it was true. Like a shy person is turned into a brave one by war, those tussles of the Juncal bathroom, one-act farce rehearsals, were going to enter now, how dreadful, into a more dangerous phase.

That's why the slap that sounded matt on Clara's face, to cut short a jealousy that I had never seen before so fully expressed, also revealed an unknown side of Tina, a loss of control which shocked me, for all that I was accustomed to my Amazon's brutal confrontations. They shouted at each other from morning to midnight pouring out insults far worse than Clara's riposte, but they would never actually touch.

I started to piece things together. Tina befriended, almost became intimate – she who kept her old friends without bothering to listen to their twice a day phone babbles while she polished her nails and only went out of her way with certain social stars to whom she offered services but no intimacy – with that *bête noire* of Clara's, more dangerous than the Second Class Amphitrite, Susi Bosch, pretty, and single, who had danced so humorously with sudden Turkish contortions at one of the ship's parties. Joaquín had had his eye on her for some time. But it hadn't been him but Tina, with her lack of suppleness, surrounded by sisters and cousins, curious in principle and totally idle, who would sidle into a corner to chat her up.

Clara with her lapwing instinct to mark her territory, started to flap at her. 'What is this sudden curiosity with Susi Bosch? She is dim, common, she's got thick ankles, and a tart who flirts even with the stewards. You seem like two excited girls prattling about boyfriends. Well you, in fact, because like all able whores she is quite furtive. Anyway, she's not after *you*. Might you be offering yourself as a Celestina?'

'Mind your own business. Run along, go after your Couturier like a mooing calf and leave me alone. Or go to play ping-pong with Isabel.'

'When we get back and I tell Matolita or Beba Vela that you've got a crush on Susi Bosch, they won't believe what they are hearing.'

'Don't be so stupid,' and she walked away with that hesitant amble that was considered charming in Mademoiselle de Lavallière.

The final great scene of the Crossing of the Line ball was the dénoument of these games. Clara must have suspected that Susi Bosch and her husband were meeting secretly, with Tina as their accomplice. Hence the lowing of the wounded beast. She couldn't bear even the slightest suspicion of the horror that her sister would get near, my God, to meddle, to take him away? no, how revolting, but to manipulate for that other whore to get in there, 'my sister may have almost died but she always had everything more than me, both united against me, but not Pepa perhaps, thank God, because though she is not that good she's hopeless or lazy or she never had any feeling for sex, but as for this crafty demon, evil by birth and evil by her sufferings, no, it can't be true, she can't be so perverse and so whorish to make the bed for this slut to take Joaquín from me.'

In my mother's rivalry with a twin-headed totem, so constant in its hostility and mistrust, there was an equally constant aftertaste of submission, perhaps because one of the heads appeared benign. Though it wasn't so much the goodness as the brilliancy which subdued Clara, the totem's masculine strength that wiped out anything caressing or maternal, and transformed it in her eyes to the cruel and dazzling Amazon, the androgynous Artemis who would bring out her own predatory side. It would be the three hunting together, an unattainable bliss that killed her.

The fear and the desire made her bristle every new day with a new fight. The nerves of an orphaned cat who would have gone to sleep with an amnesic purr if those red nails would have written love poems on her back — something that we, rescuers who arrived too late, never could, though we did try to calm down in the siestas at the estancia, writing messages that she couldn't understand: 'What is this girl saying, what is she writing?' 'Mamita, I love you,' — 'This child doesn't know how to spell, it would be better if you tried in English, good practice.'

But it's impossible to suss the motives of those liars who lied to themselves more compellingly than to one another. Of those entrenched and voluble souls who hid behind their words and seemed incapable of repentance. They looked at the world around them, ripped it up like a doll, or like a carancho would a lamb, and in the mirror they saw nothing but their well combed hair.

Joaquín, then. Was Joaquín really Clara's love, or even better, another weapon against her sisters? Would she have been capable of ditching them for the love of Joaquín, when she couldn't stop loving them or fighting them?

Sometimes I think that despite however much she was in love with loving him, she would have survived losing him more easily than them. Who were two in one. But does anyone die of love?

Pepa and Tina balanced each other well. The essential sloth of the elder one, whose writing didn't even form the verticals and looked like a line of water, her passivity, her sadness channelled into eating and sleeping, was like a nest for the diligent fraternal ant, who ate and slept merely to recharge her mined body that worked by day and partied by night with insipid determination, as if to prove that there was no chink in its recovery.

They both survived together. Although they wouldn't lick each other's wounds, they were conscious of their common destiny. They had been born and had almost died together, as Pepa convalesced for years from the break-up of her marriage. And it was at that moment of shipwreck and of land reached at last, when they were checking the damage with a side-long look and preparing for a new start, that it occurred to the youngest one, the unnoticed one, who had only ever suffered a few cuts to her face, to bring nothing less than this trophy to the house.

Of course she offered it around to everybody, like when she broke her piggy bank to help when Otropapá went bankrupt, or when she offered me to Tina as a cure. But no one forgives the rich for their presents, and if they took them and looked after them, and the change made them young and gave them hope, the door still remained closed.

It was an exile for Clara. Like being forced to live in the estancia, exiled from the horrorful loves, to be forced to endure the recurrent nightmares, excluded from the room behind the door. There wasn't a day that she didn't go up and knock. But it wasn't that they hated her, they just didn't see her. And with more reason now when she had given them such cause for envy.

Also they were religious. They didn't pray constantly like Otramamá, but made monthly confession, although perhaps Pepa had become a bit remiss after her separation, but Tina was a devotee of the Holy Ghost, Whom she visited daily in his golden shrine of the Socorro, and with Whom she allowed herself more intimate conversations than with the other Faces of the Trinity, as if He hadn't been God but one of the saints that one can adopt as guardian angels.

'On the Day of Judgment the Holy Ghost will fly from the Celestial Chair and will carry me with Him,' she said as if she wasn't convinced, although she used to reprimand Borges, who loved her silently, for his agnosticism. 'You all say that you don't believe in God, that you are not Catholics. But I would like you to explain to me what reason you could have not to repent at the moment of your death and go straight to heaven,' she is quoted as saying in Bioy Casares' diary, at dinner in his and Silvina Ocampo's house, where she had been invited so that Borges could look at her without speaking.

How could they have hated the chiquita, then, she who had paid for her triumph with her madness? But such pestering, such anger, and, at rock bottom, spoilt. Spoilt rotten. In the end we were well brought up, we were taught how to control ourselves...

Holy Ghost, Soul of my soul, teach me only to know Your Will, Tina prayed in the words of Saint Ignatius, while she wrote letters to Buenos Aires with news in equal parts from everyone on the trip, but double in length because Pepa couldn't be bothered to write her own. And she ended, from your daughter who loves you very much and misses you, which wasn't true because even if she loved them she was extremely pleased to have left them behind. Me too, added Pepa at the end of the letter, as imperceptibly as an old smudge which could have been a coffee stain.

Anyway it went on being Clara, the chiquita, who seemed so well installed in the indispensable love. And how would they, if ever, my sisters, manage without it? That polish, that soft and terse skin of Tina's that pleased me so, though less than Tía Teodé's powdered jowls, was love dispensed with. No, really? Perhaps it's what I would have liked, to believe in that chaste air where a hope trembled, etc. Tina's hope, that of a well brought-up girl with the patience of her chronic illness, spun out in letters to Buenos Aires from La Cumbre, in the Córdoba hills, where she was sent to convalesce between two relapses. 'There's so little to do that as Mama says it's better to get into bed, for me every day that passes and I don't get worse it's a blessing,' and then she embarks on an exposé over lapels for a tailleur she had commissioned from Celeste, the other seamstress of Juncal, with drawings and precisions which tried to compensate for the lost days. That tailleur to dress up in, like Don Quijote with his barber's bowl, in order to gallop into the fields. For what?

They didn't hate each other, then; but there was a fury loose around the house. Clara seemed to wield the fury as she had unleashed the strength. And the wind that shook it made those bodies tremble. Those elegant and isolated bodies, which had grown accustomed to loss, set down in the terraced gardens of Marienbad, waiting, while a blind dog stalks around them, a Francis Bacon dog with its fangs veiled by a black stain of fury.

Or was it the stain of madness of old families? The twice-crossed blood of Otramamá, the cousins' blood of Joaquín and Clara, insanities traceable due to our genealogical knowledge, ignored in families without history but which still lurk, and ambush each generation irredeemably like a flaw in the heart.

And on top of everything, the boredom. What power it had. Everything fed on it, it varnished the trivialities. It was fun to be bored but it was also fun to break free from it. That was the role of the fury, which scratched the skin of precisely tailored lapels and weary jokes, that skin as thick as a house that kept them erect on the terraces of Marien-bad, inherited like the supposed madness, and sometimes, surprisingly adaptable.

Because misfortune drove them to shake off boredom like a blanket as they jumped out of bed, and a criollo energy roused by bugles had them running to the breach with knives aquiver, knives made a bit helpless by the fury. But they persisted, for better or worse they endured their misfortunes, because boredom is the best school of endur-ance. And if the heavy and customary skin made them drowsy, there is another layer underneath, polished, ductile and able as a weapon, as resistant as chainmail, as invisible as habit, which enabled them to survive.

Whether or not Tina had been colluding with Susi Bosch, the scare ended in nothing. Clara seemed to have forgotten, the fights went on as usual, as their way of passing time, but we were approaching Europe and Susi Bosch would have other adventures waiting for her, as she was going to part from the family in Paris.

But Clara harboured a grudge against her second sister. She started to mistrust her in a way she had never mis-trusted Pepa, about her relation with Joaquín, and the attractive women who got near him. She redoubled her boasts about her successes with men, but this time it was aimed at Tina. She feared her, she needled her, she sought her out more than she did the other one, as if the totem had reabsorbed its benign head and had adorned itself with the camouflages of a sexual ambush.

Still my father was nowhere to be found.

37

THE CABIN had a powdery, persistent perfume; it was those translucent little papers Tía Teodé took one by one from a rococo-painted ivory book and rubbed on her nose before we went out, and which gave her skin the delicious down of an ageless peach, making me feel safe once more. Her travelling lamp, a lyre of glass beads studded with tiny bulbs, cast a soft firefly light in the room — it helped her drop off to sleep, as she read the book propped on a wooden rest on her stomach with a torch and a magnifying glass. Behind her closed eyes she was waiting for me.

Her lace-bed jacket stopped above her elbows, which were stained purple with eczema, her hands were crossed on the delicate forge of her breast, and her closed eyes were fringed with a row of baby's unformed lashes. Without opening them she asked, 'How did things go for my *pescatore napolitano?*'

'Not well, Totola. Not at all well. There was a real fisherman, a girl. And she got cross with me.' I burst into tears.

The Señora didn't move, but I heard her worried and affectionate voice. 'We don't treat you well, darling, but I promise you, once we reach Paris things will change. You and I will disappear, we'll let the others fend for themselves. You'll feel better when you get to Paris, one always does. It's like a better home. Go along now, wash your face and go to bed. And say your prayers, pray deeply to the Virgin, ask her to teach you to love selflessly, with detachment, something we poor things don't know how to teach you. Pobre de nosotros,' she added, her voice growing sadder.

On a grey horse
we'll go to Paris.
We'll disappear
in Paris ...
We'll walk,
we'll trot,
we'll gallop, gallop ... gallop ... *gallop*!
With Bertrand, towards Yamoidá, beyond Yamoidá, together but detached, I must learn that, he is going to teach me to be like him.

I fell asleep. I dreamed again the dream of the invaders, they tied up Otramamá and cut her up in slices like cold meat. But then the dream shifted to the corridor of the servants' quarters in the Calle Juncal that were painted a soulless, barracks grey. A young man is walking there, in uniform. Another of the invaders? In Aurea the dressmaker's room a naked and bloody body lies on the bed, in a plastic bag. I can see it clearly and foreshortened like Mantegna's dead Christ. It has the face of an old man, bald with round glasses, I see his torso and below it nothing, no legs, no sex, only a bag of bloodstained skin, stitched and distended. And next to the bag are two neat, plastic phalluses. Outside, the corridors are empty but I know they are filled with hatred; they are occupied by servants in exile from so many different places, Poland, Galicia, Sicily, people who blame us for the destruction of their hopes. And then I feel not so much horror as helplessness, for I realise that the mutilated man was murdered by the man in uniform, and that I must denounce him to the police, but he *is* the police. And it seems perfectly natural that these crimes have been committed here, in our home.

Somebody was shaking me. I was surprised to find Clara bending over me with that solemn and questioning face with which she tended to look in the mirror. For a moment

I thought I was still dreaming, but then she began to pour out a flood of information about the whereabouts of the men of the family the night before.

'They got carried away like sailors on leave and they went through every bar on the ship getting more and more drunk, even Carlitos who's usually so buttoned up, but Eduardo was the worst and your father who has no mind of his own got swept along, and they even danced tarantelas in the second-class dining room with those Italians, and your father recited *Cuore* by Edmondo de Amicis in Italian with that elephant's memory of his that you've inherited, not like me, I forget everything since I had you, the Italians were in floods of tears because they're so sad about leaving the Argentine and even sadder about returning to their *paese*, they couldn't believe a criollo spoke their language so well, instead of laughing at their gringo accents and the women were all over your father, saying *Come sei bello! Chi t'a fatto, Rafaello?* And the silly fool was so pleased with himself and Carlitos waltzed with the peasants all in their black and bowed to them as if they were duchesses, but Eduardo was so drunk that he started to strip and three men had to carry him back to his cabin ...'

She couldn't stop. I was still anxious after the dream and her outburst irritated me; it seemed naïve and also dangerous. God, how confusing, the deceit, the anger, and the anxiety of discovering that hole at the back of the house, because for the first time I understood those dreams I had when I slept with Otramamá; until then I'd simply reacted to them with either pleasure or fear. Hatred, that's what I dreamed about, a well of hatred oozing up from that disgusting hole somewhere within our house, behind the doors that screened off those who toiled for us, but it wasn't just their bitterness I was sleeping in, there was something more, something darker which I couldn't fathom, some insidious horror which stained all of us and would seep out and travel wherever we tried to escape, to the estancia, to Europe, and which would continue to mark us, inexhaustible, like an ulcer that feeds off its host.

On deck the heat was becoming unbearable, the tropical sea was a trough of molten asphalt, our spirits were low, the same people who had cheered us the night before now barely acknowledged us. Clara clung to me as though she had more to say, but she remained silent, clutching my arm with a viciousness that made me long for the ladylike touch of my great-aunt's wrist. We walked the full length of the deck, up and down, up and down, as if to purge ourselves as much as for the exercise, like the three Artayeta amazons who'd been made to march thirty blocks of the Avenida Alvear each day, between Retiro and the Monumento de los Españoles, booted and laced up to their knees, all the way up and then all the way down, six thousand metres of exercise, with their English governess struggling along beside them. And all to be able to each unwrap a thinner pair of legs on their return to the Calle Juncal.

At last my mother began to speak. 'Do you remember what I began to tell you as we left Rio? It's a long story, and it's one I find hard to remember. I was so ill. "*First things, first,*" as Miss Emily used to say' – she said this in English. 'I've never told you this, but you're not the oldest. There was one before you, who died before he was born, that must be why I was so frightened and you caused me so much trouble. Because you see I had to spend nine months in bed, crucified on my back, with the most awful stomach pains, not knowing if you would run away like the other one, looking at the sheets all the time, frightened to death of finding blood, Mamá said I looked like a *gisante* on a tomb, except that my eyes were kicking like a madwoman, what a heartless idiot she was, and she'd also lost her first daughter, although that one's in a little coffin in the Recoleta, while mine just disappeared. It happened when the Ruana bolted, I had to throw myself off, I fainted, and when I woke up the baby had seeped away like water. The horrors that have dogged me at the estancia! First my face carved up, then the miscarriage and then because there's no two without three … but I didn't move from Buenos Aires that time, because I had to break the unlucky spell.'

God, how beautiful she was. Looking at me without seeing me, outlined against the grey wall of the sea, a grey silk scarf holding her black locks like a hand. This time I didn't feel disgust, only a searing nostalgia for that part of her life that she'd lived without me. I must have blocked out the revelation of my brother; that hit me later, and even now I can't recall it without shame. Clara smiled to herself and went on speaking quite easily, with no shadow of the anxiety that had clouded her voice as we sailed out of Rio.

'I told you about the terrible labour, but I couldn't bring myself to tell you what happened next. Well, you were born, I saw you, and you were sweet if very dark. I was exhausted, it had taken a whole day, I slept and woke feeling all right, but then I started to get the most terrible headache I've ever had in my life and a high fever. I fainted, I went into a coma and then I don't remember anything, I woke up six months later and you had been transformed into a little gentleman in hat and gloves.'

We burst out laughing. Her big, wide mouth pushed up at her cheekbones and drew her eyes into a narrow and oblique line, a trace of the Inca princess of whose descent Clara liked to boast, but the laugh was Andalusian. That was all, there was nothing more to be said. Mamá had panicked, had almost died of fear, and then my manhood woke her. It was nothing more than a game between us. I saw myself reflected in the window of the bar, and my laugh was as Indian as my mother's face.

'It's not all that funny,' she said, looking out at the sea. 'I wasn't asleep. I was mad.'

She stiffened, but I knew she didn't want to stop. She grabbed my arm and because of my father's escapade, or just our shared laughter, I knew I had to encourage her. The disgust had disappeared, I was thrilled at our new intimacy, it seemed to suck away my nostalgia for her life before mine, and I felt strong, alert, and ready to elicit more secrets.

'How do you know, if you don't remember?'

'I don't remember because I am afraid to. When I woke up no one else wanted to remember either. There was a deadly silence all around me and it brought back that first memory, the one that hurt the most. It was as though an unspeakable shame had fallen on the house. They took me downstairs to the second floor where it was quieter, perhaps because of my screaming, and they had to tie me to the bed, and I didn't know who I was or where I was, but little by little I started to look at a picture. It seemed to have a message for me. I looked and looked at it, it was the only thing that would keep still, the walls moved away and came back at me and I sometimes felt like I was the horse who carried the corpse of Lavalle, or a bat nestling in a beam somewhere in the estancia, looking down on a room filled with strangers. Sometimes I sank, with a vertigo that still hasn't disappeared completely, even now. But when they realised I was looking at the picture they turned it to the wall – they didn't take it away, they turned it back to front. They meant well, of course.'

And then I saw her on horseback, mounted in that pugnacious way of hers, still side-saddle when everyone else in Maipú had given up that lovely custom, though without a skirt, her legs swathed in blue corduroy trousers, her polished English boot dangling from the pommel like an orthopaedic model, so short and *soignée*, hanging there amongst the apparatus of grand saddle and strong mare, her linen jacket shortening her long torso, and her beret and tie and gloves – all this in the middle of that sun-blasted Sahara, the thousand hectares of the potrero of Kakel, at five on a January afternoon. The hot mint and swampy air of the great laguna, the blond coat of the Ruana drenched to a seal's shiny brown, the white foam of saliva stained green by grass on the silver bosses of the bridle, the clinking bit more in rhythm with the seesawing of the sweaty neck than with the muffled hooves that were made almost silent by the mattress of marshy pasture; and her, cantering, straight as a flagstaff.

PETRO PRIMO CATHERINA SECONDA. My father was behind her, 'like a sack of potatoes on the saddle', as my brother and I said to each other, in revenge. And then I saw her in flashbacks. The solitary adolescent before she smashed up her face, manipulated into accompanying her great-aunt to the estancia at the beginning of December when Buenos Aires was humming with parties. And the child dressed for Carnival as a homemade Cupid, with heron's wings and a cane arrow. It was around this time that her father started to organise hare shooting by car, and Otramamá sang Fauré and Reynaldo Hahn, to the mortification of her elder daughters, as the catafalque of the new motor raced across the field like the runaway Ruana, tall and square and so similar to the carriages my grandfather had been so late to replace that they were nicknamed by the daughters' smart boyfriends – *Renaultsaurus, Cap Arcona*. One loves so much more those whose childhood one can imagine.

How astute they were, my mothers. One after the other, relieving each other like tireless seamstresses, they went on sewing a single tapestry for one thousand and one nights, with the pleasure of a dream that constantly renews itself. Each storyteller threaded her tales in and out without pain, without damage, without end, and even death and bankruptcy were subjected to the music of the voice. They had no need, those criollo Scheherazades, to pay for their lives with their tales, their self-indulgence made them unforgettable and inmune. Clara's role was different, but in her childhood the threads of her narrative were sustained by the estancia.

Above the noise of the hooves and harnesses the glass- needle trill of the pampa's pipit, the cachila, could just be heard as it flew in long, arched, locust-like leaps, leading the way like an invisible guide. Its pale figure, lost against even the parched grass of February, seemed too light and joyful to be pursued by the resplendent break-de-chasse, and yet it bounced along the cattle track, trill after trill, incomprehensibly faithful, offering drops of a delicious freshness to the hot morning whose edges were already blurring into mirages. Tía Justita laughed with pleasure, she was more sensitive to those things than my mother.

'Listen, Clara, how sweet the pipí pipí of that little bird. It's got the same voice as Bebecita Cossio, I always got the giggles in choir practice because she sounded like a dripping tap. Miss Midwinter used to say, "She chirps like a lark, and she's so very, very big."' And Tía Justita underlined her silliness with two dry, horizontal strokes, rather masculine, of her gloved hand.

And then, after a short ride through the fields surrounding the casco, the rumble of the carriage on the hardened ground of the Calle de Chacabuco rouses the güira cuckoos and the woodpeckers. The güiras fly from one eucalyptus to the next, with their yellow beaks, bristling crests and fanned out tails, their screams in *glissando* like a musical rattle leading us on. Like the crowd at a triumphal parade who have waited hours on the long route and when the cavalcade at last arrives run alongside and scream themselves hoarse, we seem to make the midday sun move along with us. And then, most of all, at dusk, when we return on horseback from a four-hour ride to the end of the estancia, towards the island of Kakel or the wide grey beach of the laguna of Yamoidá, and the sky ahead over Chacabuco and Maipú has gone so black that the groom announces laconically, 'Dust storm coming,' and the setting sun has inflamed the smells which loom up from the fields like walls that we must push through with our horses, and we ride at full rein so as to be home before the lightning strikes; and as we gallop, possessed by a euphoria of fear, we see the casco grow before us, its colours enhanced by the early night of the storm, the silver poplars white, the acacias phosphorescent, the eucalyptus neon-green. Meanwhile, at the entrance to the Calle de San Francisco is the silhouette of our great-uncle Bebé, who rides back at the slow pace of his great black horse and disappears among the trees, unseeing, with no urgency, like the imperturbable gaucho that he is.

In that grassy voice of the maternal pampa sea, Clara's life was encrusted within all the generations of Ramos, all brothers together and immune, so as long as we didn't lose it.

'Why didn't they take you to the estancia? It was summer. They could have put you in Madrina's bedroom, where you'd smell the gardenias, hear the oven birds and the benteveos, and you'd have known in two seconds where you were.'

Mamá smiled. 'You should have told them for me. Do you know, when I started to get my bearings, and stopped imagining I was a horse, or that your father was my cousin Canuto Martínez de Hoz, you were brought to my bedside and I'd grab your thumb and ask you to cure me. If you'd been able to talk, you'd have had me sent to the estancia.'

'You asked me to cure you?'

'Yes. Why not?' She was surprised. 'I thought you were my guardian angel. Hadn't God sent you to me as a trial?

You arrived like the angel of death, you could well have transformed yourself into my saviour.'

My mother seemed pleased, and somehow defiant. But again I felt that disgust, or perhaps not disgust but a clammy confusion, blended with the dream of the mutilated body and a sort of vertigo that separated me from my body and left it tied by that rope which entangled me with my mother. There was something I recognised in her description of madness. And then I couldn't stop thinking of that other, more horrible disgust, the thing that seeped away and never saw the light, thanks to the Ruana and the precious ground of Maipú, the odious thing I would never be able to bear or accept, nor even imagine as an older brother I'd pushed from the family tree, this *thing* which by its very mention made the rituals of my mothers ludicrous, inverted them, turned them from the celebration of a longed-for male heir into a sigh of relief for the one who had survived.

38

THE COLOUR was part of my pulse. It opened and shut, undulating, contracting and dilating with the rhythm of a heart, its beat was the colour of the water of the laguna in the shade of the tamarisks along the causeway, the brown of a bird in mist. Another recurring dream, this time bringing neither anxiety nor well-being. It was just there. But its blindness puzzled me, I was surrounded only by pulsating shades of brown. In its constant, calm compass I found nothing. And this was the colour of the day I arrived in Europe.

It was snowing. I had never seen snow before, and now the brown mist was swallowing it. Europe was a tunnel of foul weather offered up to my curiosity – I had to push through the cobwebs with both hands, and seek the hidden door at the bottom of this world without colour, except for the old colour of my dream, through which Europe would be revealed to me. How dark the tall, uniform houses that lined the Avenue de la Grande Armée, their profiles just visible like the walls of a canyon, the impenetrable mist hiding the doors. It was mid-morning. I knew by heart what was to be seen in Paris, my memory was lined with photographs and stereoscopic slides, and so I was looking at what I already knew, as the car advanced, sucking in the watery snow of the avenue. I had my nose to the window as I scanned the fog, but my own little door to Paris, private, stereoscopic and pedantic, could not match the monstrous monument looming out of the darkness.

'What's that huge great thing?'

'The Arc de Triomphe, silly. You're supposed to know your *Ville Lumière* inside out. And if it wasn't for this awful weather you could have seen the Louvre between its legs …'

'... at the end of the Champs Elysées,' I interrupted Tía Teode, disconcerted.

Napoleon's monument shocked me with its vastness, but it didn't break the link to that colour of my dream. It was the blurring of lines and the lack of colour, so unlike the tropics and heralded by the grey, grainy images of Bertrand du Guesclin, which drew Paris close to me. Closer to me than the memories of Paris of those I loved. The connection was so intimate. How can I describe it? Who would want to recognise himself in that wretched colour? But I felt its immediacy and abandoned myself to this furtive arrival.

Those memories embraced almost everything. For a hundred years the bright side of the moon had shone on our family's life in Paris. I had listened to the stories, wreathed in the eucalyptus smoke of Rafaela's kitchen, I had read them in old letters smelling of camphor and damp that were kept in the trunk in the salita of the big house. Tía Teodé hadn't been born in Paris, but her brothers had. Otropapá came here when he was seven, to be consoled for his mother's death by Mademoiselle Maillard and a whole group of cousins, more than he'd left behind in Buenos Aires. My grandmother's adolescent bliss had been so intense she'd vowed never to return. There had been weddings, suicides, state visits, embalmings; and there had been love, love everywhere. While I had rediscovered the curious colour of my dream.

At that time the city was still black with soot. Scabby black, as if with hairs and burns, a cold coal dripping with grey. Its grandeur of scale didn't impress me when I compared it with Buenos Aires. I didn't think much of the Louvre, the only building that reached my expectations was the Gare d'Orsay. Our hotel in the Rue du Faubourg Saint-Honoré had something of the Calle Juncal, although it was colder and uglier. At first Paris seemed to me like an old and shabby version of the city of my birth. But

I wasn't really disappointed. We had arrived where we were meant to be, and suddenly I felt cosy in the middle of this dirty, slushy little labyrinth, in which Tía Teodé and I had resumed our intimacy. But cosy was a word I would never again apply to that hard place.

Our rooms seemed to be older than the hotel. A cavern of velvet red worn down to brown copper, like the bruising on the petal of a magnolia, and which had more atmosphere than all the false Louis XV of the salons downstairs, it seemed the flesh-coloured focus towards which the dark winding streets converged. This apartment, with its painted ceilings, four-poster bed and draped mantelpiece was a nest and also an emblem of the family legend of our nineteenth-century travels. It had an oily but pretty perfume, welcoming but indigestible. The fragments the family had thrown at me, like bones I had to save from oblivion, began to take shape amidst those charnel house wrappings of brocade and satin and velvet.

Here, in the rooms at the Hôtel Scribe next to the Opéra, Otropapá and his brother would bath together in their father's used water, and then barge next door to the rooms of Magdalena Ramos Mejía, the builder of Kakel, disturbing their bald great-aunt at her dressing table while she, circus swift in the conjuring up of a wiglet, would welcome the orphans with the kindest of smiles. Here Otramamá's brother-in-law fired the shot that put an end to his stock market ventures after the Buenos Aires crash of 1890, the crash which made Otramamá's father Chancellor of the Exchequer. Here two Argentines dressed for the evening with the precision of their opposing styles, Vice President Madero to dine at the Elysée and the dandy Artayeta to stroll down the Avenue Gabriel and enter the Cercle of the Rue Royale for a chat with Charles Swann. And it was from here, at last, that we started for the Louvre the morning after our arrival, a rejuvenated Tía Teodé and me, straight to be bowled over by the Gallery of Apollo. It was true then, that one feels better in Paris.

'*Umbrellas and sticks! Umbrellas and sticks!*'

The feet advanced in first position and the umbrella drummed on regardless across the chequered pink and grey marble floor as if she were deaf.

'*Votre parapluie, Madame!*'

'*Ah, tres bien. Je ne suis pas anglaise, moi.* Do you realise that even here, Martinete, in this symbol of French culture, they have been infected by Anglomania? But then the French have always been frivolous. Their intelligence doesn't save them from their innate frivolity. And do you know why? Because they have no passion. You've got to hand it to the Spanish, they may be very stupid, but they are never frivolous. They are saved because they feel deeply.'

My mentor didn't feel deeply about art, and so our stroll along the Great Gallery accelerated to a bracing stride. I pulled away from her arm; I had started to recognise the originals of my photographs, although disappointingly they weren't as glossy as the Skira prints. But some of them sounded strange new voices, they threw me a look which made my head turn. I begged Totola to let me go back.

There was a voice calling to me that became a face so beautiful I couldn't understand the words. A grey portrait of a lady with a long neck cut by a black ribbon looked down at me, smiling and self-absorbed. She could well have been part of our own gallery of family portraits but for her ironic lips which seemed poised to open, filling me with a curious and quite new sensation of suspense. Tía Teodé approved of Madame de Sorquainville because of her breeding, and embarked on a story about how her brother had bought a much prettier Perronneau for a song, but I wasn't listening. It was as if the grey, the pink, the light blue and the cold yet tender brush strokes sought out the knowing eyes and that mouth but stopped without reaching them, as if on purpose. A tension, a kind of Debussyean break, was happening of its own accord, and yet it was part of the Pompadour chic of the sitter and of her sad, gallant eyes. I felt that if I could unravel that secret, it would reveal not only the soul of Madame de Sorquainville, but more important, those of the women who had made me and about whom the brushes of the Cuzco School, of Pellegrini, Pueyrredón, Bonnat and Jacques-Emile Blanche had nothing to say. Above all it would explain the enigma of the unblinking eyes of Otramamá's portrait at the estancia.

My grandmother had been painted with the official elegance of the nineteen hundreds, when the rich had acquired the bland and iconic air that only a century before was the prerogative of princes. She looked down at me from the chimney breast of the salita, on the cold nights when I was allowed to sleep down there. Those impassive faces watched over me from every wall, pursuing me around the room. Otramamá's eyes lashless like mine, long, opaque, staring but not deep, flush with the cheeks as if ready to pounce, and carrying effortlessly their black catafalque of an Edwardian hat. Its wings of tulle and satin bowed down like an umbrella rained over by cock feathers, shaped like mourning lilies. This coffin trimming on a girl of eighteen was balanced by a dress so light that the transparent material, embroidered with pink peach buds, seemed to merge with her skin. A shawl of raw silk covered her left shoulder, like an arm which linked day to night.

My grandmother hated her own image, and managed to get the portrait banished to one of the servants' rooms at Juncal, but her husband thought otherwise. He rescued it and placed it over the black marble mantelpiece, in the company of his ancestresses, ladies whose mind Otramamá despised. But it was she who stared around, in the grey gloom of the salita, shunned by the comfortable daughters of the house with their lowered lids and their profiles. In the end, her elder sister came to be hung opposite, to keep her company. But clearly Otramamá wasn't at home, as she had never felt at home there in the flesh; her disenchantment made her look as old as her hat. Portrayed twenty years later than her sister, who seemed a bourgeoise with succulently painted arms, proud of her tiara and sables, Otramamá looked sated by the luxury of the Belle Époque, and Monsieur Albert Lynch conveyed that indifference with his dry, vaporous brush strokes.

Madame de Sorquainville, however, was serene. Her detachment speaking of both religion and worldliness, and I could imagine her smiling as she offered her neck for the blade to fall straight on the line of the black velvet bow.

Tía Teodé was pulling at my sleeve.

'Look Martinete, what a surprise, here's my cousin, Pepita Errázuriz. Come and say hello. She's an admirer of Perroneau too.'

The dumpy little lady was dressed simply, in blue. She stretched out a hand without smiling, but her big face was welcoming.

'I'm so glad you like a painter who is out of fashion,' she said to me. 'It's a good sign.'

I didn't know how to answer, and so I praised her brooch, a huge enamel leaf with an insect of precious stones quivering on top, which was disproportionate to her tailored suit and loafers.

'Lalique designed it,' she said simply. 'The bug is a dragonfly that I had sent from Santa Fé. I chose it because they can sense a storm coming, and there we always need water. It amused Lalique. "*Voilá votre broche propitiatoire,*" he said to me when he produced it. The leaf is of an ombú tree. I don't want to live in our country, but I feel the need to atone. What a coincidence, the day that I put on our national badge and come to the Louvre I find my cousin.

I didn't know you'd arrived, Teodé, it's early for you. You usually come like the *muguets*, at the beginning of May.'

'This year we had to fit in with the Señor's holidays,' my aunt replied coyly.

There was nothing coy about Pepita, standing square on her haunches like a cow from the pastures of Santa Fé. But her severe voice was musical and she had an unexpected charm.

'I like to meet the new blood you bring here every so often, so that they can fall in love with all of this,' she said, and opened her short arms, offering to us the Great Gallery, the darkened Seine running beneath its snowy quays and the cold sky of Paris. 'And this boy is the grandson of the most exquisite man in Buenos Aires.'

I sensed that Tía Teodé didn't like to hear praise of Otropapá, whose good taste perhaps excluded hers, but Pepita was of her line, had grown up near Picasso and Apollinaire, and clearly inspired her respect. She treated her quite differently to her Uruguayan sister-in-law.

We set off down the gallery again, Pepita moving heavily alongside us. In profile, her high forehead curved upwards in search of the foam of her toffee-coloured hair, reaching it way back in mid scalp. After the speech about the brooch she fell silent. Tía Teodé babbled away about the trip and her educational plans – hoop games in the Tuileries Gardens, the Carousel, buying new clothes for the snow, the Conciergerie and Marie Antoinette's cell, the Musée Grévin and the wax effigy of the ill-fated queen, rounded off by prayers for her at the Chapelle Expiatoire and then tea at Rumpelmayer.

If our companion was listening, she gave no sign of encouragement. She seemed more interested in the windows, which revealed the long wall of houses on the Rive Gauche, behind the frozen trees. Her silence made me anxious, I was afraid that if she got bored she would leave. But when we reached the room of the Triumphs of Marie de Médicis she invited us to sit down.

'I get tired in museums, just walking through them. Beware, Teodé, it might happen to this child. Don't smother him with culture. Let him breathe Paris. Let him take it in slowly, step by step, without even noticing it. Let him walk, let him smell – hmm the smell of the *pissoirs* – let him look at this city whose very existence is a miracle. After two terrible wars, which have destroyed the world that created it, it's truly miraculous.'

'That's all very well for old women like us,' said my great-aunt, who seemed twenty years older than her cousin. 'To walk, to *flâner*, that's just a recipe for confusion, the child won't take anything in. I've organised a complete programme. Give him the chance and he'll lose himself in contemplation of the heavens. We don't have all the time in the world like you, Pepita. You chose to be an expatriate. Martín has to go back to school and who knows, with things as they are in our poor country, when he'll come back. But that's really as it should be. As Saint Francis of Sales said, one has to flower where one has been planted.'

I was enjoying this locking of horns, in the great arena of painted triumphs. I watched as Pepita's caramel-coloured crest of hair went erect and her Mayan mug turned violet. The two little criollo women were squaring up to one another, amidst the riot of baroque flags of such different colours from their own Pampean plumes. They positioned themselves like lapwings, inflating their already ample bosoms, and started an inner tap dance over who would win, the one who left or the one who stayed, the European or the American, two faces of the same coin who couldn't help but yearn for that which they missed from the other.

'To flower where you've been planted, *tu as beau dire*, Teodé. But how can you flower when no one waters you? When intercourse is so vapid that your ideas dry up or even worse, your desires.' Pepita went on confronting her cousin. 'And don't think that one doesn't pay a very high price for this exile. One has to reinvent oneself every day, and in making the effort one loses oneself, by forgetting who one is. The worst thing is having to explain yourself to others, that they don't care who you are, and that this should happen to people like us, we who have such a secure niche in the Reina del Plata. It is all very tiring, very wasting. But civilisation must be paid for,' she concluded with a discouraged snort.

The other one sighed and looked blindly around her; the two fat lapwings seemed shaken by their efforts and thrashed by the glorious winds of the *Grand Siècle*. Out of the corner of my eye I looked at the scenes from the life of Marie de Médicis and seized upon something. The plump heel of the Queen, who had just given birth to the Dauphin on a throne and wearing Turkish slippers, was exactly like Tía Teodé's.

'Look, Totola, look at the Queen's foot! Doesn't it look just like yours, in your Moorish portrait?' I shouted so loud that my companions jumped.

But they were not in the mood to find a naked heel in that tumult of heavens raining down gods and seas torn by tritons. Tía Teodé focussed her eyes like a matador poised to insert his sword. Before she began her next assault she threw a remark to me, as if to gather strength: 'And Louis XIII waving his orb, looking adoringly up at his mother with those silly calf eyes, he's just like you!'

'Civilisation! You pay for it with a sterile life, Pepita. Do you think it's worth it? The thing we do in Europe is learn, and then we apply what we have learnt, sowing it back into our poor, thirsty land. We can't spend our lives eating the food of others, or we'll end up like those Russians you and I met in Karlsbad before the First War, addled with culture, falling asleep at concerts, making us laugh because they seemed to be dead.'

Pepita didn't answer. She stood there silently, contemplating the naked giantesses cavorting in threesomes. She must have been thinking of that other exiled woman whose triumphs and tribulations had been inflated into three hundred square metres of apotheosis, perhaps comparing herself and her cousin to Marie de Médicis – both criollas were strong, they too had been pushed from palaces, and their power, the Sociedad de Beneficencia, had been consumed by that other Richelieu, Eva Perón.

'Teodé, Teodé,' she began, more wearily now. 'Why can't you accept that if we were planted in those deserts, where in four hundred years we haven't managed to build anything lasting, there must be some reason for it? God gives with one hand, and takes with the other, and he's left us not so much naked as confused. He plants us on a rock where we can't build our house. Isn't he telling us to abandon it? We are his prodigal children. He doesn't deceive us as he has these Europeans who believe that his kingdom is of this world. No, he loves us more, he has freed us from responsibility. Let the French take care of the Louvre, let them restore these beautiful pictures. We are his perpetual children, here to enjoy it, but spared all the worry of caring for it. Let us enjoy it then,' she raised her short arms once more, but this time she offered us nothing, 'without fear or hope.'

Tía Teodé became very serious. 'We will have to leave you, Pepita,' she said. 'I don't understand what you're trying to say, but this child can't go on listening to such sophistries. Without hope, you say! How can you dismiss one of the three Theological Virtues? Pancho used to say that I lacked imagination, and I suppose that's why I can't understand you. We shall go on now to the Gallery of Apollo, because the Señor has been pestering me for some time about the crown jewels.' And she grabbed my arm and pulled me away from Pepita, in order to save me.

And indeed, I had fallen under Pepita's spell. The short, square old woman with her toffee-dyed hair didn't conform to the canons of beauty of the Calle Juncal, yet she seemed more distinguished, more intelligent than the women there, and rather unnerving. As we walked back along the gallery on the river side I decided that she was more my style than my other mothers, she didn't love me, like Bertrand she had no plan for me. She had no plan for anybody. She had *'petites inquiétudes amoureuses'* according to Tía Teodé, who had buried hers with Tío Pancho and certainly didn't approve. How could she be ugly and yet behave as though she were beautiful? She reminded me of Adela. *Jolie-laides* with *chien*. And here in Paris, where people are meant to appreciate those subtle qualities that go unnoticed in Buenos Aires, Pepita had *chien* and let herself be cradled by *petites inquiétudes amoureuses.*

'Martín, you goose, it's this way.' The voice of poor, vanquished Tía Teodé made me feel cross with that lawless upstart. She might have been right, and her ideas might have proved more helpful than Teodé's, but I was my greataunt's protector, and I couldn't bear to see her faltering, and anyway, neither she nor I were interested in the worries of love.

No, no to the loves, those of a tart old lady like Pepita or a goddess like Clara Lenoir, no; the loves of these two arrived clothed in danger, even if it was a danger I saw coming and to which I seemed immune. For me love was fed by conversation, that unending talk of love which I would perfect at school, or at night, when I wouldn't let my new intimate best friend go to sleep, insisting in describing, analyzing and experiencing by talking the emotion we felt for each other – which was nothing more in reality than my ventriloquist's monologue, and always, of course, of a chastity incomprehensible to my father and those possessed women.

But it was different now with Tía Teodé, when love

looked for nothing more than the company of love. To be with her, to look, to eat, to walk with her, it was, like the description of lover's bliss by La Bruyère, sufficient.

Like Paris, the Gallery of Apollo was at first a disappointment. All that gold, but it was drained by the white light of the snow, and didn't show off the radiance of the royal jewel box I'd been so eagerly looking forward to. Tía Teodé redoubled her efforts, she started on Le Brun, the artistic propaganda of the young Louis XIV, Colbert's economic manipulations, but though I wanted to listen I wanted still more to understand, and I felt disturbed by her puffing and blowing, her need to reassert the syllabus which Pepita had shaken.

I threw myself on the stones, of course, the stones, my unswallowable meats, so enormous. Compared to them, the Uriburu gravel, which had left me so ecstatic on the first night on board ship were the most minimal of *amuse-gueules*.

Agates which were cups scooped out of hard, smooth dulce de leche, green jaspers veined with white, jaspers veined almost black with blood, sardonyx, jade, rock crystal, all worked with dizzying precision. They awoke in me an intense appetite, of the eye, of taste, of desire, of the spirit of complication and multiplication, and when at last I reached the serious treasures, the diamonds, ten times weightier than Tía Teodé's, rocks which had been hidden in the hair of queens and the handbags of fugitive empresses, I became exhausted and sat down and looked around me.

A new order was taking shape in my discovery of the Gallery of Apollo, sustained by the fine web of those spent golds and ivories, just as it had been by the faint smile of Madame de Sorquainville; a different beauty was beginning to dawn on me. New, because older and more mysterious than the florid opulence I had been brought up to admire. I felt as though I were finding in that gallery the real live models, who walked and talked, of those rooms which had touched something in me during my childhood – the dining room of Juncal, the drawing room of Adela's party, the tapestries designed by a friend of Le Brun. But this new beauty, rather than surrounding me quietly like the luxurious and welcoming skin of those rooms of the Argentine transplanted from Europe in Tía Teodé's lifetime, this *speaking* beauty had something horrible about it. It was a huge new eloquence that whispered to me, pointing towards a window that was intimate and closed, it was a song more lonely than the elegiac *I want a kiss but you don't wanna* of San Carlos, it was like the broken time of Debussy, and I felt it was the key to understanding, but I couldn't, I wasn't able. Perhaps if I were stronger, I might.

How difficult when compared to the poor, clear beauty of the painted slums of Rio, which Madame Blot had heralded as great art. And even more difficult was the gap between the careful artificiality of the park of the estancia and the wanton immensity of the plain that Miss Judy so loved. Both Miss Judy and Madame Blot seemed to insist that we should submit to the natural marvels that were ours already, and give up on Europe.

Apollo, incandescently pink and orange, went on conquering Python up in the heaven of the ceiling, helped by the green Hermes and the blue Pallas who dived to kill the dragon of the night, while further down a youth of ivory plaster in *contraposto* held up a golden garland. The satyrs and terms embraced; the months, the signs of the Zodiac, the muses, the lilies and the *L*s, the helmets, the urns with the sun gleaming on their breasts, the blue putti against the gold, the darkness of the ceiling, the holes in the gold, from which muscles or clouds of dirty white bulged out or hung on garlands; everything and everyone was so perfectly balanced with such fine poise that the Gallery of Apollo, like Madame de Sorquainville's mouth, whose lower lip revealed a minute brushstroke, the wound inflicted as she bit it to remain silent, was a jungle. It was the opening to something vertiginous and terrible. The archetypes of our transplanted world, filled with those things of mine that I licked to sleep in my arms, were a jungle.

39

'I HAVE been thinking, Martinete, that I'll give in to your wishes, and take you to Lourdes as a present for this famous birthday of yours,' Tía Teodé said to me one morning, when the snow had melted and the Rue du Faubourg Saint Honoré had become a ditch of dirty soup.

I was going to be ten. I felt that from then onwards, till the hour of my death, I would never be a child again. Maybe it was the break in my life produced by the great journey, and the uniqueness of a European birthday, but more than anything it was my mother's revelations. I would have to prepare carefully for such a coming of age, and Tía Teode, perhaps as exhausted as I, was appealing to this cradle of miracles.

'We'll escape, nobody but us this time, my treasure. We'll leave the girls behind, as they seem incapable of tearing themselves away from the Avenue Montaigne. We'll leave them to their *taupé* berets and their New Look tailleurs. O la lá, this sad silly war, all it's done is bring the Anglo-Saxons out on top. New Look in Paris! Whatever next. We'll rush South to Lourdes, and I'll plunge you into the Gave, which runs past the grotto and goes silent as it passes it, you'll see, so that the Virgin cures you in advance. But I won't hold you by the heel, so you won't be left with any vulnerable bits.'

I didn't find this funny. I had plunged on my own into a vertigo of self-improvement that made the European efforts of Madame de Mailly and the rest of my family seem quite trivial.

There was another consequence of my arrival in Paris: my parents had all but disappeared. Clara, having traumatised me with her horrors, forgot all about it. I don't even remember my father there. They weren't staying with us.

They had absconded to a hotel frequented by Argentines, the Regina, in the Place des Pyramides, where they found friends and a view on the Tuileries, the ever-present tower, and a pot-bellied, jaunty *tricolore* which fluttered from the peak of the Palais Bourbon over the black trees and the snow, in the centre of that pearl grey sky. A panorama which I envied them for enjoying so unreservedly, it symbolised the Paris of my dreams, the Paris seen through the eyes of Otramamá in her portrait. For some reason my parents and aunts had chosen to distance themselves by miles from this terrible birthday.

And I couldn't lean on Totola. I had tried to share my confusion with her, in the wake of my discoveries at the Gallery of Apollo, but she had answered with silence, or by changing the subject. Maybe it was the shock of her clash with Pepita, or simply her lack of imagination, anyway I didn't feel I could press her, and also I had to protect her from my sense of shame. And in her own way she went on protecting me, with her completely predictable and gentle *train-train*.

But very little, in fact. Even as I felt that we ate into the morning by lingering at the Hotel Bristol, that we were losing it because of the never ending breakfast and the baths and the powdering, and Tía Teodé who didn't bother to go out earlier, as if it was all the same to her, it was the longing to embrace a larger piece of love that made me measure that loss. Even then I loved as I did later, like a man. To go out with her into the snow covered morning, the two of us alone, to delight in it totally, was a love wish. The new morning that was abandoned to waste.

There is always one who pushes harder, and I was going to be ten while she was on her way down and tired. For her it was one more of a thousand mornings in Paris, but for me it wasn't so much to recognize the famous Paris under the famous snow, as to go out into a new day with her, into that new world where she had taken me, towards that apex of dawn light in the snow, that bronze-coloured water that flows between the snowy banks, the Seine that traverses Paris.

And yet, where was this love, that was supposed to be enough? Because this escape with her from my former life was the worst break of all. That was why I had been left alone by the others, like on the ship, that was why my father had disappeared, and this birthday would seal the cut, with no possibility of going back, towards a new life of responsibility and loneliness. And my mate, for all her little winks of complicity, would only accompany me on her own terms, terms which didn't include the Gallery of Apollo, or the real significance of my tenth birthday. I felt even lonelier than I had at sea.

The price of that liberty, salvation, call it what you like, were Mamá's confidences. I intuited them vaguely as a sort of vengeance, and now, as I am more aware of her uncontrollable jealousies, after a whole life over which the generations seem to have been born to feed them, I read them like her impulse to intrude and break, as if her son's breathing would deprive her of air, while at the same time all that envy was revealing her desperation. So vulnerable, dirty with snot and sobs, and self-shame, yet always insistent, so that if I felt disgust once, on her first revelation, afterwards it made me love her even more.

If the houses of the family — though not the estancia — if the Belle Époque portraits and the stories of its old women went on betraying themselves during the journey as riddled with lies, which couldn't live up to the truths of Mme de Sorquainville and the Gallery of Apollo, which was nothing but their beauty, and too much for me, Clara was the opposite. She was the naked Republic of Delacroix rallying her followers. But she exposed herself too nakedly for the modesty of a son. She wasn't only the dark and rubicund Republic, oddly alike her anyway, with the Phrygian cap we shared, and her flag-waving, she was something worse, she was Rembrandt's Slaughtered Ox, in the same Louvre, who exhibited his innocent wounds, for whom nobody admitted guilt.

We crossed France slowly, stopping in empty hotels that hadn't changed since my companion's childhood. In one of them I was given not a bed but a cradle – the booking had been made in the name of *Madame de Uriburu et bébé*. Tours, Bordeaux, Toulouse, the grey skies, the ploughed fields, and the old and sad cities. We were crossing the slow rivers towards the South, towards the mountains that hid Spain, to where the Virgin had made Her apparition. I looked at everything, of course, but I was carried along in a daydream of pure tension.

I slept a lot in the car that Tía Teodé had rented, driven by the Basque chauffeur she used to employ in France, so similar to the Buenos Aires servants. His garrulous chatter increased my drowsiness and soothed me. The wounded and impoverished country was like a very old hospital. Even more so than our velvet-draped apartment in the Bristol, these hotels, calling themselves de l'Univers, d'Angleterre, de la Cloche, de la Grotte, or just Grand, were like an autumn in the dead of winter, with their glass partitions opening into gardens of snow, their freezing corridors and dining rooms, long windows in the grey rooms with grey skies, the terribly white linen and the servants, so ceremonious that it added to the unreality. Like the silence which had fallen on us, Tía Teodé and I were nearing the end of our crooked loves.

Like the love that falls from the tree, like the yellow leaf with no wind, it was as if our journey had ended before its time.

I was feeling bewildered by the discoveries which were dirtying my life, I could take that, but I found it harder to understand my aunt's sulking. She didn't seem to bother to console me, although she knew everything of what Clara had told me, and also I had asked her to explain the contradictions of the Gallery of Apollo. I hardly spoke, I was weighed down by the first depression of my life, and she hardly answered, as if I had disappointed her, as if she had decided the honeymoon hadn't added up to much. The lovingly detailed descriptions of the croissants of the Hôtel de l'Univers, of the wines of Musigny that Pancho adored so at the Hôtel de la Cloche etc, all this had evaporated, and she didn't even deign to look at me.

As I felt that everything was my fault, I took it like a punishment. But curiously I also felt a kind of relief every time Iñaki and his funereal limousine stopped at the door of yet another of the venerable hospitals, where the ministrations of the servants seemed like a mortuary rite, too benign for one to take offense, so refined, so shabby and so absent, bringing hot water and towels which started to creak as they enveloped us, and a few transparent slices of bread with their tiny dollop of butter.

The big grey spaces were the purgatory. The love that had run away believing itself free from the summer of Buenos Aires didn't deserve more than this finale of scattered shadows.

I believe now that even then I didn't find it difficult to watch the leaf fall in the embalmed afternoon, falling as it does. I preferred to be released from love. It was lovelier to remember it.

I was a bit young for such a shedding. Why was it? I haven't found an answer, other than my bewilderment, torn between the mad mother's rejection and the mad mother's plea. 'Give me your hand, my baby, cure me, please, please...' As Clara would have said, in her Quixotic parlance; I had been left gored by the bull's horn, inserted in the groin, not in the ass but the groin, what wound could be more hurtful.

I must have exaggerated because Tía Teodé's bad mood didn't last long. Still she kept silent about all this. Like me she responded to the curative air of the hotels, which couldn't have changed much since she first visited at the end of the nineteenth century. They offered such a neutral repose, for they had witnessed three wars, and must have fed if not Balzac at least Maupassant, that no frustrated loves of any kind could touch them.

'*Schlafen, schlafen, ohne zu erwachen,*' my aunt started to recite to herself, like Otramamá with her limited repertoire of German, as a sort of overture. I was recovering as well. Iñaki was as affectionate as Vicente, the Galician husband of Galician Vicenta, who didn't work in Juncal, but one Christmas he brought me some silk shirts he had been given by his employer, the ambassador of the Order of Malta, stressing that he, Vicente, had never touched them. And the ever nearer Virgin of Lourdes, the purpose of our journey through France, was filling me with a fervourous unction which would substitute for any earthly sorrow. As for Totola, she was devoted to the Virgin, but as with everything else, apart from her genealogical devotions, she expressed it with reserve. I never caught her praying.

Imagination alters the experience of most into stories of importance. That's why I saw the grey spaces of the provincial grand hotels of France — so calm, austere and also nutritious, as repositories of time, as if the past, more than in castles and churches, had gone to sleep in its crannies, to be awoken by the velvet footsteps of those ghostly servants, who brought us more than our breakfast on their silent silver trolleys, they also brought to life the shadows seen from that square in Angoulême at the windows of the Cabinet des Antiques by the inventor of Victurnien d'Escrignon — charged with a richer truth. And they duped me, with the illusion that there are certain memories more privileged than others.

Tía Teodé would have agreed. The conscience of exclusion, so developed in her, was that of a class at bay. Another benefit of the mass immigration, because if it hadn't been for it the rich of Buenos Aires, instead of sharpening their genealogical superiorities, Rurikides, Sarmathians, their family slang, their elegances and insolences, though not their political power ruined by that inmigration, would have continued immersed in that Boeotian complacency described by Lucio López in La Gran Aldea, with such melancholic spite.

Neither Tía Teodé, nor even less Clara, were complacent. Warriors of their class, they were both driven in their determination to make it survive and hold up its place in Argentine history. Both, on that journey, had become the centre of my life. Hateful and lovable, Clara; altogether adorable, Totola; nobody touched me more than them. Clara, because of the unhinged humour that made her laugh at herself despite herself, and Tía Teodé because of her stubbornness. Tía Teodé was a well schooled niña, and Clara had the blind energy of the mad, an Isolda of her duty and her delirium, though she wouldn't have allowed herself to get killed for them. Both, in fact, were quite cautious. Vehement and precious criollas, I felt that they were vanishing before my eyes, in that deceitful city, covered in traps, they whose deceits had the weakness of intimacy, as they were too proud to exhibit their ambushes in public. I don't know anything, I don't know why I have decided to compare them when they hardly resembled each other.

I think I bring them together because I was trying to replace one with the other: at that time, when I thought it was possible to escape that Medusa head with four faces which emerged like an opera phantom from the steam of the bathroom of Juncal, but which now I recognize at last, after a whole life, as only one. In the end it was always Clara's face, which was used or exchanged by the other masks. And it had been Tía Teodé who came to my rescue.

It is curious that an old lady would have become entangled in the mystery of love, proposing a grand cultural excursion to a boy whom she knew not as well as she liked. And that between the swing of the boat and the swing of the car, passions would flare up and die down again, almost without the actor's awareness, which sprouted from the seeds that had flowered horribly in Phèdre.

Ah! Que n'étais-je assise à l'ombre des fôrets…. When I came across these lines on my return from France, with my French teacher, Maurice Rémy, who had heard them from Sarah Bernhardt's mouth — to her despair he was Hippolytus — I felt that they spoke for me. On the edge of the wood, beyond the reach and din of human voices, it is pleasing to sit and remember love's words.

Love, that hurricane which keeps itself in wait. One plays with it blindfold, like Tía Teodé, like my admired and ill-fated Psyche, like me, like Clara, like Orpheus, like us all, love that makes us touch the marvellous and the intangible — for only love is divine — and awakens and vanishes, and we remain blind, as is blind also the child with wings and arrows, but even so the stream of players throws itself into the ring, again and again, arroz con leche, me quiero casar, until at last we can take it no longer and we die, not of exhaustion, this time, but of death.

Asleep, we go through life. Without any awareness that the only thing that keeps us alive beneath the daily sadness, behind the idiotic rush towards the seven sins that in pure ignorance we believe give colour to our life, the only grace that illuminates us, that truly burns us alive, is love.

And as we would fall on our faces for love, if only we allowed ourselves, so I find Tía Teodé's daring so delicious, cramming her Vuitton trunks for another one of her trips, alerted this time by a new and naughty tune, a wink of the bandaged bird who struck once or twice at her windows overlooking the Plaza San Martín, no, it's nothing, don't be so silly, calm down and ask María for more tissue, she hasn't folded the dressing gowns properly, and then left so perkily behind her tortoiseshell trunks, trotting with her feet in their eternal first position, towards the port, Persea Gratissima, to decapitate the vipers in their nest.

It is true that we are aware of nothing. As my aunt used to say, happiness is invisible, like paradise, and we can only discover it by looking back, when it escapes us. This scrabbling after buried ruins is like the meal reinvented by the archeologist from a bit of china and some chicken bones, while those who sat at the vanished table, as consigned to oblivion as the table, hadn't given a thought to what they were putting into their mouths. A smell of peaches in the darkened dining room in summer, the peppery taste of the pie, can bring tears to the eyes of the survivor, excluded from the heavenly feast by the angel with the flaming sword. And it is only there, outside the gates, where he is allowed to delve.

To excavate, in order to reconstruct love. What a dire way of living it. To go back over every single look of Albertine's, like in those unendurably long passages of Proust, when she was already dead, not to bring her back but to bring myself back. If I could understand a bit more every time that I place them in front of me, just a bit more of why I ran away with Tía Teodé to escape from Clara, not only do I give myself the pleasure of spending more time with them, them at the prime of their lives coloured by my innocence, but I feel that my sadness decreases with the effort of understanding them. *La pensée qui console de tout.*

But then the excavator gets so much wrong. The chicken wing is so bare that it could well be the wing of a vampire, the mystery that we hold within us deeper than the ruins of Troy. And yet we carry the urgency to know, just as we yearn for eternity, with our only tool, the imagination, that transformed Tía Teodé during those nights at sea into Eros and me into the sightless but inquisitive Psyche; and then my aunt into Perseus, mounted on Pegasus and triumphant over the Medusa, with her erectile hair of vipers and accusing eyes, that monster Clara.

We stretch like those tiny frogs that stick to the glass of windows at night in the estancia; and when immobile resemble straw coloured moths, but wet and translucent, craving rain with their protuberant eyes and trembling throats, and which suddenly jump, pressing, uncovering, a very long and avid leg, prehensile, as able as a circus conjurer, but taking aim at the insect dazzled by the light of the room we are watching from, and then the diminutive frogs let loose another long and avid tongue to swallow the insect with a shaking of its whole body. But they are still hungry. Because they never tire of being hungry.

40

SPRING waited for us in Lourdes. Everything was green and tender and damp, and neo-Gothic and mountain-steep. My fears were atoned for by a First Communion piety. For presents all I wanted were rosaries, medals and plastic Immaculate Conceptions lit from inside, and the priest who heard my confession in Spanish gave me his absolution without listening. At the Hôtel de la Grotte I was promoted from *bébé* to *enfant*, and so I got a little bed in an alcove opening into my great-aunt's bedroom, which became a cupboard when the door was shut. It suited me. It was like a cave fit for the passing of the Gave. At night I had for company my new plastic Virgin, which glowed in the darkness like a blue-white rocket.

We visited the real Virgin at dawn. In the black dawn of the mountain, where only the suddenly silent river shone, Her image stood like a light spindle in its black niche, quite unlike the summery, friendly white grotto of my other birthdays at the estancia. She seemed about to leave the earth in a stealthy rocket burst, unattended by angels, owing nothing to nobody. She was the Great Mother of the Mountain who from the bottom of her cavern made the river silent, and She didn't even need God.

I prayed like never before, but I had no certainty of being heard. Neither Ceferino Namuncurá, nor Saint Louis Gonzaga, and least of all Bertrand, would be able to help, because I saw myself at the bottom of this dark valley, oppressed by the white light of the ascending dawn which in turn was resisted by the dark mountains, standing on the desert-like threshold of my adult life. In the past, when I had been good, I could pray with hope, when I was good it was because I was innocent, like my brother and sister were innocent. But now that I knew Mamá's secret...

Come, if you don't come who'll come? Where am I going to live, how am I going to live, what life is there after one stops being a child, what do I give, what do I pray, how much, if you asked it from me you must know, do you know? How much? How much does everything cost when one is no longer a child, I must give everything, if it's not everything it's nothing, everything, like the stairs of Versailles, and it's not that I don't want to go, you must know that I do want to go, say it again, say it clearly, come Mamá, come gracious Virgin Mamá help me, show me the way out of this darkness, this fat fruit sweetest of Virgins, fearless chaste Virgin pull me along let me ascend push me up to the cloud's eye in the dark haloed eye of bread of stars crowned hands in prayer under the beautiful feet the serpent under the roses the house the body on the bedside table glowing like a rocket when I go to sleep, maxima maxima culpa ideo precor flames flames that burn the feet pull me up hold me of ivory of marble the feet so lovely asleep dead manos sin culpa — el pié-besado — beso reverencial — brasa besada — carne abrasada — castísimo.